I0587015

THE ENERGETICS, BOOK 2

TIERRA
AND THE
WARRIOR

ELLEN BARD

archment
ublishing

TIERRA AND THE WARRIOR
The Energetics Series: Book 2
Ellen Bard

Many thanks for reading. Please consider leaving a review wherever you bought the book, or telling your friends about it, to help me introduce it to new readers. Thanks for supporting my work.

ISBN-13: 978-0-9934394-2-1
Published by Parchment Publishing.
ParchmentPublishing.com

Dedication

Sarah, Mum, Fox.
Three core pillars of both my life and my writing.
Thank you.

The Chakras and their Energies

 **Muladhara:** The Root Chakra – Earth Element
The energy of nourishment and home, family and safety.

 **Svadisthana:** The Sacral Chakra – Water Element
Fluid and adaptable, the energy of movement and connection, of practical and physical creativity. The energy of pleasure, sexuality and sensation, and emotions.

 **Manipura:** The Navel Chakra – Fire Element
The energy of the individual; of confidence, of proactivity and of drive and passion. Playful and proud.

 **Anahata:** The Heart Chakra – Air Element
The energy of healing, and of balance, located in the middle of the body and the seven Chakras. The energy of love, of relationships, of devotion. Of compassion and empathy.

 **Vishudha:** The Throat Chakra – Ether (Space) Element
The energy of communication, of conceptual creativity, and of truth. Of expression, and of listening.

 **Ajna:** The Third Eye – The Mind
The energy of imagination, of visualisations, and insight. Of clarity and wisdom. Of dreams and intuition.

 **Sahasara:** The Crown Chakra – None*
The purest of all the energies. Only experienced through the Grace of the Source (the energetics' name for the creator, the divine).

*Neither a dominant nor auxiliary Chakra for energetics

CHAPTER

1

Tierra prowled through the messy, dank garden at the back of the dilapidated property, all senses on alert. She was fully tapped in to her Muladhara energy, the magic that enabled her to track people, but what it told her about her environment made her skin crawl.

There was darkness here, in the energetic traces that she sifted through. The house itself was barely a shack, a few rooms and a musty, water-damaged basement, surrounded by weed-infested grounds that seeped into an overgrown piece of forest.

The property was isolated, twenty minutes from the pleasant, if small, town of Merrow a couple of hours east of Vancouver. This location was in total contrast to the bustling community there. Here, there was a sense of foreboding. She shivered. A sense of danger.

Tierra halted her slow progress and squatted. She rested a palm on the ground and closed her eyes. She drew on her energies, and a tingle of cool earth centered her. She breathed deeply. Her skills in this area were rusty. She needed to focus.

What could she sense?

Great anger had been expressed here. Manipura-fueled rage and violence. The negative emotions were almost overwhelming, and she wobbled on the balls of her feet. It had been so long since she'd done this, she wasn't sure she could protect herself from the negative effects of using her energies in this way. She frowned. No. She fisted her hand in the soil, and grounded herself. The ghostly storm of feelings whirled around her, and she tried to observe without being caught up, but her breath quickened despite herself.

She had been a homebody for the last few decades of her long life, enjoying a respite from the world, looking after her reclusive but brilliant cousin Cuinn and his huge house, Cathair Cuinn.

That had all changed in the last month or so. Blaize, Cuinn's new Adherent, had burned her way through Cuinn's self-imposed isolation and barriers, and into his heart. Her intelligence and passion challenged him, and brought him out of his seclusion. At the same time, he had seen a horrible prophecy that somehow involved all of them.

Tierra squeezed sticky earth between her fingers, and attempted to sift the emotional traces around her to discover something useful: people, place or thing. Anything concrete. She screwed her face up in concentration, attempting to become one with her environment.

Tierra's earth abilities allowed her to draw power and connect to anything natural in the environment around her, and sense the whereabouts of people. As part of the earth energetic training, Muladhara energetics were also trained in how to hunt. They were encouraged to tap into their primal energies and read an environment, to empathize with others and imagine what they might do and where they might go, and sense the emotions and lies in people's words. But combined with Anahata, as Tierra's energy was, she could become too sensitive.

Grim scenes whipped through her, and she gritted her teeth to stop herself crying out. A furious and broken young woman who Tierra recognized, throwing energy balls at a smoking target. That same woman hustling Blaize's drugged body into the house. Tierra shuddered at what had almost happened.

Another scene and, ah, another presence. Much fainter, but, oh, the power.

The other personality – male, from the energy – hadn't spent long on the grounds. Tierra would need to enter the house to learn more. She wasn't looking forward to that. Source knew what was in there.

She relaxed her hand and attempted to let go of the difficult feelings she'd absorbed, ready to stand. Her nerves were stretched thin.

"Can we talk?"

Tierra sucked in a breath, her pulse attempting to escape, and whirled round. But the crouch she was in wasn't made for that, and she slowly, excruciatingly, toppled over.

She lifted her head up to see the owner of the masculine drawl with a hint of Scandinavia, and groaned.

"Fintan. Don't do that when I'm concentrating." She pressed her lips together, hoping the heat in her cheeks was internal and didn't show on the outside. "I'm a bit busy at the moment. We can talk later."

Fintan's blonde-with-a-hint-of-strawberry hair was messy, and as usual it had been a while since his face had seen a razor. He wore ripped jeans and a tight T-shirt that showed off his well-muscled torso. The T-shirt had a picture of a VW van on it, and matched his twinkling sea-blue eyes.

"You're tracking. You can talk and track." Fintan stepped in front of her and stretched his clean hand out to take her muddy, sweaty one.

Tierra had hoped that volunteering to see what clues she could find at the scene of the kidnapping would give her some sorely needed peace and quiet.

When they'd rescued Blaize, Cuinn had called the friends he'd identified in the prophecy and asked them to gather at Cathair Cuinn. At first she'd been in her element. She loved looking after people. But after a few days she'd remembered she also loved her space. Her home was her safe place, her nest, and it had been decades since she'd had to deal with so many people at once.

"Tierra, c'mon. I'm bored, and I've been wanting to talk to you about something anyway. You can multitask." He sounded puppy-dog-hopeful. Fintan was easily bored, especially in times when not much was happening.

Tierra ignored his hand and pushed herself up. "I don't know why you came, anyway. This isn't your thing. There's not going to be any action here."

"I didn't think you should be alone in the house." He shrugged. "It's a nasty place."

"There's no one here. And I need to focus."

"I know you're scared."

She sniffed. "There's nothing to be afraid of here. I've tracked plenty of times before."

That had been the other reason she'd come out here. She wanted, needed, to contribute to the work the others were all doing, trying to find out who had been behind Indigo, and what the prophecy really meant.

He cocked his head. "I didn't mean of anything here. Though…it's been a long time since you've tracked anything. You're pretty out of practice."

Oh, the man was infuriating. She shook her head, trying to dismiss his comment without actually lying. After all, the prophecy had her terrified down to her bones.

He looked nothing more than a beach bum on his day off, so why was he so perceptive? She sighed. Appearances were deceiving. Fintan was a Manipura-Anahata energetic, one of the energetic race's Warriors. Battle-honed, with a keen sense of duty. Unlike Blaize's Manipura, which manifested in passion and drive, Fintan's Manipura tended towards play, risk and mischief. For all that, he was loyal, and cared deeply about family and friends. Initially friends with Cuinn, Fintan had been around for centuries.

And she'd been in love with him for nearly as long.

For most of her life, that hadn't really bothered her. It was a distant, unreciprocated love, and Tierra got on with things by ignoring it. But recently, something had changed. She wasn't sure what, exactly, but she no longer wanted to be his confidante. To hear about his numerous romantic trysts. He always fell in love with them, of course. His Anahata wouldn't stand for anything less. Unfortunately his Manipura, his fire, meant he also had a tendency to crave new things, so he usually fell out of love with them just as fast. Or, at least, in love with someone else.

She didn't need this right now. "I need to go inside the house. Someone was here with Indigo, and I want to see if I can gather more perceptions of him. It could be a lead."

"Alright." He examined her face. "Why don't we take a walk off the grounds first? You're not looking all that great."

She closed her eyes and sent a prayer to the Source for strength. "Thanks, Fintan. Just what every woman wants to hear."

Although she could do with a break. She'd opened up to the atmosphere around the house, and it clawed at her. If she was going to do good work inside the house, she needed to move away from the energetic traces here for a few minutes. Fintan was annoying, but his presence was familiar, and his energy was steady and comfortable. "Fine. I need to wash my hands. Give me a minute."

She walked around the corner to where she had seen an outside tap and rinsed her hands. Spring had definitely sprung, though the temperature was still chilly enough to wear a coat. It was the season for earth energetics. Let the fire energetics have summer – this time was all hers. From the quietness of the winter months, the earth was suddenly alive. Flowers and trees had started budding, and there was some sunshine at times. The soil was still damp enough to smell of growth and change, the breeze soft.

She tried not to drag her feet as she walked back to Fintan. When she reached him, she didn't pause, just kept moving. He, light on his feet as ever, easily caught her up.

"I thought you might want to talk," he said.

She shrugged. "Not really."

"You're the heart of the family, and Adam and Cuinn see you as unshakable," he said. "But I know what happened to Blaize scared you, and the prophecies that Cuinn has uncovered so far frighten you too. And that the danger is still out there."

"It's been a difficult month." If that wasn't an understatement, then there would be no flowers this summer.

"You don't like change. So no matter how much you enjoy playing hostess, new people in the house for this long is bound to unsettle you."

She shrugged again. *How dare he know me that well.*

"Everyone's scared, Fintan," she said, her words brittle. "Except you crazy fire energetics. And Adam. My brother has an entirely too casual attitude to danger."

"It's our job. We deal with this kind of thing more often than you know." He caught her hand in his and tugged her to a stop. "We'll deal with this threat just like we do every day. It's just another day at the office, T."

She pulled her hand free and kept marching. They'd have to walk a few minutes more for her to be out of range of the atmosphere of the house. "Well it's not my job. I've barely written a word in the last few days because of the cacophony of noise that comes with six energetics – and a dog – under the same roof."

"Well, you're trying to take care of everyone. Everyone apart from yourself." He matched pace with her again.

"Someone has to make sure the washing is done and there's food in the cupboards. Who else would do it?" Tierra was being unfair. Her brother, Adam, another earth energetic, took turns in the kitchen, and she never had to clean up. If she asked, others would help run the house. But…she didn't want to have to ask.

"It's not because we don't want to help." He attempted to put a hand on her arm, but she twisted out of his way. "No one wants to disturb your systems. I can make up a schedule when we go back if you'd like."

She wanted to shrug again, though knew she was being petulant. He was right. She was channeling fear into her housework, but wasn't taking enough time to rest and ground herself. Her sense of home, of rightness, of safety, had been shaken to the core.

Tierra's pace put her curvy body in front of Fintan again. He wasn't sure what the problem was between them, but he didn't like it. It had been a month or so now since their usual easy relationship had taken a strange turn. She'd been snappish. Irritable.

It was strange because Tierra was one of the most stable energetics he knew. Few things fazed her. She was always the rock at the center of the storm. He could count on her. They all did.

He'd have understood if she'd just been like this the last week, given how their lives had been turned upside down. It had to be affecting her. Whereas Fintan had dealt with Rogues for centuries, though it wasn't often you got a case that was as close to home as this one had been. Thank fuck Blaize was ok. He had known Blaize all her life, had been friends with her father – it wasn't uncommon as an energetic to know several generations of a family when your life span was hundreds of years.

It had been a long time since Tierra had been involved in anything so ugly. The last time was probably World War II, when Tierra's mother had been one of that war's tragic death count.

But the change in Tierra's behavior had started before Blaize had arrived. One day Tierra no longer seemed to find his jokes as funny. They'd always sparred – that was part of their dynamic – though normally she was so easy going, she never got annoyed with him. Until now.

"Let's talk about the fight." He tried once more to take her arm, which she shook off.

"What fight?" she said.

They were deep in the woods now, sunlight dappling the ground around them in short bursts, most of the forest shaded and dark. The ground smelled peaty, and flowers in early blossom were scattered across the floor of the forest, in greater density near those patches of sunlight.

"Our fight about you sharing energy with Cuinn."

"Hmph."

"I know you're still annoyed with me." he said. "But I don't know what you were thinking. It's illegal under energetic law, and it was very unlike you to volunteer. It was a crazy idea, and someone needs to watch out for you, if you won't do it yourself. You could have been seriously hurt."

She turned towards him, her dark brown skirt rippling and flowing as she turned. She could have been part of the woods, she seemed so at home in that environment. It was so unfair. He took risks all the time. "You think that's you?"

"You're like a sister to me. I don't want you to get hurt. There are times when you give too much to others, and you don't keep enough back for yourself." He struggled to explain himself under her unrelenting brown eyes.

She blinked. "A sister. Right. Well, Fintan, I might not be a trained Warrior, but I can take care of myself if I need to. I'm a strong enough energetic in my own way. I was there in World War II along with the rest of you, healing *and* protecting."

"I know. This is different. If Cuinn hadn't controlled himself, you could have been drained like the Leech was draining Blaize. There are reasons sharing energy is forbidden unless it's between Maven and Adherent. Plus, if anyone else found out, we'd all be in huge trouble."

"Given it was only you, me, Cuinn and Cara there, I don't think anyone else is likely to find out. No one else needs to know. Even if they did, I'd do it again to save Blaize." Tierra's face was set, but her foot scuffed at the floor, displacing leaves.

Fintan shook his head, frustrated. "Who'll save you from yourself?"

"It's not your job, Fintan." Tierra's tone was flat. "This little sister can look after herself. Let's walk back now. I have work to do."

They turned back. Fintan sidled next to her, body at a right angle to hers, trying to catch the attention of her chocolate eyes. Her gaze stayed focused in the far distance, and his body itched with frustration.

"I don't want to fight with you. I hate it," he said. "What's going on? Why are we arguing?"

Tierra frowned. "Not everything's about you."

They were nearly back at the house. Not especially sensitive, he could mostly ignore the disturbing energies that wrapped around the property, and anger helped drive the traces of them away. "Great. Then stop fighting with me."

"I'm not fighting," Tierra yelled, her hands in balls by her sides.

A slow smile spread across his face, as Tierra reluctantly realized what she'd said, and how she'd said it.

"Fine." She blew out a breath. "You're annoying. I've been annoyed. I *am* annoyed."

"Why am I annoying you? What am I doing that's different?" He wouldn't let this go. She was too important.

"Nothing. Everything. You're right. I'm finding things challenging with everyone here. I'm trying to keep the house going, and I don't know how to make everyone happy."

Finally, something he could fix. "You don't need to. I'll draw up a schedule for some of the key tasks for this week when we get home. Adam will probably return to his team soon if nothing else happens – though I think if Argus had his way, they'd stay. That dog loves it here. Cara will go back to the Rehabilitation Center. So it'll be back to Cuinn, Blaize, you and me."

"When are you going?" She played with the wooden beads at her throat.

"I'm not sure. It depends what Cuinn needs. And if any more snippets of prophecy come through that we can use, or if we find anything here. He and Adam are discussing it today, so we'll see where they get to after dinner. Cuinn's been a bit…caught up, with Blaize." He grinned. "Nice to see."

Tierra lifted her head and smiled. "They make a lovely couple – they're good for each other. And I'm glad he has someone helping him with the prophecies. Doing it alone was really taking a toll on him."

Blaize's training had got off to a rocky start, but she was powerful and smart, and she had taken to her training like a duck to water.

Fintan nodded. "Any progress they can make is good. It feels strange to be involved in a prophecy and only know we're involved, nothing more."

Tierra shivered. "Yes."

She put a hand on his. "We're fine, Fintan. I'm a bit, well ... off, at the moment. Bear with me."

The last of the tension left him and he took a breath, then put his arm around her and hugged her close, her scent made from delicate violets and earth. She smelled like home.

She stiffened for a moment, then leaned into him and sighed.

"Okay, Fintan. Let's go inside the –"

There was a loud noise and a clod of earth exploded next to Tierra's foot. Fintan leapt to put himself between Tierra and the direction the projectile had come from. They were under attack.

CHAPTER

2

Tierra yelped and reared back.

Fintan pulled her towards a dilapidated shed on the edge of the property. Things were happening so fast she couldn't understand the sequence of events.

Another noise, another clod of earth. Hot pebbles hit her in the shin. Fintan pushed her behind him and peered out from the cover of the shed. She shook her head in bewilderment.

"Fintan, what's going on?"

"Someone's attacking us. A Manipura energetic of some kind given the fireballs. I assume something to do with Indigo. Do as I say." Fintan ducked his head out and then jerked back as another fireball flew past him.

Tierra's breathing was erratic as her brain finally took in the scene.

"I can only see one person, but there's no guarantee she's alone," Fintan whispered.

A stream of fire hit the shed, sparks exploding. The building creaked. Tierra trembled, her stomach roiling.

"This isn't going to protect us for long. Can you shield us at all?" Fintan asked. He seemed as relaxed as ever, limbs loose, his shoulders free of the tension that was building up in every part of Tierra's body.

Her heart beat faster. The last time she had been in battle it had all gone so horribly wrong. She wasn't good at this.

"I'll...try," she said. Her hands shook and she wrapped her arms tightly around herself.

No. She could do this. She could.

She let her arms hang loose at her sides, and pulled on the Muladhara energy she had drawn in earlier. She wrapped herself and Fintan in a protective bubble, thin at first, then layering on more protection like an onion. Another stream of fire came at them, and the heat seared her back. Her bubble popped, and she staggered.

Fintan dodged the stream and sent return fire. His attacks were much smaller, like bullets made from fire. "Quickly T, we need to get out from behind this shed before it's destroyed, but we need cover."

Sweat prickled along her spine. The atmosphere of the grounds, the energetic traces she had picked up earlier, and this attack were all combining to overload her system. She wanted to retreat, to hide.

Fintan appeared so competent and in control. *There are people firing at us!* she wanted to scream.

He glanced back at her. "Anytime now."

She bit her lip and tried to still the shaking. As she made her next attempt, three balls of fire smashed into the shed, one blowing the door off with a bang that made her heart jump, and another catching Fintan's arm. He swore.

Her mouth dropped open, and she stared at the nasty burn on his arm. Apart from the curses he had dropped, Fintan seemed to be ignoring the injury for now, but Tierra couldn't see anything else. The skin was an angry red, and it needed treatment.

She stepped forward in a daze. She could heal it. He'd fight better if it was fixed.

Fintan stepped back so he was sheltered by the bulk of the building, still seemingly unaffected by the wound.

She put a hand up, and he seemed to catch sight of her. He took her by the shoulders.

"Oh, T. Okay, breathe. Breathe, T."

She struggled limply, her gaze blurry. More fire streamed past. Her breathing hitched. What was wrong with her? She needed to focus. Protect them. "Your arm."

He gripped her shoulders, and the pressure helped to ground her. She concentrated on his voice.

"My arm's fine," he said. "We'll sort it later. T, if you don't think you can do this, it's okay. We'll get out of here another way."

Her chest heaved, but she shook her head.

"Okay. How can I help?" he said.

He already was.

She tried again to pull on her energies. They came more easily this time, earth responding. It had been a long time. She should have practised. Kept up her skills. But she hadn't thought she would ever be in this position again. She wasn't a fighter.

He grasped her by the chin, tilting her head up to meet his gaze. "T. You can do this."

Her bubble grew and stretched and thickened around them. She connected the bubble to them both, so Fintan could fire out of it, but nothing could pass through to reach them.

"Great job. Can you hold it while we move?" he asked.

She nodded, and prayed to Source she could.

He let go of her, and moved to the corner of the shed. She winced and pushed power into it so the bubble would stretch. He glanced around the corner.

"The best thing I think is for us to get to the car and get out of here. If I was alone I'd try and capture one of them, but I want to get you to safety." He grimaced. "But I'd like to know if the firebrand is alone or has someone with them."

She held the protection around them, but hung her head. She was a liability in this situation.

She swallowed. And then her eyes widened. She was an idiot. She could use her earth energies to see if there was anyone else on the property. The time she had spent tracking on it so far had given her a solid sense of it. She'd know if there was more than one person. But…she'd need to drop their shields for a minute. She didn't think she could do both actions at the same time.

Fintan darted his head from the cover of the shed to look. She didn't want to bother him. A moment later, fire smashed into him, and Tierra gasped. But the flames skidded harmlessly off her shield. He turned back to look at her, a wild grin on his face. "Great work!"

Her mouth dropped open. Surely he wasn't enjoying this? "I need to drop the shield for a minute. I think I can work out how many of them there are."

He quirked an eyebrow. "That'd be helpful. You're sure?"

She nodded. "I need you to stay safe though. Don't get hurt. It's distracting."

She couldn't tell him how distracting it really was. She'd been paralyzed when his arm had been hit. She moved until her back was against the wooden shed. Then she slid down so her butt and her hands touched the earth. The more natural surfaces she could touch that were part of the grounds the better.

She closed her eyes. She sent her energies out in streaks that bounced around the ground under the house and its gardens.

The Manipura energetic was easy to spot. Tierra had no energies in common with the woman, who held Ajna as her auxiliary energy. The woman's energies were twisted, and dark, her Manipura full of rage and bitterness. Tierra shuddered. The woman was a Rogue, using her energies in a way that wasn't congruent with the Source. In ways that upset the balance of the world, rather than supported it, which was the energetics' sacred duty from the Source. Not all Rogues were killers, but given who this one was associating with, she probably wasn't there to offer them cake.

The woman was inside the house, and sending her streams of fire through a window that she had smashed.

Tierra found no one else in her fast sweep of the grounds. She needed to do the same for the house. It wasn't big, and there was a great deal of wood in it, which she found easier to send energy through. The concrete was harder.

She could hear Fintan and their attacker, though neither of them cried out. A tree near them had been set on fire, and burned brightly. She would mourn it later.

Pressure on her shoulders made her eyes snap open. She gasped.

"The house is on fire," Fintan said, urgently. "When you do your sweep, can you also track? See if there's anything else you can find? This might be our only chance if the house burns down."

She nodded, but inside her body the adrenaline was draining her faster than she could use her energies.

She tried to recenter herself. Her hands balled into fists in the earth. She could smell burning wood, and the crackle of the flames emphasized how desperate their situation was. If there was anything to find in the house, now was the time.

She sucked in a breath, and coughed on the smoke. They couldn't stay here much longer, either way.

She let her shoulders relax and sank back into herself, and the earth. She aimed her energies at the house. She passed the fire energetic without pausing, and pushed energy into the wooden frame of the house.

There! There was another person. She nudged at him. Another energetic, yes, this one with more familiar energies. Very familiar in fact, though she wasn't sure why. He was a match to Tierra, with Muladhara-Anahata.

But, Source.

Bile rose up in her throat. It had been hard to touch the presence of the first Rogue, but to touch someone who had your own energies, but had twisted them into something so corrupt, so contemptible, so evil, was horrific.

She wavered. She felt him stop what he was doing. He could tell something wasn't right. Could he sense her? He'd have to make the effort to do so, just as she was.

She wished she could read minds.

"There's two people – another one inside. Searching, I think." She squeezed the words out. Fintan flung back an affirmative.

She moved off the repugnant man and sifted through the house. The energetic traces were full of desperation, especially in the basement, where Blaize had been held, and Tierra could feel the shining traces of the presence of her friend. She had been leeched by Indigo. But there were traces of that other presence in the basement, traces that were stronger than they had been in the grounds.

The charred floorboards of the basement contained the echo of a man, his energies twisted even more darkly than the two currently in the house. It was strange, but the presence reminded her of someone. Perhaps it was the combination of energies? But twisted, and strong. Her skin crawled. If she came across him again, she'd recognize him.

She moved her energies through the rest of the house, fast. There was only the one other person currently in the building. If they could get past the woman who was attacking them, they could get out of here. And right now, she wanted nothing more.

Her mouth twisted. Was she really going to leave, having gone through all this, without any further information? Her stomach soured. If they left without making a last try for clues, by the time they came back, these two would have stripped the place of anything useful.

Her fear could have consequences for everyone.

Her body was weak, and she was shaking consistently now. She had no idea how she was going to get out of here when they needed to.

She rubbed her hands back and forth in the soil, the repetitive action soothing her body while her mind and energy focused on the house.

Could she pick up a sense of what the man in the house was searching for? She concentrated and honed in on his presence again. He was in the bedroom, low to the ground. What could he be doing?

She probed, with fragile tendrils of energy she hoped he wouldn't notice. Despite them being thirty feet from the house, she could hear the crackle of flames as it burned, warm air drifting across her skin. She could only imagine what it must be like to know that the fire could bring the house down any minute. Whatever he was searching for must be important. But all she could sense were his feelings, not his thoughts.

Moments later, his energy flooded with triumph, and he moved at speed out of the room. Whatever he had been looking for, he'd found it.

"The energetic in the house is coming out, Fintan!" she yelled it, and rose unsteadily to her feet. If their attackers came after them, she would need a clear head.

They didn't. The assault on them stopped, and an engine roared into life. Fintan shot out from their cover and headed towards it. She staggered after him.

By the time she had skirted the harsh heat that billowed out from the blazing house to follow Fintan, he had already reached the lane. A vehicle headed away from the house at speed.

"Should we follow?" She had to raise her voice to carry over the crackle of the house fire. She really wanted the answer to be no.

Fintan shook his head and gazed down the road, mouth a flat line. "Are you okay? Get anything from the house?"

"Not really." She turned back to face the collapsing building, to see if there was anything else she could pick up. Her stomach was tight. He wasn't following the Rogues because of her, and she hadn't managed to pick up anything useful. Her attempt to help had had a negative impact.

"We need to call this in to the fire service. I'll tell them we were driving past and saw it from the road." He pulled out his cell and moved away from the noise of the fire.

She nodded miserably, her gaze downcast. She drew on what was left of her energies, and tried for one last energetic examination.

But the rooms she'd searched just minutes before were turning to ash, any natural materials that might hold traces being consumed by the fire. She pulled her threads of energy back towards her – and they snagged on something. She frowned.

She couldn't get much of a read on it with her energies, only that it was a disturbance, something energetic, but not natural. It wasn't anything she could read with her magic – was there something physical there?

She took a step, but the heat was intense. She gritted her teeth. It was only another handful of feet, but the smoke from the house covered the way so she couldn't make a visual inspection.

Whatever it was was on the ground. She would need to feel for it.

She glanced behind her, but Fintan was on the phone, facing in the opposite direction. She wrapped her scarf around her mouth and nose, and dropped to her hands and knees and began to crawl towards the house. She held the strange object in her energetic perspective even as her vision was obscured by the smoke. A few more feet, that was all. It was just inside the doorway of the house.

By the time she got to the item, she was coughing, acrid smoke burning her throat. She tried to keep her inhalations short. She reached out and grasped the item, small enough to fit into the palm of one hand.

It burned.

She gasped, and then choked as smoke filled her lungs. Dizziness filled her. She gripped the hard-edged object. The burn wasn't the heat of the house fire behind her, but a cold burn.

She turned on the spot, to crawl away, but after she'd progressed a few feet, she realized that the flames and noise of the house were hotter and louder. She'd gone in the wrong direction. Tears streamed from her eyes. She shook her head, dizzy. Which way was out?

She couldn't get a grip on her energies, and the smoke wrapped around her. There wasn't enough oxygen to sustain her, even this low to the floor, and sweat poured off her from the heat of the blaze.

"Fintan!" she tried to shout, but his name came out in a croak. She dragged herself a few more feet, trying to move away from the house, but the heat seemed to surround her, and she couldn't tell whether she was moving closer to the source of the flames or away to safety. Her head drooped.

She couldn't breathe.

Couldn't make her body do what she wanted.

Couldn't get to Fintan, and safety.

And she wasn't sure how real the touch of that reassuring Warrior energy was as the smoke became too much for her.

CHAPTER

3

After a fast but necessary shower had dulled the edge of the aches and pains from the afternoon's unexpected entertainment, Fintan joined the others in the spacious living room. Its cathedral ceiling with exposed wood beams helped the room feel uncluttered despite the fact there were five of them and a dog scattered around it. Someone – probably Cara, given Tierra's current state – had pulled together some cookies and hot drinks, and the room smelled of sugar. Fintan grabbed a cookie from the plate and took stock of the room.

He loved Cathair Cuinn. It, and the people who lived there, had been a home to him like no place of his own had ever been. Its thick stone walls (so like Cuinn) and comfortable textiles (so like Tierra) had provided comfort and stability for decades. Despite his tendency to change where he lived on a whim, he knew he could always return here and be welcomed.

Adam, Cuinn and Blaize argued in the middle of the room while Tierra lay on the sofa, Cara checking her over. Adam's husky, Argus, sat with paws and nose on Tierra's legs, and gave her the occasional lick. Tierra grumbled at Cara's ministrations, her skin sallow, and her eyes red from smoke.

Cara, who had a striking combination of blonde bob and unusual bronze eyes, was Tierra's best friend, an Anahata-Manipura, and she worked as a Healer in a Rehabilitation Centre off the west coast of Canada. She looked after others without complaint – but her Manipura auxiliary Chakra meant she didn't take any shit while doing it.

Fintan gazed at her with relief. The exhilaration of the fight had nearly been wiped out by terror that Tierra might have been injured, or worse.

Fintan headed over to her and caught Cara's gaze. He lifted an eyebrow and she gave him a slight nod. His chest loosened.

"What the hell happened out there, Fintan?" Blaize glowered. "You're supposed to protect civilians."

"It wasn't his fault," Tierra rasped.

Guilt clutched at his insides. Yes, it was. He should have kept Tierra safe.

"Let him speak, Blaize," Cuinn said.

Fintan swallowed, and filled them in on what had happened with the Rogues. Then he squatted down next to Tierra. What he wanted to say was, what the fuck did you think you were doing going into a burning house? He'd turned around to call the fire service, and when he'd looked back, she'd disappeared. His heart had stuttered.

He restrained himself. "What I don't understand is why you went into the smoke in the first place."

Tierra put a hand into her pocket and brought out a bright, white stone, that seemed to glow. "I went to get this. I think they dropped it."

Cuinn's eyes narrowed. He walked over and plucked it out of her hand. He turned it over in his palm, then his gaze became unfocused as he checked it at an energetic as well as at a physical level.

When he raised his head, he looked ill. He sank down into one of the wing-backed armchairs. "This shouldn't exist. It's a white sapphire, and it contains stored Ajna energy."

He placed it on a small table in front of him and shuddered.

"Doesn't everything natural contain energy of one kind or another?" Blaize asked.

"Yes, but that's not what I mean. This stone has been used like a battery. Someone has drained an energetic and stored their magic in this stone."

There was a horrified silence.

Fintan rubbed his forehead. "I didn't think that was possible."

"Neither did I," Cuinn said, his face set. "And yet there it is."

"Are you sure?" Adam rumbled.

"There are some more checks I need to do. But I'm pretty certain, yes."

"Did the energetic they drained survive?" Cara asked. Her hand rested on Tierra's hair.

"I don't know," Cuinn said.

Fintan paced back and forth. "We have to stop this happening again. We need to find those Rogues."

"No shit," Blaize said.

"Where are we on the prophecies?" Adam said.

"We haven't made much progress since rescuing Blaize, I'm afraid," Cuinn said. "The only change we've seen is that Blaize now stands with us, rather than dies, so I'm confident that part of the prophecy has been diverted."

Cuinn, an Ajna energetic, had gone into the dreamscape at no small cost to himself to find the prophecies. He'd shared them with the rest of the group as he'd realized they were all a part of them — and now they were all in it together.

Blaize stood, and ran a hand through her hair in agitation. "This explains the jewels in the prophecy, doesn't it?"

Cuinn's mouth twisted. "Probably, yes."

"What are you talking about?" Fintan said. His body was full of adrenaline, ready for a brawl, but there was nothing and no one to fight.

"The last prophecy image that Cuinn found contained a heap of jewels, surrounded by bones. We thought it referred to some sort of treasure," Blaize said.

Cara's nose wrinkled. "The bones – it suggests the energetics probably don't survive the process then."

"We don't know that," Tierra protested softly from the sofa. Cara patted the other woman's hair comfortingly, and Argus whined.

"It's not a great sign," Cuinn said.

"Where do we go from here?" Fintan asked. He hated this helpless feeling.

"Difficult. Cuinn and Blaize can do the most." Adam turned to them. "Prophecy and stone research."

Cuinn was still gazing at the stone on the coffee table. "I need to find somewhere to store this."

"I'll go to Vancouver," Adam continued. "Follow the diner receipts we found during the first search of Indigo's place. For you, Fintan, and Cara, business as usual."

"Business as usual?" Fintan balled his hands by his sides. "Are you serious?"

"You have work. So does Cara. And we're probably going to need to pull you away from that work again in the future. So for now, we use our resources wisely."

Though Adam was a pretty senior energetic Protector, and he and Fintan had worked together often, it was unusual to see this more commanding side of him at Cathair Cuinn. Cuinn might be the person who understood the prophecies and the ether the best, but Adam, Tierra's brother and Cuinn's cousin, was the group's leader in terms of strategy and tactics in the physical world.

Adam turned from Fintan to Cara. "That reminds me. You said that the Rehab Center has had an abnormal number of Rogues this past year. Can you tell us more?"

"There's not much more than that really," said Cara. "We're the Rehab clinic for the Pacific north west of North America, and western Canada. We take a few other cases too, but that's our usual area. We're probably getting about fifteen per cent more than usual." Cara smoothed her skirt over her legs. "No links I can see. Very few have been significant – some of them have already been rehabbed and released. I don't believe we've had any cases of a Rogue being an energy Leech apart from this one."

Cuinn cocked his head. "That time frame is about the same period as for the prophecy dreams. Do you know if any of the other Rehab Centers have also experienced an increase?"

"I don't, but I can ask. Actually, has the Minor Circle been updated? I might get in touch with the Anahata Minor Guilds and ask them. They might have an overview. I'll start with mine."

There were thirty Minor Guilds, representing each combination of dominant and auxiliary powers, for example, Anahata-Manipura which was Cara's, but also Manipura-Anahata, for energetics with a dominant Manipura and auxiliary Anahata, because the two blends could be so different. Thus each energetic belonged to three guilds – their Minor guild, and two Major Guilds (Anahata and Manipura, in Cara's case). The Minor Circle consisted of a representative of each of the thirty Guilds, just as the Major Circle had a representative of each of the six Major Guilds. Since Sahasara, the crown Chakra, and Chakra of the Source, was neither dominant nor auxiliary for energetics, it didn't have any Guilds.

"Good idea." Adam nodded. "If anyone spots anything else similar, let Cuinn and Blaize know. Cathair Cuinn is our base of operations. Questions?"

Tierra sat at her workbench in her private living room. A handful of scented candles she'd made needed their wicks trimmed before they were ready to use. This recent batch was lavender scented, from herbs she'd collected and distilled.

Normally her answer to difficult feelings was to cook or clean, but she didn't have the energy for either. She was glad she had her own space in the huge house. She really needed it.

She held the scissors listlessly, and snipped the first wick. Then put the scissors down and stared out of her large windows at her little garden.

She'd tried to help, and she'd messed up. Because Fintan had had to protect her, Indigo's house had burned, and they'd lost the opportunity to find further clues. Without Tierra, he might have been able to catch the Rogues, but he hadn't wanted to leave her.

And now, everyone had a job to help with the prophecies but her. Adam hadn't even mentioned her in his summary. She was a glorified housekeeper. She was a hindrance, not a help. She snipped another wick, more viciously this time.

There was a knock and her door opened.

It was Cara. "How are you feeling?"

Tierra shrugged.

Cara walked over and put a hand on Tierra's brow, checking her temperature. She frowned, walked to the glass doors, and let in the smell of damp earth and growing things.

"Physically, you're going to be fine. But I don't need to sense your feelings to see you're sad. So what's up?"

Cara pulled up another chair next to Tierra's. A petite woman with a heart-shaped face, she was a strong Anahata, and could intuit a lot from using her energy around feelings, though it wasn't usually considered polite to do this. Tierra could sense moods when her own emotions were stable, and was fairly empathetic in the human sense, but she didn't have the strength of gift that Cara had.

The two women had got to know each other while working for a period in Anahata Guild in Cairo in the late 1800s, Tierra in Records and the Archive, Cara managing the Major Guild's relationships with some of the Minor guilds. Learning to belly dance together had cemented their friendship, which had endured to this day.

"I wish I was more useful," said Tierra.

Cara's brows drew together. "I don't understand. You're one of the most practical people I know. Look at these candles you're making."

She gestured at the pretty glass containers with their purple wax.

"I want to do more to help with what's going on, but I've barely left Cathair Cuinn and Merrow in decades. Today made me realize how scared I've become." She swallowed a lump in her throat. "I fought alongside you all in World War II. And look at me now."

Cara studied her. "You did, but it was tough on you. You needed time to heal."

"I think I took too long. I thought I was doing Cuinn a favor, coming here to look after him all those decades ago. But I got stuck. I used to travel all over the world. Now the furthest I go is to visit you on the other side of Vancouver."

"Is that a problem?"

"I froze today." Tierra swallowed. "I forgot my training."

"That's not the role you need to take," said Cara. "You have a good job in the human world, and you do provide huge support for all of us, but it's a different kind of support. Don't think we don't need it just as much though. Cuinn wouldn't have survived the last few decades without you."

Tierra glanced at her, then away. She bit her lip.

"What you do with this house baffles me," said Cara. "I could never manage to run it in the way you do. You make all of our lives better."

"But I don't want to sit at home. I want to help."

"Most of us are going back to our day jobs, like you."

Tierra, slightly mollified, rubbed a hand over her face and rested her chin on it. "I guess so. But I think Adam sees me as the little sister who's only good to look after the house."

"I wouldn't say he thinks of you as 'only' good enough to look after the house. He's as grateful as the rest of us. When there's an opportunity to help, you will."

Tierra sank down on her chair. She knew Cara didn't mean to sound patronizing, but that was how it felt. "Maybe."

"Sleep some more." Cara got up, and ran a hand lightly over Tierra's hair. "Fintan said to tell you he'll make dinner."

Tierra started. "Fintan?"

"Yes. Fintan." Cara cocked her head and gazed at Tierra assessingly. "Is there anything you want to talk about?"

Tierra's eyes opened wide. Why would Cara ask that? "No. Nothing. Why do you ask?"

"No reason." She walked to the door. "I'll call you when it's time."

The door shut behind her, and Tierra straightened in the chair, and snipped another wick. She gazed outside. Fintan was cooking? She couldn't remember the last time he'd taken charge in the kitchen. She'd like to see it. But she didn't want to get in the way.

She groaned and covered her face with her hands. *Get a grip, Tierra.*

Enough of this self-pity. She mentally shook herself and got up. She spotted her slim silver laptop on a shelf and grabbed it. She tugged a blue scarf, dotted with pretty pink flowers, from a hook on the wall, and wrapped its softness around her neck.

She'd rest, sure, but she'd also work, she thought as she stepped into her garden, leaving the glass doors that led to it open. She reminded herself that she was gainfully employed, in a job where people needed her and enjoyed her writing. And that although what she did might not be saving the world, it did help make the world an ever-so-slightly better place each week.

Outside was a shady wood, cool at this time of year, with a wooden table and chairs where she sometimes worked. She opened up the laptop and found the reader email she'd been thinking of.

"Dear Tierra,

Thank you so much for your wonderful advice column in the Vancouver Daily, which I always find helpful.

I'm having a tough time at the moment. I'm 24, and I work in an office job and still live with my family.

I know it's time to branch out and leave home, but my parents are protective, and I'm scared. They don't want me to go, and I'm finding it hard to make the leap when they see me this way.

How can I help them understand that I need this for my own independence? And how can I get the confidence to be more self-sufficient? Yours, Debbie."

Tierra started typing, her fingers flying over the keys.

Dear Debbie,

Thanks for your letter, and I'm glad you enjoy my column.

I can certainly empathize with your issue. Sometimes we can get stuck in a situation without realizing it, and it can be hard to make a change, especially when others see us a certain way.

There are two things here.

The first is to sit down with your parents and tell them that you're old enough to look after yourself, but you're happy to set their minds at ease by talking them through your move to manage any worries they have. Ask them for their objections, and then logically present the evidence to them that you have tackled each one. Keep emotion out of it.

The second is to develop your own self-confidence. Consider what, exactly, are you afraid of? What's the worst that can happen? What measures can you put in place so that doesn't happen? Face your fears head on, but in a way that's kind to yourself.

Either way, it's your life, and while you need to be aware of their feelings, you also need to set boundaries about what is your decision to make, and not theirs. You earn your own money, you're an adult, and it's okay to make your own decisions.

Take care,
Tierra

Tierra sat back, satisfied, though her fingers ached from hitting the keyboard harder than normal.

There was another knock at her door, and she turned towards it, squinting through her open doors from the garden to see who had come into her room. Cara was back.

Tierra glanced at her wall clock, where each number was a pretty bird. "Dinner already?"

"No. Adam's had some kind of call from the Circle and he's being sent to sort out some urgent problem. We need a new plan."

Fintan studied Tierra as she and Cara entered the room.

Petite and shapely, she seemed even smaller than usual. Her dark hair was pinned back, and her brown eyes were serious. She was usually more bouncy, and her enthusiasm for life infectious, but still, she seemed more relaxed than when she had left them. He'd been worried about her. She'd been injured physically, but she'd also folded in on herself, and was swathed in a rich purple cardigan. He wanted to engulf her in his arms, to hug her worries away. He grimaced. Whatever they were facing was going to take more than a hug to make disappear.

"What's going on?" Tierra asked. Her eyes were still red from the smoke, and there were smudges underneath them. She sat on the sofa, her legs curled under her. Cara perched next to her.

"Something critical's come up that the Circle needs Adam to deal with," Fintan said. Adam was highly skilled at his job. He'd taken personal time for what was going on, but without telling the Circle and the Guilds what he was doing, and as his employers, they wanted him back.

"Someone else can handle it. I'm not their only Protector." Adam wrinkled his brow, his arms crossed over his broad chest. Argus huffed at his feet. "This situation is as urgent."

"What's going on with the Circle?" Blaize asked Adam.

"I'm not sure. A problem in London. Sensitive," said Adam.

"You need to help the Circle. Our situation will have to wait until you're back. Or Fintan can go to Vancouver," Cuinn said. He didn't have his usual upright posture. He sat on the edge of one of the armchairs, Blaize behind him on one of the arms. Her hand was on his shoulder.

"Not the right skill set." Adam's voice was matter of fact. "Needs a tracker with earth energy and instincts to follow her trail."

"We're not out of options yet," Cara said. She glanced at Tierra, who narrowed her eyes.

"What do you mean?" Cuinn absently stroked Blaize's hand on his shoulder.

"Well, we have more than one tracker," Cara said. She put a hand on Tierra's arm.

Tierra sighed. "Me."

"You?" Adam frowned. "After earlier?"

"Absolutely not." The words were out of Fintan's mouth before he'd really thought them through. But, really, what a ridiculous idea. He'd seen today what Tierra was like in a defensive situation. The last thing they should do was send her out again. She'd be scarred for life.

"I don't think it's your decision to make." Cara said, her tone warm, but firm. She caught Tierra's gaze. "It's your decision. This is something you can do. If you want to."

"If I'm brave enough," Tierra muttered. "But yes. I can do this."

"We're all involved in this," Fintan argued. "I have a say."

What the hell is Cara thinking?

"Only as much as anyone else," Tierra said. "Let's vote. All those who think I should go to Vancouver, raise your hand."

Tierra looked around the room, meeting everyone's gaze in turn, daring them not to raise their hands.

All the women raised their hands immediately. Blaize nudged Cuinn, and his hand followed, albeit slowly. When Fintan looked at him, mouth open, Cuinn said, "I don't love the idea, but she has the experience. Don't be sexist."

"I'm not being sexist. She's not a Warrior. You weren't there today. It affected her badly." *Was the world going mad?*

Tierra scowled at him.

"I'll take Blaize or Cara with me," said Tierra. "Either way, I'm going. I'm the right person."

Argus whined, and trotted over to stand next to Tierra.

Adam glanced at him, and then around the room, and he rested his hands on his hips. "Huh. Alright. You can, but not without protection. Unfortunately, Blaize is needed here, and Cara is needed at the Rehab Center." Adam's gaze moved to rest on Fintan. "You can go with her. I'll square it with the Circle."

"Haha," said Fintan, wincing at Adam's unexpected and terrible attempt to lighten the mood. "This is still a bad idea."

His whole body was tight. Tierra didn't track killers. She was the heart of Cathair Cuinn, the only real home he had.

Tierra looked torn, presumably at the idea of him accompanying her. It didn't feel great, but she'd be safer with him. She looked at Adam mutinously.

"You can track," said Adam to Tierra. "But you're rusty. You haven't defended yourself for decades. You need someone with you and Fintan is the only Warrior here who doesn't have another pressing job. And he can work with you on your defensive skills in the downtime." He shrugged. Decision made.

Both Fintan and Tierra were scowling now.

"Okay?" Adam had already moved on.

"Fine," said Fintan.

Except that it wasn't even close to fine.

Elrian stood in his closet. His crisp white shirts hung neatly in a row, several pairs of black pants pristine beneath them. Shiny black shoes were lined up on the floor. He reached and took down a shirt, and pulled it on one arm at a time. His movements were calm and measured. Deliberate.

Today would be a good day.

It hadn't been a good couple of weeks. His Adherent, Indigo, who had been with him, helped him and served him for many years, had been killed. Through her own stupidity, of course. He frowned.

As her Maven, her death had hit him hard. Her Haven—her 'safe place' in the dreamscape—had been destroyed when she died. As it had been tethered to his own Haven, he had needed to shore up his defenses in the dreamscape. His power had been severely depleted.

He took a pair of suit pants out of the closet and shook them, hard. He hated creases. After all, outer order created inner calm.

Ensuring things were neat, tidy, and in their proper place helped to quiet the tangle of voices inside his dreamscape.

It wouldn't do for Cuinn to find him. Not yet, anyway. Indigo's death had also meant Elrian had lost his opportunity to hurt Cuinn's partner, Blaize. Now that would have served a two-fold purpose, breaking the prophecy and devastating Cuinn.

Elrian took a breath as he shut the wardrobe door, then smoothed his shirt down over his chest. There were other chances coming.

He was confident he was still ahead of the game. His work in the dreamscape meant he had more pieces of the prophecy than Cuinn did. Elrian had been working on it longer, after all.

But Cuinn and the others were seeking Elrian out. They would follow Indigo's trail back to Vancouver. He had prepared for that. They were unlikely to find the upscale house where he was right now. They should find the nasty motel she had spent most of her time in. Despite the fact he had set her up in this affluent community, she hadn't wanted to spend time here, preferring the fire of the metropolis to the suburbs, which she had considered lifeless. But he would limit his time here anyway, and soon jettison this place. He had no attachment to it, and it was one of a number of places he moved between for work.

The prophecy slivers he had picked up that morning suggested this was a turning point. Cuinn's people had choices about who they set on Elrian's trail, and whoever was sent would determine the next of the six possible couples that he needed to derail.

They had two trackers, the brother and sister.

Adam and Elrian had never gotten along, and Adam was strong enough that he could be a problem, especially when you added in that mutt of his. Not every Muladhara energetic needed an animal. That kind of bonding with a lower species had always seemed unsavory to Elrian.

His sister, Tierra, on the other hand, was weak. The intelligence he'd gathered told him she had fossilized in that pretentious house of Cuinn's. She wouldn't be a challenge.

Elrian hoped they'd send Tierra.

CHAPTER
4

There was silence in the car as they left Cathair Cuinn behind them. Tierra shifted uncomfortably in her seat and took a sip of the coffee in her travel mug. Fintan's vehicle was fast and powerful, a Chevy Corvette – red, of course. Their overnight bags were in the trunk; his worn khaki duffel bag, and Tierra's small, barely used wheeled suitcase.

Fintan reached down and switched on the radio, finding a soft rock station that Tierra couldn't really complain about. Even though she wanted to. She was scratchy today.

She had mixed feelings about this whole situation. When Cara had suggested she go to Vancouver instead of Adam, Tierra had realized she didn't have a choice. She'd complained she didn't have a way to contribute, and Cara had offered her one. So she could make up for the day before.

Yet at the same time, there was an icy core of terror inside her. There wasn't any question she wanted protection. Yesterday had shaken her up and reminded her how vulnerable she was.

But, Fintan? He would protect her, there was no doubt. But would he also try and control her? He hadn't wanted her to come. Hadn't supported her need to play a part in the hunt for Indigo's co-conspirators. And that had hurt more than she'd wanted to admit.

Tierra needed to step up and show she could protect herself. And that didn't include a nanny.

Then she caught sight of the burn on Fintan's arm, and hunched her shoulders, remembering how he had looked after her the day before. She blew out a breath.

What had she replied to Debbie? *"Ask your parents for their objections, and then logically present the evidence to them that you have tackled each one. Keep emotion out of it."*

She'd take her own advice and address this awkward silence between them head on.

"Why don't you want me to do this?" She kept her gaze on the road as she sipped her drink.

The music filled the car with lyrics about love, holding on, and being a small-town girl. She turned it down.

"I was with you in World War II, T. I saw how much the violence affected you, the deaths of your mom and aunt especially," he said. Concern layered his tone. "How long it took you to recover. Yesterday was like turning back the clock. You were in shock last night."

"We're not at war. We're going to Vancouver to find out where Indigo was staying. We're looking for leads, not fighting an army. Those thugs have no idea we're going to Vancouver." She made an effort to relax her hand around her coffee. *Keep emotion out of it.*

"We don't know what we'll find, but the signs yesterday weren't good. There are at least two of them, and they're not afraid to use violence." He took a turn to the right onto a main road, heading towards Vancouver.

"So we track them, and then bring the others in when we've found them. We don't need to engage." Tierra kept her voice level.

34

"If we do, you take the lead. But don't forget, it was my bubble shield that helped us escape yesterday. I'm not without resources. I just need to blow away the cobwebs on that aspect of my energies."

Right?

They sped along the highway, a road that followed the glittering ribbon of the Harrison river. Tierra loved the scenery in this part of the world. It had helped in her transition from the Mediterranean, where she had lived for many decades before relocating to Canada. She'd moved because Cuinn had needed her, but she'd also welcomed the break from Europe after the wars that had ravaged it.

Energetics tried to live in a place lightly, given that they often had to leave a location to prevent their long lives being discovered, but their connection with their natural environment went deep. She'd had a lot of self-healing to do after the wars, and her sorrow had been over the land as well as the people. Canada had been clean and fresh, with few people and a great deal of open space.

"We need to bring your training up to date," Fintan said.

"What training?" Tierra frowned at the change of topic.

"Your offensive and defensive abilities."

Oh. Not such a change. Tierra's shoulders slumped. He was right. But she wasn't enthusiastic.

"It's okay, you know," said Fintan.

"What is?"

"You're not suited to combat. Not everyone is. Source gives us all different aspects, different gifts. Violence isn't one of yours." He shot her a glance. "It's not a bad thing."

He was right again. So why was there a tight ball in her chest? Why was it hard to swallow? Why was she feeling so angry? It was as if all the emotions from the last twenty four hours were being squeezed into a tiny hollow between her breasts, making it hard for her to breathe.

"Let's talk about what we're going to do when we get there," said Fintan.

"We'll go into the diner on Hastings that was on the receipts. Have some food. Look around. See who we can talk to." She stared out of the window and rubbed the spot just above her heart Chakra.

"I should take the lead," he said.

"Oh, you have tracker training, do you? Know how to get inside someone's emotions? Because if so, you haven't been demonstrating that much lately." *What is wrong with me?* Tierra wasn't usually someone who made sarcastic comments. Or not with the angry edge that had made those words slice at him. She took a deep breath in a futile attempt to calm herself and slow her pulse, which hammered in her chest.

"It's better if I draw their focus. And I don't think you should go anywhere alone. If we're together it's much less likely you'll have trouble." Fintan's tone was oh-so-reasonable, but Tierra had had enough. The thin veneer of control she had clung to since the first fireball the day before splintered and fractured.

"Stop the car." If she didn't get into some open space, she was going to explode. Her energy, her magic, demanded that she connect to the natural world before she burst her skin.

"What?" Fintan's forehead wrinkled, but he didn't take his foot off the accelerator.

"Stop the car. Now." She was going to prove to him – and more importantly, to herself – that she could do this. That she didn't need to be wrapped in cotton wool.

"Why?" said Fintan.

Tierra drew a little power, and sent energy through the tires, asking the land to grip them and slow the car. She realized as she did how rusty she was – it hadn't even occurred to her to do the same the day before when the Rogues were leaving.

Fintan grappled with the wheel as the car skidded. He applied the brakes. Within seconds he had pulled the car over to the side of the road. "What the—"

Tierra threw her door open, and headed for a glade of trees on the right. After a few strides, she ran. The freedom of the forest surrounded her, and she drew deep breaths of fresh air into her lungs. She could have blended with the forest, hidden herself from him, but that wasn't the point of this exercise. She wanted him to follow.

Fintan stumbled out of the car and shouted her name, but she had a good lead. She stopped a minute or so later, in the middle of a thick glade of pines, and pulled power, waiting for him to catch up with her.

He entered the clearing and walked cautiously towards her. She sent tendrils of her power into the earth, stirring roots, branches and vines. She riffled through them as if she was looking for a file in a cabinet. She chose the vines.

Before Fintan had taken more than two steps, she'd caught him. Her vines, thick, strong and supple, reached out of the earth and wound themselves around his muscled calves. He glanced down at them, his eyebrows raised. "Tierra, what the hell are you—"

The vines grew quickly, and she drew them up his body, and wrapped them around his skull, so his jaw was bound. His eyes narrowed, though he seemed merely irritated, not angry.

She, on the other hand, was furious. The tight ball of emotion that had sat so heavily on her chest exploded through her body, and the earth shook. Fintan, his legs tied by vines, fell. She wrapped more vines around him and he made a stifled noise, struggling. He glared at her as he tried to speak.

"I'm showing you I can protect myself!" The words burst from her. "I'm not helpless. I was surprised yesterday. I can do this, Fintan!"

He stilled, and cocked his head, considering her from his position on the ground. He nodded once, and she felt him pull his power, Manipura, fire energy. She forced panic down. Was he going to defend himself? If so, she needed to show him she knew what she was doing. Because she did, didn't she?

She did a fast scan of the environment. What might he do? Ah. He could burn through the vines.

She used her power to lower some of the longer, higher branches, tying the vines to them and lifting him high, high up in the air. He'd be a lot less likely to set alight the branches from up there, where he'd fall if he freed himself.

She tipped her neck to stare through the boughs. He wasn't struggling, but watched her with the patience of a hunter. The pleasant glade hummed with power, the animals and birds hushed. She bit her lip. Having that assessing gaze directed at her was disconcerting.

She wanted to talk to him, explain, before he did anything rash. She sent her power into the trees, and several branches bent towards her, their leaves whispering gently. She stepped onto one, held on to another, and lifted the branches up so she was close enough to Fintan that he could hear.

It had taken less than a minute, and she'd neutralized him.

"I. Can. Protect. Myself." She shook a little with the aftermath of the adrenaline that had flooded her system. "Stop seeing me as the little sister you need to control, and treat me as an equal. A partner. Because that's what we are for the next day or two. If we don't work together effectively, we waste time, not just for us, but for everyone. What's at stake here is a lot bigger than the two of us. Do you understand?"

She released the vines that bound his jaw.

"You made your point. We'll train later, and I'll show you exactly why you do need me. Let me down." A vein pulsed at his temple. Okay. Perhaps he wasn't so relaxed about what she'd done.

"I wouldn't have needed to do this if you weren't such an arrogant idiot." She moved her branch a little further away.

"Arrogant? Me?" His hands, down by his hips as he was still wrapped in the vines, balled into fists.

"Yes. You. Just treat me as if I was any of the others. And let's move on." She drew on her energy to take them both back to the ground and release him.

"Okay. I'll treat you like any other Warrior who tried a trick like this," said Fintan, grimly.

The hum of power around them intensified as he pulled energy. A heartbeat later, he burned through his bonds, and he propelled himself over to her branch, his weight sinking it, and them, to the ground at an alarming rate. Oh. Apparently being up high wasn't the deterrent she'd thought it would be.

He, anticipating the landing, took it in a graceful roll, whereas she tripped as she landed, and had to put an arm out to catch herself.

As he came back up to his feet, he dived and snaked his arm around her throat, lifting her head up at an awkward angle. Fire rose up around them, heating the air.

Oh dear. She was trapped in a circle of fire with an angry fire energetic.

Her back and butt were pressed into him, and his solid arm was hot against her neck. She could hear the rasp of his breath in her ear. Her brain fogged over.

And then her anger was gone, chased away by a pulse of something that was one part fear, and – disturbingly – three parts arousal.

Fintan's blood was up. Tierra was being so, so, irritating. When, exactly, had that happened? All their lives, she had been the sweetest, most loving of energetics. Since running Cathair Cuinn, she'd always been welcoming, always been supportive. She always listened to him. Provided an ear.

So who was this?

She had attacked him. What had she been thinking? There was no way she could best him, as he'd just shown. There was a move she could make to get out of the stranglehold he had her in, but he doubted she'd remember. Perhaps this could serve as the first of Adam's suggested lessons. Though he wasn't sure this was exactly what the big man had had in mind.

Tierra moved against him, and he got wind of the scent of her hair. Which smelled of flowers. She was soft, and the curve of her back, and, Source help him, her ass, was pressed into his groin. She tried to twist in his arms, and that movement stirred something in him.

Something that had never noticed Tierra before. His groin twitched.

He let go of her as if she were hotter than the flames he had conjured.

She yelped and fell towards the circle of fire around them.

"Shit!" he said, and dropped the flames and grabbed for her at the same time.

She flailed as she fell, and ended up awkwardly in his arms, off-balance, clinging to him. Her fingers dug into his forearms and they stared at each other.

He righted her as if she were made of glass, and let go. He stepped backwards, putting some distance between them. She had a dazed look in her eyes.

The silence stretched uncomfortably.

The forest air suited her. Sunlight through the forest canopy made her hair shine dark and glossy, and her skin was once again smooth butterscotch rather than the yellower color it had been the evening before. Her Latina genes were highlighted by the browns and greens of the woods. She was a curvaceous dryad, apple-cheeked and innocent.

Whatever insidious part of him had woken up when she had been pressed up against him wasn't going away. He growled, and her eyes widened.

Damn.

He'd never seen Tierra as anything other than family. An honorary sister, as Cuinn and Adam were like his brothers. Part of him craved a sense of family, a sense of home, and while his many-years-dead biological family hadn't been up to much, his chosen family was vitally important to him. The love that she'd always provided him with was crucial to his wellbeing, to his purpose. It gave him the strength to carry on when things were tough and he had moments of emptiness, or loneliness. Not that those happened often. He was someone who could always find a beautiful woman to keep him company. After several centuries, even the most inept of men had a better understanding of seducing women, and he had never been inept.

Tierra was different though. Her love was steady. Constant. It was part of his foundations.

And he wasn't going to fuck that up just because of a brief and weird moment of sexual desire.

They needed to get out of this forest, where some kind of wicked magics were at work.

"You need more work on your self-defense," he said.

She bit her lip and nodded. "You need work on your social skills."

He raised his eyebrows slightly, but decided discretion was the better part of valor.

They walked back to the car. He hoped like fuck she hadn't noticed anything. What the hell was going on with him? Adam and Cuinn would kill him if they knew what had crossed Fintan's mind as he'd held her in that chokehold.

At his car he hesitated again. "Do you want to drive?"

She smiled. "No thanks. But I'll choose the music."

"Okay."

They drove the two hours to Vancouver, breaking their silence only to discuss the best place to park. Fintan suggested—carefully to make sure it didn't seem like a command—that they park some distance from the diner and walk.

She agreed, and he parked a few streets away.

"Will you put a protection warding on the car?" Fintan said. "This doesn't seem the safest of areas to leave it."

She nodded, and looked around the dull concrete environment. "There's not much here for me to draw from."

Muladhara energetics didn't enjoy built up environments. He needed to remember that. He pointed towards a spindly looking tree that stood in a patch of dry earth, part of some previous gentrification project that hadn't taken. She nodded, and after a few moments, said, "I've warded the car to appear less expensive, and less flashy."

She raised her eyebrows at him, and he rolled his eyes. And those childish gestures of teasing did a lot to resettle him.

The drab and dirty diner was no improvement on their surroundings, the smell of bacon fat and the cleaning agent used to wipe tables down assaulting his nostrils as they entered. A sullen waitress gestured to the mostly empty room behind her, to indicate they should seat themselves.

Fintan scanned the other occupants before choosing where to sit. An old man in his eighties sat hunched over a newspaper and a greasy looking all-day breakfast in a booth near the windows. A tired mother, her two children squabbling opposite her, picked at a plate of fries. And a handful of teenagers, most of them sporting piercings and tattoos though none of them looked a day over eighteen, were draped over the booth furthest from the door.

He weighed up the room, and judged none of these to be a threat. That didn't mean he wouldn't take his usual precautions, and he chose a seat where he had his back against the wall. One of the teenagers made a lewd gesture about Tierra behind her back, but a look from Fintan, and the kid's hands fell to his sides. The teen muttered something. Fintan smiled.

Tierra sat, and looked around. "Poor Indigo. Adam said from the receipts she ate here almost every other day for a month."

"Poor Indigo?" Fintan gave Tierra an incredulous look. The woman's heart was uncontainable. "She leeched from Blaize. She'd have drained her dry if Blaize hadn't stopped her."

"Who knows what her background was? Maybe she didn't have our opportunities. Our families. No one would choose to spend so much time in a place like this if they didn't have to," she said. The corners of her mouth turned down.

Fintan picked up the laminated menu from a plastic stand embossed with a perky tomato. "All families have their issues. Cuinn's father isn't exactly a peach, for example. Do you want something to eat?"

"Not really. But we'd better have something. Otherwise, it'll look a bit strange. Plus my stomach is unsettled. Food might steady it." She craned her neck to see what others were having. "Omelet and hash browns? They have to cook that from scratch, and there's not that much that can go wrong with it. And coffee."

Fintan gestured to the waitress, who ambled over on her own schedule.

"What?" The waitress drawled the word.

"Two omelets with a side of hash browns each. And two coffees."

"Whatever you say." The waitress walked off to the counter. She ostentatiously repeated their order to the cook, who, given he was only a couple of yards from them had probably heard it the first time. She returned with a stained coffee pot in her hands, and two mugs.

She poured coffee for each of them, pointed to the creamer and sugar on the table, and walked off again.

"I guess Indigo didn't come here for the service." Tierra tore open a couple of sugar packets and tipped some creamer into her mug, and slid the condiments towards him.

"What's the plan?"

"Can you pick up any energetic traces?" he said.

She glanced around the room. "It's mostly metal composites and manmade things in here. Plus this is highly trafficked. I'll scan, but it's unlikely I'll pick anything up."

"Sure. See what you can do," he said.

She leaned down and looked under the table and made a satisfied noise.

"The table's made of wood under the laminate." She put her hands underneath the table, touched it, and drew in a breath.

She pulled power, and the air shimmered around her. He watched and waited while she worked, her eyes shut. Her long lashes rested on her cheeks. Her face was serene – and bewitching.

He grimaced. It was like a switch had been flipped inside him, and he was suddenly seeing a completely different Tierra.

He was someone who had a lot of relationships. He enjoyed the company of women. He liked cuddling, and he liked sex. But his relationships never lasted that long – for an energetic, anyway. A handful of years, max. His schedule, away from home for long stretches, usually frustrated women after a while. He got bored easily, too. There weren't many people he could spend long periods of time with without wanting more variety.

Though he'd never felt that with Tierra.

He shoved his hands in his pockets and leaned back, his eyes widening in alarm. He needed to nip this in the bud, now. Tierra was the heart of his adopted home and family. That was far more important to him than her being some sort of sexual conquest. His mouth twisted in disgust at the thought. She deserved better than him. He snorted. Way better.

Her eyes popped open. "Everything okay?"

"Fine. Anything?" He winced internally at how curt he sounded. They'd just made up, he didn't want to upset her again.

She frowned. "No. There are some energetic traces here, and I would say they fit Indigo and the male presence I found in the basement, but they're too diluted for me to get much off them. So no progress."

She took a sip of coffee and stared despondently at the table.

"You confirmed this is a place that Indigo came to. That's progress." He reached over and squeezed her hand. "Next step is to offer the waitress cold, hard cash. She's not exactly the friendly type. You can read her if she gives us any useful info."

He opened his wallet under the cover of the table, and checked to see what he had. "But we eat first."

"Let's see what it looks like when it comes." She traced invisible patterns on the table with a finger. "About earlier—"

"Forget it. I was an idiot, you were angry. We're definitely going to refresh your self-defense skills soon though."

"Okay." Tierra's answer seemed meek considering the emotions she'd displayed in the woods. "Just treat me like a partner, and we won't have any problems."

Like a partner. Yes. He tried to blink away the sensory impression of her body tight up against him, his arm around her smooth throat, and took a swig of coffee to distract himself.

"Euhhh." He tried not to spit it out. He forced himself to swallow it, grimacing as it went down.

"I told you it needed sugar."

"There's not enough sugar in the world." He tipped in several packets anyway. Maybe as sweet tar it wouldn't be so bad.

The waitress, whose nametag said 'Betty', brought over two plates and put them on the table with poor grace. As she was about to walk away, Fintan said "Betty."

She turned, eyebrows raised.

"We're looking for a woman," he said.

Betty's nose wrinkled. "I may not be much, but I'm not that desperate, thanks."

Tierra's lips pinched together and she shook her head. "Sorry, that's not what he means. We're looking for a friend of mine. We heard she's been in here a lot recently. In her last phone call home she told us how much she liked the place."

A small 'oof' came from Tierra as he kicked her under the table to prevent her from overdoing it. He added a $50 bill to the table to help her out.

The waitress caught sight of the money, and stopped in her tracks. "What's her name?"

"Indigo. She has dark hair, and she's thin. Pale."

"Maybe I know her. Maybe I don't. What's she to you?" Betty asked.

"A distant cousin. She's been in some trouble recently, but she was planning on coming home. We haven't heard from her in a month or so." Tierra clasped her hands in front of her. "We really need to find her. We're worried."

The waitress thawed a little, though whether in response to the money or Tierra's doe-eyed pleading, Fintan wasn't sure. Betty slid the money from where Fintan had wedged it under the grimy container of creamer, and slipped it into her apron, her gaze never leaving Tierra's.

"I can't tell you much. She was in here every couple of days for about a month, then she disappeared. I thought she was a druggie to be honest. She had that thin, desperate look that junkies get when they're looking for a fix."

"Did you hear where she was staying?"

Betty shrugged. "Probably at the Motel 72. There's not much else around here. It's down the street."

Tierra nodded. "We'll try it. Thank you."

Before the waitress could walk away, Fintan added one last question. "Did you see her eat with anyone else? We'd like to find her friends. They might know something."

"She met up with a guy a couple of times, they left together. Older man. If he hadn't been dressed so fancy, I'd have thought he was her dealer, because she always looked better after they met."

Fintan tried not to seem too interested. "Can you describe him?"

The waitress turned away. "White guy, fifties maybe. Like I said, well dressed."

She walked off to another table.

Tierra let out a breath, and poked her omelet.

"Pretty good." Fintan raised his eyebrows. "And you told no actual lies. Apart from the one about Indigo being your cousin."

"She is, in human terms. She's an energetic. I said distant." She gave up on the pale and greasy omelet, and ate a fry. "That seemed to go well."

"Yeah. Time for our next delightful stop on our tour of Vancouver's finest establishments, Motel 72."

CHAPTER

5

Tierra rolled her shoulders uncomfortably as they walked down the road towards the motel. All around her were the signs of a deprived area. Angry graffiti, broken windows, boarded up shops. The smell of trash because it was heaped in piles of garbage bags rather than in a dumpster. Passers-by avoided eye contact. She hooked her hand into the crook of Fintan's arm.

Then wished she hadn't.

She'd forgotten, for a moment, their strange encounter in the woods. She wasn't quite sure what had come over her. It was so unlike her to behave in such a crazy-person way. But Fintan was incredibly irritating.

And gorgeous.

Putting her hand on his bicep, the muscle flexing as he walked, was giving her some very inappropriate thoughts.

It was odd. She'd loved him for centuries. But she hadn't lusted after him in the way she had since the moment he'd looked down at her, anger in his eyes, flames around them, his arm stretching her throat out like an offering.

She could let go of his arm. She really didn't want to though. Alright. Time for a change of topic.

"How do you want to play it at the motel?" she asked.

"The cousin thing worked well. It'll probably be a guy on reception though." He scratched his chin and narrowed his eyes thoughtfully. "So…why don't you open an extra button on the cardigan?"

Her mouth fell open. "What?"

"Nothing too much. Just…encouragement. It might distract him enough to let his guard down. Your figure is pretty captivating."

She gaped at him. He'd called her body captivating. And possibly insulted her at the same time.

"That ok? You don't have to. You did a great job with the waitress. Wow, she was a piece of work."

She pulled her arm out from his, and stopped. She used the dirty window of a car to redo her lipstick, a subtle rose color, and undid her scarf, stuffing it into her shoulder bag. An amber pendant hung above her cleavage. She popped another button on the nut-brown cardigan, and turned to Fintan.

"How's this? Slutty enough?"

"You look lovely." There was a strange look on his face, a look that didn't match his words. A slight wrinkling of his brow. And was there the faintest hint of disapproval in his voice? She sighed. *Oh well.*

Tierra kept her hands well away from Fintan's biceps as they continued on. He held the door for her and scanned the street to see if anyone watched them enter.

In the motel foyer, an unpleasant dank smell struck her. Like clothes that had been left in a washing machine for too long, and had started to mildew. She headed to what could loosely be called the reception desk, behind which, as Fintan had guessed, was a scrawny man watching a TV. He barely looked up.

"Rooms are $30 for an hour, $70 for the night. Reductions for longer stays. Whaddayawant?"

Tierra leaned over the desk, putting her cleavage in the man's line of sight.

"We're looking for my cousin, Indigo," Tierra said in her best sultry voice. Well, her first ever attempt at a sultry voice. "She was staying with you for a month or so. Dark hair, pale skin, thin. We haven't heard from her in a few weeks, and we're worried."

The man, drawn to her cleavage like it was a magnet and his eyes iron filings, appeared to have been rendered senseless. *Not entirely unflattering. If only I could capture Fintan like that.*

"Maybe. Your cousin, eh?" The man's cynicism was strong enough to get past the view, though his gaze didn't shift.

"Distant cousins. You remember her, then?" Tierra leaned towards him.

"Maybe. What's in it for me?" He leered.

Tierra stepped backwards into Fintan. She could almost feel his eyes burning into the man's face.

Fintan waved $50. "Eyes up, dickwad."

The man mumbled an apology. Fintan put the money on the counter, and it disappeared into the guy's pocket.

"She stayed here about a month. Left a few weeks ago." The man avoided eye contact.

"Do you know what she was doing?" Fintan asked.

"It's not like we had long conversations, Mister. Most people come here for privacy." He snickered.

"You might have overheard something. A man in your position hears a lot of secrets I'd imagine." Fintan gently moved Tierra to his side so they stood next to each other. He leaned a casual hand on the desk, and bent over the counter. It forced the weasel-faced man to look at him, though he had to tilt his head to meet the much bigger man's eyes.

"Maybe, maybe. I might've heard something about research a couple of times." The man leaned back in his seat, putting distance between him and Fintan as casually as possible.

"What kind of research?" Tierra jerked in excitement, the amber pendant swinging.

The man's eyes followed the pendant's path, hypnotized. "No clue. Something about a man? Irish name maybe? It sounded like she was trying to get information about some kind of hippie commune to the East. Talk about dreams and earth, fire, that kind of thing."

That sounded like energetics. Thank the Source, they were on the right track. But who was Indigo researching? Blaize? And who was this other man? What was his relevance to the prophecy?

"Did anyone come here to meet her? Or did she get any phone calls?" said Fintan.

"She had a cell. Didn't make or take many calls from her room." The guy shrugged.

"She had some? Can we see the phone records? Her final bill?"

The man narrowed his eyes and assessed Fintan. "Not strictly legal, that."

Fintan held up another $50 and the man smirked. And did nothing.

Fintan glared at the man, but held up one more $50 bill.

The manager got up and went into a back room. Tierra turned to Fintan. "There's no need to act like my bodyguard. Partners, remember?"

He eyed her and lifted one eyebrow. "It's part of the act. Just like your new and improved voice."

Not much she could say to that.

The man came back out, a piece of paper in his hands. "Here's her bill. There's not much on it. A few phone calls. She didn't use much here apart from the room. We don't have food, or many extras. Just a bit of pay-per-view porn."

"Of course," said Fintan.

Tierra rolled her eyes.

"But she didn't use that."

"How was she? How did she seem mood-wise?"

"Moody's a good word for it. You'd never know whether she was up or down. Not my place to say, though if you ask me, she was doing some kind of drug. High as a kite one day, then a grumpy bitch the next." He caught Fintan's gaze, and said, "'Scuse my language."

50

Tierra took the paper and beamed at the man, while her skin crawled. "Thank you for your help."

"Sure. Next time, come alone with the money, and maybe I can help you a little more." He sniggered.

Tierra hunched her shoulders, and Fintan growled. A jolt of panic went through her at his face, and she took him by the arm and dragged him out of the motel.

Back in the blessed fresh air, Tierra shuddered. "I need a shower."

"It's probably a good idea to book in somewhere for the night now we have a couple of leads to follow," said Fintan. "I'll text the numbers to Adam and he can check on them for us."

His gaze was on his phone, and his fingers moved as he spoke. He didn't see one of the teenagers from the diner sidle up to them.

Thin and bedraggled, she had three piercings in one ear, one in the other, and her eyebrow and nose both sported rings. She looked to be Asian, and wore heavy biker-style boots, ripped jeans, a white t-shirt with a unicorn on, underneath which it said 'go to hell' in rainbow bubble writing, and a battered leather jacket over the top.

"I heard you wanted Indigo." The teen glared at them both.

Fintan tensed. Tierra put an arm up to stop him moving. The girl's demeanor was a front. Anxiety came off her in waves. She wasn't a danger.

"Yes, that's right. Do you know her?" Tierra kept her voice gentle.

"Do you have money?" The girl brought her chin up.

"We can pay you a little for information." Tierra hesitated. "Why don't we buy you a meal?"

The poor girl was slender to the point of too thin. And she could have valuable information. Maybe.

"You can buy me a drink." The glare softened slightly.

"Okay. Where do you want to go?" *Not the diner, please.*

"I know a place." The girl shoved her hands in her jeans pockets, and, head down, strode away.

Tierra followed her, and she heard Fintan sigh behind her, but he'd joined her side within a few strides.

"What's your name?" Tierra asked.

"What's it to you?" The girl mumbled from ahead of them.

Tierra had to strain to hear her, she was so quiet.

"Just something to call you," Tierra said.

"Whatever. I'm Ai."

A couple of blocks later, the girl stopped at the entrance to a bar.

Fintan whispered to Tierra, "This could be a trap. Stay alert."

She nodded, and kept watchful. Fintan's eyes moved constantly, scanning for trouble. Despite all Tierra's confident words of the last twenty-four hours, she was glad of his presence. While talking to the waitress and the guy at reception in the horrible motel had felt like a game, Ai's demeanor made her uncomfortable. Something was very wrong, though Tierra had sensed no threat from Ai herself, despite her angry tone. It was a puzzle.

Ai pushed open the door and went in, without any indication that she was bothered if they joined her.

"Let me take the lead." Tierra put her hand on Fintan's arm to pause him following Ai.

"You think she'll listen to you?"

"Maybe," said Tierra. Hopefully. "There's something about her. I'm not sure exactly, but yes, let me take the lead. If anything happens, you can take over."

Her tracker instincts were on alert. She hoped they would get something from Ai that would move the investigation forward. Then Tierra would have done her part and they could go back home.

Fintan nodded, and led the way through the door. There were a few steps down to the dingy bar, which held more customers than the diner. The floor was grimy, but the bar was well polished, if worn. A few of the patrons drank in a focused fashion, and many of them looked like they had been here for a while. This was a place for serious drinkers, not socializing, and there was little conversation between the customers.

She scanned the room, and found the girl sitting in a booth. Tierra slid in across from her.

"What do you want?" Fintan asked.

"Soda, please," Tierra said.

"A beer." The girl traced circles on the table in old beer with a slender finger.

"How old are you? You're not old enough to drink." Fintan raised an eyebrow.

"Old enough to give you information about your *cousin*. So old enough for a beer. Or two."

Fintan shrugged and went to the bar, leaving the girl and Tierra together.

There was something unusual about the girl, but Tierra couldn't put her finger on what, exactly. Tierra considered reaching out with her energy, but even humans could sometimes feel that, and Tierra didn't want to upset her. At least not until they'd had a proper conversation.

Tierra wrinkled her nose. She was starting to think like Fintan.

"What do you do, Ai?"

"Not much." The girl's chin was still up and her defensive glare held a lot of anger. What kind of life had the girl had, to have such rage in her eyes for strangers? "This and that. Some errands. Whatever needs doing."

"Do you live around here?"

"You could say that."

Tierra gave up, relieved, when Fintan came back with the drinks.

He sat next to her in the booth, his muscular thigh pressed against hers, the heat of it burning through her dress. She frowned, and turned her attention to the girl. "So. Ai. How do you know Indigo?"

Fintan divided his attention between Tierra and Ai's conversation and the room. This would be a good place for an ambush. There were only two exits, the door where they'd come in, and another that appeared to lead to a backstage area. If Ai had set them up, he would be ready.

"Met her in the diner," Ai said. "A couple of months ago. She offered to buy me a burger. I told her I wasn't into funny stuff, and she said that wasn't what she wanted. Said she recognized herself in me. After that we hung out in the diner a few times."

What had Indigo seen in this young woman? They both seemed to have had a shitty deal from the world. Maybe that was it. And street smarts – they reminded him of urban foxes, feral creatures that could turn on you at any time.

"Did she tell you what she was doing?" Tierra asked.

"She said she was working for a guy. And looking for info on another guy. I couldn't help her there." Ai took a sip of beer.

"What else did she tell you? Or do?" said Tierra.

"She met with a few people in the city."

"Do you know who they were?" said Tierra.

"One of them. Said she'd introduce me to a guy who needed a kid to run errands. The money sounded good. We went along to a place in Upper Delbrook. Fancy place. House in north Van. Plenty of glass and wood."

She took another sip of her beer.

Fintan willed his impatience down. The girl was enjoying the attention.

"Trippy from the start. He was weird. And I know weird. He had the same vibe as the girl. I thought they were both on drugs." She shifted in her seat. "Though he was less wired than she was. More in control. He said he could always use people like me. Then they both laughed. Something was off. I decided to disappear. Waited till they were in the other room. Went out a window."

"What made you leave?" said Fintan. He sat back in the booth and stretched an arm out along the back of the seat. The stink of stale beer hovered in the air. Was the weird guy the man who had been in Merrow?

"Just a feeling. I'm good with feelings. Learned to listen to them. Helped me out of bad situations a few times." Her mouth twisted. "The one time I didn't listen, things got ugly. Learned my lesson. Don't take chances now."

Tierra's hands were flat on the table, and she was practically vibrating with excitement. What was she seeing he wasn't? "What happens when you get a feeling, Ai?"

"Not much. A tickle in my brain. Feeling in my gut. Heat."

"Do you ever get dreams? Dreams about real life? And the dreams come true?"

Oh. Surely not. If it was what he thought, then this mess had just got even more complicated.

Ai's eyes widened slightly, and met Tierra's gaze for the first time since the street. "Why?"

"I have … a feeling."

"That's what Indigo asked me. Said she had them too." The girl had stopped clutching her beer and had begun to scoot towards the edge of the booth.

"You're free to go at any time, Ai," said Tierra. "We're not like Indigo, you know that. Because your gut, and the tickle would tell you if we were. And it hasn't, has it?"

Ai shook her head slowly. "Do you have dreams?"

"No. But both of us have gut feelings. Like you."

Sacred Source.

The girl was an energetic.

CHAPTER

6

Tierra's heart raced. Lost energetics were few and far between. She and Fintan needed to be careful, as the girl seemed skittish at best. Tierra refused to lose her. They needed her to find out what was behind the situation with Indigo, but Tierra also wanted to bring the girl home.

The name Ai, which meant love in Chinese, indicated she'd been named by energetic parents, as all energetics' names had some kind of link to their dominant Chakra – Tierra came from the Latin for earth, while Fintan was Irish for 'white fire'. An energetic's dominant chakra was usually evident right from birth, though their auxiliary could take a while to settle.

Ai hadn't moved away from the edge of the booth. She was poised to run.

"I'm not crazy. Neither are you. We're cousins too, in a way," Tierra said.

"Like you and Indigo?" Ai snorted.

"Sort of. Indigo was in with some bad people. We're trying to find them, to make sure they're not taking advantage of any other kids, like you."

"I'm not a kid." Ai crossed her arms over her chest, her beer bottle held in one hand.

"You can help us," Tierra said.

"If you show us where the house was, we can tell you more about yourself," Fintan said.

Ai narrowed her eyes, but she settled back into the booth. Tierra's heart rate slowed. Fintan's appeal to Ai's self-interest had worked.

"What else can you tell us about the man she met?" Tierra asked.

"Tall. Thin. But wiry-strong, rather than thin like Indigo. As I said, in control. He was the boss-man. Not her. Grey hair. Looked like a lawyer off a TV show. Rich."

"Anyone else there?" Fintan said.

"I didn't see anyone. But maybe. The house felt wicked strange. I didn't stay to find out." Ai rolled her shoulders back and thrust out her chin. "What do you know about me?"

"Did you know your parents?" Tierra asked.

"No. I was in the foster system. What do you know about me?" she asked again, insistent.

Tierra spread her hands out, palms up. "I think … I think you've always known when something bad was going to happen. At first you told people. But they ignored you, and bad things happened anyway. Sometimes they blamed you. So you stopped telling them. But you didn't like to get close to people because of it."

Ai turned her head away, her arms wrapped tightly around her slender body. "How do you know that?"

Tierra's heart squeezed. Ai's name and her 'feelings' indicated Anahata. The tickle in Ai's brain, the dreams? That was Ajna. The energy of the mind.

She was an Anahata-Ajna energetic, who had somehow fallen outside the world of the energetics. Both Chakras were dormant, but untrained energetics were dangerous. Volatile.

They needed to get Ai to a teacher as soon as possible.

"Because we're like you," Tierra said. "We get those feelings too. And we know a lot more people like us."

"Where's Indigo?" Ai asked.

Tierra blinked at the change of topic, and bit her lower lip, hesitating. Now wasn't the time to tell her that Indigo was dead. They needed to win Ai's trust.

"We're trying to find her, and we think the man you met might know where she is," Tierra said. "How about this. We'll check into a hotel, and you can meet us again later. In the meantime, listen to your instincts about us."

The girl relaxed her arms and took another sip of her beer. She put the drink down, and slid out of the booth. "Fine. Seven p.m., Gabrielle's. You can buy me dinner."

She disappeared out the door.

Tierra let out a breath. It had been like handling a wild animal, which at any point could have turned on her. "Don't say it."

"What?" Fintan cocked his head.

"That I let our best lead go."

"I think you did great."

Tierra lifted her head and looked at Fintan, her eyebrows raised. "Really?"

"You figured out she was a Dormant long before me, and she responded much better to you."

Tierra swallowed, her throat dry. The compliment was appreciated. She picked up her soda and took a sip. "The poor girl. I wonder who her parents were, and how she slipped through the net. The Circle is usually so good at keeping tabs. Her parents must be dead, surely, for her to be in the human foster system. Do you think she'll come back?"

She really hoped she would.

"I do. Letting her go was a stroke of genius." Fintan patted her hand. "It'll show we can be trusted. Let's find a place to stay."

Fintan drove them to a nearby hotel. Tierra fiddled with her necklace the entire journey, her face drawn. He hoped she wasn't worrying too much about Ai. Sometimes her compassion got the better of her.

It wasn't long before they were in their room – one room, two beds. Thankfully, it was a lot nicer than the motel they'd visited earlier in the day, with fabrics in soft pastels and more cushions than any man knew what to do with scattered around every surface. As he threw his bag down on the bottom of his too-soft bed, the thought triggered the memory of the softness of Tierra's body against his own hardness in the forest.

Sister. She's like a sister to me.

Tierra headed straight for the bathroom. "I need to wash the diner off me."

After a few minutes, the shower started, and fragrant steam leaked out under the door.

He tried hard not to think about her, the soap, water, and bubbles. He shook himself, and called Cuinn, which had the same effect as reciting algebraic equations.

"How's it going? What have you found?" Cuinn sounded tired.

"We have a lead – apparently Indigo met with a man a few times, and a girl has told us she can take us to the place he lives."

"That's great news. Should I send reinforcements?"

Cuinn always had his back. "Not yet. We'll scope the place out and see if he's really there. If he is, we'll find out what he's doing, and who he is. Then Blaize and Adam, or whoever, can come and help us if we want to go in."

"Okay, if you're sure. I trust your judgement. How're you and Tierra? I hope you're not still arguing."

"We're good." *Apart from the fact that I've started lusting over her.* Fintan ignored the feminine scents coming from the bathroom and filled Cuinn in on Ai, and after a bit more conversation, they hung up.

The walls were a uniform cream, with pictures of British Columbia's impressive scenery.

Scenery like that which had surrounded them in the forest. He shifted on the bed, reached for the remote for the TV, and turned it on, flicking through the channels to try and distract himself from the thought of Tierra in the forest, or, perhaps worse, in the shower.

After what seemed like an age, she came out, already dressed, her skin flushed from the heat, in a cloud of the musky perfume she always wore. Fintan's cock hardened slightly, and his eyes widened. Shit. He focused his mind on Cuinn and Adam. *They will kill me. And they would be right to.*

She wore a long skirt that swirled as she walked, and a tight-fitting vest top that showed off every delicious curve.

"Are you going out like that?" It came out of his mouth before he'd thought about it.

She looked up, frowning. "What? Like what?"

"With just that vest top on. You'll freeze." While he, on the other hand, might overheat.

Her forehead creased. "Of course not. But it's a bit hot in the bathroom to wear cashmere."

She searched through her suitcase as she spoke, and pulled out another of those soft, touchable sweaters.

She tugged it over her head, and as she raised her arms, a little of her stomach showed.

A little more of his blood diverted into his groin. *No, no, no.* He tore his gaze away. "I'm going to shower."

"Sure." Tierra tugged the sweater into place. "I'll email a few people to see if they know which energetics were in the Vancouver area, what, about seventeen years ago?"

"I'd say more like fifteen to sixteen."

"Really? Okay. See you in a bit."

She leaned down, looking into the bottom of her bag as she poked around to find her laptop. This stretched her skirt tight over her bottom. Thankfully, that also meant she didn't see the now very visible bulge in Fintan's pants.

He went into the bathroom with a sigh of relief. *This isn't acceptable.*

He stripped off his clothes, his erection jutting from his body. He flushed, and turned the shower to cold, and stepped in with a shudder. He'd wash away the lust. Freeze it out. He'd focus on their plans for the evening, and getting Ai to trust them, and following the leads.

He definitely wouldn't think about the fact that Tierra's warm, soft, naked body had been in here and covered in soap suds minutes before.

CHAPTER

7

Sitting on her bed, Tierra sent emails to five energetics who had been in the BC area between fourteen and eighteen years ago. She, Adam and Cuinn had also lived here then, though she couldn't remember anything that might be relevant. Maybe one of the boys would. She emailed them both.

Then she put the laptop down, and sighed. Why was this hotel room so stuffy? Why did windows never open in these places? She wished she'd thought to bring one of her homemade candles with her.

Then she forced herself to examine the real reason she was feeling a bit suffocated – what was she going to do about her feelings for Fintan?

Truth, integrity, and being open and honest were core parts of her being. Her values. She drew her knees up to her chest, and hugged them. She hated lying, and she felt as if that's what she was doing. She put her head on her knees.

She wasn't acting in accordance with her values when it came to Fintan.

She'd told him that her grumpiness towards him was to do with the situation they were in, which was only partly true.

When Cuinn had first started having the prophecy dreams a few months before, Fintan had been one of the few people Cuinn had confided in. The unshakable loyalty that Fintan had shown to his friend, and his genuine offer of 'whatever Cuinn needed' had reminded Tierra that there was more to Fintan than the couldn't-care-less persona he usually projected. Tierra's love for Fintan, love that she had always been able to put into a box in the back of her mind, had started to shift into something new.

Something uncomfortable.

When Blaize had been kidnapped, Tierra and Fintan had worked together. Tierra had used her rusty tracking skills to see if they could trace the whereabouts of either Indigo or Blaize.

They hadn't been successful, but working with him had given her another glimpse of a different, more professional Fintan.

Fintan the Warrior.

Her carefully managed love for him wouldn't pack back into the box she'd contained it in. It scratched and prickled and frustrated her, and it was harder and harder to ignore.

When she'd given energy to Cuinn in a highly illicit and taboo ceremony so that he could find Blaize in a dreamwalk, Fintan's protectiveness of Tierra, and his care for her afterwards, had shattered the box entirely.

But it had still been love. Something she could consider pure, and unsullied.

That moment in the forest had destroyed that illusion too.

She loved him. She also lusted after him. When she was with him, her emotions were muddled, and there were times when it was hard to put thoughts together. It wasn't ideal.

So what was she going to do about it?

She rubbed her hands over her face. She knew what she needed to do. She needed to tell him the truth. Or she needed to find a way of dealing with her emotions without affecting their friendship. She grimaced. She was a very open person. She needed to tell him.

How would she approach it? She should be good at this stuff. She did it for a living, didn't she? She could pretend she was advising one of her readers. *Let's see.* She pulled her laptop to her. What would the letter read?

Dear Tierra,

I need your help. I've been in love with a friend for years. It's not reciprocated. He's someone who falls in and out of love all the time – he needs variety. He's just not a one-woman man.

I thought I could live with it – I have for years, but recently something's changed. I've started to lust after him as well as love him. I don't want to hear about his latest conquests.

It's affecting the way I treat him, and I don't like the person I am when I'm with him. He doesn't understand what's happening, and it's upsetting him.

What on earth should I do?

Yours,
Anguished of BC

That was about it. She drummed her fingers on the bed cover. So, pretend she'd just got the letter. What would she write?

Dear Anguished,

I'm so sorry to hear of your problem. That sounds tough. Have you been able to tell any of your friends about your problem? Sometimes it can help to share things, get them out in the open.

It sounds like it might be a good idea to have a conversation with your friend. Have you ever told him how you feel? People can sometimes surprise us. Even if he doesn't reciprocate your feelings, you can ask him to be more sensitive in his conversation with you – I'm sure he can find other people to tell about his conquests.

Find a quiet moment, and just let him know how you feel. Don't make too big a deal out of it. Something like: "Can we have a chat? I have something I want to share with you. I don't feel very comfortable saying this, but I have romantic feelings for you, feelings that go beyond the friendship we currently have. Nothing needs to happen, but one thing I find challenging is when you talk about your lovers, or your feelings for other partners. I wanted to ask you if we could stop having those conversations until I move on."

Now, that probably sounds a lot harder than I made it seem.

If you tell him the truth, you'll feel in integrity with yourself, you'll have explained why you've been unhappy with his company lately, and he can change his behaviour so he's not upsetting you.

Try not to dump it all on him. He has feelings too. Let him respond.

And perhaps once you've let go of your secret, you can start thinking about moving on – how often do you get out and about and meet new men? Just a thought.

Wishing you luck
Tierra x

Tierra sat looking at the screen in surprise. Where had all that come from? She met new men all the time, didn't she?

Did she?

Ah, heck.

She hadn't thought about that aspect of hiding in Cathair Cuinn all these years. When you were long-lived, like the energetics, sometimes decades passed before you realized it.

Tierra tended to keep her dating within the smallish energetics community, given that relationships with humans usually meant a lot of secrets and heartbreak. But she hadn't run out of new energetic males to meet yet.

She nodded, resolved. She'd tell Fintan, get that over with, and then when they got back home, she'd suggest to the also-single Cara that they go out and meet some new men.

She'd be over Fintan in no time.

Elrian opened his eyes, then smiled. He was on his mat, and had been in the dreamscape, searching for the latest on the prophecy.

Searching through the tangle of voices and the....mess that his dreamscape could sometimes be, it was still easier for him to navigate than it was for Cuinn. Elrian knew what he was looking for, had been working with this prophecy for years. Cuinn flailed about blindly, hoping to stumble across information.

Though it was true that something had happened in the last day that had tipped the scales against Elrian – something which made it a fraction more likely that Cuinn and his friends could beat him, though he hadn't been able to work out the specifics – at the same time, Elrian had found his next target. And she was no match for Elrian. No match at all.

Tierra.

When Fintan came out of the shower ten minutes later, he found Tierra sitting on her bed, as still as a statue. Not wanting to disturb her meditation, he crept around the bedroom to hang up his towels and put his dirty clothes in his suitcase. In a room this small, with a neat freak like Tierra, he wasn't going to leave them in a heap like he normally would.

Eventually Tierra opened her eyes, more cheerful than she had been when he'd gone into the shower. Relief saturated him and tension he hadn't realized was there melted away.

They headed out. At the front door, he looked up and down the street to get his bearings. "If we want to go through a park so you can recharge some, it's this way. We have an hour or so before we need to be at the restaurant with Ai."

She nodded, and they walked in comfortable silence till they reached the entrance to the park. Tierra stopped for a moment and took a deep breath. He could feel her pull a little energy, and she seemed to brighten.

She let go of his arm, and danced into the park. It might be in the middle of Vancouver, but there was a reasonable amount of plant life, green and natural materials. Fintan looked around to check no one was watching, because if you didn't already know she was something supernatural, you'd guess from her reaction to her element after only hours with concrete and glass around her. No wonder she didn't live in a city. Manipura energetics didn't get drained in the same way, as long as they spent time in the sun every day. He mainly preferred hot countries, with plenty of sunlight and heat, but growing up in Scandinavia, with short days in the winter, had toughened him up.

He wandered along the path behind her, as she appeared to be greeting every tree and flower in the park. Finally, she sat in the middle of a patch of grass, and he dropped down beside her. He took off his jacket and enjoyed the gentle breeze on his skin.

The sun started to set, and dusk grew around them. The evening felt intimate, the two of them together without the hassles and demands of others. A bubble of tranquility in their currently difficult lives.

"Fintan, I wanted to talk to you about something."

"Sure." He leaned back on his elbows. Clouds floated through the sky above him. He was at peace for the first time in a while.

"It's no big deal, but I want to get it off my chest." His brain caught up with the words, and, confused, he twisted his head to look at her.

"What?"

"You remember you said that you love me like a sister?"

He nodded, and reminded himself that not only had he said that, but it needed to be true, despite his strange reaction to her recently. Because Cuinn. And Adam. And family.

"I love you too. But it's not very sisterly." She bit her lip. "I've been in love with you for a long time."

A slow second passed, and a thousand times a thousand choices of response whistled through his mind. He was stunned, exultant, terrified, and complete. In his mind, he said yes, he said no, he reasoned with her, and swept her into his arms and kissed her thoroughly.

The strangest thing was that none of the responses was disinterested.

Nonetheless, there was no way they could be together. They were entirely wrong for each other – that is, he could never be good enough for her. She needed someone with a deep and true Anahata, their heart Chakra full. That would never be him. And he didn't feel the same way about her.

At the same time, he tried to put out the nascent and unexpected spark of something, something he couldn't identify, that her words had roused.

He opened his mouth to speak, though what he would have said, he had no idea, but she put up a hand to stop him.

"Nothing has to change. I just needed to tell you. But I'd rather you didn't talk to me in such detail about your love affairs any more. It seems to make me cranky. One day I'll have hearts and flowers of my own, but right now, that's not my path. I know it's not very enlightened of me, but I get grouchy when you talk about all the girls." She rested a hand on his arm.

His mouth remained open, and his brain had stopped functioning. "Ah ... what?"

"I don't want to make a big deal of it. But if you could just keep your adventures in that area to yourself, that would be great." Her brown eyes were wide and trusting.

"Of course, I'm sorry that – wait, I'm sorry, what?" He shook his head to try and clear it, and catch up with the conversation. She'd just said she was in love with him. As in, 'in' love. Not love in a more general way. Right? Something inside him quivered, expectant.

But at the same time, she didn't want them to be together? The only reason she was telling him was to ask him to stop sharing?

She'd already risen, and was brushing off that damned skirt.

What did she want from him? His brain wasn't responding, conflicting feelings chasing around in there like an out-of-control pinball machine.

"Thanks. I'm so glad I was able to be honest with you. I feel better."

He scrambled to his feet, and she put her arms around his waist, and laid her head on his chest. She looked natural there. He put his hands gingerly on her upper back, but before he could really connect with her, she pulled back.

"Let's go see Ai." She walked in the direction of the park exit. He walked several paces after her before he remembered his jacket was still on the ground. He turned back, picked it up, and then had to run after her, as she marched to the gate.

What. The actual fuck. Had just happened.

He caught up with her and got into step. "What you said, back there."

It was a smooth opening. And he had no follow up.

"Yes? I hope Ai comes today, don't you? Poor girl. It would be great if we can take her back to Cathair Cuinn. We have plenty of space."

"Tierra, I'm not quite sure…what do you want me to say?" He was entirely at a loss. She'd dropped a bombshell, one that could explode their friendship, and now was carrying on as if everything was the same.

She looked at him, puzzled. "Say? What do you mean?"

"To what you said, in the park. Although I don't understand, exactly, what you said."

"I'm in love with you, is what I said." Her voice was just on the tart side of apple pie. "But, that's ok! In fact, it's fine! What wasn't fine is the fact that I was keeping it a secret. Which is never good between friends, hmmm?"

She patted his arm, and continued walking.

He stood still for a few seconds, before he realized she wasn't stopping. He hadn't lost control of his energy in centuries. Not when he'd been in a ten person bar brawl over his ex, when some country bumpkin in 19th century England called her a doxy. Not when a human business associate he'd invested with in 18th century France had gambled much of Fintan's savings away. And yet now flame appeared around his fists, which hung clenched by his sides. Tierra looked back over her shoulder and paused.

He drew on his heart center, limited as it was, and tried to be calm. His Manipura, the fire, was far too close to the surface right now. The flames flickered and went out.

"Tierra. You've just told me you're in love with me. And that, apparently, you have been for a long time. What do you want me to say?" He tried to stay reasonable.

"Nothing." She looked surprised. "Weren't you listening? I just needed to tell you. Now it's out in the open, we can move on."

"Move on? Move on?! I haven't even caught up." His whole body had begun to heat up. His skin seemed to burn.

She stepped in close again, and put her hands on his arms, then took them off hurriedly. "It's ok. Really. I've told you, and assuming you're okay not to talk about your, um, flings with me, then we're fine. I know you don't feel the same way. Let's meet Ai and see if we can find out who this energetic is, and where he's located."

She smiled, but it faltered as she caught his gaze.

He needed time to process this. Time to work out what the hell he was going to do. He was not nearly as sure as she was that 'nothing' was the answer.

He pulled Anahata energy to cool himself. After a few moments, when the heat had subsided, he held out a still-not-quite-steady-arm for her, and they walked to the restaurant in silence.

CHAPTER 8

They entered the restaurant just before seven p.m. A perky waitress showed them to a table. There was no sign of Ai.

Tierra wasn't sure what to make of Fintan's reaction to her words, but now she had dealt with that difficult business, she was relieved and ready to talk to Ai. He might need some time – he had seemed a little more taken aback than she'd expected.

She squirmed in her seat as the waitress poured them iced water. Was the idea of her loving him so difficult and unpleasant? She wasn't using any energy when she talked to him, but he'd emitted an onslaught of emotions that she couldn't help but pick up. Emotions that were so muddled, however, she hadn't been able to decipher them. She grimaced. They needed to focus. Maybe she should have waited. She hadn't thought it would matter that much to him. Perhaps she hadn't thought it through enough. She'd just wanted to get it off her chest. Get it out there and over with. She hadn't really thought through the consequences. She shifted again. She couldn't get comfortable in her chair.

Ah. She'd forgotten to let him respond. Okay, not her finest moment maybe. But they had other things to focus on now. They needed to get back to normal.

"It's too soon to worry," she said to Fintan.

He fiddled with his napkin, smoothing it out again and again. He looked across the table at her. "Too soon? Source is right it's too soon. You only told me five minutes ago. I haven't even processed it yet, let alone worried about it."

What? "What?" Tierra said.

They stared at each other blankly.

"Where our pierced teenager, Ai, is?" She persisted.

Comprehension dawned on them both a few seconds later, but only Tierra smiled. "Put it aside for the minute, Fintan. We need to focus on Ai, and what she has to tell us."

She took her phone out of her pocket and checked the time. "Assuming she comes. Which she will, because we're buying her dinner. And because her gut will tell her she can trust us."

They couldn't deal with the personal stuff now. Tierra felt a twinge of guilt as she glanced at Fintan. He looked a bit, well, wild. And the flames on their candles were a lot taller than those on other tables. Surely that couldn't be because of their discussion?

"Fintan," she hissed. "You need to control your energy. You're affecting the candles."

She blew them out. They lit again, and the smell of hot wax and smoke wound around them. "Stop it. We're out in public. With humans. We're not at Cathair Cuinn where you can play. Settle down."

"I'm not feeling very stable right now." The words came through gritted teeth. She could practically hear them grinding.

"We're going to have a teenage girl with us any minute. One we don't want to scare." The flames increased in size. Tierra bit at her thumb, worried now. "Fintan. Please."

He looked her dead in the eyes, and her stomach churned. His Manipura Chakra was burning, and the energy was starting to twist.

Twisting energy, eventually, was how someone became a Rogue. Energetics were alert to any sign of it, as it could be the start of a negative progression – though many energetics had come up against tests of self where their energy had wavered, due to a lack of control, or to intense negative emotions, most were able to catch themselves. Having healers around while energetics were in physical adolescence, and also while they were learning each energy as an Adherent, was helpful for grounding and to mitigate the risk of twisting. Energy twisting didn't mean one automatically went down the path to Rogue, but a person whose energy had twisted once had a tendency to seek out the darker side of emotions, which could eventually corrupt the person into a Rogue, someone who had given up their connection to Source.

This is not good.

She made a decision to earth him. Literally. Trained as a healer, she could stabilize him with her energy, take some of his within her, and ground him. Which, given she seemed to have been responsible, she felt she should. She'd missed a trick here. She hadn't considered his reaction to her news – well, she had, and she'd assumed it would help him understand why she'd been cranky recently, and there might be a smidge of embarrassment between them, but that it'd soon pass. She hadn't really counted on him ... being actually affected by it.

She put her small hand on top of his large one. It burned. She winced, and knew her hand would be pink when she pulled it back, but there was no help for it. She pulled a little energy of her own, and spooled it, weaving together a lot of earth energy with a little air energy.

He was deep inside himself, looking at her as if he didn't know her. Also not good.

She squeezed his hand, and took a breath. And pulled. She drew the excess energy from him, the twisting energy, like a poison. It caught in the net she created for it, but still it burned. She captured it, and dissipated it, and he shuddered, his eyes closing. She sent a pulse of pure Anahata, healing energy, into him.

"Stop." His voice was hoarse, and she took her hand away from his to pass him his water glass. He drank, fast. She poured him another when he held his glass out. He drank that too.

She watched him glancing over to the door every now and then to look out for Ai. This wouldn't be a good time for her to come in.

Fintan was pale and looked more believably like his Scandinavian roots than he had for decades. "Are you ok?"

"Sorry." His voice rasped, despite all the water.

"That's fine. I guess we should probably talk a bit more after all." Yeah. She had probably messed that up.

He opened his mouth to speak, and she hurried on with, "Not now. Because Ai will be here at any minute, and we can't afford for you to burn this place down to the ground before she even gets here. Okay?"

He pressed his lips together.

"More water?" she asked.

He shook his head, and they sat there. Tierra wasn't quite sure of the way forward. She wanted to help him – and clearly he wasn't feeling as sanguine at her information as she was – but she couldn't afford to upset him again. Especially when she wasn't completely sure what had set him off in the first place. Was he angry that she was in love with him? That didn't seem fair.

Ai came through the door, her face a mix of swagger, apprehension, and awe. She ignored the coat check girl, and headed over to their table, the maitre d' following. When the maitre d' realized the girl was with them, professionalism won over her disapproval, and she pulled out the chair for Ai.

Ai was made up to look years older than she actually was, with a sweep of black eyeliner at the corner of each eye. She wore a long black skirt that was slit all the way to the top of her legs, and the 'fuck you' t-shirt was gone, replaced by a charcoal vest top. Over the top she had a black trench coat, which despite being somewhat battered, looked amazing. She didn't remove the coat.

"Thank you for coming." Tierra said.

"I'm here for the food." The girl didn't meet her gaze.

"We're happy to be buying. Have a look and see what you'd like."
She pushed the menu in Ai's direction.

Ai picked it up as if it might contain something nasty inside. Or
explosive. She opened it, and couldn't keep the deadpan look on her
face at the many different menu items – and their chichi
descriptions – inside.

Tierra knew how she felt. She loved food, loved cooking. Few
things gave her greater pleasure than sharing food she'd just put
together with those she loved. And it usually meant she didn't have
to be the center of attention in other ways. She turned her focus
back to the menu.

"There's a lot of choice," Tierra said. *Well, duh.*

"Yeah. What's up with him?" Ai gestured at Fintan with her head.
Fintan hadn't spoken. Hadn't stood when Ai arrived, hadn't
acknowledged her presence other than with a nod.

"Nothing. We've just had –" What could she say. "We've just had
a difficult afternoon."

This seemed to satisfy Ai. But Fintan spoke. "I'm fine. Sorry Ai.
It's good to see you."

She nodded, and went back to her menu.

Tierra looked at Fintan, putting a question in her eyes. He
nodded back, if perhaps a little less vehemently than she might like,
and started to read his own menu.

Fintan stared down blankly at his menu. He couldn't make out a
word, whatever his reassurances to Ai and Tierra.

He couldn't remember the last time he'd lost control of his
energy.

He ground his teeth in a mix of humiliation, outrage and shame.

Tierra had had to rescue him. To ground some of his energy,
which had to have taken a toll on her. And now they were sitting at
the table, choosing their dinner as if none of the last hour had
happened.

What was he supposed to do with her words at the park? Did she really think she could drop that kind of information on him, then move on? The candles at the table flickered, and Tierra flashed him a warning glance. He gritted his teeth again. *Get back in the game. Idiot.*

"How was your afternoon, Ai?" Tierra asked.

The girl shrugged, though he sensed she was pleased to be asked. Had anyone ever taken an interest in her like that before? Without an agenda. Although he supposed they still had an agenda.

The waiter came over, and they ordered. The girl tried to hide her satisfaction at being called 'Madam'. Fintan had to hand it to the man, he wasn't fazed by the girl's dark attire and multiple piercings.

Once the waiter had left them, their water glasses refilled – Fintan wasn't ordering beer for the girl again, not twice in one day – Tierra asked her how she was feeling.

A loaded question.

Ai was smart. She knew exactly what Tierra was asking when she talked about 'feelings'. "I'm here, aren't I?"

Ai's gifts had told her she would be safe with Fintan and Tierra.

"How do I know what you're saying is true?" said Ai. "What you're saying, what you're talking about – it's magic, right? How do I know you're not just talking shit?"

"We have…other talents," said Tierra. "As you will, with a little training."

"What?" Eyes narrowed, arms folded.

Tierra hmmm'ed, then reached out to take a stem from a pretty posy of white flowers in a vase on the table.

She held the flower, still in bud, low in front of her. "Watch."

Fintan felt Tierra pull earth energy, pushing it into the flower. The flower's tight bud rippled, and slowly, gradually, unfurled. There was a strange tug in his chest at the sight of Tierra, prettier than any flower, concentrating on this tiny piece of loveliness in front of her.

Ai's eyes got bigger in proportion with the flower's opening. By the time the flower was fully in bloom, they were huge. Tierra, with just a hint of glow around her, handed Ai the flower.

The girl cradled it in her hands, examining it from every angle.

"We call ourselves energetics," said Tierra. "We're like humans, but we evolved from a more...elemental source. Have you ever heard of the Chakra system?"

It probably wasn't the time to tell the girl about their homeland, Atlantis, and its mysterious destruction, Fintan supposed.

The girl shook her head.

"It's known in some Eastern philosophies," Tierra continued. "Essentially, it says that there are seven 'Chakras' or energy centers, in a person. In human beings, these tend to be very underdeveloped. Occasionally a human is born with one activated, or manages to activate it in their lifetime, but their energy is still weak."

Fintan hadn't seen Tierra in teaching mode for a long time. She was patient and relaxed. He enjoyed watching her.

"Energetics, on the other hand, originally evolved from this energy." Tierra was leaning forward, and moved her hands as she talked. "Our existence helps maintain the energetic balance of the earth."

As Tierra continued her lecture on the basics of the energetics, Ai's posture loosened. When Tierra introduced the idea of Dominant and Auxiliary Chakras, Ai's eyes gleamed.

"What am I?"

Tierra smiled. "We think you're Anahata-Ajna. That links to air and mind. You must be strong to have coped for so many years on your own, with no one to guide you. And to keep your energy pure, and not twisted."

"What do you mean, twisted?" Ai's forehead creased.

"Sometimes in our community there are those who become 'Rogues'. This, I'm afraid, is what Indigo is. Her energy has twisted, and she's using it in a negative, rather than positive way."

The girl's cheeks had spots of color, and she looked down at the table. "What do you do with those whose energy is twisted? Do you kill them?"

"That's not our way." Tierra shook her head firmly. "There are few we can't help in our Rehabilitation Centers, given time."

The girl toyed with her starter, which had arrived a little while ago.

"How do you know if someone's energy is twisted? And what if someone did something with their energy that wasn't good, but they didn't mean to? Maybe they were protecting themselves?" The girl's face was a picture of misery. Fintan was glad that Tierra was handling this and not him. The girl was clearly worried about something, and he had an inkling of what it might be, given her background.

"What kind of thing?" Tierra asked. "If it wasn't her fault, we'd help her sort it out, and make sure her energy was kept untwisted."

The girl shrugged, and stuffed some of her garlic bread in her mouth. She addressed Fintan through the mouthful. "What can you do then?"

Fintan leaned over and blew the candle out.

"Watch." He held a fist up to his mouth, and blew it open, as if he were blowing a kiss. The palm unfurled in the direction of the candle – which sparked to life.

Ai gasped.

He grinned and took another mouthful of pasta.

They spent the next hour eating and explaining some of the energetics' history and background to Ai. She was intrigued by the possibilities of her powers, and keen to try them out.

"How old are you, then?" Ai asked.

"Hmm. Well, think in terms of centuries, rather than decades," Tierra said.

"Woah. You only look in your thirties. How long will I live?" Ai asked.

"No reason why you wouldn't live as long as us," Fintan said through a stolen mouthful of Tierra's dinner. "Your Guild will help you manage the details of pretending to age normally. One of our Guilds, Vishudha, whose powers include communication, have expertise in creating new identities. It's much easier to move to a new city or country and start again, though it can be tiring. And we do age, it's simply slower than humans."

Tierra scowled at him and poked him with the fork. "Some of us should be old enough to know better."

Fintan smirked at her. He felt a bit better, teasing her. It seemed more … normal.

"And do you get like, a black belt in it?" Ai asked.

"How d'you mean?" Tierra said. She was eating more defensively now, an arm around her plate, which made Fintan smile more.

"Do you take magic exams or something?" Ai said.

"Er, no. But there are different levels. You're a Dormant, which is how all energetics are born. Usually their parents can tell the Dominant chakra of their child very early, and that's how names are linked to chakras. Once you train with a Maven, you're an Adherent. Eventually you do a Chakra Trial, and you become a Practitioner, and then eventually, after many decades, your Guild can affirm you as a Master."

"Huh," Ai cocked her head. "How long does it take? And what are you two then?"

"Anything from five to twenty years per Chakra. I'm a Master in Manipura, Practitioner in Anahata," Fintan said. "Tierra, though, is a Master in both her energies."

Tierra flushed. "Yes. Well. I'm a bit rusty these days."

He wondered why her usual sense of self was letting her down. The current dangers they all faced were really affecting her. His mouth flattened into a line. That was fine. He would protect her, and keep her out of trouble. No one would hurt her while he was around.

Ai ate every scrap of her food, and seemed to enjoy it. But he could see something still nagged at her. He thought he knew what it might be. Perhaps he could help.

"I grew up in a remote part of Scandinavia, and trained with a Maven called Gunhild for Manipura, my fire energy. She was a good woman, but tough. She trained new energetics by tiring them out physically so they had better control of their energies."

He tried to speak casually, but the story brought up a slew of memories. Friends and family who were gone, and growing up as a youth in a difficult era.

"Each day I would muck out the various stalls of the animals with a shovel and barrow. It was hard work. Though I loved the animals."

He paused to sip at his water, his throat still sore.

"I was an angry young man – the dark side of Manipura. You don't have to turn Rogue for your energy to slip and twist a little."

He tried not to look directly at Ai as he said this, but he could see he had her attention. Tierra had grown up in a happy family. She had a lot of empathy, but she couldn't know what it was like to live every day with that anger inside you.

"Anahata can use others' feelings against them – manipulate or humiliate them,' he said. "Some can even cause illness – purposefully, or, if we're not in control, the very force of our feelings can cause sickness in others. Just as our joy is perhaps more infectious than others' might be."

Tierra was watching too, listening, lines on her forehead. He wasn't sure she had ever heard this story before. He hadn't considered that. He hoped it didn't affect her view of him.

"Anahata's element is air, so we can cause winds. Hurricanes even, if we're powerful enough."

He blew another kiss at the candle on the empty table next to them, and it flickered and went out.

Tierra shook her head.

He shot her a quick smile to reassure her, and continued.

"So, angry young man. Isolated, because Mavens are responsible for the damage their Adherents do, so most Mavens live a little away from any human community. Lots of feelings I couldn't understand, not being the well-adjusted, emotionally mature man I am today." He didn't feel he could meet Tierra's eyes on that one.

"One hot summer day, I'd been cleaning out the barn for hours. The animals were in the fields. Gunhild came into the barn, and pointed out, very matter-of-factly, several spots I hadn't cleaned properly. My energy leapt inside me. I couldn't contain it. I started to burn."

He had Ai's full attention.

"Luckily, it's rare for us to harm ourselves with our own energy. I didn't even realize I was alight. My Maven smelled my clothes burning, swept me up with her air energy, and dumped me in the stream. But half the barn had burned down before she was able to douse the flames. Thankfully, none of the animals was hurt."

Even centuries later, the story still caused him shame. He hated the fact he'd lost control to that extent, even as a youth.

"She wasn't happy, though she understood it was a mistake. She upped the intensity of the physical effort, but changed the direction of my training. She explained what had happened, and we talked about ways to manage it."

"Were you in trouble?" Ai asked.

"A little. She made me rebuild the barn. Without my energies." He winced. "I can still remember the blisters – in the days before power tools, it was quite the job."

Ai looked thoughtful, and gave her spoon one more lick before putting it down. "I'll take you to his house. The guy's. The weird one. But I'm not coming inside."

Tierra put her arm out to touch Ai. "Thank you. We'll keep you safe, don't worry. You're part of our extended family now."

The girl shrugged. But didn't move her hand away.

9

They went their separate ways outside the restaurant, with plans to meet up again the next night to scout out the house of the 'creepy guy'.

Tierra and Fintan walked back together to their hotel without much talking. They didn't go through the park this time, Fintan's gaze just glancing over Tierra as they passed the now-locked gates. He didn't bring up their conversation. He hadn't quite decided what he was going to do about it.

She had dropped a bombshell. One that he had no idea how he was supposed to respond to. The only thing he did know was that however he did respond, it would probably be wrong. And not only wrong in the eyes of Tierra, but Adam – oh hell, Adam – Cuinn, and Blaize too.

The other, more humiliating, part of the evening had been his own loss of control. He didn't understand where that reaction had come from. Before he brought it up again with Tierra, he needed to work out exactly what this was about.

The person he'd usually talk to about this kind of situation was Adam. *So not an option.* Cuinn would usually be a close second – again, not an option.

Perhaps this was one he was going to have to figure out on his own.

He looked at Tierra, who was walking next to him, her smaller size meaning she had to take one and a half steps to his one stride. He slowed his pace to match hers, and she looked up at him. "Everything ok?"

"Yeah, just realized I was walking a bit fast for you."

She angled her head to the side. "No faster than usual. But thanks."

He shrugged.

They took a few more steps.

The evening darkness seemed to accentuate the intimate bubble they walked in, rather than conceal the fact he didn't know what to say to her.

Yeah, this was awkward.

"What's our plan tomorrow?" Tierra said.

A plan. Okay, he was on more familiar ground here. "We meet Ai at ten p.m. and then drive to wherever she says we need to be. We leave her somewhere safe, and you and I go and scope out the house. We should probably give her Cathair Cuinn on speed dial, just in case, but if we're only checking things out, there shouldn't be any need for back up."

"Sure. So we have the day to kill? What do you want to do? We'd better sleep in if we're going to be up late," she mused.

A flash of Tierra waking up, her hair messy and loose, and her chocolate eyes sleepy, hit Fintan's brain. Ouch. He was going to have to shield his feelings a little more carefully around Tierra if this was going to happen.

"What about a hike tomorrow?" he suggested. Physical exercise sounded good right now. A lot of it.

"Sure," she said.

"Okay. Sleep, breakfast, head to the park for a hike. Late lunch somewhere. Rest and recharge in the hotel room before the evening."

"Great. Less time for me to get nervous that way."

Tierra reached the doors of their hotel first, having bounced up the steps. As they walked through the quiet lobby, he said, "What are you worried about?"

She shrugged.

"All of it? I'm fine, but it's been a while since I've done anything like this. I'm totally capable, before you say anything –" he held his hands out, palms up, as if to suggest he had no intention of doing anything like that " – but like I say, it's been a while."

"We can talk it through again if you like," he said. "With some 'what ifs?' thrown in. What if he's there, what if he's not there, what if there are other people there, what if he's got someone else, just like Indigo had Blaize. That's what I do with my team. Worst case, or almost every case, planning. Of course, life always throws you a new curve ball, something you just didn't have on the list, but it helps to work through possibilities. Especially when you need to make fast decisions in the moment."

"Alright," Tierra said. "How do you throw your Anahata intuition into the mix? Your feelings?"

"I make sure I listen to my gut. I've had a few times when listening to a nagging feeling that something wasn't right about what seemed to be a perfectly normal setup saved my ass." He shrugged. "That's a good reason for us to spend a bit of time in meditation tomorrow afternoon, just tuning into our energies. We'll both need to listen to our feelings, and we'll also need our other energies."

"We might need your Manipura and your fighting skills, but what do you think we'll need earth for? We don't need tracking skills, we know where the guy lives."

"Maybe he'll have moved. Maybe there'll be a garden, grounds, and I'll want you to check if anyone else is there. There are plenty of uses for earth. Remember, I've worked with Adam a lot over the years, so I know how Muladhara can help."

"I'm not Adam." They were in their room now, and Tierra sat heavily on the bed, lines appearing on her brow. "I don't want to let you down."

"You won't let me down. We're on a scouting mission, we're not going to engage."

She nodded, though the creases on her forehead didn't disappear. He came over to sit next to her, and put his arm around her. She fit snugly into his shoulder. He gave her a squeeze, and dropped a kiss on her forehead. Her skin was soft, and she smelled good.

She tilted her head up, and a thousand thoughts swirled around his head.

Heat flooded his body, and he froze, his gaze on the sweep of her eyelashes, the curve of her brow. Her nose was so cute.

Without considering it further, he leaned down and gently bopped his larger nose against hers, squishing it. Their heads were so close together that her breath fluttered over his lips. His mouth watered.

Her eyebrows raised, her mouth open a fraction.

He bent his head at the slightest of angles, and an inch of movement brought their lips into contact.

His breath stalled as his mouth captured hers with the pressure of a butterfly's wings. His skin tingled and his brain went fuzzy, confused.

What was he doing? He couldn't change their relationship, especially after what she'd said in the park. He couldn't give her what she deserved.

But it was fine. This was a chaste kiss. No tongue, no touch.

He drew away from her, and wondered if he had a similar dazed look in his eyes.

"Let's go to bed."

Tierra woke up to the sound of the shower running. She was used to being first up. She wasn't feeling as perky as normal this morning.

Last night had ended in the strangest way. Fintan had given her a hug that had started like any other of the thousands of hugs he had given her over the centuries they had known each other.

It hadn't ended that way.

She couldn't remember him ever kissing her on the mouth before.

But the kiss hadn't been sexual. Not really.

Not…exactly. *I mean, it might have made my entire body prickle with sexual heat, but it didn't have any effect on Fintan.*

The kiss had been almost absent-minded. An after-thought. A kiss of a child before bedtime.

She frowned and sat up. She grabbed the hotel room's guidebook. She needed to take her mind off that moment. They'd planned to go for a short hike this morning around Burnaby Mountain, which was why Fintan was already up.

When the bathroom door opened, she looked up, and then blushed when she realized that Fintan only had a towel round his waist. His sculpted, manly waist. He was rubbing at his hair with a second towel as if he was in a shampoo advert. She went mute.

What did you say, after all, when the man of your dreams came into your room, all chiseled abs and wet from the shower?

"Hi." Start simple, and work up.

"Morning. How're you feeling?"

"Um, good. You?"

"Yeah, better than yesterday, thanks." He threw the towel, damp from his hair, down onto his bed, making his skin move over his chest muscles in a distracting – delicious – fashion. She hadn't seen him like this for a while. It would certainly give her something to think about on cold winter nights.

Fintan was lean and muscled. With some interesting scars. She knew where some of them had come from – had been with him for one of them in particular – but there were some she didn't remember.

She realized he was looking at her. "Is everything alright, T?"

"Oh, yes, sorry. I…I just woke up." She tried not to babble, and was glad that fire energetics couldn't read minds. And hoped his

Anahata wasn't picking up the waves of lust his outfit – or lack thereof – was causing in her. Happily he wasn't a strong empath. Usually.

She scuttled in and out of the shower, feeling more together once she was washed and dressed.

"I assume we're staying another night here?" she said. "If we're only going to this house at ten p.m., we won't be back till the early hours of the morning."

Fintan nodded. "So you don't need to pack. In fact, why don't you leave your stuff untidy? Live a little."

She scowled at him. "There's no need for sarcasm. And there's nothing wrong with being neat."

He suppressed a grin. "Let's go get you caffeine and breakfast."

They headed to a nearby bakery, where the smell of bread and pastries wafted out and enticed patrons in. Tierra chose a window seat so that she could watch the passers-by on their way to work. There were still a few yoga bunnies here, but the crowd was mainly a work one, given it was a weekday in the city. She had a moment of gratitude that her job as a writer meant she could work wherever and whenever she liked.

Plus the fact that, as a long-lived energetic, money was never a problem. You lived long enough, it built up. Tierra had worked in a lot of roles over the few centuries she'd been alive – energetics hadn't had the gender stereotypes humans had – though as often as not, behind the scenes. She'd had a lot of fun running an Inn outside London in the late 1800s, on one of the routes down from London to the coast, in a market town called Kingston-Upon-Thames. Working in different professions helped to keep a long life interesting, and also was sometimes necessary given one had to move around so humans didn't realize you still looked about the same age at 60 as you had at age 30. Learning new things also helped the energetics' minds and attitudes stay flexible, a plus when you were trying not to get stuck in the last century's attitudes.

Her favorite job had probably been as an apothecary in the 1800s after her time as an Anahata Adherent. Being a nurse during the two great wars had been some of her most important work, and contributed to the energetic race's purpose of maintaining balance in the world. But it had been some of the toughest.

Fintan eyed her cautiously over his first croissant. His blond hair was tousled, and he was casual in jeans and a sweater, though his jeans had seen a lot more wear and tear than hers, and his sweater was a giant hoodie with the mascots from the 2010 Vancouver winter Olympics on it. Tierra's favorite was Miga, who was a combination of mythical sea bear, killer whale and spirit bear, and managed to be both cute and a little dangerous. *Much like Fintan.*

"We'll work on refreshing your self-defense moves while we're out today," Fintan said. "That okay with you?"

She was unenthusiastic, but given all the protesting she had done to get herself to Vancouver, she couldn't show it. "Sure."

"What you did in the forest wasn't bad. Now you need to keep your emotions under control when you engage. If you fight angry, your emotions can cloud your moves."

"What about scared?" She was only half joking.

"It's harder not to be scared. Better if you keep calm. It's like going into a meditative state, and fighting from there."

"Do you get scared?"

"Sometimes. Not too often. I know I'm big and bad."

She took a bite of her almond croissant, which she was eating in small bites to make it last as long as possible. Fintan had long since finished his first pastry, and was onto his second.

As she reached out to pick up her cup, Fintan's eyes flashed and he put a hand out to stop her.

"What? What's the matter?" She put the cup back down. "Did you see a bug in it or something?"

She peered into the cup to see if she could see what he was staring down at. He hadn't released her hand, and she let go of the cup, thinking he was trying to make sure she didn't drink anything.

When he just took her hand in both his hands, she tugged ineffectually, trying to make him let her go. But he held her fast. Her heart jumped. "What's going on, Fin?"

CHAPTER

10

Fintan stared down at her hand, feeling sick. Her hand, the one that she'd grounded him with the night before, was burned.

He'd burned her.

He didn't know what to say. Sorry seemed so…inadequate.

He realized she was trying to get her hand back, and he dropped it. She pulled it back into her chest and cradled it against her. Oh hell, he'd hurt her again.

He stood up, his metal chair clattering on the stark black and white tiled floor.

"I have to go to the bathroom." He walked off, eyes averted.

In the small room, he glared into a mirror with a cheery 'Please wash your hands' sign with tiny hearts drawn around it stuck to the bottom of the glass.

He'd burned her, and she'd never mentioned it.

He leaned on the sink and bowed his head as her words from the day before came back to him. She was acting normally, as if having divulged her feelings for him the day before, she'd been relieved of a burden.

A burden that she'd shifted onto him.

He washed his hands for want of something to do. Running his hands through his hair rather than waste a paper towel, he made a decision. He wouldn't worry about Tierra's feelings today. Well, he would, of course, he amended, but not her, er, romantic feelings.

He walked back out into the cafe, teaspoons clinking against cups, mothers chatting, their children sleeping in strollers next to them, and the aroma of ground coffee beans scenting the air.

Tierra squinted at him as he sat down. "Is everything ok? Is there something wrong with your stomach?"

"I'm ok." He took her hand back, cupping his larger hands around it as if it was fragile and expensive.

Her face added puzzled to worried.

He turned her hand over and examined it. He took a breath, and pulled energy of his own. Air energy. Healing energy. He'd been too addled, and possibly, he thought to himself, too ungrounded, to think of it last night. And of course, she'd never waste it on herself.

She looked startled as his energy crept into hers, cooling, healing. The antidote to the energy she'd grounded for him the night before.

The faint pinkness of the skin on her hand, that had turned her butterscotch skin to a dusky rose, faded back to normal. Although her cheeks remained pink.

"I'm sorry about last night." He gave her hand a final squeeze between his palms before placing it on the table.

"That's ok." She sounded uncertain.

"Really. It won't happen again."

And neither of them was sure what, exactly, he was talking about.

Fintan drove them a little way out of Vancouver to Burnaby Mountain. In the car park, he got out a backpack containing water and some provisions, as well as light rain jackets that could be folded up tight and small. It was spring, and the weather was unpredictable. Although it was clear and dry at the moment, it could easily rain later. Perfect weather for hiking, though, if you liked that kind of thing.

They walked up the rocky trail, and he quizzed her on the ways she could use her energies to protect herself. She wasn't enthusiastic. She might be a Master in her energies, the highest level of Practitioner, but she wasn't keen on using them in that way.

They reached a plateau, and Fintan beckoned Tierra over. She went to him, caution in every step.

He slid an arm around her, and before she knew it, she was in a headlock.

"You know what you need to do to get out of this," he coached.

Tierra struggled to breathe, but was determined not to tap out too quickly. She croaked, "Yes, but knowing what to do and doing it aren't the same thing."

Tierra put both her hands on one of Fintan's, the arm currently locked around her head. She pulled down sharply on Fintan's hand, then stomped down hard on the earth next to his foot to simulate stamping on his foot. Then she moved her shoulder into Fintan's arm, breaking the lock. She twisted her body around to come up for air behind him.

"Good," Fintan said. "Now, don't forget, if you've broken out of the headlock you either need to run, or you do some damage to the person from behind, fast. You need to train for that. If you just train for the move itself, the muscle memory will stop there, and you'll just get caught again as you'll hesitate while you think what you should do next, and you'll just be standing behind them while you think."

Tierra's shoulders drooped. "Neither's a great option for me. I'm not exactly a runner, and I can't imagine hitting someone, let alone from behind."

Fintan turned towards her and put his hands on her shoulders. "If it's you or them, make sure it's not you. We're not talking about you attacking some innocent here, Tierra, but someone who's already initiated an attack on you, or someone you love."

Tierra shrugged off the feel of his warm, solid grip, off. "I know. It's just...hard."

She made as if to sit on the ground, but before she could, Fintan narrowed his eyes. "That's not the end of the practice. We need to step it up a bit. Make it more real."

He grinned at her, and Tierra's eyes widened, and she halted her progress.

He jerked his head, and a sheet of intense fire surrounded Tierra. She gasped, heart pounding.

Fintan grinned. "Let's play."

The crackle of fire burned close to her skin, but didn't touch it. She was pinned in place.

She looked around her, took a deep breath, and pulled energy. She gestured with an arm at the earth, and lifted it up, up, and then down again onto the fire, putting the fire out with the damp scattering of earth.

"There," she said. "Happy?"

Fintan's smile grew. A wind stirred her mounds of earth, blowing them out of the way.

How do I counter his wind?

A tree behind Fintan, with long slender branches, caught her attention. *That's how.* She made it move, its leaves and twigs like fingers reaching for him. She made a grab for him with the tree, aiming to tie him up like last time. But he burned the ends of the branches away. The tree drew back quickly, its leaves singed.

She sent an apology to the tree, then shot a pulse of energy into the earth, and made it ripple underneath Fintan. He staggered, and nearly fell. She did it again, keeping the ground under her own feet steady.

What now? Fire was tricky for an earth and air practitioner to counter. *Hmm.* She wasn't able to use the energy of water, but she could move it if she found it. She sent tendrils of energy into the earth, seeking a source of water near by.

Fintan drove a small whirlwind around her, which trapped her as effectively as the fire. She planted herself in the earth, letting it grip and hold her while the wind whipped around her. She struggled to suck enough oxygen to breathe, and concern flooded her. This was a game, wasn't it? He wouldn't actually hurt her, surely?

She pulled on air. It came into her body from the ether delicately, a very different feel from the solid earth energy which felt almost tangible.

Air energy was like pure love entering her. Her heart swelled. She channeled the love into the earth, combining her powers. Every buried, dormant seed in the ground germinated and grew.

In seconds, Fintan was surrounded by a meadow of flowers. But the flowers weren't the only seeds. Saplings sprouted and she wove the springy trees around him, a new prison.

She counted on the fact he wouldn't destroy the plants with fire when it wasn't truly necessary. Energetics supported life, they didn't destroy it, though those with Muladhara were the most connected to plants and animals in that way.

He didn't need to. He used air energy to lift him in a huge jump over the new growth on the clearing's floor and landed in front of her. He tackled her by the waist, and took them both to the ground.

She fell with a thud, and Fintan's weight pinned her there.

"You can't forget the physical," he said. "Just because we can fight with energy, doesn't mean we have to, or we will. How will you protect yourself from this?"

He levered himself up so he was sitting astride her waist, holding her left wrist with his right hand, with his left knee grinding into her right arm.

She struggled to move.

I can do this. Don't think, just do.

Her legs were free, and in one swift move she shifted her hips and bent her legs up at a right angle, hooking a foot around his neck. It didn't shift him off her, but it rocked him slightly as he reacted to the threat, and his knee slid off her arm. Without hesitation she thrust down with one foot and lifted the same hip, which shoved him further. Her free hand came up to catch his forearm, so every aspect of her body was concentrated on moving him to the side, muscles straining.

He pressed his weight down hard, but her movements dumped him from her body onto the dirt. She rolled away from Fintan, and got to one knee, ready to get up. She was trembling with the effort she had exerted, and sweat coated her back despite the cool day.

Fintan grabbed her ankle and slid her to him. Rather than trying to get away, she went with the movement, and when she got close enough, she kicked at his face.

It didn't connect, but he let go of her ankle, and she scrambled to her feet. He shook his head, rolled, and got up as smoothly as if he was tugged upwards by strings.

They faced each other, Tierra panting hard, Fintan balanced lightly on the balls of his feet.

Still grinning inanely, he seemed to be waiting for her next move. She wanted to growl. And she really wanted to wipe that smile off his face.

She sent energy into the forest to see if she could find any animals. She connected with a handful of squirrels. Tierra linked to them, and sent a silent request for their help. She didn't want them to hurt Fintan, she wanted them to disorientate him.

She gave the 'go' to the squirrels, and five of them scampered out of the trees and ran up his body, racing up and down his limbs. He batted ineffectively at them, and she ran forward and shoved him.

Blinded by the squirrels, he staggered back, and fell over the short earthen ridge she'd been building behind him.

She released the squirrels, and as fast as she could, she drew earth over Fintan and packed him in mud. He was horizontal in the earth, buried, with only his head out.

She drew a breath, pulse pounding, body shaking.

He laughed. "That was good. Creative."

She sat, keeping several yards between them. She could barely move. It had been the most concentrated use of her physical and energetic powers at the same time for many decades. *Damn him for showing me how out of practice I am.*

Branches rustled as the wind picked up. Leaves blew through the clearing, and the earth started to shift away from Fintan. Air loosened the packed earth, building to a whirlwind. She could no longer see him for the mixture of earth, branches and leaves that blew around where his head had been. She scooted away, her forearm over her face to protect it. She was too tired to create her own air shield.

Her eyes stung as particles of mud hit them, and she squeezed them closed. The air was warm and insistent. Pressure built around her, as the hot air compressed her. She opened her eyes to find him standing a few feet away, covered in mud, smiling. She tried to move, and hit what felt like a wall of heated air.

She was in a cage, and she had no idea how she would break out of it.

Elrian sat in the back of the luxurious town car and seethed.

Indigo's death continued to affect him, and it had made him sloppy.

He had taken the leeching of his most recent victim too far. The girl had managed to get under his skin. Elrian and the others in the room had taken too much energy, and the girl had died. He'd captured most of her energy in a Remnant stone, but some had been lost. And they needed twelve full stones for the next part of the prophecy. He cursed again for the loss of the Ajna stone at Indigo's shack.

At the same time, he'd been called back to the house in the country. There was an urgent problem there he needed to sort out.

They needed to move the body out of the Vancouver house. But a neighbor had had a break in – some mundane burglary – and there were more cop patrols than usual. He'd decided to leave the body where it was for the time being. They couldn't risk a body being found in the car right now, whatever the camouflage he could provide.

Elrian had put extra warding and protection on the suburban house, and Dagon was driving him to the place in the country.

Once there, Elrian would draw more Muladhara energy from the land, and supplement the Ajna energy he had taken from the girl. As soon as he was up to his usual strength, he would return to the city and clear things up.

And then it would be time to start again with a new victim. He would find the street brat that Indigo had brought to them before this current one, and this time, he would forget the niceties.

He would simply drain her dry.

CHAPTER

11

"I think you need to remove some of the silver." Fintan had to hide his amusement at Ai's outfit. She'd really gone to town on the goth look for the evening, taking their suggestion to wear black in a completely different direction to his own black jeans and sweater, along with a black watch cap stuffed in his pocket to tuck his blonde hair under. "It kind of reflects the light."

Ai was wearing all black. And silver. A lot of silver. A pair of baggy black jeans, with a black belt and big silver buckle. Black Doc Marten boots – now those he approved of – and a tight black t-shirt that had strange holes cut out of the sides and around the top. It looked lopsided to his eyes, but what did he know about teen fashion?

She had silver bangles that clinked as she walked, as many rings, studs and other face jewelry as she had piercings, and what he could only call a collar – black and silver, of course.

She made quite the picture, and certainly didn't blend with the local environment as he'd hoped – even in the coffee shop they sat outside, she stood out. Tierra, with her earth training, was capable of blending into the background. His own more mundane military training helped him be capable of the same. But Ai had no training, and a lot of shiny.

"Let's go to the bathroom, Ai," suggested Tierra. She stood, and winced.

He shifted on the chair and averted his gaze. She was going to ache after their workout together, but it had been a useful day. Being in nature was good for any energetic, and he always enjoyed practising his own self-defense, drills, and attacks. He'd gone easy on Tierra today, but not that easy, and she'd fought till he called time. She might never be a Warrior, but with a little more training, she'd get back up to the skill levels she'd had in World War II.

He'd almost offered to give her a massage after she'd showered, had wanted to take care of her for a change, but the thought of his hands on her body had been too awkward. He had a lot of confusing feelings about her at the moment, and he couldn't afford to let them distract him. Tonight was a time for action. Careful action, but action nonetheless.

His phone bleeped. He turned it over, and Cuinn's name came up. A text.

"Progress on the prophecy from some of the older prophecy texts. Confirm the six roles the Ajna Farseer noted – Sage, Communicator, Healer, Warrior, Creative and Protector – are archetypes linked to each Chakra. Not much on the stones. Still searching there."

He texted back a thanks.

He was the Warrior, and he supposed, Healer if he counted his own pitiful Anahata. That was obvious enough. Tierra was both Protector for Muladhara, and Healer for her much stronger Anahata. But battles were coming, and she would need to fight. Or at least protect herself properly.

She always looked after others. Always. She'd handle the situation with Ai's outfit as kindly as she did every other. She'd talk to the girl in that soft voice of hers, and Ai would come out of the bathroom dressed more appropriately, self-esteem intact.

Not a skill he was blessed with. His fire was too dominant.

It was rare that anyone took care of Tierra. He'd tried to do it when Blaize had been captured and Tierra had offered her energy to Cuinn. Crazy woman. Not only was it forbidden by the Circle to share energy with anyone with whom you weren't in a Maven-Adherent relationship, but there was good reason for that. The taker could easily become addicted, and end up as a 'Leech', with the person who was providing the energy becoming drained, with the possibility of death.

He'd tried to dissuade her, and she'd held firm. He'd sat behind Tierra for those minutes when Cuinn had taken energy from her, and felt physically sick at the risk she'd taken.

He hated sitting around, and the days since he'd realized the import of Cuinn's dreams had been challenging for Fintan. Others might think that he rarely took anything seriously, with a temperament that contained a large amount of Manipura mischief and love of variety and change, as well as an Anahata's more dreamy distraction, but there was one thing that was sacred to him.

Family.

He didn't have any blood relatives alive. All energetics were related pretty much if you went far enough back, but his own immediate family, parents, grandparents, were all dead. And he and both parents had been only children, not uncommon in energetic families.

Their race had been a lot more populous when nature ruled the earth. But as the oily machines of the nineteenth century had come into being, fewer and fewer energetics had been born. Which made it all the more important that lost sheep like Ai were brought back into the fold. The other side of the noise-dampening glass, Tierra and Ai stepped back into the harsh fluorescent light of the coffee shop, weaving their way between animated patrons to the door.

Ai didn't catch the light in quite the way she had, but energetically, she was still an angry flame in the darkness. He wasn't sure how either he or Tierra had missed the fact that she was an energetic. He and Tierra seemed to be off their game.

"All good?" he asked. He pushed his chair back from the small table.

Tierra nodded. Ai shrugged.

"Let's go."

They took the black sedan car he'd rented that afternoon after their hike. The Camaro not only drew more attention than they needed this evening, but it only had two seats, so nowhere for Ai to sit. They'd park a couple of streets away and then walk to the house.

Ai had refused to give them any more detail than the general area, and he hoped this was because she wanted to feel useful rather than because she didn't remember the address. He still didn't completely trust her.

Tierra got in and gestured to Ai to sit in the front, so she could direct Fintan. They buckled up and he pulled away from the curb. A few miles after crossing the Ironworkers Memorial bridge, they came to the outskirts of an upper-middle-class neighborhood. Spacious houses set back from the road had driveways with one or more expensive cars. Doctors, lawyers and bankers lived here. Maybe consultants, psychiatrists and CEOs.

At Ai's uncertain direction, the car glided down the street. They passed a cop car, and Tierra made a thoughtful noise.

She pulled a little power, and the reflections in the car windows they passed no longer showed every detail of their vehicle. She had blended the car with their surroundings. They wouldn't be invisible, but they'd be less noticeable.

He should have thought of that.

Ai's face was pale in the moonlight, and her eyes were too white in the darkness of the car.

"Recognize where we are?" he said.

"Yeah. We're close." Her words were clipped.

"How close?" He kept a wary eye on their surroundings.

"A street away. Left at the end and then it's on the right. I think."

He nodded. Tierra put a hand through from the back of the car onto Ai's shoulder in support – a hand that the girl didn't shake off. Perhaps they were getting through to her.

"I'll go past it the first time. As slowly as I can without attracting suspicion. He'll have no reason to think anyone is coming, but there's no point in drawing anyone's notice. Then we'll park and come back on foot," he said.

He put his signal light on to turn left as they approached the intersection. The tick-tick-tick was loud in the car.

They made the turn.

His heart beat a little faster, but it was excitement rather than anxiety. This was a straightforward recon job, nothing more, due to the need to bring the girl.

"Say when Ai," he said.

"It's coming up." Her words were jagged.

Seeing only lights on in the driveway at the house she indicated, he slowed a little more. The house was contemporary, and he estimated four or five bedrooms. It had a vaulted roofline and huge windows, and there were no cars parked in the spaces that belonged to the building.

His brow furrowed. He'd expected there to be at least one car. That kind of house rarely had just the one occupant. And he didn't know any energetics who couldn't drive. They might not all love being enclosed in metal boxes, especially some of the really old energetics, but with the long timespans they all lived, most of them had learned in the last hundred or so years.

Why are there no cars in the drive?

As they passed it, he checked one more time. He gestured with his head towards the darkened house. "That one?"

"Yeah."

"We won't let anyone hurt you, Ai," Tierra's voice came from the back, low and soothing.

"Sure. Whatever." Ai shrugged the words off, voice tight.

Fintan drove a few streets away and parked. This neighborhood was more blue collar, with people working shifts. Less likely to pick up on a car coming and going after midnight.

"Okay. Suit up." He pulled the watch cap from his pocket, and the others also put on gloves and hats. The place they'd parked afforded them a quiet walk to the house.

"What did you notice?" he asked.

"No cars." Tierra's voice was still pitched low.

"Yeah. Strange. Makes it less likely anyone is there. Which is odd because…?" He was treating them like any new members of his team, seeing how they responded to the environment.

Ai stared at him, and Tierra put a comforting hand on her forearm and spoke. "The house was big. There should be a few people living there, even if some of them are staff."

"I didn't see anyone apart from the old guy and Indigo last time," Ai said.

"Yes. Though there could be a garage. Or maybe no one drives. More likely, no one is home. The last would be best for us. Ready?" They nodded, neither enthusiastic, and he started moving, continuing their discussion in a low voice that matched Tierra's. "Right. What's the plan?"

"We've been through it, 'Dad'." Ai's voice emphasized the last word with a sarcastic tone. "We know what we're doing."

He was glad to see a bit of spark in the girl, but made her talk them through the plan anyway. The most critical part of which was that Ai couldn't join them until they'd checked the house was safe.

"Which is stupid because I'm the only one who's been in the house." Ai muttered this, an argument they'd had several times already.

They ducked down a side alley and brushed through some scraggy bushes at the edge of a new housing development.

"We're coming up to a road where we don't have much cover. We should walk normally. As normally as anyone coming home at this time of night on foot would, anyway," he said.

He turned to Tierra and tugged off her hat. "Hey!" she protested, slowing.

"It's just for a minute. Take my arm. Keep walking." Puzzled, she did so. "And Ai, take my other one."

Ai, not nearly as obedient as Tierra, shook her head. But she sensed what he was up to, and slipped around him to take Tierra's other arm.

"Playing at happy families are we?" *Hmm.* The girl was sharp.

"Something like that. We're just a family walking home from our friends' house," he lectured.

"In the dead of night," muttered a scowling Ai.

They approached the street with the house. He looked around to see where Ai could hide.

He scouted out a likely looking place by some shrubs, where she could remain unseen both from the house and the street. When she was safely stashed he stepped away, Tierra pulled a little energy, and the bushes swayed slightly. When they were still, there was no longer any sign of Ai. He nodded his approval.

They approached the house from the rear, which meant cutting around the back of several other houses, which he hoped wouldn't have dogs or alarm systems. Tierra could calm dogs, but every one she had to reach out and connect with took a little of her energy, and he wanted her as primed as possible.

Going along the backs of the houses they passed several large lawns, a swimming pool, and one property which was entirely walled off. A good place for an energetic to blend in. Anonymous suburbia.

They arrived at the rear of the target property, marked by a line of trees and bushes. Tierra put out subtle tendrils of energy to check for wardings, and her eyebrows rose.

"This place has a lot of protection. It's going to take me a while to unpick. You want to take a walk and scope the rest of the house out?"

He frowned, unwilling to leave her.

"I'll be fine here," Tierra said. "I need to concentrate. The person who lives here is either a reasonably strong earth energetic, or they paid one to secure the home. Go get the lay of the land. See if you can get a sense of anyone in there physically. We don't think anyone is there, but you can check. You need to treat me like a real member of the team."

He nodded, and wished for the millionth time in his life that he had the Ajna power of mind speaking. It would come in really handy.

Fintan walked away. Tierra scolded herself at the millisecond she let herself be distracted by his very nice butt. She went to work.

These wardings were complicated. A sophisticated and powerful energetic had put them together. She hoped the house was as empty as Fintan thought it was, because whoever lived here would be able to tell she'd gone through the protection they'd created. She tried to slide through them gracefully but what she was actually doing was hacking at them with an energetic machete – which was taking a lot of power.

She traced one of the wardings that surrounded the house. They glowed with power. They were connected like knotted string. She tugged at one of the ends. It was like unraveling a knitted sweater, though one with the power to bite if you unraveled it in the wrong place. It was the type of guardian energy that stopped you getting in, not out, so she picked at it to make a hole where they could enter, and then they could leave anywhere.

After many minutes, she was sweating in the night air, and she was almost at the limit of what she could do with her earth powers. She hoped they wouldn't need them inside. Her body was high on adrenaline, hyper-sensitive to the environment around her, and to the task at hand.

But she was proud. She'd managed to make a hole big enough for the three of them to get through, and she'd deactivated three or four other wardings that connected to it.

There was no sign of Fintan. But there was no sign of anyone else either. The property was almost certainly empty.

Should she go in alone? Perhaps she should pop through the hole she'd made and check for other wardings. She wouldn't go into the house, but she might as well be thorough.

She used some of her air energy to tag the hole to Fintan so it would shine if he came by. The circle she'd made glimmered a white-blue color for a moment before it faded. That was as big a clue as she could leave. Not that it mattered, she'd be back by the time he returned.

She bent down and put her hand on the earth, and 'asked' the hedge to let her through. The branches moved out of the way, rustling as if the wind was moving them, but in a very specific direction. After a few moments there was easily enough room for her to creep through.

She moved through the hedge without incident, and stood on the other side. It was a big garden for a suburban house, a well-tended lawn with the odd flowerbed and some small trees. It wasn't a working garden – no vegetables, no herbs, nothing useful.

There was also very little cover. Anyone who was in the house and looking out at the garden would be able to see her if she moved across the lawn.

Except that she was an earth energetic. She pulled power, which had begun to be a strain, and wrapped it around her. She blended with the night, and moved across the lawn, sticking to the side of the garden, next to the hedge and going towards the house. She kept her energetic senses open the whole time, checking for more wardings.

She didn't find any.

She crept to the back door, her heart pounding. She'd investigate the house's protection, and for signs that there was anyone inside.

She put her hand on the brick and she sent whisper-thin tendrils of power into the house, seeking. She touched each room in turn, surprised at how big the place was. After a few minutes, she let out a breath. There was no one in the house. No signs of life at all, not even a cat or a dog.

It was safe to disable the last of the protection, and then she would get the others. She turned her attention to the house. She found another security warding linked to the house itself. It took her a few more minutes, and more energy, to disable it, but she managed it.

She needed a break. She sank down on the grass, her back against the house, and put her hands into the damp earth, seeking support from her element. It wasn't the same as rest and recharging, not with the amount of energy disabling the protections had needed, but it would help.

Somewhat refreshed, she got up and prowled around the house, checking for anything else energetic. She kept a hand on the house at all times, trailing it round behind her as she used every sense to see if there were more. She was more relaxed now she knew there were no people inside.

At a large window, she peered inside to see into the darkened room.

And reared back, her gorge rising.

Because she'd been wrong. Well, half-wrong. There was someone inside. But she'd been right that there were no signs of life.

A lump the size of a sleeping bag lay on the otherwise very tidy living room floor. She forced herself to step back and focus on the lump to check she was right. She squinted, and couldn't look away.

It was a dead body.

CHAPTER
12

Fintan flowed between shrubs and trees, if not as quietly as Tierra, near enough. Certainly no human would come close to his stealth. He crept past several cats, a fox, and a squirrel, but none of them startled.

Once he'd circled the house, found nothing out of place, and checked on Ai, he returned to the place he'd left Tierra.

She wasn't there.

His belly squeezed. As he moved into the spot he'd last seen her, a shimmer of something touched him, and a faint circle of air energy appeared, surrounding a low gap in the hedge.

Bloody woman. This wasn't the plan.

It wasn't like this when he worked with other Warriors. They knew to follow instructions. He pressed his lips together and got down on his hands and knees to maneuver through the small hole in the hedge. He and Tierra were going to have words.

He got halfway through the opening, and slammed into something solid. He rocked back and moved into a defensive posture on his knees, unable to see anything as his head spun. The hedge's spiky thorns pricked and scratched.

He searched the dark to see what he'd ricocheted off, and a human cannonball barreled into him. Its momentum took him down to the floor with it. It took a moment more for the 'ouuff' noise the other body made to filter into his stunned brain.

And for him to realize that the warm, soft body he had in his arms was Tierra.

Tierra ended up on her back in the alley with Fintan on top of her. She panted hard from her short flight from the house, and her back and butt hurt from tiny stones digging into her.

She blinked and shook her head.

"Fintan? Fintan, get off of me," she said. She struggled to catch her breath.

He was as dazed as she, his cap askew so some of his reddish blond hair poked out at the side. "Fintan!"

She arched her torso slightly to nudge him off.

"Sorry." He moved to the side and put an arm out to pull her into a sitting position.

Tierra pressed a hand to her forehead. Her heart drummed in her chest. She didn't want to close her eyes in case the image of the still body came back.

"There's a dead person in the living room." She couldn't swallow over the lump in her throat.

He slid to face her, both of them still on their butts on the ground, and grabbed her by the arms. "Did you go into the room?"

She shook her head vigorously. "Of course not. I saw her through the window and came back out to get you."

She couldn't have gotten away fast enough, in fact. A blush of heat rose up her neck. Should she have done more?

"Did you sense anyone else in the house?"

"No." She wanted to be home, in her garden, where it was peaceful, there were no dead bodies, and no one tried to attack her. This was such a horrible mess.

"We need to get Ai." He stood.

She rubbed her hands over her face. If only her head would stop pounding. "We can't bring Ai in with a dead body in there."

His face was impassive. "The body means we need a new plan. And if we leave her outside much longer she might join us on her own – we're lucky she's obeyed up until this point. I don't trust her to follow orders. You didn't."

She closed her eyes, her face hot.

"Maybe she'll know the body, or have other information. Better to have her with us."

Tierra's nod was slow. She still reeled at the sight of the body. Should they really expose Ai to the same? But Fintan made a good point about her coming to join them anyway. Ai was a wild card. Tierra would just have to try and protect Ai however she could.

Fintan had already disappeared, and reappeared a few short minutes later with a pale and vibrating Ai.

"Did you tell her?" Tierra asked.

"It's not my first stiff," Ai's tone was flippant, but her hands clenched and unclenched.

"Tierra, can you open the back door?" Fintan said.

"I've ripped through a lot of the wardings. Given our lack of subtlety so far, I think you might as well burn through the back door's lock."

"There might be no other live humans, but we don't know what other nasty surprises might be hiding there." His hand rubbed his chin. "We do a sweep before we look at the corpse. No lights. Actually, give me a second."

There was a light buzz as he reached for the energy of fire. He shaped the energy into a small glowing ball that he kept muted.

"That should seem enough like moonlight that it won't be too suspicious in the unlikely event that anyone sees it from the outside."

"Can I do that?" Ai whispered.

Tierra shook her head. "Manipura energy."

Ai sighed.

"Are you ready?" Fintan said. "Understand the rules?"

"Yes." She wasn't going off-script again.

"As much as possible, try not to leave any traces of yourselves." He drew latex gloves out of a pocket and handed them each a pair to put on.

Too soon, they were ready.

"Let's go," Fintan said.

He gestured to Tierra to lead them through the hole in the hedge. She ducked down and wriggled through the space, coming up on the other side in the garden, where she waited for the others.

It was hard to believe that a body lay on the other side of the manicured lawn. The last corpse she had been up close and personal with had been in World War II, a lifetime ago. A bad time. Her mother and aunt had been two of the bodies, which Tierra had helped sift through the remains of a hospital to find and identify. The miasma of cordite that had hung around the wreckage, combined with the smell of wet burning and damp cement had blended together into a unique and horrible perfume that Tierra hoped she never had to smell again.

The sound of Ai coming through the hole was audible in the crisp night air. Tierra shook herself.

Fintan came through the gap without leaving a trace. "After you."

Tierra nodded, and set off towards the house, taking a circuitous route that kept them to the edges of the gardens. She could hear her heart thud in her chest, and sucked in deep breaths to attempt to calm herself.

When they reached the back door, she moved aside, and Fintan put his hand on the door handle. He traced a laser-sharp blade of fire around the lock mechanism, until he was able to open the door while the lock stayed in place.

He sent his energy-ball low into the room, its glow dull but helpful. Tierra took in a spacious kitchen, full of gleaming metal and marble. It looked like a show kitchen – everything in its place, nothing ever used.

She followed Fintan through the house, room by room. The rest of the house was just as impersonal. The pictures on the wall were bland art that could have come from IKEA, though had likely cost a great deal more.

Nothing revealed anything about the owner.

The house had been mostly cleared out apart from one room, where there were a couple of boxes stacked up by the door. Tierra pulled off the lid of one of the containers, and poked through the contents.

Ai, looking over her shoulder, let out a muffled noise.

"What?" Tierra turned to her. "Is everything ok?"

"I think this is Indigo's stuff." Ai moved forward and started her own inventory, pawing through the contents. "This is a necklace she wore, and I think this was one of her t-shirts." She yanked out a black shirt with the name of a heavy metal band on it. "Why's her stuff piled up? Do you think he's done something to her?"

They still hadn't told Ai that Indigo was dead. They hadn't gotten around to changing their original story that they were searching for her. But now wasn't the time.

"Hard to say," Fintan said. "Let's keep going. I don't think we should stay here long, and we need to spend some time with the body."

Tierra closed up the box again, and stared down at it. Poor Indigo, a woman whose life had ended up stacked into a couple of boxes, most likely to be thrown into the trash.

They worked their way through the rest of the house, finding nothing else, then approached the doors to the living room.

Fintan cracked the door, and held his hand up. "Let me go in first."

He slipped silently into the room, his light ahead of him, and left the two women standing in the hall. Ai moved closer to Tierra, and she put a hand on the girl's shoulder.

After a few tense moments, he came out again, his face grim. "Okay, you can come in. There's not much to see, but she's been dead a while. Don't touch anything if you can. Whoever did this is likely to come back to clean up."

"They'll have seen that someone has been here from the wardings I took down," Tierra pointed out.

"Let's keep it at a minimum. There's no point in letting them know who we are." He slipped back into the room.

Tierra took a breath, and followed him, Ai trailing after her.

The living room was stuffy, and the nausea that she had tamped down surged up again at the stink of the body.

She wasn't sure if she could do this. Her feet dragged on the plush carpet as she walked to the window where Fintan stood surveying the body.

It was a teenage girl, perhaps a few years older than Ai, with streaked blond hair and nails bitten down to the quick. She was thin and dressed in some baggy jeans, nondescript trainers, and a hoodie. Her face seemed pinched even in death.

Tierra's hands sweated in the latex gloves. She pushed up the sleeve of the girl's hoodie, left side and then right side. The girl had the look of a junkie, but there were no track marks that she could see. She frowned and checked other possible injection sites. How had the girl died?

"Do you think she was…like us?" Ai's voice was thick.

Tierra mentally kicked herself. How had she not thought of that? She needed to examine the body from an energetic's perspective, not a human one. She really was off her game.

"I'm not sure," Tierra said.

"Can you read the room?" Fintan asked.

Reading a room was something only powerful energetics could do. Tierra could, but she rarely practised it. Emergencies only. It took huge effort.

"I'm not sure I have enough energy left. But I can try."

Fintan rubbed the back of his neck. The glow of the light showed up the shadows under his eyes. She'd barely thought about the impact of the situation on him, assumed it was commonplace for him, but he was still sensitive. Just because he could deal with it, didn't mean he welcomed it.

"Don't do it if you don't have enough." He glanced around. "Let's start with a physical exam."

He searched the room methodically, checking for hidden spaces, and examining every possible detail. Tierra stayed with the body, Ai looking on, her arms wrapped around her thin frame, bravado gone.

Tierra might not want to read the room, but she could have an energetic look at the body. Her Anahata energy was a healer's energy, and would let her see inside. She wanted, needed, to help.

She removed one of her gloves, and pushed up the girl's hoodie so her sunken stomach was revealed. The closer Tierra could get to the girl's own Anahata Chakra, even if it wasn't activated, the better. Not that Tierra had done this often on dead bodies.

She drew a breath, and pulled what little energy she had left. She'd mainly used Muladhara, earth energy on the house's protection, and so it was good that she was using Anahata here. She went inside the body, and sought out anything unusual. It didn't take long to see what the problem was.

Ai was right. The girl was an energetic. Her life's energy had been sucked away by a Leech, leaving her drained, with nothing to sustain her system.

Tierra drew her awareness out of the body, and opened her eyes. She rose to her feet in a smooth motion, but she swayed when she was upright. How could any energetic, sworn to protect the earth and its life, do something like this?

"She was drained," Tierra said.

Fintan turned. "Drained?"

"Yes. She was an energetic, an active one. I don't know her, but..." She pulled the girl's left sleeve higher, displaying a dark stripe of what looked like a tattoo. "She has an Adherent mark. She'll be known to one of the Guilds."

"Someone should be missing her. That's interesting. Which Guilds?" Fintan asked.

"Anahata-Ajna."

Ai's ears perked up at this. "Like me?"

"Yes. Like you. But she knew she was an energetic. She would have had what we call a Maven, which is someone who trains you in one of your energies. Most likely she was an Anahata Adherent as that's what her stronger energy was. It's hard to tell how developed it was given she's been drained like this." Tierra stood to face Ai. "Draining someone else's energy is one of our greatest crimes. It's a type of vampirism, cannibalism almost. It's extremely rare."

If Tierra got out of the house without throwing up, she would have done well.

"Yet we've seen it more than once in a matter of a month." Fintan mused.

"What does he mean? Where did you see it before?" Ai asked.

Tierra hedged, unsure of what to tell Ai, so new to their world. They would need to tell her about Indigo, and what had happened, if only to show Ai how serious things were. Later. "Let's talk about it when we're not in a room with a dead body."

Her stomach twisted. It wasn't a deception if she held off the full truth for a while, surely?

"The house doesn't look as if it's in use at the moment, but I need to talk to Adam about the best approach from here. We don't have infinite resources, but it's one of our best leads. We can also look into a paper trail for the property, which might give us another place to look." He took out his phone and snapped a few shots of the dead girl. "It's hard to know how long she's been here. And whether whoever did this intends to return and…dispose of her, or has left and doesn't care."

"A paper trail will help us there, as we might be able to track it to a person. Besides, they're likely to come and move the body. In which case we'll have them," Tierra said.

She couldn't imagine that person. Would that person be evil, or mad? How disturbed did you need to be to break the darkest taboos of their society? Her nausea returned.

"Either way, we need to get out of here," Fintan said. "We're not in a position to capture an unfriendly at this moment. We also need to find out who she was – I'll send the photo to the Anahata Guild when we get back to the hotel."

He took a final look around the room. "Let's go."

It had been four a.m. by the time they'd all hit the sack, and Tierra had insisted Ai stay the night, so Fintan had ended up on the floor.

He got up early and went for a run to help him think. He'd barely had a moment to himself in the last few days. He'd been with Tierra the entire time. Which hadn't been bad, but it had been different.

He spent that kind of time with his unit, but rarely with a woman. Okay, lots of those he served with were women, but Tierra was, well, a *woman*. A woman he didn't quite know how to interact with right now.

His feet pounded the pavement, as he built from a jog to a run. Sweat beaded his forehead. Physical activity had always been the way he'd processed difficult feelings or events, and the last few days had been as confusing as fuck.

He had a few issues he needed to work out: next steps on the investigation; the girl and what to do with her; and then, Tierra. His mind shied away from that last, and he sped up.

Investigation first then.

He hadn't expected the body at the house. He would never have brought Tierra – let alone the girl – to a house with a dead body. Tierra had seen enough of that in the war, and he didn't want to expose her to it again. She was softer, gentler than him, and she suffered more at other people's distress. He needed to protect her.

He hadn't seen the body coming, and neither had Cuinn predicted it in a dreamwalk. They needed to find the girl's identity, watch the house, and discover whatever they could about the owner. This was solid ground for Fintan, an area where he had plenty of experience. He knew how to run an investigation. Since the war, he'd been a trouble shooter for the Manipura Guild. He preferred to work alone – he didn't enjoy managing a team – but he had access to plenty of resources. As did Adam. They'd catch up, work out the details of the op and take it forward between them. Fintan had already sent the other man a few brief texts giving him a heads up, and there were people on the way to stake out the house.

He turned right at a corner with a huge steel and glass building. At this time of day he'd passed plenty of typical Vancouverites, with yoga mats over their shoulders and Starbucks cups in their hands. Fintan had dated a few girls like that in the past. They didn't seem as appealing now.

He picked up the pace, sweat pouring off him. Ai was a harder problem. She was untrained, and a liability in several ways. She was also, one way or another, family. They needed to find out who she was, and bring her in so she could learn about her magic and how to use it safely. Would she, though? Would she trust them enough to come in? Leave the world she'd known behind? He grimaced.

Tierra wouldn't want to let the girl out of her sight, for fear they might lose her. It would be easy for Ai to disappear in a city like this. It was important that the girl made her own choice. If they forced her, the chances of keeping her were slim. He hoped Tierra would be on board with that. Once they got her to Cathair Cuinn, he hoped she'd be intrigued enough to stay. The ideal would be to get her to one of the Guilds. She had a lot to catch up on.

The last problem was Tierra. He swiped at the moisture on his forehead with his forearm, drops falling behind him as he ran.

In the park Tierra had told Fintan – in the same way she might offer him a sandwich – that she loved him.

He groaned. What was he supposed to do with that?

Yet, she didn't seem bothered. She'd told him with her usual grace and warmth, and then seemed to move on. Surely if she was able to do that, she'd mixed up her feelings. She couldn't actually love him.

At the same time, he'd found himself having some disturbing feelings in relation to her. Disturbing, because it was entirely unthinkable that they could ever be together. They would be a terrible match. He couldn't give her what she needed – someone who was able to love with a full heart, and who was able to be a rooted presence for her at Cathair Cuinn. Fintan, on the other hand, had a role that involved danger and travel, unpredictability and change, none of which Tierra enjoyed, even by proxy.

What was the way forward here?

His usual approach was to face a problem head on. Should he talk about this with Tierra again? But what would that gain them? She'd said her piece, and he agreed the idea of them trying to date, whatever his willful dick said, was incomprehensible.

She was prepared to pretend it wasn't a thing, and so would he. Their attention right now needed to be on the prophecies, and whoever was draining young women. After that, he'd get back into his work in Europe for a while. Have a break from Cathair Cuinn. He gritted his teeth. Some space would be good.

He slowed his pace, more relaxed. His feet hit the pavement with satisfying thumps, and his breath puffed out in little clouds as he jogged back towards the hotel. Exercise always cleared his head.

He stopped at a coffee shop on the corner near the hotel and picked up a Caramel Macchiato for Tierra – her favorite – but hesitated over Ai. He went with a mocha as a balance of sweet and coffee. Though knowing her, she'd probably want a double espresso. He got a triple-shot Americano for himself and went to the room.

The room was warm and smelled of flowers and moss. Like Tierra. The beds were made, and the room was tidy, their bags packed.

"Keen to get back?" he asked.

She smiled. "Yes. There's stuff I can do there."

She stopped, her brows lifted. "Oh, you brought coffee! Thank you, Fintan. That was really thoughtful."

Fintan flushed at Tierra's disproportionate delight. He did nice things for her usually, didn't he? Why was she so surprised? He handed the drinks out quickly.

"Where do we need to go to pick up your belongings, Ai?" he asked.

She looked down into her mocha, one arm wrapped right around her thin frame. "Um, about that. I can't just, you know, pick up and leave. I need a bit of time, to sort things out. Say goodbye to some people. I can get the bus over in a few days, and we'll see."

Fintan rubbed the back of his neck. Not pressuring her to come back with them would help her to trust them more. Plus, she might need a bit of time to come to terms with the very different turn her life was about to take. Before Tierra could say anything, he spoke. "Okay Ai, that's fair."

She took a relieved sip of her drink and jerked her head in response.

"But please, keep in touch," Fintan said. "All you need to do is contact us, and we'll help you however we can. We'll see you within the week – there's plenty more to tell you when you arrive. Do you want a phone?"

He stated her arrival as fact, leaving her no room for argument. He might not know how to deal with teenage girls, but he had dealt with a lot of unruly subordinates. He was going to treat her like that from now on.

Ai shook her head. "I have one."

"Do you want us to drop you somewhere?" he addressed her, not hopeful, while wanting to see if she would trust them a little more.

She shook her head. "Nah. I can walk from here."

"Okay. I'll walk you downstairs." He caught Tierra's frown, but he had a couple of things he wanted to say to Ai in private.

They walked from the room to the elevator, and he checked around to see no one was watching before he pulled out $500. He stepped in with her. "This is to get you to Cathair Cuinn. Get a case or something to pack your stuff into, and make sure you pick up some more clothes here in the city. There's probably not much in Merrow that will suit your dress sense."

She looked at the cash in his hand and to his surprise, paused. "I can earn my way you know. When I get to the house. You can give me jobs and stuff. I learn quick."

"I'm sure you do. And no doubt we'll have a fair few for you. Helping Tierra in the kitchen and garden, helping Cuinn and Blaize with research."

Ai didn't look thrilled, but she nodded anyway. "Whatever. But I don't need charity. Give me room and board? I can pay you back."

Fintan was hoping to find out who her parents had been, to see if they'd left an estate or anything valuable behind them. He'd quizzed Ai on what she could remember of them, and of her life with them — which wasn't much — and he and Tierra had agreed between them that this should be high on their list of priorities once they got back to Cathair Cuinn.

"We can work it out when you get to the house," he said. "One other thing. You asked how we know if someone's energy is twisted. Unless the other person is shielding, it's something we can tell by sending our own energy threads into theirs to check."

She had frozen, her face pale.

"I think you might have a personal interest in the answer. You've lived on the streets for a while. Probably faced some tough situations. I wanted to tell you neither of us picked up any sign of your energy twisting."

The girl's eyes welled up, though nothing escaped. She sagged back against the wall of the elevator. "Okay."

"Okay. Look after yourself, and make sure you're with us within the week — check in every couple of days so we know you're good. And please, Ai, don't go back to that house on your own. He's still out there somewhere and you may be a target given you've already had contact with him."

She shrugged one shoulder, feigning indifference — the tears unshed but still glittering. "Why would I? There's already one dead girl there. I'm not stupid. But if Indigo comes back, what should I do?"

"Let us know," said Fintan smoothly, without taking a breath.

Ai hadn't seemed to like Indigo especially, but he'd detected a hint of hero worship there, especially once Ai had found out about Indigo's powers. They'd tell her what had happened when she was safely at Cathair Cuinn.

He was happy taking the wheel of the Camaro again. He loved driving, and it was a good trip from Vancouver to Merrow. Plus there was no 'new car' rental smell in this one.

Tierra was silent in the car, unlike her usual chatty self. He was pretty sure what she was thinking.

"I didn't like leaving her either," he said.

"She's a child, Fintan! A child!" The words burst out of Tierra like a flood breaking down a dam. "And we just left her, again!"

"When did we leave her before?"

"Energetics did. And we're energetics. Should we have pushed harder? Showed we cared? Was it a test?"

"No. We did the right thing. She needs space to absorb everything. It's a lot." He hadn't liked it, but it was the best way to get her to come to the house.

"Why didn't you tell her about Indigo?" she said.

"It seems too complicated. We can tell her when she gets to the house."

Tierra shifted in her seat. "I suppose. I just don't like hiding the truth from her."

"It's only for a week," Fintan pointed out. "Then we can explain everything."

The urban sprawl of Vancouver transformed into the rich green countryside, the imposing mountains in front of them. Fintan cracked his window to let the air, with its hints of spring, into the car.

He put a hand over to touch Tierra's leg for comfort, his eyes not leaving the road. Her leg was warm through her jeans. The car felt smaller, and he moved his concentration back to the road, and his hand back to the wheel.

"Let's talk about something else." *For my sake as much as yours.*

"Like what?" Tierra wasn't too interested, her eyes on the landscape they were passing through.

"What's the most unusual topic you've had in your advice column?"

She looked back over at him at that. "What?"

"Your column."

"No one ever asks me about that." She was frowning.

"Why not?" This was not the reaction he'd been expecting.

"Because...it's not important. Not really. Compared to the jobs everyone else does." She shrugged.

"You don't believe in what you do?" He was baffled. She took care of everyone around her, and held down a job in the human world, and still she didn't feel she was worthy?

She didn't say anything, just picked at an imaginary thread on her sleeve.

"You might not be doing one of the high profile energetic jobs, but you're fulfilling your energetic role as much, if not more, than most of us. How many newspapers is your column syndicated to?"

"About two hundred and forty."

"So every week, across Canada, you bring comfort and support to many thousands of humans. You bring a little balance to their worlds. How can you say, as a Muladhara energetic, whose energy centers around safety, security, and grounding, that you're not carrying out your role?"

She was looking at him as if she'd never seen him before.

"What?" he said.

"I've just – that's not something anyone else has ever said." Her words were halting.

"How long have you been working for the newspapers?"

"A few decades I guess. Writing under different names, of course, so the non-ageing thing wasn't a problem. And sometimes I 'retired' and handed the column down to a protégé. Dealing with people digitally has helped a lot. It took me a while to settle here when Adam and I first arrived, and I needed to get the house properly set up. Cuinn had built it, but it wasn't a home. And then I was looking for something to do, and met one of the newspaper editors at some mixer of Cuinn's at the university. He wanted to add a female touch to his paper, and Cuinn convinced him to give me a trial." She shrugged. "And it built from there."

"And you do a gardening column too?"

She blushed a little. "Yes. I could do more to keep myself up to date. Attend more courses. I just never seem to get around to it. I'm happy in the house, doing my thing. Being part of the community here. And writing the columns."

"The degree in horticulture must help though," said Fintan, dryly. "Let alone your degrees in psychology and social studies."

She wriggled in her seat. "What does your role consist of at the moment? You always seem to be doing something different. Adam's had a similar role for decades now, or at least, he's been in the same area, just gaining seniority. But not you."

Her tone was curious, and she'd abandoned the view to focus on him, shifting to look at his profile. He felt bathed in sunshine.

"I'm more of a trouble-shooter. I help out in difficult cases where there's a Rogue issue. This situation with Cuinn is actually just the sort of thing I'd be assigned to. I have quite a lot of leeway as to what I get involved in. Sometimes the Major or Minor Circle will direct me to investigate something. It's rarely boring."

"What do you enjoy most?"

"I love the variety. And I love problem-solving. I like people, but I'm not necessarily a team player, so I like the autonomy that the role brings me." He paused to overtake a battered truck that was chugging along the road. The driver, probably a farmer, Fintan thought, raised a hand to wave at them, and Fintan waved back.

"I like the travel, too," he said.

"Where's home for you these days? I know you have the apartment in Italy, the cottage in Ireland, and the penthouse in Hong Kong, but which is home?" Tierra asked.

He ran a hand over the stubble on his chin. He couldn't tell her the first answer that had come to mind, which was that Cathair Cuinn was the place that felt most like home. He'd even given it its name – in jest, originally, as Cathair meant castle in Gaelic, Cuinn's original language – but the label had stuck. An answer that was as much a surprise to him as it would be to her. He made short visits there every few months. And he'd been coming to visit for as long as Adam and Tierra had lived there. It added up.

"I'm not sure. They all contribute different things to my life. I like the variety remember?" He realized she'd neatly turned the tables on him, and was now asking him about his life rather than the other way round. He wondered if she even knew she was doing it. Tierra was humble – she never put herself in the spotlight, and always found a way to get the other person to talk and share their secrets.

Luckily, we're nearly home. He turned the car down the long lane that led to Cathair Cuinn. *Otherwise who knows what other secrets – secrets I didn't even realize existed – she would uncover?*

Elrian stood on the threshold to his property, and glared at the broken wardings. He and Dagon had come back to the house to remove the body, only to find that Tierra and that good-for-nothing Fintan had found the house, and worse, discovered the body. The disgusting…taste of their energies was everywhere.

Elrian's manicured nails dug into his palm. This wasn't part of the plan. Indigo's stay at the motel should have ended the trail there. How did they find this house?

He stalked around the edges of the land, using his earth energy to see if there had been anyone with Fintan and Tierra. He was surprised Tierra was powerful enough to get through his protections, but she hadn't done it gracefully.

Dagon unlocked the front door, and Elrian walked into the house and headed for the back room where they had left the body. It was still there, and to the naked eye, at least, it appeared untouched. But Tierra's energetic traces were all over.

Discomfort crept along his shoulders and back, and he shrugged it off, annoyed. He couldn't shield as well as he would like when reading the house like this.

In the living room, he stared down at the body of the girl, ignoring the stink. He twisted the thick ring on his right hand. The ring contained a tiny chip of stone, a Remnant, that he had recharged from the girl's energies.

Elrian stood in the room and closed his eyes. He reached out with tendrils of earth energy and riffled through the energetic tracks in the room. There was Tierra…there was Fintan…ah ha. There was a third, who also seemed familiar. Was it another of Cuinn's friends? Elrian drew his brows together. He couldn't quite place the energy. Female, definitely. Was it Cara? No, though Anahata energy was present in the traces, hard to pick out because both Tierra and Fintan also had that Chakra activated. And...the auxiliary...was Ajna.

The energetic scent tickled the back of his mind. He knew it. Who was it? He tried to relax, to let the tracks settle so the name would come to him. He took a couple of deep breaths, his body motionless in the center of the room.

Ah. A loose end. His eyes snapped open and he gritted his teeth.

That little bitch, Ai. Indigo had brought her round as a gift for Elrian's lover and mentor. His nostrils flared. He needed to find that girl. Either way, if he found the girl, he'd likely find Tierra and Cuinn, and vice versa. And if he knew Cuinn and his family – and he did – then if they'd found the stray, they'd adopt her. But Elrian needed to get to her. She'd serve more than one purpose.

She knew things about Elrian he didn't want Cuinn's family to know – yet.

And she could be the exact bait that Elrian needed to destroy them.

CHAPTER

13

In her living room, Tierra opened the glass doors that led to her garden. The peaty air would freshen the room up. She was so pleased to be home, in her space.

She had just put the kettle on when there was a knock at the door.

"Come in," she called.

Blaize's auburn hair appeared around the door, and Tierra smiled and took another mug out. "I was just making tea."

"Great." Blaize flopped onto Tierra's sofa. "So, I'm up to date on the difficult stuff, now give me the important stuff. What was Ai like? Does Fintan snore?"

Tierra had liked Blaize from the first moment she'd arrived. Young for an energetic – in her late twenties – she was confident, and her green eyes twinkled with fun as much as they were serious.

Tierra laughed. "No, he didn't snore. He was a good roommate actually, if a little messy."

"Huh."

Tierra brought their tea over and sat at the other end of the sofa. She tucked her feet under her.

"I had one interesting chat with him." She kept her tone casual.

Blaize perked up again. "Yes?"

"We went to the park for me to recharge." Tierra sipped her tea. "I decided it was a good time to share something."

Blaize's eyebrows rose. "What?"

"I told him that I loved him. And that I didn't need anything from him, but I felt I wasn't being honest with him by keeping it to myself. It was making me awfully cranky with him," she said, her tone confiding.

Blaize had almost choked on her tea at the first few words, and was still recovering.

"You told him – what?"

"That I loved him."

"And, how long … have you, hmm?" Blaize gestured weakly with the hand that wasn't holding the tea.

"A long time. As long as I can remember."

"But, Fintan? Really?" Blaize's forehead was furrowed.

Tierra frowned at Blaize's tone. "Yes, why?"

"Well…he's just so…unsuitable for you."

Tierra bristled. It wasn't that Blaize was wrong, exactly…but. Okay, but what? Why was she annoyed? She took a deep breath and let it out slowly.

"I realize we're not a good match," she said. "All I did was tell him, and ask him not to share details of his romantic life any more."

Blaize sagged back against the sofa. "Okay. Good call. I love Fintan, really, but he can be a disaster in relationships. He's always falling in and out of love. I remember my Aunt and Uncle teasing him about it when I was a teenager."

Tierra frowned. "It's not like he's fickle. He only ever has one relationship at a time, and he cares for them."

Blaize fidgeted, getting comfortable in the seat. "Well, sure, but you're so different. He loves travel and variety, you love stability and home. He loves to go skydiving and have sex outdoors. You love baking and snuggling up by the fire. You're chalk and cheese."

"It's not like opposites can't attract. Anyway, I like sex outdoors." Her words were very slightly defensive and she added. "Not that we're going to get together. Or we should. Or I want to."

"How long have you been crushing on him?" said Blaize.

"A long time," said Tierra. She wasn't sure she wanted to talk about it now. It was one thing for her to choose not to pursue something, another for Blaize to tell her it was crazy. What, she wasn't good enough for Fintan? He wasn't good enough for her? She was also embarrassed to say quite how long she'd pined after him. It had been back of mind as long as she could remember. It had faded when she'd done her training for her energies, fading from a burn to an ache. It wasn't like she hadn't dated or had relationships in the meantime.

Blaize's expression was sympathetic, which irked Tierra more.

"He's an attractive man," Blaize said. "I had a crush on him growing up. He always looks like he's just about to play a joke on everyone. And with those bright blue eyes and that surfer hair, well. He has that bad-boy-with-impulse-control-issues thing going on. It's pretty hot."

"Hmm." Tierra drank more tea. She wished she hadn't said anything.

"You're right though," continued Blaize, oblivious. "He falls for each woman head over heels, but they never seem to keep his attention. Not that any of them ever seem to hold a grudge. He must do the most charming break-up speeches in history. He could probably write an advice column of his own on it."

"I guess," said Tierra. She felt scrunchy, and she didn't want to talk about it any more.

"What did he say?" Blaize asked.

"Not much. Though it obviously annoyed him, because later on that night he lost control of his energy for a little while." Which had been weird, in retrospect. Perhaps Fintan also thought the idea of dating Tierra was unthinkable, horrible. Enough that the thought of it made him so ill he'd lost control. Tierra rubbed the back of her neck. Her muscles were tight.

Blaize's forehead wrinkled. "He did?"

"Yes."

Blaize smirked. "I bet that hasn't happened to him in a while. That's not the kind of impulse control issue I was thinking about. You should probably have told him that it happens to all guys at some point or another."

Tierra rolled her eyes.

"Have you talked about it since?" said Blaize.

"No."

"Why not?"

"I've told him the situation, what else is there to say?" Tierra got up and began fluffing cushions. She was done with the topic. "I don't expect anything from him. I just wanted to get it off my chest. Oh, and not have to hear endless stories about his latest conquest."

Blaize gazed at her thoughtfully, silent for a while. "When are we expecting Ai?"

"Another week or so." Tierra's chest loosened. She'd process her feelings about Fintan by herself in the future.

"You want help getting a room ready for her? Cuinn's had me reading through old prophecies for days. I'm going a little stir-crazy. If it wasn't for exercise – which I'm still not allowed to do at full tilt – I'd be going mad."

"I bet you get some exercise." Tierra's grin was teasing.

"What do you – oh. Well, yes, you're right, I do get some. That can be pretty exhausting." Blaize grinned in return.

"How are you and Cuinn doing?"

"Really well." The smirk on Blaize's face was a little self-satisfied.

"Enjoyed having the house to yourselves?" Tierra hugged a cushion to her chest.

"Well, we've had a lot of work to do. Of course. But yes, we did manage to explore a lot of the house I hadn't yet seen."

Cathair Cuinn was a sprawling residence, with several outbuildings, one of which was a small house in its own right where Blaize had stayed when she'd first arrived. Cuinn, Tierra and Adam had quarters of their own which had everything they needed – living area, kitchen, bedroom and work space, though each was decorated quite differently. There were guest quarters with the same, and other simpler rooms with bathrooms. Many of them were closed up, but the house could easily accommodate a large number of people. Tierra wondered, not for the first time if Cuinn had considered bringing more students here to teach, not simply in a Maven-Adherent role, but more like his day job as a Professor at Vancouver University, from which he was currently on sabbatical. Having decided to opt out of his Guild for a while, perhaps he'd thought one day he'd want to offer something and would need the facilities to do so.

"I'll help you with getting a room ready for Ai, ok?" said Blaize. "Don't do it without me. I'm sure you have your own work to catch up on, and you do a lot more than your share around here."

Disconcerted, Tierra frowned. Had Fintan said something? "I don't mind looking after the house. I enjoy it. And I can't help with the prophecies the way you and Cuinn can. It's what I can contribute."

"Hmm. You contribute in lots of ways, Tierra. It doesn't mean you have to be everyone's maid."

At supper a few hours later, Tierra and Fintan explained to Cuinn and Blaize what had happened in Vancouver.

The kitchen was cozy in the evening dark, the lamps were lit and the four of them were sitting around the sturdy wooden kitchen table together. Tierra felt able to relax for the first time in days. Cuinn opened another bottle of wine, and filled their glasses. "A night off for all of us. We deserve it."

He looked a little hollow around the eyes, but not nearly as bad as he had before Blaize had entered his life. She had managed to heal some of his old wounds, but he still carried the weight of the world on his shoulders.

The three men in Tierra's life – Cuinn, Adam and Fintan – were a study in contrasts. Cuinn was cerebral, conceptual, and scholarly. Adam was the opposite – not that he wasn't highly intelligent, more that he channeled his intelligence into a pragmatic, practical outlook that aimed to get the job done.

Where did Fintan fit? He was practical like Adam. A Warrior, so he'd have to be. He had the air element too, which meant he was also conceptual. He liked ideas, that was for sure. Though he didn't tend to stay serious in a discussion for long. She loved his mischievous side.

"When's Adam due home?" she asked. "Do you know why they needed him?"

Cuinn shook his head. "He knows you're both here though, so he wanted to try and come back within a couple of days."

"What are our next steps?" said Blaize.

"We need to follow the paper trail on the house," said Fintan. "Tierra's going to contact the Anahata Guild to see if she can find out who the victim in the house was."

Cuinn nodded. "Sounds good."

"What's the latest with the research?" said Fintan.

"The only new sliver of prophecy we have is: *The one you find at first shall not be the one you ultimately seek.*" Cuinn shrugged. "I don't think it adds much – apart from confirming that Indigo is only the tip of the iceberg."

Blaize reached out a hand and put it over Cuinn's slender fingers, which tapped the table, restless. "Confirmation is still useful, especially when it's as hard won as it is."

Cuinn's nod was a little stiff, but he thawed as she wrapped her fingers around his, lifted his hand to her lips and kissed it.

"We've found a few possible avenues in the prophecy books," he continued, "but nothing that we've been able to pinpoint with any certainty. We're pursuing the Archetypes, as we said the other day – Warrior, Sage, Healer and so on. And the stones. Though they're considered a myth by most."

"I could help more if I was allowed to dreamwalk on my own," said Blaize, wrinkling her nose.

"You need to strengthen your Haven first," said Cuinn. "It needs to be as real and as solid as this house before you can start wandering off. You need to be much more strongly tethered."

"I know, I know." Blaize turned to Fintan and Tierra, rolling her eyes. "I have training wheels on."

Cuinn opened his mouth to speak again, but stopped when he saw she was smiling. "I just want to keep you safe."

"And I, you."

Tierra looked down, moisture in her eyes at this intimate moment. There was an ache inside her chest. Would she ever have that? Perhaps now she had let go of this Fintan nonsense, she could. Her mouth twisted. She took a breath and raised her gaze to find Fintan staring at her in a peculiar way. She broke eye contact quickly and looked at the floor.

The conversation moved on. Eventually they got round to Ai.

"She needs a home, and some education before we find her a Maven," said Tierra. "I'm going to talk to Anahata Guild about that. In the meantime, we have a flexible household, with energetics in and out that she can learn from, and an extensive library. I want her here."

"I'm happy to teach her combat and self-defense," said Blaize.

"Okay,' said Cuinn, rubbing his chin. "We need to find out more about her parents too. Ask Anahata about that. Someone out there must have missed her. It worries me that she fell through the cracks. It shouldn't be possible."

Tierra was grateful for her family, then. That they would be open to taking in a child they didn't know, on Tierra's say so.

"Given all the things we want to ask them, you'd have better luck visiting the Guild in person," said Fintan.

"What, go to Egypt?" Tierra was taken aback. She hadn't left Canada for years. Actually, decades.

"Why not?" said Fintan.

"I can't leave Cuinn and Blaize again."

"Sure you can." said Blaize. "We're working on the prophecies – Cuinn barely lets me out of the work rooms. We can feed ourselves. And you can work on your column anywhere, right?"

"But – but I like it at home." Not a great argument, and she flushed, realizing she sounded like a child. But she felt like she'd been brave. Done her travels. Got out of the rut. Surely now she could stay at home a little while?

Fintan put a hand on her shoulder. "Maybe I can come with you, before I head back to the office."

'There's no need for that." His palm was distractingly hot on her shoulder, and she shrugged it off. "We're spread thin enough as it is."

"I don't mind,' said Fintan. "It might be fun. I haven't been to Anahata HQ for a long time. It's probably time I reminded them I still exist."

"I'm sure they haven't forgotten you, Fintan," Cuinn's lips quirked. "Didn't you nearly burn the place down at some point?"

"I was much younger then," said Fintan, affronted. "By several hundred years. I'm sure most of them have forgotten that."

"I heard that they warn young Anahata energetics about you as part of their training – and that they're especially wary of anyone who is a Manipura-Anahata," Blaize snickered.

Fintan threw a balled-up serviette at Blaize, who ducked and laughed. "Rumors aren't facts."

"That's settled then,' said Cuinn. "Tierra and Fintan, you leave tomorrow."

"But, what about Ai? What if she comes early? Who will take care of her?" Tierra protested.

"I think we can manage," Cuinn said, somewhat dryly.

"But she won't know you," Tierra said. What if Ai bolted before Tierra got back?

"You won't be gone long. Fintan said she wasn't likely to be here for at least a week, right?" Blaize said, with a brief frown at Cuinn, in a more gentle tone. "We'll let you know if she turns up. And we can operate the stove and the washing machine. It'll be okay."

Tierra's gut swirled and she bit her lip. It didn't feel okay. And if she admitted it, it wasn't only Ai she was worried about. Tierra herself could do with time at home to regroup. She wasn't ready to be out in the world again so soon.

But she was the one who had wanted to contribute. So it didn't look like she was going to have much choice. It was time to step up.

The flight to Cairo was straightforward, if long. Tierra insisted on driving from the airport to the Guild, citing Fintan's tendency to road rage when he was in Egypt.

He'd protested, but it was true he'd learned to drive early in the 20th century when there weren't many cars on the road. He loved driving places like Canada, where the traffic was orderly, but in Egypt the roads were obscenely busy, slow-moving collisions were an everyday occurrence, and every car they saw bore dents and scrapes. He had no problem dealing with this by yelling out of the window and beeping like every other driver on the road here, but Tierra had steadfastly refused to let him.

She rolled her shoulders and drove them out of the crowded airport. She seemed more relaxed in the car than she had in the airport, where the throng of people had jostled her petite frame. He'd tried to put himself between her and them when he could. Her passport worked fine – she'd kept her formal human-style identity current, as energetics were taught growing up. Vishudha Guild, responsible for communications, had a department responsible for keeping the papers of energetics from giving away their secrets. In the age of surveillance their longevity could be harder to manage, but when you could create perfect copies of country documents, you could 'belong' to any country, and be any age.

Dust covered many of the cars they passed, the close desert heat in the 90s as the long hot Egyptian summer began. The washed out yellows of the buildings were familiar to him, but there were many more structures than when he was here last.

When the Guild had re-located near Memphis, after the destruction of Atlantis and at the height of the Ancient Egyptian civilization more than four thousand years ago, the plains had been spacious and bare, with plenty of room for the energetics of air.

Since then Anahata had moved buildings a number of times, but had stayed in the region, despite political and religious turmoil and an increasing population. The energetics had watched with dry amusement the excavations of the so-called Egyptologists of the early nineteenth century. They could have shed some light on a number of mysteries, had it not been their rule by then not to interfere with human progress.

He glanced back at Tierra's profile. He was glad to spend more time alone with her.

He'd realized that it was rare that it was just the two of them. Usually someone else was around. Tierra was most often at the heart of the household, visitors gravitating towards her. She always seemed to have plenty of time for everyone, despite her job.

It was because, he mused, she made everyone feel as if they were the center of the universe.

Whoever she talked to felt cleverer, nicer and more important just by the way she interacted with them.

She was humming to herself in between grumbles. She'd chosen the music for their trip. A mix of rock ballads, not what he'd choose himself, but he'd found himself singing along to an ancient Bon Jovi track, so he couldn't really complain.

He snuck another glance at her. Her focus was on the road, her speed not exactly sedate, but just a whisper over the limit. She navigated the traffic like a pro.

Her hair curled over her shoulders, loose today. He liked it loose. Its waves set off her body's soft curves. Her eyes were ahead. He'd obviously been staring at her too long when her glance shifted off the road and onto him, eyes narrowing. "What?"

"Nothing," he said, easily. "Just thinking."

"Hmph. That'll be the day." But she smiled as she said it, and her attention went back to the road.

An hour later they reached the Guild headquarters, the sprawling buildings in front of them. It was the hottest part of the day, and the sun baked the sandy ground. The buildings looked no different from other buildings in the area – the flat, middle-eastern style, in a pale yellow, a little off-color from age. Energetics didn't draw attention to themselves. The humans who lived in this area thought it was some kind of research institution, anonymous and boring.

The Anahata Minor Guilds were also housed in the midst of big cities. There were many Rogue Rehab Centers run by the Guild too, each one a hospital of sorts for energetics, as well as what might be considered a jail in human terms.

That wasn't how energetics thought. They weren't interested in retribution. Energetics who acted against the good of society – Rogues – were taken to a Rehab Center, assessed, and wherever possible, rehabilitated. It was rare for an energetic to act against the greater good. Energetics didn't have the same kind of societal problems that existed in the human world. That was one of the reasons that Ai's case of abandonment had shocked Fintan and Tierra so much.

In the main, energetics were brought up in a strong family unit. The birth rate for energetics was low, their population barely maintaining over the millennia. Children were wanted and brought up knowing their heritage.

Fintan and Tierra stretched and got out of the car, Fintan grabbing their bags. Stepping through the front door was an odd experience. It had been a long time.

Tierra and Fintan were both auxiliary Anahatas, but still trained as healers. They used these skills in different capacities – Fintan often did double duty in his unit as the unit medic. Tierra had worked for a few periods over the years with different Rehabilitation Centers, and was currently on call for emergencies at the center off the coast of British Columbia where their friend Cara worked.

Energetics weren't exactly considered second class citizens at their auxiliary Guild, but it was definitely easier asking for favors at the Guild of your dominant energy. Always hard to put your finger on, perhaps it was just more the energetic resonance – by definition, an energetic had a stronger resonance with the energy of their dominant Chakra. Fintan wasn't sure. All he knew was that sometimes, all the love and peace of the Anahata Guild was a bit much for his Manipura side. And some bad experiences here in the past meant he didn't have much love for this place.

It had seemed like a good idea to come with Tierra, a way to protect her, but he was less sure now.

Tierra seemed comfortable enough as they checked in and headed to their rooms. "Don't look so grim. I set us up an appointment with a friend, Jebediah. He's been here a few decades, and has a good handle on who's working with whom. He'll give us somewhere to start."

"Lunch first?" he said. An army marched on its stomach, after all.

She laughed again at the hopeful look in his eyes. "Yes, lunch first. Who knows who we might meet in the hall."

They had a two-bedroom suite with a living room between the bedrooms. Tierra had perked up when she'd seen they had a bathroom each.

Fintan threw his duffel in his room, and himself onto the sofa. "Ready."

Tierra, who was opening all the drawers and cupboards, gave a tut of annoyance, and said "You'll just have to wait. I want to freshen up. Didn't that plane journey tire you out at all?"

"I'm used to it. A lot of traveling. You need more practise," he said, and flicked on the television. He found a sports channel after a bit of hopping around, and slouched down on the sofa to watch two Asian nations play some kind of handball.

CHAPTER 14

Tierra showered, pulled on a blue summer dress patterned with tiny woven daisies, added sandals, and was ready to go. When she went back into their living area, Fintan was in exactly the same place she'd left him.

They walked down the hallways out of the accommodation area to the main living quarters. Anything between fifty and one hundred and fifty energetics lived here at any one time, and so the buildings were flexible enough to account for that, with parts that could be shut off or opened up depending on need. Just as at all the other Major Guilds, a large library was housed here, and many of the Guilds' most experienced Masters and Mavens came to share teachings or to learn.

It was easy to tell when they were close to the hall, as the noise level increased. Usually seventy-five percent of the inhabitants of Anahata Guild would come down for meals. People could be heard chattering to each other, with laughter and the clanging of cutlery against plates.

Lunch was a buffet system, with food at the side of the room, and a free table system of long benches, where you could sit with whoever took your fancy. A great deal of networking and swapping of information – and gossip – took place here, and Tierra's gaze ranged over the hall to see if there was anyone she knew.

Well, anyone she knew and wanted to spend an hour with.

She'd lived a surprisingly solitary life in recent years for someone of her energies and nature. She grimaced. It was time to push herself out into the world again. She walked over to the buffet and picked up a tray, handing a second to Fintan. Scooping up cutlery and a napkin, she moved along the buffet table taking small portions of various tasty looking dishes.

She didn't see anyone she knew, so moved to the closest table with spaces and put her tray down. A striking blonde woman already at the table gave her an assessing look. "Hi."

"Do you mind if we join you?" Tierra asked.

The woman nodded slowly. She wore a lightweight cream skirt suit, perfectly pressed. Her face was beautiful in a sharp way, like the glint of sun on a blade. "Be my guest. I won't be long. I'm teaching a class shortly. Have you just arrived?"

"Can you tell?" asked Tierra, self-conscious. The woman was gorgeous, and Tierra wondered if jealousy was the reason she had a sudden chill.

"I don't remember seeing you around." The woman ate a delicate mouthful of salad.

"We've come to use the libraries. It's been a while since I was here." Tierra sat opposite the woman.

"I'm sure it hasn't changed much." She shrugged.

Well, this was awkward. It was rare that Tierra's social skills weren't up to the task, but she wasn't doing well in this interaction. Where was Fintan?

"What are you teaching?" said Tierra.

"A course on weather manipulation."

"Sounds interesting. I'm Tierra, by the way."

The blonde jerked her head in acknowledgement. "I'm Maya. You were one of Jebediah's Adherents, correct?"

"Some time ago, yes." More than a century, in fact.

"He uses you as an example sometimes when he teaches, as one of the stronger auxiliary Masters in Anahata. He said you were 'remarkably balanced', your energies almost as strong as each other." Maya put her palms face up and moved them up and down as if they were weighing scales.

"Maybe you have me mixed up with someone." Tierra frowned. Fintan walked over, his plate laden with food, and at the sight of the woman next to her, stopped.

"Maven Maya." He gave her a short nod.

"Fintan. It's been a long time."

Tierra glanced between them. They knew each other, clearly, but where was the tension coming from? Her stomach clenched with unease. She hated friction. She patted the bench next to her, and he grimaced and slid onto it reluctantly.

"You know each other?" She'd address things head-on.

"We did, a long time ago. Fintan was a student here in one of my previous phases of teaching."

Interesting. To all intents and purposes, Fintan had had a difficult time as a student here, though he didn't talk about it much. Perhaps this woman was a reminder of a different time.

Fintan stuffed a forkful of food in his mouth and gave a short jerk of his head in response to Maya, who responded with an amused eyebrow lift.

"I was saying that Tierra – who appears to be modest as well as talented – is still talked about by Jebediah, in his lectures to new and prospective Mavens."

Heat crept into Tierra's cheeks. There was something in the woman's tone that was almost mocking. Was she...smirking? Okay, this was strange. Tierra wasn't sure she resonated with this woman.

"That sounds like a surprisingly accurate statement." Fintan waved his fork at Tierra's plate. "No need to be embarrassed, T. Eat something."

She picked at her fried rice. Fintan focused on his food. Was Tierra being oversensitive? "We're here to see Jebediah actually. We have a couple of mysteries we think he might be able to help with."

"Oh yes?" Maya finished the last couple of mouthfuls of her salad. "Sounds intriguing. Maybe I can join you all for supper tonight. Get to know you both better."

It wasn't like Tierra could say no, whatever vibe Maya was giving her, and whatever Fintan's odd reaction. The woman was clearly a senior member of the Guild, and she might be helpful in their search even if interpersonally she was difficult.

"Sure," said Tierra, weakly.

"Have a great afternoon." Maya strode off.

"Hmph." The noise escaped Tierra before she could stop it. She waited for the women to get out of earshot, and turned to Fintan. "Who is she?"

Fintan was still shoveling food in his mouth as if they were about to ration it. He shook his head.

Tierra hesitated. Something about the woman was off, but she had nothing concrete to back that up. She'd sound snide if she said anything without something more solid. She gazed into her food, thinking.

"Don't get caught up in the flakey day dreaming they all do around here," commented Fintan.

Tierra looked at him in surprise. "You don't really think that about Anahata do you? It's your auxiliary energy too."

He shrugged. "My Manipura's stronger. I never really fit in here. It's not a big deal."

"Okay. Seems strange, that's all. It's been a long time since you've been here, right?"

"Yep."

"So, give them a chance. It was Caradoc who was the Major Circle member then?"

He nodded.

"I think the culture's changed a lot since Aiko became Guild Leader. Different leadership styles."

"Damn straight," said Fintan. "Maya worked pretty closely with Caradoc."

Caradoc, who had been the Anahata Major circle member for an unusually short time of about a decade, had been more of a broadcast empath than a receiving empath. He was a highly skilled healer, but he had also tended to broadcast his feelings – which because of his auxiliary Manipura, had at times had a hot edge to those around him. *Had Fintan and Caradoc had a run-in of some kind? How was Maya connected?*

"Anyway," said Fintan. "Tell me about Jebediah. I don't think I remember him."

"Um, sure. Probably one of the longest serving Mavens in Anahata I would think. Kind, smart, strong. He's currently the go-to person for new Anahata Mavens, sort of a Maven's Maven. Skilled in both healing and empathy, with great instincts. Sometimes almost too sensitive for his own good – he can read others' emotions like you'd read a book."

Fintan nodded. "And he was yours?"

"Yes. I was lucky, he was a great teacher." She smiled. "Now, my own intuition tells me that you want another helping."

Fintan watched as Tierra knocked on Jebediah's heavy, old-looking door, the nails and studs even darker than the knotted sycamore. It was a door with a lot of character.

Fintan was intrigued to meet Jebediah. Tierra seemed to have a lot of respect for him. Though he'd sounded a bit like a boy band singer, the way she'd described him.

He hoped to the Source that the guy had a sense of humor. That wasn't always – necessarily – the case with Anahata energetics. Fintan wasn't usually a fan.

Tierra had told him that Jebediah had been sequestered in the Anahata headquarters for a long time. After the Second World War, he'd been almost drained by the amount of healing energy that he'd expended, as well as having been surrounded by the horrors of the war, even when it was just in others' minds, for so long.

"A kind of PTSS, we'd call it now," Tierra had said. "He's a lot better than he was, but he's chosen to stay here to keep himself out of the world. He finds other people – intrusive."

After a 'Come in,' Tierra pushed open the door to reveal a large, pleasant room, much lighter and brighter than the door had indicated. A slender, though solid, man was standing next to a desk in the same rich wood as the door. He shook Fintan's hand, and took Tierra in his arms. The man's looks were unconventional – his cheekbones sharp, his eyebrows dark slashes despite hair that was a lighter brown with some bronze hints. His features indicated mixed heritage of some kind, though predominantly Caucasian. It was hard to pin down, but the man was striking, certainly.

They hugged for a long time. Fintan suppressed a twinge of – what, exactly? protectiveness? – as the man's face showed an unalloyed happiness as he held her close. And Fintan could appreciate the man was attractive, and his combination of stability and the intuition that Tierra had told Fintan about was bound to make him a hit with women.

They settled themselves in comfortable chairs that were in the lightest area of the room, in front of several large windows, black lead crisscrossing them. One pane even had ancient-looking stained glass in it, though Fintan couldn't make out any detail. The room was a study in blues and creams, the only dark notes being the door, the desk, and the shelves on which the books were placed. The sofas and chairs were modern, though very much in keeping with the style of the room.

"Tierra. I'm so pleased to see you. It's been a while." Jebediah's voice was deep. *What was his auxiliary energy?*

"It's Svadisthana, Fintan." Jebediah smiled, and Fintan narrowed his eyes. He hadn't sensed the energy of Svadisthana at all. Perhaps it was a weak auxiliary. He didn't love mind readers though.

"I didn't read your mind. There's no Ajna here. Just your emotions. I usually remind people early on in the conversation that this is part of my talent. Not everyone's as comfortable being an open book as Tierra here. It's easier to get it out of the way, rather than accidentally shock you later by answering a question you didn't ask." He kept smiling, but Fintan could sense weariness behind the words, which had clearly been repeated many times.

"It's not an easy gift, for me or the people around me." Jebediah shifted in his chair, his hand resting on his abdomen, but his dark blue eyes were steady. The guy didn't seem to be hero material, but there was something engaging about him, almost like a charisma he was reining in. Fintan wanted to like him, despite the annoying head stuff. Hmm.

Tierra put a hand on Fintan's arm, though whether in support or in warning, Fintan couldn't be sure.

Jebediah offered them a drink, and they got down to business.

"Thank you for seeing us. We have several things we'd appreciate your input on. We've found an unattached energetic, a teenager, in the Vancouver area. She didn't know anything about our world, and she's an Anahata-Ajna. She's been caught up, peripherally, in a problem that Cuinn's investigating for the Minor Circle." Tierra filled him in, but kept the detail light.

"We want to know which energetics might have been in the Vancouver area about ten to fifteen years ago. Probably a couple with either Anahata or Ajna as their linked energies."

Jebediah was rubbing the multi-hued stubble of reds and browns and blonde on his chin, eyes gazing into the distance as he thought. 'Okay. We can look into that. You can try Records. And I'll have a think as to who was in the northwest of the Americas then. It's not that long ago, someone will know."

Fintan's attention wandered to the room around them. It was a study, so there were a number of books – that was common with most Mavens. It wasn't a role that Fintan had ever sought out himself.

As well as the books, there was evidence that Jebediah had had his lunch at his desk, a laptop propped open and an empty plate beside it. There weren't any photos on the desk, or any evidence that the man had any family himself. The study had a reclusive feel, isolated despite being at the heart of the Guild.

Fintan tuned back into the conversation.

"There is another area we'd like your help with Jeb." Tierra hesitated. "This is – darker."

"Darker than an abandoned child?" Jebediah questioned.

She nodded and reached down and picked up her bag, rummaging through it to pull out an envelope. "Fintan and I tracked a person of interest in one of Fintan's cases to a house in Vancouver. We found a body."

Jebediah's lips thinned, but his voice was gentle, a rumble in the hole left by the words. "I'm sorry, Tierra, love."

Her head made a shallow acknowledgement. "I did a reading of the body."

Before she could go on, Jebediah leaned forward, his brow creased. "And I'm sorry again. What did you find?"

"She was an Anahata-Ajna mix, just like Ai. That's how we met Ai, actually. She'd also been to the house, but ran before anything happened."

"Did you get a reading on how the girl died?" Jebediah asked.

"She was drained."

There was no shock on the man's face, just a deep sadness, the lines on his face becoming even more pronounced. Fintan wondered just what the man had seen and endured for this to be his reaction to such a violation of energetic law. Perhaps it was better not to know.

"We were hoping you might be able to help us find out who she was." She hesitated again. "I have her picture, and I hoped you'd take a look for us."

They stared at each other for a long moment. "I will, of course. But I need to recharge my energies first. Tomorrow? You can talk to others and search in the records in the meantime for Ai's origins."

Tierra nodded. "Thank you, Jeb. I really appreciate it. I wouldn't ask if I – if we – didn't think it was important."

"I know." The words were simple, the emotions complex. *I'm missing something.*

15

"Blaize had a great idea." Cuinn's voice came over Tierra's cellphone's speaker, tinny and far-away.

Fintan and Tierra were back in their suite, sitting at either end of the sofa. A lazy breeze blew through the open wooden shutters. They had both been around heat enough in their lives to be comfortable without air conditioning. Fintan was sprawled out once again, and took up at least two thirds of the long, comfortable piece of furniture. Tierra sat with her arms around her knees, chin resting on those same knees. Fintan tossed an apple in one hand.

She was trying to focus on the conversation, but she was still thinking about Jebediah, and how he seemed so much more muted than before. She knew he still had an injury, sustained in the war, something that she didn't know much about but seemed to still be there, decades later. The war had affected them all, she thought. They'd paid a high price to help the humans.

"What idea?" Fintan prompted, when Cuinn's excited voice didn't continue, clearly expecting some reaction. "Tell us and we'll get excited, I promise."

"We've been working on sharing mental images. Blaize isn't quite up to sharing words with anyone apart from me yet, but she's able to send a picture to someone she's close to and resonates well with, as long as they're physically close. She's a fast learner." His tone was animated.

"So is it just the fact that Blaize is amazing that we're pleased about, or is there something more?" Fintan's voice was lazy. He took a bite of his apple.

"No, no, that's not it. I mean, you should be, because she's brilliant –" that was all pride "– but she had an idea about how we could use it. We've seen the face of another energetic in the ether, and I don't recognize him. Blaize suggested she could share the image with Nixie and Nixie could draw it. That way, we can show it to people, and we don't have to just rely on my own memories."

Nixie was Blaize's best friend, living in Thailand. Tierra hadn't met her in person, but she seemed to be a fun, vibrant personality who didn't take life too seriously, quite the contrast to Blaize's confident intensity.

"Great idea," Tierra enthused. "The more visuals you can get of everything in the prophecy dreams the better. You never know what detail one of us might spot. Don't just draw faces, do every aspect."

Fintan nodded. "Definitely."

"How are things at your end?" said Cuinn.

They shared their plan to work with Jeb the next day, and to visit the Records department again, which so far had yielded nothing, but there were many more relevant Records to review. They were likely to spend another couple of days in the Guild.

"I don't need you to be here," Tierra pointed out, when Cuinn had signed off. "I'm fine on my own. Jebediah can help if there's anything I need."

"It looked like he was the one that needed help," said Fintan. "What's the deal with him and the photo? Why did he need to recharge? Is his energy really that weak?"

150

Tierra's eyebrows rose. "Not at all. Did I not explain?"

"Explain what?"

"His gift."

"I thought his gift was mind-reading, or whatever it was."

Tierra shook her head as she got up and put the kettle on. "No. I mean, yes, but he has more Anahata gifts than that." She took out two white mugs from a small cupboard underneath the kettle. "He's a sensitive, and able to do psychometry."

"He can read objects?" Fintan crunched the last bite of the apple and tossed the core at the garbage in the corner. It hit the back of the container and dropped in with a thunk.

"Yes. He needs to touch, then he can read them."

"We only have a photo. He can't read that, surely?"

"He can, if someone who was there when the photo was taken is with him. So, us."

"That's extremely unusual." Fintan frowned.

"Yes, it is." She poured the water into two cups. "And it takes a great deal of energy to read from a photograph. And the kind of photograph we're asking him to read from? He wouldn't usually take it on." She sighed. "I wouldn't ask him if I thought there was another way. But we have no idea who she is, or who killed her, and we can't afford to involve the human police at this point, it's too risky. And with the kind of darkness that Cuinn's foreseen? We need to know what we're dealing with."

Her stomach squeezed. Jeb was her friend, and she was asking him to do something that could harm him. At the very least, he'd have the images of the dead girl in his head, to add to the many sad scenes he'd read over the ages. At the worst, they might bring trouble in the form of the prophecy to his door.

Was she being selfish, asking him? Did he have the strength to do this? Was there another way?

Jeb, always more serious but once the sort of man at the center of romance era sagas, had turned into a tragic hero after the war. He considered himself fallen, she knew, and had closed a part of himself off because of that, but his sexuality could be glimpsed in brief moments if you knew where to look. He was a magnetic, even seductive, man who tried to hide that fact as much as possible.

She brought the mugs over to the coffee table where her phone was still resting, and nudged it aside to put them down.

"Thanks." Fintan looked into his cup and back at her. "Peppermint?"

"We had enough caffeine earlier." She ignored his eye roll. Though maybe she was fussing over him some.

"And I didn't get any sense of Svadisthana energy at all. Is he, well, is he ok?"

And that was the heart of the matter.

She settled herself back down on the sofa. "You don't get a sense of Svadisthana? Really?"

Svadisthana, the energy of creativity and sexuality.

"No. Why, you do?"

"Yes. His voice alone…" There was no doubt in her mind about Jeb's sexual energy. It was there. He was holding it in check, dampening it somehow, that she would agree with, but he was a deeply sensual being. "But you're right, his Svadisthana isn't as strong as his Anahata. He hasn't had a partner in many decades. He's moved from eros to agape, he says."

She frowned and wrinkled her nose. "It's all very well to forego sexual love for brotherly love, but I'm not sure it's healthy to shut down part of yourself."

"I see." Fintan studied her face. "Then what are you worried about, T?"

Tierra sighed. "He's such a good man. He's been like a brother to me. I'm scared this reading might hurt him. And he's already injured."

"Injured? How?" Fintan asked.

"I'm not sure. His stomach perhaps? It happened during the war, and it was part of his reason for retreating to the Guild. He needed to recover."

"I'm not sure he has. Is that why he was holding his abdomen?" Fintan said.

"He was?" She felt bad she hadn't noticed.

"Why doesn't he just heal it? Seems odd. Anyway, don't feel guilty for asking him. He's an adult." said Fintan.

"Why do you think I'm feeling guilty?" She flushed. Every time he showed an insight into her thoughts or emotions, it threw her.

"Because you always worry about other people more than yourself. Reading the body took a toll on you, yet you did it." Fintan rolled up to a sitting position, reached out and cupped her cheek. There was comfort in his touch, and she leaned into it, despite telling herself it was a stupid thing to do. "You're not asking Jebediah to do anything that you wouldn't do if you could. And there's probably only a handful of energetics who can even do this."

"I'm aware. But it doesn't mean that I have to accept danger to my friends without regret. I'd feel the same if it was you." No. She'd feel worse. Despite the fact that Fintan was a Warrior, the idea of him in danger made her nauseous. She shuddered.

He slid his hand round to rub her neck. "It's going to be okay. He'll help us, we'll find out who killed this girl, and take them down."

She nodded, her throat tight. She wanted, for a moment, to believe him without argument, to pretend that he was right, and all would be well. He massaged the nape of her neck, and some of the tension seeped away. Her shoulders relaxed.

His words would be comforting – if only she could believe it would be that simple.

Fintan showered, and toweled off roughly. He ran his fingers through his hair, considered it brushed, dismissed the idea of shaving, and pulled out one of the shirts that Tierra had made him pack. It was a pale blue. He scowled. *A very Anahata color.*

Dressed, he left his room. There was no sign of Tierra in the living area of the suite, though the scent of lavender lingered, as Tierra seemed to have brought some of her candles from home. She really knew how to make temporary digs more cozy. He looked at the clock on the TV. They were dining with Jebediah and Maya in a private room shortly.

He was not enthusiastic about eating with Maya. She'd seemed keen to have dinner with them, though he wasn't quite sure why, considering their history. She was attractive in a hard sort of way – all diamond edges and sharp points, but he had no interest in her. At this moment he yearned for something softer. Warmer. He frowned.

Perhaps this prophecy business was taking more of a toll on him than usual.

He texted Adam a quick "What's up? Any news?" and received a typically terse reply. "No. You?" He sent back "Met Jebediah. You didn't tell me he was a hermit. Doing a reading tomorrow. Is he strong enough for this stuff? Health doesn't seem the best. Nothing from Records so far."

He looked around the room as he waited for Adam to reply, or Tierra to come out. *Maybe I should call her?* But, no. He'd known Tierra through centuries of women's clothes and fashions, and she wasn't a woman who took ages to get ready. She pampered at times, yes, but she didn't primp.

Sitting down, he flicked on the TV. Fifty-seven channels and nothing on. He switched it off and considered Maya some more. Bitch. They should have said no to her for dinner. They could have been freer with conversation with only Jebediah. Tierra, open-hearted as ever, hadn't wanted to say no.

His phone vibrated. "Jeb's a hero. Tougher than he looks. Deserves to be relaxing on a beach somewhere, not the politics of Anahata."

Fintan raised his eyebrows. That was high praise indeed from Adam, whose idea of tough was very tough indeed. The guy must have some hidden steel in his spine. He'd have to ask Adam about Jebediah next time he and Adam had a beer. Though the likelihood of that happening any time soon wasn't looking that great.

He couldn't figure Jebediah out. Fintan was pretty puzzled why a guy living in the Guild of the Healers had a wound so bad it wasn't healed in over half a century. Something was up there.

The door to Tierra's room opened, and he forgot about Jebediah as Tierra appeared in an elegant green dress that hugged her curves and flattered her petite frame. It also showed a lot more cleavage than usual. The discomfort in his body that had been building since he'd got dressed stretched across his upper back. He stood and rolled his shoulders.

"That's a nice dress." It really was. These days he only saw Tierra in casual clothes. It was strange how a dress could change her appearance so much. She was so elegant. But he wasn't sure if he liked it, if it was his Tierra that was standing there. She looked like someone new. Someone different. Someone who might not be interested in a friend like Fintan, who was casual down to the very bone. Why had she dressed like that? Was it for Jebediah? He wished he'd shaved after all.

She was scowling. "Don't be sarcastic."

"I wasn't." He kept his tone mild, and hid his alarm at the idea of Tierra changing and growing away from him. "It's a nice dress. And you look nice."

"Hmmph." Tierra muttered as she walked across the room to open the door. "Okay. Let's go down. Nicely."

He raised his eyebrows as he got up and followed her out. What was that about? "Hey, what about me? Don't you think I look nice? We men like to be appreciated too, you know."

And to his surprise, he found he was only half-joking.

Nice. Pah. Tierra hated herself for bothering to dress up. She'd made the effort knowing that if she didn't, Maya would hopelessly outclass her. Maya's casual daytime dress was more stylish than Tierra's evening wear, for Source's sake.

And Fintan's response was that she looked nice. Nice! Who wanted to look nice? She wanted to look sexy, like a goddess. A movie star. She bet Maya didn't look 'nice'.

Screw nice.

They passed through corridors and halls until they reached the main dining hall. Tierra headed to one of the rooms off to the side. It was a paneled, high-ceilinged room that spoke of age and history. Jebediah and Maya were already there, chatting in low voices. Jebediah's seductive rumble was easy to place, even before they got to the room.

She gave Jebediah a quick hug, unable to resist the love he radiated. It was always so safe, being held by him, and it melted a little of the spikiness she'd been feeling. Though she'd seen many women become infatuated with him, she'd never had any romantic or sexual feelings about him – he was like a brother to her. She'd been grateful for that, as she'd seen energetics get distracted by his magnetism in the past. That would have made it hard for Tierra to be his Adherent.

He'd been there for her to support her through the growth and development of her auxiliary Chakra, as it had grown almost as powerful as her Muladhara. She'd been scared of her own power. She hadn't the maturity then, she thought, to be a powerful enough vessel for the energies. They'd spent eight years together as she'd developed not only her power, but her confidence. It had been towards the end of the Spanish Empire, and she had travelled with Jeb around what was now Mexico, where the culture of Europe mixed with the ruins of the Aztecs and other native peoples of the Americas.

Tierra herself had been from a family of energetics who had left Egypt, where the energetics had based themselves immediately after the destruction of their home, Atlantis, in 200BC, to live in the city of Teotihuacan. Like many energetic families, the occasional mixing with humans – generally not approved of, but not forbidden – had given rise to her family's eventual Hispanic appearance.

The travel, meeting so many new people, keeping their powers hidden while still using them to do the good needed to maintain the region's balance – especially after some of the horrors the Spanish inflicted on the native people – had built her experience and confidence. Tierra's shoulders drooped. Somehow, since the 1940s, she had lost some of that confidence. She frowned as she walked to her chair. Well, she was traveling again now. It was time to get it back.

They sat at the formally laid table. Maya wore a pair of hip hugging pants that flowed around her legs as they fell from the waist. They had a slit down one side that showed glimpses of pale flesh as she moved. She topped that with a turquoise corset that put her breasts front and center. It was an unconventional and striking outfit, especially against the simpler decor of tile floor and wooden furniture.

"What are we having?" Tierra asked.

"Pumpkin soup, Eggplant couscous, summer pudding for dessert. Or cheese. As you like," said Jebediah.

"I ordered white wine," said Maya.

Anahata's Major Guild had a small core of permanent staff to keep up with the ever-changing group of energetics who moved in and out. Many energetics took a turn to help out in their Major Guild, and Anahata was no different. Energetics who came to take courses here would take their turn in the kitchens, or cleaning up. Anahata energetics like Tierra, with earth as their auxiliary, tended to enjoy roles cooking, cleaning and serving best.

So the staff wasn't as large as one might expect. This evening, a dark haired young male energetic entered, carrying their soup on a tray. His eyes widened slightly as he caught sight of Maya.

Jebediah greeted him by name, speaking Arabic. "Good evening, Darrell. How are you today?"

Speaking many languages was one of the side benefits of living a long life. Tierra had learned Arabic herself while studying in Egypt.

"I'm good, Maven Jebediah." Darrell rested the edge of the tray on the table as he took their plates off one by one. The tray only shook a little. Tierra helped him by passing Fintan a bowl, and taking one for herself. The boy sent her a grateful look.

"Have you been practicing your defenses?"

The boy nodded, his dark eyes wide. "Yes, Maven."

"Well done. Let me know if you have any trouble with it."

The boy nodded again and hurried out the door.

"Sweet," Maya drawled, switching them back to English.

What was up with her? She was supposed to be a teacher here. Was that how she interacted with her students? Tierra was starting not to like this woman. Tierra bent to take a mouthful of her soup to hide her annoyance.

"He's a good lad," said Jebediah. "Shows promise. We're experimenting with new pre-Maven-Adherent schooling now. They come and spend time here, to be exposed to other Anahata energetics, and we teach them some basics."

He sighed. "The nature of Anahata is that many of them are so sensitive. And I don't mean with a capital S, just empathic to the point that they take on other people's feelings and issues, and worry so much. We try to build them up before they start working with a Maven. It's also enabling me to place Mavens and Adherents together in a more matched way. While matching to a Maven used to be haphazard, and based on who was local, or who the parents knew, now we focus more on matching personalities."

Tierra was impressed. "That sounds great. Not everyone is as lucky as I was. And it's a long time to spend with someone who rubs you the wrong way, for the Maven and Adherent."

Jeb nodded. "It is. It's still experimental, but it seems to be working."

"Aren't you exposing them to other people's feelings more by putting them in this environment?" Fintan questioned.

"To some degree. But it's contained. We keep them in small classes – there aren't huge numbers of energetics who are ready for the Guild each year. They've all completed normal human schooling at least, that's a prerequisite. That means a little of the tumult of adolescence has passed. We encourage them to go to human university too, if they have the aptitude. Gone are the days when energetics could get better schooling from their Mavens than the human system."

"Anahata is a powerful energy," commented Maya. "But don't you think it's odd that in the last hundred years or so we've seen more Anahata energetics' energy twisted and turn Rogue than almost any other energy?"

Fintan raised his eyebrows. "Really? I hadn't come across that statistic."

"Ask Adam. Or Blaize Blackfire," said Maya. "I heard she was training with Cuinn these days, is that correct? She'd know about the twisting of Anahata with what her father did."

How did the woman manage to make it sound like Blaize's fault? Tierra bristled.

Jebediah studied Maya. "You're right. I've been researching the phenomenon, and trying to understand it more clearly. We have a team of Healers here working on the problem of how Rogues are created, how they're formed."

"I thought we knew how they were formed?" said Fintan. "Their energy twists and becomes the opposite of itself. Anahata, love, becomes jealousy, or hatred. Manipura becomes anger or pride. Muladhara becomes lethargy, exhaustion, laziness. And so on."

He ticked them off on his fingers.

"The Rehab Centres report that some of the Rogues, especially recently, have been very strong," said Maya. "What do you think of the theory that they're simply harnessing others' negative emotions for their energy? And that they're doing those from whom they take them a favor?"

Tierra's spoon hovered in mid-air, her eyes widening. She couldn't believe her ears. Anahatas were trained to bring balance, but that didn't mean stealing emotions. It might feel hard at times, but everyone had the right to feel both sides of emotion, positive and negative, and be in balance themselves. Negative emotions could get out of control, but they didn't need removing, the individual needed training in how to bring that pain and discomfort back into balance. What Maya had suggested, that what Rogues did was acceptable, was…unthinkable.

Jebediah leaned back, one hand spread on the table. "I think, Maya, that it's a damaging idea, spread by a few heretics who want to cause trouble."

"For some energetics, harnessing negative emotions can mean they are more potent though? And surely it's a way of rebalancing energies, by siphoning some off?" Maya persisted, one perfect eyebrow arched.

Fintan had finished his soup, and studied Maya, his head to the side. Tierra considered him in turn. Did he think Maya was attractive? Well, she was attractive, clearly. Rather, was he attracted to her? Tierra's nose wrinkled.

"Individuals as well as the earth need to be in balance. But they have to find that harmony themselves. We can help them, but the answer comes from inside, not outside," said Jeb. He didn't waver, and was as polite as ever – though perhaps firmer – and he watched Maya carefully. Despite Tierra's unease – and disgust – at the topic, she was glad to see him braced.

Maya laughed, bright and quick, the sound more like breaking glass than bells to Tierra's ears. "I'm playing devil's advocate, of course. But it's always good to know what the man at the top thinks, so I can refute any misguided students who come to me with thoughts on it."

Jebediah's eyes narrowed. "Have any? And did you mention it to Aiko?"

Aiko was the head of Anahata. Maya shook her head. "Just being prepared."

There was a taut silence that stretched out, almost unbearably long. What was the relationship between Jebediah and Maya? And who was she? Did she believe any of the dangerous ideas she'd proposed? Tierra found herself twisting her napkin in her lap. The benefit of not spending much time with people was a lack of conflict in her life. She'd never enjoyed it, unlike more fiery Manipuras, who enjoyed nothing more than a good, rousing argument. Perhaps Maya was Anahata-Manipura?

Fintan caught her eye, and cocked his head. Checking on her. She gave him a weak smile. He pressed his lips together.

"So what's your research about, Jebediah?" said Fintan.

"There's still much to learn about Rogues," said Jeb. "For example, why do some go Rogue, and not others – what triggers it? Are some energetics more susceptible? Does energy, family history, environment, or any other factor make a difference? These are just some of the questions we're exploring."

"That sounds fascinating and useful. How far have you got?" Tierra pushed away the rest of her soup, though what she had eaten had been delicious. This conversation was putting a damper on her appetite.

"The Guilds didn't like sharing their records. Still don't, really. Anahata, as the energetics' healers, has a lot of data, but we need the Guilds to share their records more openly. While most Rogues come through a Rehab Center, not all do. When we get the data, we enter it into a database. Everything we know about Rogues goes in there, each individual case."

Maya toyed with her wine glass. "Will you share your results?"

"Of course. We're nowhere near that yet though. Maya, what are you working on at the moment?"

Tierra tuned out Maya's answer. The other woman had expressed some strange ideas, and Tierra wasn't quite sure how she felt about them all.

CHAPTER

16

When they arrived at Jebediah's room in the morning, Tierra's stomach was queasy. Her memories of him were colored by a time when his psyche was strong, her role model and mentor.

She hadn't been involved in his rescue, or helping him to recuperate after the war, but she'd heard about it. A little from him, a lot from others. His mind was stronger than it had been then, but there was still a sense of precariousness, as if he could snap at any moment.

She just had to hope his strength was like spider silk, and could hold more than its own weight.

She knocked at the door.

"Come in," the low voice said.

They entered, and this time, Jebediah didn't immediately turn to them. He was looking out of the windows, and Tierra could see only the back of his head. A sadness surrounded him.

"Are you ok?" Tierra kept her own voice soft.

He turned, and there was a moment when he seemed to expect someone else. He shook himself with a visible effort, and smiled, though it was a pale imitation of what they'd seen the night before.

"I'm fine. I didn't sleep well. Let's do what you came to do. The sooner I help you, the sooner you can get moving on the case.

Tierra hesitated. "We could try someone else. Or come back another day."

He shook his head, and held out a hand. "No. Give me the photo."

"You don't want to sit down?" Fintan said.

"Would it make you more comfortable if I did?"

"It would, actually. I understand it's an intense emotional experience from your perspective." Fintan gestured at the seats they'd sat in the day before. "We'll join you. Do you need anything?"

"No." He moved across the room to the armchair that seemed to have seen the most use, and he seated himself with neat, efficient movements, though he winced almost imperceptibly as he did so. It seemed that Fintan was right, and his injury was still somehow active.

He held out his hand again.

Tierra dug into her bag for the photo. She held onto the envelope for a few seconds longer, reluctant now to hand it over. Were the answers to the girl's death worth impacting Jebediah's sanity and health? Was that what she was risking?

Jeb's gaze was implacable. His eyes were deep blue pools that showed nothing of what he was feeling. He was good at shielding his own emotions from others. You couldn't work in a place like this and broadcast without inviting trouble – you only needed to look at what happened with Caradoc's leadership of the Guild to know that.

She took a breath. And handed the envelope over.

The silence in the room was tangible. Jebediah's fingers closed around the innocuous flat white rectangle, and he sat back in his chair, holding it in his lap. He didn't need to hold it, any skin contact would do. It was why she'd kept it in her bag, to avoid any chance of that happening.

She'd tried to understand it once, how his gift worked – how it could work – but he'd talked about energetic resonance echoes, and then eventually admitted that it wasn't as clear as it was with objects, where the energetic imprint was still held within the object, in the same way a holograph held every piece of information about the whole picture within every single aspect of that picture.

Today, she didn't need to know how it worked, she just needed it to work.

Jeb was sitting in the chair, and he slowly pulled the photo of the dead girl from its protective wrapper. He let the envelope float to the floor, and held the photo loosely in his fingers, his eyes closed. His eyelids fluttered rapidly without opening, as if he was watching a film on the inside of his eyelids. She and Fintan watched intensely, monitoring his vital signs.

He paled steadily, sweat dewing on the stubble on his upper lip. After a few more minutes, a tear began to form at the corner of his left eye. It beaded, slowly gathering weight, until after what seemed like an aeon, it trailed slowly down his face, slowing its pace when it reached the stubble on his cheek.

Tierra itched to comfort him.

She could see Jeb's thready pulse. His systems were performing as normal, and he seemed to be experiencing more of an emotional, than physical, impact.

After about five minutes he froze for a long moment, and then, without Jeb visibly moving, the photo slipped from his fingers. It caught an updraft for a second, and seemed to hover in the air, the girl's face upturned, pasty and staring.

Tierra almost reached for it, but she knew not to disturb Jeb in this processing stage. He needed time to make sense of the emotions and impressions that the photo had given him.

To her surprise Fintan reached out, and took her hand in his. His larger hand folded over hers in a warm, firm grip that spoke volumes. She nearly burst into tears. She was glad he was here.

After many more long minutes, Jeb spoke without opening his eyes. They had agreed with him that they'd record what he said, and Fintan held his phone ready on his lap to start recording. At Tierra's look, he tapped the button for record.

"They met by chance, I think. She knew him, a family friend, perhaps. An older energetic male. There was no sense of threat at first. A little awe, perhaps, or at least respect."

Jeb's voice was almost inaudible. He gained force as he got the first couple of sentences out, and Fintan relaxed back with the phone, which he'd been holding out to catch the words.

"He took her for a hot drink. The feeling is safe. He asked her back to his home. She agreed. She still felt safe. And honored."

Neither Tierra nor Fintan said a word, despite long pauses between sentences or phrases.

"At the house – the house where this photo was taken, as she never left that house again – she feels uneasy. Uncomfortable. Not scared, not yet.

"There's another young woman there. Our girl's confused. I'm not sure why. She's disturbed by the girl. She also feels, I think, the sort of anxiety-fear-respect you get from a less popular adolescent when a more popular student comes along. Intimidation perhaps.

"I can't tell the timelines on all this. But quite soon after the other young woman comes along there's a great deal of fear. It's sudden. Something happened. Something that burst open our girl's feelings of safety, and security. Her bubble of trust is not just burst, it's exploded.

"There was physical violence."

There was another longer pause. The color had not yet returned to Jeb's cheeks, and his deep, usually melodic voice had become flat in the telling.

Tierra realized she was holding her breath. She opened her mouth slightly and released it, the warm air rasping like a saw inside her head.

Nothing else moved in the room.

"After this, fear colors every other emotion. It has peaks and valleys, but it's always there. She didn't live another moment of that too-short life without fear."

A dust mote floated down in front of Tierra, the sunbeams coming through the windows showing its out of place movement in the quiet stillness of the room.

"The violence, and the fear, were only the start of the girl's torture. You were right. She was drained. Repeatedly, over a long period, by several energetics. Her energy was put into Remnant stones, and also used by individuals. There was a casual violence to the way she was treated.

"Sometimes it's just one of them. Eventually, it's always just one of them. The girl is desperate. Desperate to die."

Another pause. Another tear grew at the corner of Jeb's eye.

"She has barely any resources left, but she seeks a vision, to find some way, anyway, out. Instead, it tells her of her death – and something more. She moves through the emotional spectrum at that point. Anger a little. Until finally, acceptance. She accepts her fate.

"She wants to die on her own terms. There's a feeling of ... determination, almost. Though it's faint. So faint. The male comes back, and she says something to him, baits him, and it pushes him over the edge. He takes too much from her. And her final feeling is satisfaction."

His eyes still closed, he bowed his head. "I'm glad it was satisfaction."

Fintan moved his hand with the phone slowly back into his lap. He looked grim, muscles tensed and ready, though there was nothing to fight. He was still holding Tierra's hand, and he squeezed it now, once, before letting go.

Jeb hadn't finished. "When her killers moved the body from the basement, they found she had scratched something on the stone floor underneath her. It said 'Balance and harmony depend on all. 12->6->1.'"

Tierra sat for a moment, wondering why she couldn't see.

Before she realized that her eyes were full of her own tears.

Fintan had been shaken by the session they'd spent with Jebediah. The man was talented. He could be doing so much more than moldering away in this heap.

But seeing the man after the session, barely moving, exhausted, wrung out, he'd understood how much the activity had taken out of him.

Tierra had given him a little earth and air energy, the most healing and nurturing she could draw on. And still, it had barely put color back into his cheeks.

He'd just sat, his head resting on the back of his chair, his hands in his lap, as still as a statue, until they'd left. Tierra had made him a cup of tea before they'd gone, and Fintan suspected she'd also dosed that with healing energy. He hoped to Source the man drank it.

Back in the room, neither was ready to talk. After a short period of this, Fintan was going crazy.

"Come on," he said, tugging her by the hand.

She eyed him. "I don't feel like going out."

"Me neither. But it's that or sit here. And I don't want to sit here either. So let's go out. It'll be good for both of us. This place has huge grounds."

She'd acquiesced, although he thought more because she didn't have the energy to disagree or argue with him than because she'd been persuaded by his argument.

Cairo at this time of year was hot. But Fintan liked that. It also, once they'd walked a little way away from the buildings, had a view.

The huge pyramids dominated the flat desert landscape from any high building or hilly vantage point in Cairo. The heat shimmered in the thin haze of pollution that covered the city in the modern age.

They stuck to the shade, and walked away from the Guild's buildings. Fintan found a bench underneath a huge and ancient sycamore tree, and pushed Tierra, who'd followed him like a zombie, down onto it.

"Sit." She turned her face, that expressive face, up to him, and there was such a depth of grief in her eyes, that he sat next to her and pulled her roughly into his arms. "Tierra."

She crumpled against him. He could smell her delightful musky perfume, and her hair tickled his nostrils. He didn't care. All he wanted to do was to wipe the sadness from her eyes.

What could he say, after all? Everything will be alright, was facile. There there, seemed meaningless. I'm sorry, wasn't quite right either, as it wasn't his fault.

So why do I feel so responsible?

Why did he feel the need to turn the world upside down in his quest to make it alright again for her? He wished, for a moment, that he was a man worthy of her. That he could be someone that Adam and Cuinn would be proud to see their sister and cousin with.

He hugged her more tightly, as her grief turned into wracking, wet sobs that tore from her body. He cursed himself for not being a handkerchief man. Cuinn would have had a handkerchief. And Adam wouldn't have had a handkerchief, but he'd have had something manly that he could turn into one, like a bandana.

After several long minutes, her sobs subsided, and she just lay against his chest, quiet. He could hear her gentle breaths, no longer hitching. She radiated grief.

He tapped into his own healing energy, the energy of air, of Anahata. In his mind, he drew it into a sort of energetic balm. And he sent it to her through his hands and his arms.

She gave a small laugh. She knew what he was doing – after all, she was the mistress of stealth healing herself. She was always sharing healing or soothing energy with her family when they were tired or ill. She'd dose drinks, food, or her own hugs. Rarely did any of them use it on her, mainly because it wasn't necessary.

He could feel the balm settle on her, despite her laugh. She hadn't blocked it, or turned it away. So that was good.

She gradually disengaged from his arms, pulling away and sitting up on her own. Her face was streaked with tears, and her skin was blotchy.

She had never seemed more beautiful to Fintan.

She cared so much. Her depth of empathy for a girl she'd never met. Her ability to open her arms without judgment to the girl Ai. Her open heart and optimism.

He realized he was entranced. But Tierra was looking out at the ancient monuments in the distance, her gaze far away. When she brought it back to his own eyes, he could see that the effects of the last few days had caught up with her.

"So we know more about what happened to her. And how she felt." Tierra's voice was flat. "But we didn't get more than that. He couldn't see who the man was. And we don't know where they took her from. We're no further along."

"We are," he told her, firmly. "We didn't know the stones Cuinn mentioned had a name, Remnant stones, and we can connect Jeb and Cuinn to pool their resources on them. We know that the girl liked and trusted the Leech, and that he's an older energetic, which will hopefully reduce the number of suspects once we know who she is. And we have the numbers."

"Numbers which could mean anything. How do they help us stop this?" Tierra's tone was forlorn. He found the lack of her usual optimism disturbing. He hated to see her like this, and would do almost anything to fix it.

"We will, T, we will." Fintan wasn't just reassuring Tierra, he was doing it for himself. They needed to stop this man and send him to a Rogue Rehabilitation Center. This was a nasty, nasty business.

The cold rage that had been building in Fintan since he first heard of Blaize's kidnapping had blossomed into a true anger. *If we catch the man, and he doesn't make it to a Rehab Center?*

I can live with that.

Elrian, still not strong enough to leave his country house after the psychic and energetic injuries that Indigo's death had caused him, gritted his teeth. He spent a lot of his time in his Haven in the ether these days, venturing out into the wider dreamscape to collect and hoard slivers of the prophecy.

His latest venture had shown him the prophecy had moved forward another fraction – in the wrong direction. His own goal had been pushed a little further away due to the ridiculous pairing of the layabout Fintan and the coddled Tierra, which had somehow become a little more likely.

His eye twitched. He wanted to destroy them all, but he had to be more subtle. He needed them to destroy themselves – or to thwart the prophecy by splitting the five potential couples up before they got anywhere near love.

On the plus side, the impetus was now with Fintan. A guy whose relationship style wasn't exactly long-term, and whose external confidence hid surprising issues around his own worthiness to be with a woman he considered to be of any consequence.

Really, what were the chances of Fintan not screwing it up?

CHAPTER
17

An hour or so later there was a knock at Tierra's door. She sat in the armchair by the window, and watched a group of birds dart and wheel in the bright blue sky above. The poor young girl who'd died would never enjoy that freedom. Tierra, on the other hand, had had the freedom to do whatever she wished, but had barely used it the last few decades, shutting herself at home with Cuinn. Guilt weighed on her.

"Come in," she said.

The door opened slowly, and Fintan put his head in. When he saw her in the chair he entered, carrying a sandwich. Tierra's stomach growled. She hated her body at that moment. Her needs seemed so basic and irrelevant compared to the problems they were working on. Fintan's caution in opening the door also irritated her.

"What were you expecting to see?" She tried for amused at the way he'd crept through the door, and instead heard annoyance in her tone. He raised his eyebrows, and she wrinkled her nose. *Gah.* "Sorry. Thanks for the food."

She took it from him, two fresh falafel and hummus wraps that smelled delicious, arranged on a plate, a knife and fork wrapped in a blue cloth napkin with them. "Looks good."

He perched on the bed. "How are you feeling? Did you sleep?"

Of course she hadn't slept. How could she sleep? She shook her head. "I spoke to Cara. I'm already out of synch enough from the travel. A nap would only make it worse."

He leaned towards her. "Are you going to be okay? Really? Can I do anything to help?"

She took a breath, and poked at the lettuce on her plate. She was about as un-alright as she'd been for a long time. And then on top of that, she was annoyed that she wasn't alright. That she couldn't take everything in her stride like the others seemed to. Reliving the young woman's death with Jeb had hit her on several levels – empathising with the poor, betrayed girl, and at the same time feeling for Jebediah who had to experience it so viscerally.

"I think…" She made her words slow and deliberate, "that a lot has happened recently. And I'm out of practice dealing with so much in so little time. And I didn't realize how out of practice I was, and that's upset me."

"Can I do anything?" Fintan looked so downcast, Tierra gave an almost-smile.

"No," she said. "Thanks for trying though. It'll pass. I need to get grounded."

"Do you want to work on your self-defense again? They have a gym here; we could go and train."

She gave a quiet snort. "No. Training's your way to ground, not mine. I might do some work on my column for a bit if you go down to the gym. Then we could hit the archives again to see if we can find anything else on Ai's parents?"

"Okay, that sounds good. I'll be back in ninety minutes or so." He hesitated. "And then maybe we could have dinner, just the two of us? And talk?"

She looked up and met serious cornflower blue eyes. She blushed a little. "Sure."

Fintan sweated in the quiet gym, running on the treadmill. He had never seen Tierra this off-balance. The feel of her tears soaking into his shirt when he held her wouldn't leave him. He upped the intensity of the run, letting the treadmill's computer include more inclines and sprints than usual to run off the worry. It made a small difference, and when he stepped off the machine, panting, he was more himself.

He switched to weights, and thought about their next steps. He ticked them off in his mind. First, they'd go back to the archives, and get to the bottom of the Ai situation.

Then they'd go to the dining hall for supper, and see what other connections they could tap for information on either of the situations. Both were somewhat delicate, but he trusted Tierra's intuition to know who the right people were to share with, and who weren't. And, he winced, they'd probably need to touch on what had happened in Vancouver. It was like a cloud hanging over their interactions, and they needed to get past it.

They also hadn't talked yet about Maya. Fintan disliked her as much as ever. She hadn't changed. Though it had been a while since he'd come up against anyone proposing openly that encouraging the darker side of emotions, or even creating situations to make others feel them, was positive. It was a dangerous philosophy to hold.

He'd put most of those who did into Rehab Centers.

Should he report her views to anyone in Manipura Guild?

No. Jebediah was a smart guy, and Fintan wasn't exactly objective when it came to Maya. Fintan frowned as he finished his last set of reps. Or maybe not. Jeb was smart, but also a bit, well, unworldly. Did he keep some of himself back because of his gifts? Undergoing other people's worst experiences in the way he had with the photo must take a toll.

Perhaps he'd drop by and check in on the guy, and bring up Maya. They could chat about Tierra too, and maybe see if anything else had come to mind about the photo.

Fintan's initial suspicions of Jebediah had been lessened, although Fintan still felt the guy was too good to be true – and that he was somehow deliberately minimizing his Svadisthana energy rather than it being naturally more slight than his Anahata as Jeb claimed. Which made Fintan wary, as he could see no good reason for it. Fintan was a practical person, and he didn't love mysteries.

Hitting the gym – which was quite basic compared to the one at Manipura Guild HQ, and only had one other person working out – had helped his mood. He'd have liked to go a few rounds of hand-to-hand, but there was always a lack of people to spar with in this Guild.

He had a quick shower and strode down to Jebediah's room. He tried not to think about whether Tierra would approve of him visiting Jebediah on his own.

He knocked, and at the acknowledgement, went in.

Jebediah had more color in his cheeks than previously, and greeted him graciously, gesturing at a chair the other side of his desk. "How can I help?"

"I wanted to see how you were doing." Fintan dropped down onto the seat. The study was a calm but cool place.

"I'm fine, thanks. It takes a great deal of my energy, and can be rather unpleasant. But food and rest and meditation all help me get back to normal." He waved a hand.

"It looked it. It was good of you to help us."

"I'd do a lot for Tierra," said Jeb. Fintan believed him. "The situation you've discovered is a nasty one. And Rogues are of particular interest to me at the moment, with my research, so perhaps the awful situation might lead to a new understanding."

"Have you worked much with Leeches?" asked Fintan.

"They make up a big part of the Rogue population, along with unstable energetics." Blaize's father, whose energies had been unstable, had eventually gone mad and killed her mother in a horrible murder-suicide. "But at the moment I'm examining trends, and I haven't dug into any one area in too much detail. Getting the data has been the initial challenge."

"If I can put in a good word at Manipura, I will."

Jebediah stroked his chin. "I might take you up on that at some point. For now, I'm working on the Svadisthana Guild. What does your work at Manipura involve?"

"I'm a troubleshooter for the Circles. So I have credit with some Circle members. I might be able to help out."

Fintan had started as a Warrior, after training. It had seemed simple at the time. There were bad people, and he fought them. His training in Scandinavia had been harsh, but it had suited that time, and that bleak and barren snow-covered land. His own parents had died one tough winter, when even their own magics hadn't been enough to heal them from a pandemic that had swept the region.

He'd taken longer than most to be ready for his Anahata Practitioner test, and had passed by the skin of his teeth. Anahata had left a bad taste in his mouth for more than one reason. It had been another sign to him that he'd been meant to be a Warrior.

He'd gone to Ireland to help support both the Warriors and the Healers there, and the people fighting against the English Crown to retain some semblance of independence. He'd met Cuinn there, and Cuinn's gentle mother and distant father, as well as Marius, Blaize's uncle.

He'd earned his stripes, risen to Master level in Manipura, and learned to help defuse conflict as well as fight in it. He'd fought in wars, and he'd worked alone to hunt down Rogues and dispatch them to Rehab Centers, until finally he'd started working for the Manipura Guild in his current role.

Jebediah nodded. "Do you enjoy it?"

"Life's rarely simple. My role allows me to color outside the lines more than most of my Guild. Though I belong with Manipura." It had been one of the reason he wasn't a Warrior anymore. As he'd got his hands bloody, he'd grown up, he'd understood that it was rarely as easy as good against bad, right against wrong.

"If you don't mind me saying, you strike me as a man who feels like he fits everywhere, and belongs nowhere."

Fintan tried not to bristle, and sat up straighter in his chair. Where had that come from? And who the hell did he think he was? "What are you talking about?"

Jebediah regarded him steadily, leaning back slightly behind the desk. "What's going on with you and Tierra?"

Fintan scowled. This was none of his business. This was just one of the reasons he hated this Guild. Everyone always wanted to talk about their feelings all the time.

"Nothing. And it's going to stay that way, don't worry."

"Why would I worry?" Jebediah made an open handed gesture. "You seem like you would make a good partner for her. Someone who would have her back, and make her laugh. Someone who'd help her be the best version of herself."

"You know nothing about me," stated Fintan, flatly. Heat rose from his belly.

"You think she can do better."

Of course she fucking could! He ground his teeth. The heat grew in his Manipura Chakra and spread through his torso.

Calm. He needed to be calm. He wasn't usually so on edge.

"What's your relationship with Maya?" he asked. Jebediah was a nice enough guy, but he had no right to ask Fintan about his personal life. He would shut that shit down.

Jebediah shrugged. "She and I get along, while not really being close. Why?"

"The ideas she was floating at the table are subversive." Maybe subversive was stretching it a bit, but they were certainly…troubling.

"I'm aware. She's caused some issues in the past. For you, too, I believe?"

Fintan flushed. Okay, so somehow, Jebediah knew. He'd been around Anahata for a while, after all. And it wasn't like it was a secret. His body tingled.

"I'm sorry. I didn't mean to upset you," said Jebediah.

Dammit, the man was too sensitive for both their goods. That was enough.

"It's fine. I don't mean to pry –" okay, maybe he did "– but are you injured?"

Jebediah's calm was ruffled for the first time since Fintan had entered the room. "Yes."

There was an awkward silence. *Okay.* Fintan pushed his chair back with a scrape and stood up. "I need to go meet Tierra. We have more records to go through."

And he needed to be out of this room. He'd had enough of Jebediah, well-meaning though he was, poking at Fintan's sensitive spots, keeping his own strange secrets, locked away in the Guild.

Jebediah nodded. "I'll keep an eye on Maya."

Fintan grunted, and headed toward the door, and tried to ignore the knowing look he saw in Jebediah's eyes.

Still. He was pretty sure the guy was okay on balance, and this thing with his Svadisthana energy, and his injury, whatever was happening, was his business. Surely someone in the Guild could heal him. And there were greater reserves of Svadisthana energy in the guy than he was displaying, Fintan was sure of it. He was suppressing it, whether consciously or unconsciously.

Personally, Fintan couldn't imagine going without the company of a woman for more than a month, let alone decades.

Perhaps that was at the root of Fintan's own issues. His last date had been a while ago. He shrugged. Easy enough to rectify, after this current business was done.

In the meantime, though, he needed to take care of Tierra.

CHAPTER 18

"Ready to hit the archives again?" said Fintan. "Another scintillating couple of hours poring over old paper and trying to puzzle out who Ai's parents might have been?"

"I'm ready. How was the gym?" She walked ahead, along the corridors of the Guild, her big purse over her shoulder.

"Fine. Do you really need that bag?" He needled her as they walked towards the archives, trying to get a rise. He knew she liked to be prepared for everything – was always the one with sun cream, a band-aid, a snack or a hairbrush, so he didn't really need to ask, but anything was better than her sadness. He'd take annoyance or irritation directed at him if it bumped her out of this passive despair. "Or are you going to stash all the archives in the library in it so we can do our research in our room?"

She heaved a sigh and rolled her eyes.

Pleased, he darted ahead to open the heavy wooden door to the archives for her with a flourish. If he could make her laugh, perhaps all wasn't lost after all.

True, sometimes his flippant sense of humor got him into trouble, and there were those who couldn't see through his beach-bum looks and relaxed attitude, to the committed Guild member that he was. Though that element of surprise had helped him more than once in fights, where opponents hadn't appreciated his speed and his understanding of human psychology and tactics.

Tierra though, knew him inside and out. And still laughed at his jokes.

A couple of hours later, in the archives, neither of them was laughing. Their research had netted them nothing. As at many of the Guilds, the archives here weren't yet digitized, and consisted of books and papers loosely categorized according to whatever the system of the current Records Keeper was.

They stood at a high table, papers and books of all ages spread across the green felt surface. Both of them wore gloves to protect the records. Tierra's piles, naturally, were neater.

Tierra knew the current Records Keeper – of course she did, she knew everyone, even one of the most introverted energetics in the Guild. He was an Anahata-Ajna of Chinese origin called Feng, who Tierra had somehow managed to build a relationship with when she had studied in the Guild, a century or more ago. Fintan would have to get that story from her sometime. This short, thin man had slender fingers, and a distracted look, although he seemed to know where every record in the library was kept. Which was both a help and a hindrance.

Fintan knew Feng had numerous advanced degrees from Universities in a number of languages, but, delighted by Tierra's presence in the archives, he kept bringing her more and more books and papers, heaping them on her desk with all the adoration of a puppy bringing toys to its mistress's feet. When Tierra smiled and thanked him, the man looked like he'd died and gone to heaven.

Every time he brought something new, Fintan had to suppress a groan. *We'll never get out of here.*

They'd been working their way through the birth records of energetics in North America between fifteen and twenty years ago. And it was taking them a long time. It wasn't that Fintan couldn't do this kind of work. Much as he had found himself enjoying the time with Tierra, he preferred action, and being out in the field.

He was starting to think they should make an appointment to see Aiko, the current Anahata Major Circle member, to get her take on things. He wasn't sure how much the Ajna Circle members, who Cuinn had been updating, had shared with the other Guilds. Or whether Jeb would share details with her.

Fintan really didn't want to get involved with the Anahata leadership. This trip hadn't been as bad as he'd expected, but he preferred to stay off the radar. Unease spiked through him and he sighed.

Tierra had gone to use the bathroom when Feng skittered up to Fintan, his forehead wrinkled, mouth a worried line.

"What's the matter?" Fintan said.

"I think...there's a book missing." Feng hunched his shoulders, stricken. He spoke in a permanently low voice that meant Fintan had to strain to hear him.

"What book?" asked Fintan. There could be a hundred thousand books in the archives, all as dear to Feng as children. Feng had to have some kind of magical affinity with them.

"The one that contains the recorded deaths in North America among the Anahata members in the last twenty years. I thought it would help as it's a shorter list than the births, but I can't find it," said Feng.

"It's been misplaced?" That was annoying. They needed all the information they could get, and on the chance Ai's parents had died in the area, it would have been helpful. The sooner they got out of here, the better. He rolled his head, stretching out his neck.

Feng shifted from foot to foot, agitated. "No, not lost. I don't lose books."

Fintan tried to keep the disbelief from his voice. "Feng, there are a lot of books here. Misplacing one happens. Do you want us to help you look for it?"

"It's not lost," Feng insisted.

"What happened to it then?"

"It's been stolen."

Ah, hell. Feng was quite the neurotic. Maybe Tierra should handle this when she came back. Though she probably didn't need that right now.

"Perhaps another energetic needed to consult it and took it?" Fintan suggested, trying to keep his voice soothing.

"No! We have a system. Everything is checked in and out. And there are wardings around the library. I'd know."

"So it couldn't have been taken from the library?"

Feng shook his head firmly.

Fintan wasn't sure what he was supposed to do. Offer again to help look for it? Feng knew his books, but who would have stolen it? It was more likely it had been taken for a project and not been returned to the right shelf. It was probably in here somewhere. "It will turn up. We have other sources to consult."

In fact, it had given him an idea, which he should have thought of previously. He'd take the names of all those who had been born during the approximate period, and see if he could track them down. If there was anyone they couldn't find, they'd see if the child might be Ai.

When Tierra returned, Fintan shared the idea with her.

"That might work for identifying the dead girl too," she commented. "Just increase the age range by another 5-10 years."

"I'm going to hit the phones. I think the administration here might be able to help with tracking some of the energetics down." Fintan straightened, feeling better with more purpose, and action to pursue. He grabbed their notes of possibles from the table.

"Sure. I'll keep working with the paper records," said Tierra. She bent back over the papers, her glossy hair obscuring her face. He stared at her a moment longer, struck by a feeling he couldn't define, then shook it off and headed back to their suite.

Several hours of phone conversations later, his long list of possibles had been whittled down to four. These were all couples who had had a girl child in the right time period, they had the right mix of energies to produce Ai, and he either couldn't track the couple down, or the couple were dead and he couldn't find out where the child was now.

He checked his watch. Nearly dinner time and there was no sign of Tierra. He'd have to go and haul her out of the library.

Back in the Records he was surprised to see her talking to a solemn-faced Jeb who stood by the table, hand on Tierra's arm.

Fintan hastened towards them. "What's happened?"

"Jeb knows who the dead girl is," said Tierra. She didn't meet his eyes, her shoulders drooping.

"There's a girl who attends Vancouver University, and is missing. I looked up her photo, and it's the girl."

"What did you tell the parents?" Fintan's tone was sharp. Tierra looked at him, eyes wide. He tried to soften his tone. "We didn't recover the body, and we haven't made it known that we found it. If he told them we had her, we'd have some difficult questions to answer."

Jeb nodded. "I know. I didn't speak to them. I'd asked a colleague who deals with such matters to let me know if anyone went missing in the northwest area. When the notification came in, he called me. I didn't say anything about my suspicions, and it took me a while to find her on the system. But when I did, I knew."

"Who is she?" Fintan sat down on the bench that Tierra was perched on, her body tight as a bow string. He put an arm around her.

"Aimée Fortin. A 20 year old medical student who was in her second year at the University. She was living in human dorms, and two of her friends called her parents after she was away for a few days without letting them know. They said she'd gone to visit a family friend, but never came back. The parents knew not to get the human authorities involved until they'd spoken to their Guild, so they haven't – yet. They're desperate."

"Complicated." Fintan said. "I better let Adam know."

"We can't let her parents think she's still alive." Tierra's voice was soft. "We need to tell them what's happened."

"I want to speak to Adam. We need to do a check on the parents, the friends – and then we need to rediscover the body. But we have to do it quietly. We can't lead the human authorities into what is an energetic death." Fintan pushed his hair out of his face and sighed.

Jeb nodded. "Whatever you think is best. But talk to Aiko. This business has to be brought to her attention without delay."

Fintan's heart sank. Dammit. Exactly what he'd tried to avoid.

Fintan went off to call Adam and Cuinn, and Tierra tidied up the papers she'd been reviewing. She loved the smells of the library. She'd spent a lot of time here in the past. It was a comforting place for her, which she was grateful for at this moment.

She gestured to the stool next to her. "You should sit, Jeb. I'm so sorry to have brought this to you."

"It's okay. Perhaps it's time that I engaged a little bit more with the world."

"You already engage. You run the Maven program. You're doing great work here," Tierra attempted to reassure him. Though she was hardly one to talk about engaging with the wider world. She had been just as hidden at Cathair Cuinn as perhaps Jeb was in the Guild.

"But there's more I could be doing." He stared down at his feet.

"There's always more all of us could be doing," she said. "But we can all only do so much. What you're doing is enough. More than."

Was it?

"Those poor parents," murmured Jeb.

Fintan returned. "I couldn't get Adam. But I spoke to Cuinn and Blaize. Adam still has a watch on the house where we found the body, a couple of trusted members of his team. They're keeping it quiet. They haven't seen anyone come or go since they arrived. The house seems deserted. They've been trying to chase up who owns the house, but it's a rental, under false documentation."

"So what are we going to do?" said Tierra. This was such a mess.

"The parents are on their way to Vancouver. They live in Montreal. Blaize and Cuinn are going to talk to them, to tell them what's happened, and to work out a story to tell the human authorities. The body needs to be discovered, but not in a way that leads them to the real crime scene. Cuinn and Blaize are going to work with members of Adam's team to retrieve the body and move it someplace else."

Tierra shuddered. "That's just horrible."

Fintan looked at her. "Yes. But we walk a line here. The body needs to be found, and the parents need to be told. But we could lose our only lead on the case, and that would endanger other energetics."

He shook his head. "I didn't really think someone would be back, but I hoped. We'll keep a guard there, just in case, but it seems unlikely now. We don't think that the parents are involved, but there's always a possibility –"

"No, surely." Tierra looked at him aghast.

Jeb nodded his head slowly. "It's the kind of question that has to be asked."

"And I don't know the answer," said Fintan. "That's another reason why Blaize and Cuinn are going to see them. It's unlikely – to all intents and purposes they haven't left Montreal in months, but looks can be deceiving. They're also going to try and find out why this girl, specifically, was taken. And explore the family friend connection a bit more, as that's the best lead we have at the moment."

Jeb nodded again. "Because if you combine that piece of information with my vision, where the girl felt safe at first, she was almost certainly taken by someone she knew."

"Her name was Aimée." Tierra's voice was dull. Her head was empty and slow.

"What, Tierra?" Jeb asked.

"Aimée. Not 'the girl'."

"Are you okay?" Fintan's voice sounded unsure.

"Now she has a name…a family…friends, it all seems so much worse. And I didn't think it could." Tierra remained staring at a wall of books. "She had a future. And it was taken from her, at twenty. Not just taken, but torn, in fear and in pain."

She felt like a statue. Rooted to the bench. Still as a stone. There was a low-level buzz inside her head.

Both men moved. They paused, and Jeb gestured for Fintan to go ahead. He put an arm round her shoulders. She didn't stir, her body as tight and as motionless as it had been since Jeb had told them the news.

"The best thing we can do is to get her justice. And we will." Fintan promised.

"Can I go and help Blaize and Cuinn?" She muttered the words. She needed to help. To do something. To take action and get out from under this crushing sadness and regret for a life lost so young. The Records were suddenly suffocating her.

"We need to find Ai's parents. Ai is alive, and she's alone. You can help her more by finding her parents than you can Aimée right now." Fintan spoke in low, soothing tones.

Movement flowed back into her face and limbs and she lifted her chin up. *Yes.* "I can."

She focused on this new path. "Jeb. We found several possibilities for Ai's family. Can you take a look?"

"Of course."

"Do you have them, Fintan?" said Tierra.

"Yes." Fintan handed the paper on which he'd scribbled them to Jeb. "We think she could be the daughter of one of these families. They match the parameters. Can you rule any out?"

Jeb looked at the paper for a long while. "I know one of them. She's alive and well and living here. There are two more I want to check on my computer upstairs. If I can't find out, then you can try Aiko. Ask her if she'll check the Guild database. The other families should be on that, and what's happened to them. Assuming we know."

"There's a Guild database?" Fintan was incredulous.

"Yes," said Jeb. "It's all part of the work we're doing around the Rogues. We have a lot of paper records, as you'll have seen, but Aiko's forward thinking. She wanted to see what we have in the

Guild in terms of combinations of dominant and auxiliary Chakras, where we tended to settle, what people are doing, and the birth rates."

Jeb rubbed his forehead. "The Healers in Anahata have always been interested in the birth rates of energetics, as keeping them stable helps to ensure the world remains in balance. Every energetic counts. But Aiko hasn't made the project public. She hopes to encourage the other Guilds to do a similar thing, but given the trouble she's had over cataloguing and understanding the Rogues, she's put the full records on hold for the minute."

"There would be a lot of energetics who wouldn't like the idea of being on a database. Even for the good of the race," remarked Fintan. His voice didn't betray his feelings, but Tierra could tell he'd probably be one of those who weren't happy about it, though she wasn't sure why. Perhaps his own less-than-positive experiences with Anahata Guild.

"Perhaps." Jeb was noncommittal. "But there is much to be gained. And much of the information – as you've found – is in the paper records anyway. Why not put it onto a computer?"

"There's something different about having 'Archives' of the past, compared to a database of the present." Fintan frowned. "Haven't you read any George Orwell?"

Jeb smiled. "Of course. But that's not what this project is about."

"Anyway." Tierra, distracted for a moment by the potential for argument that was hovering in the air, stood up. "We've made a lot of progress today. Let us know what you find, Jeb, and we'll try and get an appointment with Aiko either way. I hope she can fit us in."

"I might be able to help you with that. She's in residence at the moment. Let me call her. I'll get back to you if I can help. Otherwise you'll have to go through her office." Jeb's emotions were locked down so tightly Tierra found it hard to get a read on how he was feeling. Her gut twisted again for getting him involved in this mess.

They went to dinner, but the talk Fintan had suggested didn't happen. They ate in silence, Tierra's head full of anxiety about all the balls they had in the air.

They headed back to their suite. Fintan's cell pinged as Tierra put her bag down.

"Ah," said Fintan. "Jeb's set us up with Aiko. She'll see us in the morning, first thing. Eight a.m." He didn't look that pleased, and she wasn't sure why. "He's also ruled out another one of the families. Two possibilities left."

"Alright. Helpful on both fronts – I thought Aiko might be too busy. There must be other people who can use the database. She can't be the only one," said Tierra.

"I expect it's more about making sure that we've got a good reason to check it," said Fintan, "rather than the actual checking itself."

"Oh. Yes, of course." Why did she always feel so naive?

"Do you know much about her energies? What's her dominant-auxiliary combination?" Fintan asked.

"She's Anahata-Vishudha."

"Interesting. Heart and the throat Chakras. Air and space as her elements. I wonder how she stays grounded enough to run a Guild?"

"I've met her a couple of times over the years, but not since she's been Anahata's Major Circle member. She's a great communicator. Quite the change in style from Caradoc's reign."

"Let's hope she can help us." Fintan frowned. "There's something not adding up with Anahata."

"What? Why do you say that?"

"Gut feel," he said.

She narrowed her eyes. "That's not good."

That meant Fintan's intuition was sparking.

Fintan slumped on the sofa. "It's really not."

CHAPTER
19

Fintan and Tierra were in the living room area of their suite. Night had fallen, and the faint smell of shisha tobacco floated through the room from outside.

To say Fintan's feelings for Tierra were complicated would be a huge understatement. He'd wished for Cara, or even Cuinn, to talk to about the unexpected confession in the park, a hundred times or more. His embarrassing and unprecedented loss of control over his energies had been a stone in his shoe since then.

Fintan tended not to dwell on things. He preferred action to endlessly talking things over. And yet he'd barely stopped thinking about Tierra since that morning in the park.

Today, throughout his time in the gym, archives, and discussions with others, Tierra had popped into his mind multiple times. And how much he'd wanted – needed – to make it better for her.

Her confession in the park had taken him by surprise. He'd thought he saw her as a sister. As a friend, despite the odd moment of sexual attraction he'd felt recently.

Since then, he'd been watching her. Watching her curves, and how touchable all the material she wore seemed to be. How it draped over her body in a way that both hid and enticed. How she moved her hands when she got excited when she was talking. How still she'd seemed when she was holding in the sadness in Jeb's study.

And he'd realized that he could see her as a lover – and it had stopped him cold.

Whatever Jeb said, Fintan knew Tierra deserved more than someone like him. Which meant he needed to be cruel to be kind. He would have to knock any idea she had of them being together romantically on the head. She might be angry at him in the short term, but she'd see it was for the best, later, when she was free to be with someone who was right for her.

Some guy who could be relied on. Who was steady, and stable, and had his own family and friends. With a smarmy smile maybe – he growled as he imagined it – but someone who would always be there for her. Not a rootless loner like Fintan. He ground his teeth as he envisaged Tierra in the arms of the nameless man.

He'd decided to wait till after dinner for conversation, wanting to make sure Tierra ate properly. She needed to look after herself. He'd brought an extra bottle of wine with him back to the suite to help the conversation. He didn't think she was going to like what he was going to say. Even if it was for her own good.

He poured them both a glass now, the pale gold of the wine sparkling in the simple room.

Tierra sat on the sofa, her feet tucked up beneath her as usual. He handed her a glass, and sat on the couch next to her, leaving a careful distance between them.

He began. "I've been thinking about our discussion in the park."

She swirled the wine around in her glass, and took a sip, eyes downcast. "Hmmm?"

"It was flattering. But we're not suited. I don't feel that way about you." His face flushed. It wasn't a lie, exactly. His feelings for her had changed, but it was true he thought they weren't suited.

"Right." She clutched her wine. No eye contact yet. Is that all she was going to say?

"I'm sorry."

She shrugged, lightly. "Thanks. But I didn't ask anything of you when I told you. Well, apart from to stop telling me about your many women."

"It's important," he said. Had she really listened to what he said? She didn't seem bothered at all. Maybe her feelings had changed. There was a twist in his gut at the thought. Which was stupid, because that would be the best thing all around.

He needed to see her eyes.

He reached out and put his hand under her chin, tilting her face up.

"Tierra." Then he stopped, uncertain how to continue. Why was this so awkward?

"What do you want me to say?" She jerked her head back away from his touch, irritation in her tone, and her dark eyes sparked, the wine casting gold flecks into them.

She's beautiful. He frowned. He knew she was attractive, but he'd never really considered her in that light.

Her eyes narrowed as she saw the emotion flit across his face. "What?"

"You're stunning." The words fell out of his mouth without censorship, without thought. "You deserve someone who is worthy of you. I'm not that man. I can't be that man."

She narrowed her eyes and hunched her shoulders, wine held protectively in front of her. "I don't need empty compliments, Fintan. I knew you weren't attracted to me. I told you because it felt wrong to keep a secret like that from my best friend. But I know I'm not the kind of woman that men flock to. I don't have someone like Maya's glamor, and I don't have the kind of model looks you go for. And that's fine."

Anger burned his chest and his muscles clenched. How could she think he could find someone like Maya, who had no substance, who was brittle like glass, who was nothing, *nothing* compared to Tierra, more attractive than her?

"It's not an empty compliment," he said. His fists balled.

She'd backed into the corner of the sofa, her body curled into itself, and she'd put the wine down. Her chin trembled, even as she held it up defiantly.

A desperate need gripped him, a need to show her that she was beautiful, exquisite, wonderful.

He shifted towards her, and she held up a warning hand, even as moisture gathered in her eyes. His body filled with heat, with anger and desire and despair combined.

He took the hand she held up in his own, and gently moved it to the side. She hung her head, hand limp in his. He wanted that spark of defiance back. Wanted her to realize how amazing she was.

He used his free hand to raise her head up, and to gaze into her eyes, eyes that didn't want to meet his.

He leaned towards her, his chest against her knees, and dipped his head, as slow as honey flowing from a spoon. He gave her every opportunity to stop him.

His lips touched hers gently, sweetly. Her mouth was so soft and full. His lips clung to hers, and he moved his hand from her face to cradle the back of her head. He opened his eyes to see that hers were closed, her dark lashes resting on her cheeks, which had a blush of color to them. He butterflied another kiss on her lips, and pulled back.

His breath came a little faster. Her eyes opened, surprise and sexuality battling in them.

"Never think you're not beautiful. Desirable. I'm the one who isn't worthy of you, not the other way round."

He released her gently, an ache in his chest, went into his room, and closed the door.

The next morning, Tierra and Fintan waited in embarrassed silence outside Aiko's office.

Tierra wore a light gray skirt, soft brown sandals that wrapped around her ankles, and a subdued pink top that flattered her skin tone. Pink eyeshadow echoed the pink of the top, and a lick of mascara and some lip gloss completed the look. She was erratic about make up, but today she'd felt the need for it – and she looked every inch a woman in total control.

She did not feel it.

There was a tension between them that Tierra didn't know how to break. She didn't know what to make of last night. On the one hand, he'd been firm that he wasn't interested in her. On the other, he had kissed her like she was the only woman in the world.

The kiss had stunned her. It wasn't the asexual kiss of the hotel. This had contained a hunger, and a wanting, but also a sorrow that she couldn't interpret. Had it been a consolation prize? In bed she had puzzled over it for hours, replaying it in her mind, and trying to sort out the mess of emotions that had come with it.

This morning they'd been polite to each other, but it had been the forced politeness of strangers, not their easy familiarity. Something had broken between them, and she didn't know how to fix it. She swallowed. What if she was never able to?

This part of the Guild still had the exposed beams and historic look of the rest of the building, but instead of beds and wardrobes in the rooms, there were filing cabinets and desks. This early, there weren't that many people in the offices, at what was clearly the administrative heart of the building.

She considered saying something, anything, to try and mend things, but they weren't alone. Aiko's Executive Assistant, Sajan, a tall man with dark hair and eyes, sat at a desk outside Aiko's office, behind a sleek laptop.

A few minutes later, at an unseen signal, Sajan disappeared through a door, and Tierra clutched at the opportunity to fill the silence. Maybe something related to the meeting might get them back on track. "Do you know if Aiko is in the loop on Cuinn's prophecies?"

Fintan startled, in his own world. "Yeah. The Major Guild leaders are aware of Cuinn's prophecy dreams, and the Rogue incident with Blaize. I imagine it's not high on Aiko's radar though. Ajna has a lot of prophecies, and with something as amorphous as this, even the Ajna Guilds aren't putting resources into it until there's more to go on. And it's not like Anahata is the most...diligent of Guilds."

She frowned, unsure of what he meant. She'd thought the tension in him was about them, but was there something around Aiko, too? He'd seemed okay about their time in the Guild so far, seemingly relaxed about being there as they'd stayed under the radar, but perhaps this opportunity to look the Guild full in the face was causing him more agitation that she'd realized. She grimaced. She needed him to help her in this meeting, not to hinder her.

Sajan returned and gestured for them to follow him. The door led to a small hallway, where another door opened onto a spacious office. Aiko was sitting behind a large desk, signing papers. A small, delicate woman of Japanese ethnicity, she sat behind a desk dwarfed her. Tierra could see a foot rest under the desk on which the woman's feet perched.

Aiko rose and came around the desk. "Welcome, Tierra, Fintan."

She greeted them in the traditional Japanese style, bowing to them with her hands on the tops of her legs. When she rose again, she smiled, and came over to each of them.

"But let us greet each other in the way of the Guild." She opened her arms and hugged each of them in turn, deeply. Every fiber of her being was contained in the hug, and calmness and love flowed into Tierra from the embrace.

"Thank you Aiko-san. You honor us." Tierra bowed back in turn after the hugs, and Fintan followed suit a few moments later, his own hands at his sides.

The Guild leader smiled, and moved them to several comfortable chairs in front of the large windows. Tierra took a longer look around as she walked over to the chairs. The room was airy, the windows letting in plenty of light, and showed the view that Tierra and Fintan had been looking at the day before. There were plenty of bookshelves, but also technology. Tierra saw wireless speakers, a smartphone, and a thin silver laptop open on the desk. A classic Japanese print by the artist Hokusai was mounted on the wall, but apart from the general minimalism of the office, there was little more that spoke to the energetic's human-world ethnicity.

They settled themselves into the chairs, tea on the small table between them. Tierra picked up a small cup, and took a sip. Fintan didn't touch his.

Aiko spoke. "Jeb tells me you have important information for me, to do with Cuinn Ahern's prophecies. Come, tell me your news."

After a glance at Fintan, Tierra related the full tale, holding nothing back. She spoke of Blaize's kidnapping, of Indigo, the trail to Vancouver, the dead body, Ai, and their discoveries while in Anahata Guild. Aiko listened carefully, and delicately drew out every detail from Tierra.

When it came to Ai's identity, Fintan pulled out the paper with the two possibilities on it and handed it to Aiko.

Aiko studied it, then looked out the window for a long moment. "I know who she is."

Tierra sucked in a breath. She couldn't help herself. She'd been expecting more drama. More buildup. Thank Source. At least something positive would come out of this crappy day.

"That poor girl. We'd thought she was dead, along with her parents." She showed them the paper, and her shapely nail pointed at one of the families. "It's a sad story. But nothing to do with the energetics. They were involved in a horrible accident on one of Vancouver's bridges. Something beginning with P?"

"Pattullo Bridge?" Tierra asked. "It crosses the Frazer river and joins New Westminster and Surrey."

"That sounds right. They were in their car driving home from the daughter's parent-teacher conference, and they were hit by another vehicle that was speeding. Their car spun and flipped over the barrier railings. They were incredibly unlucky. At least one of them was seen in the water after the car went over, but it was dark, and there was bad weather, and only the husband's body was found." She sighed. "He was called Ji, and was Ajna-Anahata. The woman was called Shu, and was Anahata-Svadisthana."

Tierra was nauseous. Those poor people. What a tragic death.

Aiko frowned. "But I don't understand how the girl is still alive. She was supposed to have been in the car with them. She was assumed to be dead. How did she survive? And how did we miss her?"

"Good question," Fintan said roughly. "Anahata failed that girl. It should take a good, hard look at itself."

Tierra put a calming hand on Fintan's thigh.

His rock hard thigh.

"Uhh. What matters is she's alive and well. We'll educate her around her energetic heritage and powers. Luckily we've found her before they're fully developed, so we can still help her to adjust. We intend to ask her to come and stay at Cathair Cuinn for a while in Vancouver. She's not ready for the Guild right now, and I don't think human education is right for her given her background."

She looked Aiko in the eye. "Would the Guild have any problem with that?"

Aiko smiled. "No. I'm happy that Ai has found someone with your capacity for love, but I'd be glad if you included Anahata in her education. Once she needs a Maven, Jeb can help. She needs a human education first, but you might have to home school her."

"She's smart," said Fintan. His posture was still alert, wary. Tierra couldn't understand why. There was no danger here. "She'll catch up quickly."

"You like her," Aiko commented.

"I do. She's prickly, but she's kept herself together despite a tough life. She deserves better."

"I'll assign someone to look into how we could have missed that she was still alive," said Aiko. "I find that strange. And I don't like the implications."

"Agreed. But I will look into it. There's no need to put a stranger on the case," said Fintan.

Aiko nodded. "As you wish."

Tierra squeezed his thigh again. Not that she was sure he'd even notice the limited pressure she was able to exert. "You weren't Guild leader then, Aiko. You weren't responsible."

"No. But still. I've changed a lot in the Guild in the last decade, but worms still keep coming up out of the apple. This looks like another." For a moment Aiko looked weary.

Tierra hated to burden her further, but they needed to talk to her about the information they'd gained from Jeb. "There was a second puzzle which the Anahata Guild has also helped us with. I'm afraid it's another tragic tale."

"This is in reference to the death of Aimée Fortin? I'm aware. I, and the other Major Circle members, have discussed Cuinn Ahern's dreamwalks, and the terrible situation with Blaize. However, we are divided as to the true import of the prophecies. Some believe that the situation with Blaize, and even now Aimée, could be a coincidence. His prophecies are – troubling. And there is little detail to help us to understand exactly what we should be doing."

"And you, Aiko? What do you believe?" Fintan asked. He seemed so confrontational today. So angry. Tierra's shoulders were tight.

"It seems an unlikely coincidence. The fact Jeb saw several people involved, not just one Rogue, is alarming. And I am distressed that whatever the situation, it has caught an innocent in its wake." Aiko drew in a long breath through her nose. "Do you need anything from me at this time?"

Tierra looked at Fintan. He shook his head. "No. The family may. We need to keep the fact that we've discovered the girl's death quiet for a time, as we're still hoping that those involved in this crime might come back to the house. That may be difficult for the family. Perhaps you have somewhere you could offer them sanctuary for a while until we have resolved the situation?"

"We can do that," said Aiko. "Please let me know once they have been informed of the death, and I will call them personally."

They took their leave of her. On the way back to their rooms Tierra said, "I'm going to let Jeb know what we found out."

Fintan changed direction to follow her, and she waved him back. "It's fine, I can do it. You head back to the rooms and start packing.

We're done here now. Let Cuinn and the others know what's happened."

She walked off without waiting for him to protest. She needed some time away from him. And she wanted to see Jeb before she left and see if he was feeling better. And, she admitted to herself, she wanted to feel his comforting energy herself. She felt exhausted and lost.

She knocked on his door, but it took longer this time for him to answer. When he did, she saw hollows under his eyes, as if his own night had been even more troubled than hers.

After they greeted each other with an embrace, Tierra curled up on one of the armchairs and tucked her feet underneath her. She hugged one of the cushions to her chest. Jeb followed and sat opposite.

She filled him in on their meeting with Aiko. "So we've managed to find the answers to both our questions, and can head home."

Jeb nodded. "I'm glad, though I'll be sorry to see you go. But you know that."

He smiled at her and she smiled back, though a wave of sadness choked her and stopped her from saying anything.

He got up and went over to his desk, picking up a notebook. He came back and handed it to her. "This is every detail I can remember about my vision. It's mostly just a series of sense impressions, but there might be things you can use. I hope it's helpful."

She gripped it. "Jeb, thank you so much. I know how hard this was for you, and I can't tell you how grateful we are."

"I enjoyed seeing you again. And meeting Fintan." He left an expectant pause.

"What do you mean?" Tierra was cautious.

He laughed. "Tierra. Come now. Even if I wasn't an empath, your love for Fintan shines out from you."

She put her hands to her face as her cheeks burned. "Jeb. I…"

He waved it away. "It's fine. I wish you happiness with him. He may not realize it now, but he loves you just as much."

She looked out over her hands. "Thanks Jeb, but I don't think so. I mean, he does love me, but not as a partner. He loves me as a dear friend."

Shame stopped her from mentioning the night before.

Jeb gave her a long look. "Perhaps the time isn't now, but it won't be long. You deserve joy, Tierra. You give so much to others, without expectations or demands."

She turned the question back on him. On this one, he was mistaken, and it hurt her to talk about it. "And you Jeb? Do you have someone who loves you? Who you can love?"

Jeb looked away then. "That part of my life is over. I have nothing to offer a woman."

"You're wrong, Jeb." Tierra's voice was firm. "Any woman would be lucky to be with you."

He got up and walked over to the window. "I'm happy enough as I am. My life here in the Guild lets me contribute and support others in a way that keeps me content."

She got up and walked over to stand next to him, putting her hand on his arm, looking up at him. "Is contentment enough for you, Jeb?"

He laughed, and the sound was harsher than normal. "It's more than I deserve. Really." He turned and dropped a light kiss on the top of her head. "Thank you for coming to see me. I'm glad I was able to help you a little. And come back if you think there's anything else I can help you with. If I can, I will."

She knew she'd get no further. "Thank you. It's been good to see you. Keep in contact – I'd like to hear from you more often."

He nodded. Their discussion was over.

CHAPTER

20

Somehow, Fintan and Tierra had departed the airport for different destinations – she home to Canada, he back to New York – without any further discussion of the night before. His body hummed with a constant sense of unease, as if something were out of place.

Instead of clarifying the situation the night before, he seemed to have royally fucked things up with Tierra. And he had no idea how to fix it. Every time he tried, he seemed to get into more trouble.

It wasn't like he'd started it, he thought, with a sense of righteous indignation. She'd been the one to open the can of worms that had caused all of this.

He arrived back at his apartment, the fourth floor of a walk-up in the Meatpacking District. He'd owned the place for decades, watched the area evolve from gritty to sophisticated. His neighbors used to be hookers and meat truckers, and now they were designers and hipsters. There was a sense of relief as he walked up the wooden stairs into the familiar space. Perhaps he could throw himself back into work for a while, to give himself a sense of perspective on the situation with Tierra.

Fintan had never really had a problem with women. His ability to connect with them attracted them to him in plentiful supply. He kept things light and playful, always keeping some of himself back. There weren't many he let in to the deeper parts of him, and after a while, the women got frustrated and left him. But they usually stayed friends. Occasionally, Fintan played matchmaker, using Anahata and his own intuition to find someone who was a better match for whoever he was dating. That worked even better than the commitment issues.

In his bedroom, he tipped his duffle bag upside down on the bed and shook it, his clothes and toiletries falling out into a heap. He threw all the dirty clothes onto the floor ready for the wash, and scooped up the clean ones and dumped them in a drawer in the wardrobe. He'd spent enough time in the military over the centuries that he took pleasure in being untidy at home.

He had the entire top floor of the building, the glossy modern interior a contrast to the stone it was built from. Long thin windows let in plenty of light.

Tierra … she wasn't like the other women in his life. They were friends. She did know him. He'd never hidden any part of himself from her. And he couldn't bear to lose that friendship.

What had gone wrong?

It wasn't as if he could talk about it with Adam. And he hoped Tierra didn't tell her brother. Or Cuinn. Or Blaize.

He winced and sat on the bed, head in his hands.

He was going to get his ass kicked if he didn't sort this out. Though he probably deserved the kicking if he didn't resolve the situation.

He reached for his cell and called his team in Manipura Guild to see if there was anything that needed his attention. There was nothing pressing, but enough emails and ongoing work that he decided to head into the office as soon as possible to catch up. It might be that he was needed again by Adam fairly quickly, and it would be better to be up to date on this part of his life if that was the case.

He showered and changed, and was in the office within an hour, picking up a couple of PB and J bagels on the way. One thing about the current century he loved was the diversity of food in one place. You no longer had to travel for hundreds of miles to get a different kind of food. You just switched to the restaurant on the other side of the street.

Fintan had an office to himself at Manipura HQ. The Guild owned a collection of brownstones on Washington Square Park, nestled in among New York University buildings. They were a warren architecturally, having been acquired as the Guild needed them, and Fintan loved them. It still amused him that the Americans considered them old, but the hustle and bustle of New York made it one of his favorite places to stay, and he found the mishmash of buildings, people and scents exhilarating. Let alone the secret rooftop speakeasy close by.

His space was a messy room off the bullpen where many of his colleagues worked. It was still early, and there weren't many others in. He shut his door, preferring to be alone a while longer. He worked through what felt like a million boring emails, the ones he'd ignored while away, which updated him on various ops. This wasn't the image most people had of Manipura Warriors, the fighters of the energetic world. But he stuck with it, rather than using his preferred method of 'delete all', because he wanted to see if there were any other leeching cases that had come up in recent weeks. He had a hunch that the ones they'd come across weren't isolated.

And he was right.

Several hours and hundreds of emails in, he came across something that looked promising. A report of a leeching of a teenage Ajna-Muladhara energetic across the Canadian border in Seattle. The young man was drained and killed. The police had discovered him and assumed he'd died of malnutrition, but local energetics had checked it out and had found signs of leeching.

The teen had had ligature marks on his wrists, indicating he'd been held. No prints or other useful physical evidence had been found at the scene to trace who the perpetrator might be.

It could be the work of the man, or his colleagues, who'd killed Aimée. Typically, because the taboo against killing in their society was so strong, energetic Rogues who got involved in leeching didn't kill their victims. Sometimes leechings were accidents. Sometimes they were addictions. In either case, the perpetrator wasn't in control of himself enough to clean up and remove physical evidence from the scene this well.

Fintan stared at the screen and rubbed his forehead. This was a nasty case. He frowned and went back to the report, and the date of the crime. Buried in his emails, he'd assumed it had happened a while ago. The report said the body had been found in the last three days, and the search for the perp was ongoing.

He took notes from the report. This could be the break they needed. At least it gave them a more recent location. Seattle was only about two or three hours from Vancouver. Close enough for it to be a short trip for the Rogue, or Rogues, and it also suggested that there was a reason they were staying in the area. *What was it?*

He was considering whether it was too early – or rather, late – in Seattle to call the energetic who'd been looking into the death, when his phone rang.

"Fintan."

"Adam here. We need to talk."

CHAPTER

21

Blaize met Tierra off her plane at Vancouver airport. The slender, toned redhead looked like a dancer – though a dangerous one. All muscle and lithe grace, her naturally pale skin had lost most of the tan it had had when she arrived in Canada from sunny Thailand, but she was still a striking woman. Today her expression was grim.

"What's the matter? Is everything alright?" Tierra's stomach fluttered. There was a constant sense of anxiety in her life at the moment. She was much closer to the reality of the jobs that Blaize, Fintan and Adam did daily, and she didn't like it.

"It's Ai." Blaize headed for the exit as soon as Tierra reached her. Her pace was determined, and other patrons veered out of the way as she stalked through it.

"What's happened? Is she ok?"

"We're not sure. She'd been staking out the house you found."

"The house where Aimée was killed?" Tierra's stomach lurched at the danger Ai had placed herself in, and she hurried to catch up. "How do you know?"

"When Cuinn and I went back in to check things out before they removed the body, she came in." Blaize pulled open the door to the car park and let them both through. "She had a gun."

"She what?" Tierra stumbled. "What happened?"

"I disarmed her. I think she was surprised about that." The corner of Blaize's mouth quirked. "Anyway, once she realized who we were she apologized. She'd been waiting for someone to come back to the house. I think she was trying to impress you and Fintan by catching the bad guys."

Tierra winced at the thought of the teenage Ai going up against the Warrior Blaize. "But she's okay now? And you're okay?"

Blaize clicked the lock on the car with her remote, opened the door and slid in. Tierra put her suitcase in the back and hurried into the passenger seat. Blaize turned on the engine and continued. "Not exactly."

Tierra's stomach flipped. "Tell me, please."

"We didn't realize you hadn't told her about Indigo."

"Oh." A blush suffused Tierra's face. She wanted to explain their reasons, which had seemed right at the time, but the tingling in her face and sweat on her palms were an indicator that perhaps at a deeper level she was less sure.

"It came up in conversation. We didn't know it was a secret," Blaize said.

"Oh, Source." The tingling spread down her neck and across her chest. "How did she react?"

"Not good. She ran." Blaize crossed her arms over her breasts. "We haven't seen her since."

There was a thickness in Tierra's throat. She'd had niggles of doubt at the time that it hadn't been a good idea to keep the reality of Indigo to themselves, but she'd wanted to protect Ai.

She grimaced. No, let's face it. She'd thought that Ai would run if she pegged Tierra and Fintan as part of the group that killed Ai's friend.

"We might never find her." There was a sinking feeling in her chest. "We don't know where she spends her time, where she lives. If she doesn't trust us, we might never see her again."

Tierra slumped in the seat, everything catching up with her at once. She wasn't cut out for this life. She couldn't juggle the dangers and the risks not only to herself but to others, that her friends and family seemed so comfortable with.

"I'm sure it won't come to that," Blaize said, her tone brisk. "I'll take you to the house, and maybe you can track her from there."

Tierra's brain teemed with images of Ai injured or dead, as she watched the scenery pass. Ai might be alone forever, because the first people she'd trusted in years had let her down. "What about the cell phone we got her? Adam or Fintan might have connections at Vishudha Guild with some of their comms energetics – maybe we can track that."

Blaize shook her head. "It's off. We're monitoring it, but it's dead so far. The last cell tower it bounced off was near the house. We haven't seen her since."

Tierra bit her lip. "Okay. Don't go to the house. Let's go to where Fintan and I first saw her. Perhaps she'll go back there."

"Can you put the directions into the GPS? And text Cuinn to let him know?"

By the time Tierra next looked up, they were approaching the area where they'd first seen Ai. They drove up and down the streets for half an hour. No sign of Ai.

"Okay, park anywhere," Tierra said.

Blaize pulled the car over, and loped over to two teenage boys who were playing a card game while pretending not to watch her approach. Blaize was in her work gear, which was tight jeans that had plenty of stretch so she could move in them, a black T-shirt, and a black jacket. It was sunny enough for her to be wearing a pair of sunglasses. She looked pretty bad-ass. Certainly compared to Tierra's own small frame and floaty skirt.

Blaize came back, smoothing her jacket and humming.

"What were you doing?" said Tierra.

"Paying those kids to keep an eye on the car. This isn't a neighborhood where I want to take chances. It's twenty bucks well spent."

Tierra was already searching the street around them. "Let's try the hotel first. That's where we first talked to her."

She walked quickly along the pavement, boots tapping. Blaize walked along next to her.

"We'll find her, T." Blaize's voice was firm. "I'm sorry we scared her off."

Tierra rubbed the back of her neck. "You're sorry? Fintan and I should be the ones who are sorry. It's our fault. We should have told her. It just seemed easier not to at the time."

They were nearly at the hotel doorway.

"How do you want to do this?" asked Blaize.

"He seemed to respond well to cleavage last time." Tierra wrinkled her nose.

"Eww. One of those. Let's see how he responds to a woman who can kick his ass."

Tierra trailed behind Blaize as she burst through the doors into the reception. The odious man Tierra and Fintan had met previously glanced up from behind the desk with little interest, saw Blaize, and got to his feet in a hurry.

"Can I, uh, help you?" He caught sight of Tierra, and his shoulders relaxed. *Not this time, buddy.*

"Remember my friend here?" Blaize jerked a thumb back at her. "She's looking for the girl she met when she was last here. Dark hair, skinny, teens, goth look. Where does she hang out?"

"I don't know what girl you mean."

"Listen, pal, there's fifty bucks in it if you help us, or a broken nose if you don't." She shrugged, checked her nails. "The nose is cheaper for me, so it's your choice."

His eyes widened. "I don't know. I've seen her sometimes, around this street, or sometimes near the bus station down the road. The diner, a couple of times. I don't know where she lives, I swear."

Tierra's eyebrows raised at this side of Blaize, who exuded menace as she leaned on the counter and put her face close to his. "Are you sure?"

He shot backwards, almost falling over the chair. "I'm sure. Give me your number and I'll call you if I see her. I promise."

Blaize shook her head and her lip curled. She took a leaflet from the counter and scribbled her number on it, leaving it on the wood. "Don't let us down, pervert."

Back outside in the sunshine, Tierra was open-mouthed. "Wow."

Blaize shuddered. "He was gross. And easily scared."

"You were pretty intimidating." In a way that Tierra knew she could never have been. When they had last been here, it had been like playing a role, a sex siren who could vamp information out of a guy. She wished she had Blaize's confidence. Her shoulders dropped.

"To a worm like that, sure. At least he gave us a few more places to check. Somehow I don't think he's going to call." She gave a wry smile.

They were both quiet as they made their way down the street, searching the alleys and roads they passed. It would be easy to miss Ai. At the end of the road they turned and looped back again, heading to the diner.

"When did you last eat?" Blaize asked.

"I don't know. I had some food on the plane." It wasn't important. And her sense of time was pretty messed up after the flight and with the time difference.

"Let's get something in the diner. It'll give us a reason for being there. And you need a break. We can sit in the window so you can still watch for her."

"I guess." Tierra's body was heavy with fatigue. She hadn't slept much on the plane.

Tierra's shoulders hunched at the sight of Betty the waitress, who gestured them towards a clear table.

Blaize ignored her and steered them to a different table, a booth in the window where they could see in both directions by sitting opposite each other. The plastic seat was grimy, and slightly sticky.

Blaize searched the menu for vegetarian options. Energetics were too connected to the food chain to eat meat.

"Don't have the omelet," Tierra said. "Or the coffee."

"Hmm. I might have a shake. And pancakes."

"Don't say I didn't warn you."

"You should eat something too." Blaize pursed her lips and tapped Tierra on the hand.

"I'm not that hungry."

Betty came over. "Yeah?"

"Two pancake stacks, and a chocolate shake and a strawberry one."

"Sure." Betty scratched something on the pad. "You find your cousin?"

"Yes, thank you. And one of her friends, Ai. Do you know her?" Tierra asked.

"Perhaps. What's your name?" Betty rested a hand on one hip.

"What? Why?" Tierra frowned.

"Maybe Ai left something for the right person." Betty's thin lips were pursed.

"She left something? What?" All Tierra's attention was on Betty.

"Name?" Betty's voice was obstinate.

"Tierra. I'm Tierra." *Please let that be who she was looking for.*

"Right. She said you'd give me $50 for delivering it to you." A glint of avarice shone in the woman's eyes.

"$50?" Blaize's voice was incredulous.

Betty shrugged. "If you don't want it, that's no skin off my nose. But she seemed to think it was important."

She ambled off in the direction of the kitchen, calling over her shoulder, "I'll put your order in, and you can think about it."

Tierra rose slightly, as if to go after her. "Sit down," Blaize said.

"We already gave her fifty for the information about Indigo. She knows we're good for it." *And it's not like they didn't have the money.*

"You gave her $50? Ah, Source. She's taking advantage of you," Blaize said.

Sure. Because everyone was. An ember of something lit for a moment in Tierra, then suffocated. "Sometimes it's easier to catch flies with honey."

"Like you did with that repulsive guy in the hotel?" Blaize reached across the table and poked Tierra playfully.

The ember flared again. Tierra flushed. "I was with Fintan. It seemed more like a game. I didn't have to threaten to break his nose and we still got the information."

"Hmmph. I like my way better," Blaize said, but when she caught Tierra's gaze she continued hurriedly, "Sorry, T. We can give her the money. It's just the principle of the thing."

"It was actually Fintan who gave her the money last time." Tierra lowered her eyes and reached into her purse. She pulled out a $50 bill. She did not want to feel ashamed for what she'd done. She had to contribute in her own way.

Blaize plucked it from her fingers. "I'll deal with it. Otherwise you'll end up giving her more."

Did everyone else think she was a soft touch? Tierra shoved sugar packets around the table while Blaize looked around to attract the waitress's attention.

The woman didn't come back for a while, and when she did, she had their shakes in her hands. She put them on the table, and paused.

Blaize slid the $50 bill across the table. "This is to cover our check," she said. "You can keep the change as a tip. How about that?"

The woman frowned, but then she shrugged and pulled out a plastic bag and handed it over. Inside there was a phone, and piece of paper, folded over and stuck together. There was no envelope, but in order to read it the woman would have had to tear it, and that didn't seem to be the case.

"Thank you," said Tierra. They were making progress, and a spark of hope ignited inside her. Perhaps they would find Ai today.

Betty shrugged again, and headed off.

Blaize ripped open the paper, and money fell out. She fanned it out on the table and frowned, then held the opened note out to Tierra. "It's yours. Can you read it aloud?"

Tierra nodded, and took it from Blaize's hand, her fingers trembling. She hoped it would tell them where Ai lived, or give some kind of clue as to where she might have gone.

She unfolded it and scanned the scrawled letters. She read them out loud as Blaize requested.

Tierra / Fintan,

You lied to me about Indigo. Did you kill her?

I guess my senses don't always give me good information. Seems like I was pretty much wrong about you. Here's your phone and money. I don't need you. I'll find answers myself.

A.

Tierra tried to read more into the stark words. Her stomach roiled.

"We didn't get a chance to tell her the whole story about Indigo. She's inferred a lot more from the conversation than we said." Blaize shifted in her seat. "I'm so sorry."

"It wasn't your fault." She didn't need to reread the note. The words burned in her mind. How could the girl think they might have killed Indigo? Tierra wrapped her arms around her body. They'd betrayed Ai's trust, and treated her like a child by not telling her. And they'd given her reason to doubt her gifts. Ah, Source. They'd really messed this up.

"I know it feels like everything's gone south, but enough of the guilt for now," Blaize said. She tapped the table to get Tierra's attention. "We're going to sort this. Let's think practically. How would she try to find the man who lived there? What could she do that we can't?"

"I don't know. We have much greater resources than she does." The guilt wasn't shifting, despite Blaize's order.

"Unless she's found something else out from her contacts. It wasn't from watching the house." Blaize frowned. "Adam's had his team watching it almost from when we left, and no one came or went. Though…they missed Ai who was also staking the place out."

"It's possible she got something from her gifts. She's Anahata-Ajna, which is a powerful combination for prophecy, even untrained. She told us she'd always had feelings about people, always had thoughts about what might happen to them, or about whether they were good or bad." Tierra bowed her head. "That's why she trusted us. Her feelings about us were good."

Blaize stretched out a hand across the stained Formica. "You are good, T. You're one of the most selfless people I know. She's got this wrong."

Tierra clutched at Blaize's hand as if she were drowning. "We have to find her. The man in that house is depraved. He killed a blameless girl, and who knows who else? If he gets his hands on Ai, she's likely to be drained and killed just as Aimée was."

Blaize nodded. "We will. I'll call Cuinn and update him. Drink your shake. You'll need the fuel." She reached for her cell and slid out of the booth, heading outside.

Tierra sat, her hands wrapped around her glass. The cold seeped into her hands. She kept them there, deliberately punishing herself with the small gesture.

Betty returned with their pancakes and slid the plates onto the table. She hesitated. "You okay?"

Tierra looked up at the previously surly waitress, her eyes overflowing at this small indication of concern.

"Shit," Betty muttered, and grabbed a handful of napkins from a dispenser on the next table. She dropped them in front of Tierra. "It's a hard world, lady. You're luckier than most. You have friends or family to help you. Lots of people don't. So suck it up and get on with it."

Tierra gaped at the woman's retreating back. It was an unexpected kindness from the hard woman, and demonstrated to Tierra once again there was good in everyone. Trying to dislodge a lump in her throat, Tierra took a swallow of the milkshake in front of her. It was a great deal better than the awful coffee from the last visit. More solid with something in her stomach, she ate some of the pancakes. It was slow going, but she'd managed one of the pancakes and half her shake by the time Blaize came back.

She set her phone on the table, and settled back into the booth. She took a sip of her shake. "You doing okay?"

"Yes." She wasn't great, but the food and the moment with Betty had helped. Now she just wanted to take action.

"I've let Cuinn know. He'll fill in Adam and Fintan. Cuinn's been dealing with the parents of the dead girl –"

"Aimée." She had a name. Her name was important.

"Aimée, that's right. They told them this morning. They're devastated, of course, but they're going to keep it quiet. Apparently Aiko, the head of the Anahata Guild, called them personally and offered them the use of one of the Guild's safe houses to grieve privately."

Ahh. Aiko had come through. More of the inner tightness that had come from reading the letter released. There was kindness in the world. "She offered. She was sympathetic – they're members of her Guild."

"You helped with that? Good work. It keeps them out of the way."

"Blaize." Tierra dropped her chin and shook her head, but couldn't help but smile at Blaize's efficient practicality.

"You know I'm right. It's for their good as well as ours." Blaize took a bite of her pancakes. "So. What now?"

CHAPTER
22

They searched the streets for hours but found no trace of Ai. Some time later, Tierra and Blaize were back in the generic hotel room with Cuinn.

Blaize sprawled on the large bed, her head in Cuinn's lap. He sat up against the headboard, absent-mindedly playing with her hair.

"The parents are on their way to Aiko's sanctuary. That will give us some time to sort this mess out." He sighed deeply. "I didn't see this coming."

Blaize twisted to look up at him. "You – we – can't see everything. We're still trying to put the pieces together."

She addressed Tierra, who sat in the room's only armchair. "Nixie's coming next week and I'm strong enough now to mentally share images of all the vision pieces we have had. She and I have a previous energetic connection that I think will enable me to do it. It will help us with finding out who all the figures standing with Cuinn and me are."

Cuinn's first visions of the prophecies had seen eleven figures standing with him. So far he'd identified Blaize, Adam, Tierra, Fintan and Cara, and Blaize had recognized Nixie, but there were six figures who were either too blurred for Cuinn to see clearly, or who he – and now Blaize – hadn't recognized.

"Great idea," Tierra said. She slumped in the chair, her mind dull. What in Source's name were they going to do? And where was Ai? Was she just in a burger joint somewhere chatting to her friends? Or had she somehow found the owner of the house and was even now being drained? Tierra shuddered. "We need to find Ai. But we don't have the first idea where to start."

"She might not have found the Rogue," Blaize pointed out. "Just because she said she's going to look for him doesn't mean she'll find him."

"She's a determined young woman, with Anahata-Ajna energies. When she spoke to Fintan and me previously she talked about having 'gut feelings' about things that came true. Perhaps she had a feeling about – or even a vision of – the man involved." Tierra bit her lip. She wanted to be out there, taking action, except – she didn't know what action to take.

"Either way, Tierra, we don't know." Cuinn's tone was gentle. "We should work with what we have, and not with 'maybes'."

Blaize nodded. "Okay, so what do we know? Let's start from the beginning."

Tierra closed her eyes and stifled a scream. She didn't want to go through it all again. She took a deep breath. "We know that there's a threat to the energetics, as per Cuinn's vision. I think we have to assume that these events are all linked."

"Definitely," said Blaize.

"The threat is undefined, but potentially to the whole race, not just us and those we love. We know that eleven energetics stand with Cuinn against this threat, and we're included in that number," said Tierra.

"The Ajna Guild leaders gave me some information before Blaize was taken, that led us to research that told us two things. First, that at the start of our history, each of the Chakras corresponded to a single Archetype. And secondly, each energetic had access to all the different gifts of a Chakra, unlike the diluted gifts we have now. If they were Ajna energetics, for example, they didn't just have the gift of prophecy. They could mind-speak, were great teachers, had drum-tight memories, and could even manipulate others' minds. This was their Archetype."

Tierra's mouth made an 'o'. She'd never heard this. Cuinn was one of the stronger energetics she knew, with several Ajna gifts, but he couldn't manipulate minds. She didn't know anyone with all the powers and gifts possible for their dominant and auxiliary chakras. "Which Archetype is which?"

Cuinn sketched out a list on the notepad by the bed.

Manipura – Warrior – Blaize / maybe Fintan

Ajna – Sage – Cuinn

Muladhara – Protector – Adam

Anahata – Healer – Cara

"Creator and Communicator were harder, but by process of elimination, we think that Svadisthana is Creator, and Vishudha is Communicator," Cuinn said.

Tierra counted in her head. "So if Nixie counts for Svadisthana, we have five of the roles covered, but no one with Vishudha? We're missing the Communicator. And do we only need one of each Archetype?"

"Maybe," said Cuinn. "We can't be sure. It's likely we need two of each though, male and female, if we go on the personal prophecy I got at Ajna guild. That makes it more complicated."

"Okay. What about the bracelets?" Tierra asked. "I thought you said each of those in the vision had a bracelet on their wrist? Only you and Blaize have them so far."

Tierra knew that Blaize and Cuinn's twin bracelets, made of entwined threads of the colors of their chakras, had appeared when they were in the dreamscape together. Blaize had told Tierra that this had happened after they'd made love for the first time.

"Yes," said Cuinn. "We don't know why. We're trying to research that too. Blaize helping has been very beneficial. I've made more progress with her working with me than I did in twice the time alone."

Blaize gave him a quick smile. "Okay, so that's the prophecies. What about the real world?"

"Indigo kidnapped you because you were an energetic match, and leeched from you. Aimée was Anahata-Ajna, and so is Ai. Which suggests, if they're leeching, that one of the kidnappers is also Anahata-Ajna, possibly the man, but we don't know how others are involved. But then we also have the Remnant stones." Tierra spoke slowly as she reasoned it out. "Jeb said that Aimée knew her attacker, and her friends said he was a family friend, which suggests he's older."

"He rented the property under false documents, so that's a dead end. And he hasn't been back," Cuinn commented.

"You didn't get any Ajna readings from the house itself?" Tierra asked.

"No. Nothing. I was impressed you were able to do an Anahata reading. Most of the house was wiped." Cuinn shook his head.

"Oh," Tierra breathed. "That makes sense. I only got a reading from the girl, not from anything else in the house. That explains why some of the details were blurred. I couldn't see the faces of her attackers at all. And Jeb said that the faces of the attackers were blurred for him too."

"We don't know if Indigo was the other woman you saw, or whether it was a third person. And there seemed to be other figures, but it's uncertain," Blaize said.

"Where does that leave us?" Tierra asked. "Do we have any leads at all?"

"We've asked the parents to write down every family friend or acquaintance they know who's an older male. However, they're each a couple of centuries old, so they've had time to accumulate a lot of people. I'll suggest they start with prioritizing the Anahata-Ajnas." He shrugged. "That might be a dead end. Or an impossible task."

"At least it's something. The parents will feel better taking action too," Tierra said.

"I'll talk to my grandmother and ask her to explore things with the other Minor Circle leaders," Blaize said. "I think it's worth tugging on any lead. She knows about my attack as she leads the Manipura-Ajna Minor Guild, and might have heard a rumor or have some suggestions."

Cuinn nodded and turned to his laptop. Tierra got up, and walked to the windows of the hotel room. The sky was clouded over, the day gray. She looked out at concrete and cars, and longed for the peace and nature at Cathair Cuinn. *But not until we've found Ai.*

"So what can we do?" She could hear the frustration in her voice.

"Adam's on his way back," said Cuinn. "A fresh pair of eyes might help."

"Really? He didn't know Ai," Tierra said.

"He knows you," said Blaize, gently. "And he trusts your opinion. Plus, you know, Protector. Looking after the innocent is kind of his job. He's going to go over the house one more time. We don't expect anyone to come back now. He can't justify the surveillance resources much longer."

"This is so frustrating!" Tierra exploded. "There must be something else we can do apart from go over old ground."

Blaize lifted her head from Cuinn's lap and unfurled to a sitting position. She took one of his hands in hers, and he looked alarmed. "What?"

"Cuinn. I know you don't want to. But I think it's time you explored the connection with your father."

He pulled his hand out of hers and stood. His tone was clipped. "I don't think that's a good idea. He won't help us, even if he could."

Tierra frowned. "What do you mean, the connection with your father? What's he got to do with it?"

Cuinn's father was a difficult man with whom none of them had spoken for decades.

"We don't know."

"Probably nothing."

Blaize and Cuinn spoke at the same time. Cuinn shook his head and squeezed out, "The last thing Indigo said to me in the ether was, 'Give my love to your father'."

"She said that? You didn't mention it." Tierra felt a little bruised. How was she only just hearing this information?

Cuinn looked even more uncomfortable. "I thought she was probably trying to get under my skin. It's no secret that my father and I are estranged."

"That's one way to describe it." How was that cantankerous old bully with the stick up his butt related to this mess? It had been a long time since they'd heard from Cuinn's father, and that was no bad thing as far as Tierra was concerned. He'd caused Cuinn a world of hurt. She accepted the man had his own burdens, but Tierra was of the opinion he'd treated Cuinn badly, and she had little time for that.

"He made it clear that he wasn't interested in a relationship with me, and he's the reason I left Ireland and came here. I can't see how he's relevant," Cuinn said.

"Why didn't you tell us?" Tierra tried to keep her voice neutral, but the idea that she wasn't Cuinn's first port of call with personal things anymore stung a little.

"Ah, Tierra. It just didn't feel like something worth sharing. It was a difficult conversation, and Indigo was mentally ill."

"Did she say anything else you didn't share?"

There was a long pause. Cuinn rubbed the corner of the duvet between his fingers while he thought. "She said she knew secrets about me, and about my friends. She said that my cousins have challenges ahead. And she said that the blond one – who I assume was Fintan, though I can't be sure – has a temper. And that there were surprises in store for all of us."

He sighed. "All typically vague and unhelpful. Nothing that could actually give us a lead, and lots that could cause people anxiety, which is what I assume her motive was."

He looked back at Tierra. "See, anxiety. I can see it on your face."

She shook her head. "No, no. Well, perhaps a little. But you're right, she was unstable, so we do need to be careful with everything

222

she said. Cuinn, you need to share this information with everyone. Adam and Fintan especially, as it's about them as well as me."

"I agree with Tierra, my love." Blaize's face was serious. "And Fintan does have a temper, that's true. But it's rare he loses it. He has great control over his energies."

Tierra blushed. He had great control, past tense. She seemed to have messed with that, recently. She ducked her head and hoped no one noticed the color in her cheeks.

"Yes. It's time. I'll speak to Adam when he comes, and I'll call Fintan. He's back in New York, Tierra, right?"

She shrugged. "As far as I know."

"I'll contact my father, assuming I can find him. As you say Tierra, it's been a very long time. Do you know his whereabouts?"

She shook her head. "I think Adam was keeping track of him. Ask him. And if he doesn't know now, he's the person most likely to be able to find out."

"What are your father's energies? Maybe that will give us a clue as to how he can help." Blaize's tone was supportive.

"Ajna-Muladhara." Cuinn's response was terse.

"Oh … Nothing new to add then," Blaize said, weakly. These were the same as Cuinn's energies.

"I think that the best thing to do is for us to go back out and ask more questions around the streets where Ai seemed to spend her time," said Cuinn. "We'll go back to the bus station, and the diner. It's frustrating we don't have a picture, so we'll need to describe her verbally as much as we can."

Tierra nodded. "I wish I could draw."

"It is as it is. We found her in the system now that we've connected her to her parents, but she fell out of the system when she left the group home she was in at thirteen, and so there are no up-to-date photos of her there we can use. If she has any online presence in terms of social media, she's using another name."

They went back out, and spent several more fruitless hours asking questions and attempting to find any trace of Ai. Cuinn even re-questioned Betty the waitress.

But it was as if Ai had vanished into thin air.

❧ ❧ ❧

Adam arrived early the next morning and put away a mountain of breakfast in the hotel's restaurant while they updated him, dropping bacon regularly, if clandestinely, to Argus, his husky, who sat by his feet. They arranged to go back to the Leech's house to talk Adam through everything from scratch, hoping that it might trigger some fresh insight.

Back in her room to get ready, Tierra tidied her few things, thinking ruefully she'd have to buy some new clothes if this trip continued. She'd only expected to be away a couple of nights, and it had already been twice that.

She frowned down into her suitcase at something that didn't belong to her. She plucked it out and held it at arm's length. It was one of Fintan's socks. The V between her eyes deepened. How dare it be in her luggage. And at the same time, she was flooded with a fondness and a longing so deep she crushed the sock in a fist and clutched it like a lifeline.

She wished he was with them. Then immediately wished she didn't wish it.

"Argh!" *Why is life so complicated?*

She'd thankfully regained her senses and stuffed the offending item into her dirty washing when Adam's knock came.

"I'm ready." She stepped out and shut her door behind her.

"We're not going yet. We need to go back to Cuinn and Blaize's room. Something's come up." Adam's voice was a low rumble.

"Is everything ok?"

"Not exactly." Adam set off down the corridor without explaining further, Argus trotting behind him, a faithful shadow. Tierra sighed, but, used to her brother's taciturn nature, she followed him to the other room, where Blaize paced and re-paced the few steps between bed and window and Cuinn sat on the bed, his face neutral.

"What?" Tierra stepped into the room, the churn in her stomach that had started yesterday now full-blown nausea.

224

"Cuinn got a message." Blaize didn't stop her pacing.

Adam pushed past her and scooped up the cell from the bed. He pressed a couple of buttons, and handed it to her. She wanted to refuse it, dread spreading through her.

She listened, and a voice came through the line, its identity obscured by crackles and computer modulation. "Blaize and Tierra for the girl, Ai. Beaver Lake, Stanley Park, midnight tonight."

Tierra wobbled and sat down hard on the bed. "Ai's been ... kidnapped?"

"It seems so. If we trust this." Adam's terse voice penetrated the fog in her brain.

Argus padded over and butted his head against her legs. She put a hand down to pat him, then clutched at her usual optimism. "So... we can rescue her? It's good news?"

Blaize and Adam exchanged nonplussed glances. "I wouldn't call it good news exactly," said Blaize. "We don't know who's holding her, who will be there, and they've asked for you and me to be exchanged for her. Or if it's even real. Might be Ai pushing our buttons in revenge."

"No," said Adam. "Tierra's not going. Not Warrior trained. Or Cuinn. Team is Blaize and me, and two of my team. We'll check it out. Get Ai back, if they're telling the truth."

"My, what a long speech," said Tierra. As if she was going to stay behind. No, just no. "I thought we'd agreed I could make my own decisions."

"My op." Adam responded.

"How is it your op? You've just got here." Her body was heavy with anger. Her power throbbed deep inside her, and she wished the kidnapper, a kidnapper cowardly enough to take children, was here so she could make him or her hurt.

"Best qualified," said Adam.

"In what way –"

A crack echoed through the room.

Everyone but Adam and Blaize froze. He went to the window, and Blaize to the door. They exchanged signals, but before they could check for further danger, Cuinn raised an arm and pointed at the floor, his mouth open. "Uhhhh…"

A teeny, tiny green bud had split one of the polished floorboards in two. It was very out of place.

"Oh. My," said Tierra. "Oops."

Elrian stared at the drugged and bound girl who lay on the floor in his country house.

He'd sent Dagon and Jowaki to the area where Indigo had first met Ai. When they'd found her she'd been easy prey – the girl was as untrained physically as she was energetically, despite her years on the streets.

Elrian had given the do-gooding idiots ranged against him an offer to swap the girl for other, higher value pieces, but he had no intention of swapping Ai for the other two. He wanted them all, as potential sources of energy for him and his subordinates. He had matches for all of them. Or, perhaps, they would serve to fill another Remnant stone – a harder process to manage, but where the reward was much higher.

At this point in the game, though, his priority was Tierra. She was the strategic piece. If he drained her, destroyed her, at this juncture, he would derail the prophecy.

His breathing sped. He drew in a deep breath and relaxed his hands, which had clenched at his sides.

Luckily, he knew a way to relax. There was no need for Ai to be one hundred percent healthy for the meeting. He gestured to Dagon. "Lift her up onto the bed."

The man picked up the girl by the arms and dropped her on the mattress, where her body bounced before stilling. She gave a quiet moan. She wasn't quite unconscious, wasn't quite conscious, though what he was about to do would wake her up quickly.

He sat on the bed next to her, and put a hand on her forehead.

He could only access her underdeveloped Ajna energy; her Anahata was no good to him. But it would be enough for today. He drew in a deep breath, and reached inside her with his energy.

23

Fintan's head was spinning as he raced to the airport to get to his friends. Tierra needed him. He should never have left her.

He had never been a fan of doing nothing, so the flight from New York to Vancouver was agonizing. With no business class seats left on the flight at this short notice, he crammed his broad frame into economy. He drummed his fingers on his thigh during take-'off, garnering a narrow-eyed look from the business woman trying to read her book next to him. He must have checked the flight info on the screen in front of him a hundred times, watching the minutes count down.

He trusted his friends, Adam especially, though Adam didn't know Ai. But Adam would move mountains to help Tierra, and as a Protector, took the world on his shoulders for those he loved.

Fintan gripped the plastic glass the air steward had given him, then gulped some of the water in it. How could they have let Ai down like this? He rubbed at his forehead, the chill of the plane's air conditioning gnawing at him.

What if Adam missed something? Something that Fintan would have caught? Fintan would never forgive himself. Adam had talked him through the plan, and Fintan knew the two energetics he'd have as back up. As a Protector, Adam had some experience with hostage negotiations. He was better qualified than Fintan. It was better this way round, with Fintan on the plane and the big guy on the ground, but Fintan still wanted to be there. They owed Ai. He'd told Tierra they'd keep the girl safe, but his decision to let the girl come to them may have cost her her life.

An acrid scent caught his attention, and he looked around before realizing it was his plastic cup, softening under the heat of his hand. His eyes widened, and he put it down and wrapped it quickly in the napkin, hoping his seatmates hadn't noticed.

He had to keep better control of himself.

For Ai.

And for Tierra.

The day passed at a snail's pace. Adam finally relented when Tierra enlisted Blaize's support. Tierra would not miss this. Fintan had been told, and was on his way, but he wasn't going to be back in time to make the meeting.

She had missed him more that day. If he'd been there, he'd have lightened the atmosphere, made her laugh, and told her it was all going to be ok. She was a lot more intense when he wasn't around, she realized.

When she wasn't arguing with him.

They crowded into Adam's room for a final briefing. He introduced the two men who would join them, Clay and Ymir, both Muladhara-Manipura, earth-fire combinations, both Protectors who worked with Adam. Clay was short and stocky, his strength obvious in his wince-inducing handshake. Clay had a lot of search and rescue experience, and was both an experienced tracker and able to manipulate earth. Ymir had a talent for working with metal and minerals, and was taller than Clay, with hard eyes and a serious expression. He seemed to be assessing them all, and Tierra felt she'd come up wanting.

"Blaize and Cuinn, stick together. Clay, stay with Tierra, and Ymir and I will get Ai back," said Adam.

The fighters had scouted the meeting point for potential hiding places and traps that morning, but they didn't have the resources to keep a constant watch on it. And it was a big place, one of the largest urban parks in North America, surrounded by sea on three sides and connected to the city on the other.

"Beaver Lake has a park police patrolled trail around it, so we need to stay off that. We don't want any humans hurt."

Adam's a lot more talkative in mission mode.

"We believe at least one of them is an Anahata-Ajna. They may have access to empath or intuitive energies. And Indigo, the Leech who took Blaize, suggested that they had access to prophecy. We have no idea what energies they have otherwise."

"We're going in blind," said Blaize.

"Yes," said Adam. "We focus. Go in, get Ai, get out. If we can gather information on the enemy or capture anyone, we will, but that's not our aim. We're risking enough taking two civilians with us –" he gestured at Cuinn and Tierra "– but both of you have been in battle before, even if it was a few decades ago, so I'm counting on you not to do anything stupid."

He looked at his sister, and she scowled back, but the churning in her stomach wouldn't let up. The danger ahead was sinking in, as she listened to Adam's quiet, efficient voice set out the plan. Cuinn might be a civilian, but his comfort in battle was greater than hers, and he'd been a fighter in his youth, if not for a long time. She wished she'd practised her self-defense harder. She wished she'd trained in offensive energies when she was younger.

She wished for many things to be different.

She got a hold of herself. *If wishes were horses … but they're not.*

Adam seemed to have finished. "Questions?"

No one spoke. "We leave in twenty."

They all took different routes to their assigned places in the park. Clay drove defensively, checking for tails, taking a circuitous route. Every moment tightened Tierra's nerves further.

She closed her eyes and whispered a prayer to Source that they get through this safely. She tried to use her breathing to calm herself. It didn't work. She needed to be in the park, with her element around her. She gritted her teeth. It wouldn't be long.

In the meantime, she needed to calm down. So Clay was just going to have to suck it up and talk to her. Because people helped her center herself, and she was so utterly terrified right now of what was about to happen, it was that or ask him to turn the car around.

"Sorry you got stuck with me." She watched his face for any reaction. He shook his head very slightly.

"Are you from England?" People loved to talk about themselves. Normally. But either Adam's taciturn nature had rubbed off on Clay, or Adam recruited for similar qualities.

"A long time ago. Now I'm of no particular country." He glanced at her.

"Do you have family? A home? A place you go back to after missions?"

"No. Too hard in our work." Something flickered across his face, but she wasn't at the right angle to read it.

"That must be tough. I find that for my Muladhara, home is an essential part of who I am." It really was. She longed for a day at home, baking or preparing food for family and friends. Instead, the prophecy and its consequences put her in situation after stressful situation out of her comfort zone, where she was barely managing to keep up.

"Home can be people as much as a place," said Clay. "My team are my home. I don't need to be grounded in a place."

She considered that as the city passed by the windows. Perhaps it was true for her, too. When she and Adam had moved to Cathair Cuinn, it was because family was her safe place. She loved the house, but if it was a choice between the place or the people, there was no contest.

And Fintan was as much part of that as the others.

The thought of him soothed the edges of her fear, and instead of her usual practice of stamping down on her foolish romantic fantasies around him, she let herself dream for a moment of a life with him as a lover, instead of just a friend. She sighed. The knot in her stomach eased a fraction.

They arrived at the park where the night was quiet and the abundance of earth energy soothed her further.

She followed Clay into the woods, and he stopped for a moment when they were hidden by shadows in the trees. He drew her off the path, into a wooded glade. Butterflies plagued her stomach and she was cold despite the layers she had on and the night being warm for the season.

"I'm going to connect with the earth," he said. "You might want to do the same."

She nodded and listened to the sounds around them. An owl hooted, and she followed the sound as it moved through the trees. Her attention was caught by a rustling, and her mind followed that. It was a grey squirrel, which should have been asleep in its den. Her attention swept the surroundings as she connected to the earth. To her energies. To her power.

She used the fear inside her as fuel. She was determined not to hinder the group. To do her part as best she could. She drew on the energy, connecting to the ether and pulling power so it spooled within her, ready. She could feel Clay's presence, his aliveness on the other side of the small clearing in the trees, as he too, drew in power.

He was pulling both Muladhara and Manipura, she sensed. For her, this evening, Muladhara was enough, as she'd drawn on more than she had in a long time. She would use it to scout their surroundings, to find what was hidden and to protect those she loved.

She sent her attention further through the woods, seeking what was alive there. She passed over skunks and racoons, and even a stalking coyote.

The lake was a couple of kilometers away from where they were, and she sent her attention that way. There were a couple of mounted police patrolling and moving away from the lake. She drew in a deep breath, grounding herself in the earth. She felt steadied. Connected. Energized. Her power was like a calm, deep pool within her. She only needed to draw on it when it was time. She could do this. She whispered a Muladhara prayer. *I am grateful the earth supports me and meets my needs.* It would.

She drew power over herself like a veil, hiding herself from possible trackers. She was warding herself as she would ward a property, to keep herself hidden. And protected. If she was attacked energetically, it would need to be someone who was at least Master level, like herself, for the attack to break her wardings. And even then, not every Muladhara energetic could do it. She was powerful.

She just needed to remember it.

Opening her eyes, she watched Clay come out of his own sequence.

"You sensed the police?" he asked.

She nodded. "Anyone else?"

He shook his head, no. "Are you ready?"

"I am." And to her surprise, she really was.

They walked quickly and quietly through the trees, staying off the trails. Their energies meant that they were both easily able to walk through the woods as if they belonged, making little or no noise, and leaving the smallest possible trail.

They came closer to the lake, and Clay waited for her to catch up. He breathed his words into her ear. "Go. I'll be watching. If you need me, I'll be there."

She nodded, and he melted into the trees. She was on her own.

CHAPTER

24

Tierra crept through the last few trees towards the spot where she had agreed to meet Blaize. They exchanged nods, and Cuinn materialized from the trees beside them. The groups had split up to scout more area on their way through the park.

The three of them stood in silence, facing different ways, and scanned the area. The meeting was scheduled by the lake, but the lake wasn't small. They weren't sure which direction their adversary would come from.

Tierra could hear the gentle splashing of the nocturnal beavers, unbothered by the energetics standing close by. A sense of dread crept up her spine. What was out there?

A jarring sound came from over the water. A girl's stifled cry, cut off. Tierra spun around, and surveyed the lake, her heart pounding.

Across the other side of the water, Ai stood, her arm held behind her at a painful angle by a man Tierra couldn't see clearly, but who seemed familiar.

Oh, Source. Ai. Fear tore through Tierra, leaving her gasping. She clutched at Blaize's hand, who squeezed back, briefly, then let go, positioning her body in readiness to move, attack or defend, whatever was needed.

"Cuinn Ahern, leave us." The whisper was sibilant, an oily poison floating across the water.

Cuinn shook his head. "Return the girl."

"In exchange for the two women only."

The man jerked Ai like a rag doll, and she gave a despairing cry. Tierra bit her lip. They needed to do something. The plan wouldn't help them if Ai was half-dead.

Cuinn seemed to feel the same, as when the man across the lake had demanded Tierra and Blaize, Cuinn had drawn a huge rush of power, and the usually calm man was pulsing with his Muladhara. There was a tremor in the earth underneath them, and Blaize put a hand on Cuinn's arm. Their role was to keep the kidnapper talking until Adam and Ymir were able to take him down. If Cuinn attacked them, or even angered them to the extent that they left with Ai, or hurt her, everything up to now would have been pointless.

"Why are you doing this?" Tierra's voice was shaky, but she put a thread of power in it to make it carry across the lake, just as she presumed the kidnapper was doing.

"Come here, Tierra, and you'll learn everything you need to know."

She shivered. There were few things she wanted less in this life than to be on the other side of the lake. She extended a thread of energy, seeking to learn more about the owner of the voice. And recoiled, as her energy was thrown back at her with the force of an electric shock.

She gasped.

"What?" Blaize's gaze raked the landscape around her for the threat.

"It's the energy. Male. Nasty. Protected. Ajna-Muladhara. He's the one who was at the house." Tierra was breathing hard. She drew on her center to ground herself.

Cuinn turned to look at her, a frown on his face. That was the same as his energetic combination. He shook his head and focused back on the small figures across the water.

A soft, unpleasant laugh drifted their way. "If you're not interested in the girl, I'm sure I can find another use for her. She's truly full of life."

Ai lurched again, and another cry echoed on the water.

Tense seconds passed, the night expectant around them.

"I should go over there," Tierra murmured to Blaize. "We need to make sure he stays. If he thinks we're not going to swap ourselves for her, he might leave. Or do something horrible to Ai."

Tierra hated the idea of getting any closer to the male figure across the lake, but she would do anything to get Ai back. The ice water in her veins could not, would not, hold her back this time.

"Absolutely not," Cuinn said, his voice hushed and calm. "We stick to the plan we all agreed on with Adam. It's the logical thing to do. And that does not involve you or I engaging with the kidnapper."

Tierra opened her mouth to protest, but he continued, "However, I agree we need to do something to keep Ai and her captor there until Ymir and Adam attack."

"Clay's here. I could go. You're protected, but it looks like the kidnapper is alone." Blaize almost vibrated with energy. She had her own defensive shields in place and was ready for an attack.

Or to attack.

"We seem to be alone too, and we're not," Cuinn said. "But yes. Go. Distract them. Be ready to take Ai when Ymir and Adam attack and bring her back here."

Blaize pulled Cuinn to her in a fierce embrace.

He leaned his forehead against hers for a moment. "Thank you, my love. Stay well."

"I'm on my way," Blaize pushed the words across the water. "I need to check you really have Ai, and she's safe."

She took off at a run, disappearing round the dark edges of the lake.

Tierra and Cuinn were left standing together. Tierra searched the trees for a sign of Clay. He was out there, but she didn't want to search with her energy in case it drew the man across the lake to her somehow. She'd be happier if she could see Clay. For all her bravado, the energy of the man across the lake was so twisted, so uncomfortable to touch, she didn't think she could protect herself from him.

Thoughts become things. Thoughts become things. She chanted the mantra in her mind and tried to picture herself beating the figure. Picture herself winning in a fight. After all, she was a Muladhara Master in her own right. She was powerful. She connected to the ground again, topping up the energy she held spooled inside her.

Blaize arrived at the two figures, and Tierra crossed her fingers at her side. Blaize's power shimmered as she talked to the Rogue, her shields up and ready for an attack. They were no longer projecting their voices and Tierra strained to hear what they were saying. As the man's attention was on Blaize, Ymir, Adam and Argus appeared from the scrub to the east of the man, and the Rogue was distracted enough to let go of Ai.

But the Rogue didn't release her easily. He shoved the teenager to the ground and kicked her, hard, in the stomach while he put strong Muladhara shields up around himself and Ai.

Ymir and Adam attacked. Adam caused the earth to move, the ground mounding and flattening underneath the Rogue male's feet. Argus darted in and out to nip at the man's ankles. The Rogue stumbled but didn't lose his footing, pulling energy to make the branches and the bushes turn on Adam. Tierra clenched her fists. Adam was an earth energetic too – did that mean the Rogue was stronger than Adam? Oh, Source. What could she do to support their earth attacks from here? She'd promised to stay out of danger.

Ymir was much closer to the man, and added physical attacks to his energetic ones. He threw out a snap kick, aiming at the man's side. The Rogue retaliated and swept Ymir's other foot from under him. Ymir went down hard, then used the energy of the fall to roll backwards and up on his feet again.

It was all so fast and hard to follow. Tierra was unable to think of a way to help.

In the meantime, Blaize burned the plants and trees that had captured Adam, freeing him. As Adam leapt forward, she forced her way through the strange man's shields with a blast of Warrior fire while he was distracted by Adam and Ymir.

It was enough to give Blaize time to pull Ai away, although the girl was no help. She looked injured. She cradled her arm, protecting it as Blaize dragged her behind her. Ai struggled to keep up. Before they could get more than a few paces, the Rogue sent a blast of greasy energy at both the women, who froze in place.

Cuinn startled and shook his head. He turned to Tierra, his face pale.

"He's using Ajna on them," he said. "He's really strong. He's keeping them still with a suggestion. I need to help. Watch my back."

Cuinn sat on the ground and closed his eyes, drawing yet more power, preparing to aid them.

Tierra's limbs were so cold, she was shaking. Everyone was helping except her. But what could she do? She looked at the forest behind them again, hoping Clay was still with them, a silent watcher. Her neck prickled, and she listened over the sounds of the struggle across the water.

She saw the next few moments in slow motion.

Blaize and Ai moved again, presumably as Cuinn broke the Rogue's hold on them.

Cuinn, Adam, Blaize and Ymir attacked the man, using different energies, and he held his own.

His power must be immense – there weren't many in the energetics world who could hold off the combined powers that were focused on him.

Surely they must be able to identify him after this, at least.

She swept another anxious glance at the forest behind her, full of adrenaline and anxiety with no outlet. Cuinn was still and focused beside her. Perhaps she could give him some of her power again? Boost him by sharing? It was forbidden, but they had done it before, in equally desperate circumstances, and there hadn't seemed to be any negative consequences. She hoped.

Funny how it was easier to break a taboo the second time.

She drew in a deep breath, and glanced across the lake to check events there. She had to force the nausea down at the sight of her friends in battle.

Her side of the lake, a beaver slapped his tail on the lake as a warning, and a raft of ducks quacked in fear and outrage as their normally serene home was disturbed.

She dropped down to push her hands into the earth, to see if she could read the terrain and see what was disturbing this side of the lake. She connected with the earth, power sending tingles up her arms, her body between the forest and Cuinn, the lake protecting his other side. There didn't seem to be anyone this side of the water. All the action was over there – where she should be. Her body vibrated with power, and after another quick glance, she stood and stepped towards Cuinn. She would give him a tiny part of her power. He was more likely to be able to use it than her.

She bent, hands reaching for him, and agonizing pain seared through her skull. She tried to cry out, but a hand was over her face, stifling her, toppling her backwards, off balance.

The pain receded, and she crumpled into the arms of her assailant.

And everything was quiet.

Fintan was on a motorbike, driving from the airport to Stanley Park.

The bike was a dream to ride. Big, powerful, its throaty roar muted by the padding in his helmet. He kept his body low over the bike, reacting to each bump in the road, other vehicles and traffic signals by instinct as the wind pushed against his body. He was forced to be fully in the moment, be fully present. Air was his element, and he spared a touch of power to cloud his passing with a mist to obscure himself from any human law enforcement. He could do without that problem tonight. He was wary, though, of spending too much power. He might need it.

Which stopped him thinking about the danger his friends were in. That Tierra was in.

She was so stubborn, so brave, and he knew she wouldn't think twice about putting herself into danger if she thought she could rescue Ai. She needed someone to protect her from herself.

The bike soared through downtown, and streaked past lights and other cars on late night errands. He flew through the entrance to Stanley Park, but Beaver Lake was in the interior, and eventually he had to leave the bike and run.

Another five minutes and he was close to the lake. He slowed his pace, and crept through the trees, being careful to keep any noise to a minimum. No energy use needed, this was woodsmanship, learned from many hard years of fighting in forests similar to these – if a lot colder – in his native Scandinavia.

He came to the edge of the trees, where a path cut around the lake. There were figures to his left. A girl on the ground. Ai. A woman standing next to the girl, her hand on the girl's head. Too tall to be Tierra. It must be Blaize.

His body was ready to fight, desperate to help, but years of training and discipline forced him to scout the situation before rushing in. He swallowed, mouth dry.

The moon had gone behind a cloud, and, in the darkness, it was hard to make out who was who. There didn't seem to be any fighting, but he could see two men, most likely Adam and Cuinn, were nose-to-nose arguing.

What the fuck was going on here? What had happened? He swept another last look, before he sprinted the last few hundred meters to join them.

Adam gave another man some kind of instruction, and he took off running into the forest. Was he looking for someone? Chasing someone?

Where is Tierra?

There should be one more man present, as well as Tierra. Perhaps they had gone back to the safety of the hotel. Source, he hoped so. He loped round the side of the lake, keeping his eyes open for anyone else as he moved.

And fell right over a body.

CHAPTER

25

Fintan twisted in the air so as not to land on the body.

He sucked in a breath as, on his hands and knees, he stared into familiar eyes. Eyes that no longer held any light. Clay, a man he had known for over a century, and had worked with probably hundreds of times, had been killed. *Shit.* Grief stabbed his chest.

Then icy fingers crept up his spine as he realized the implications.

Clay had been protecting Tierra. Adam had promised him in his last conversation that if Tierra went with them – and Adam had implied that he wasn't going to be able to stop her – he would ensure she was protected. Not left alone. Fintan and Adam trusted Clay as a first rate fighter, and unfailingly loyal. He would protect Tierra to his last breath.

And it looked like he had.

Fintan swore again. Tierra wasn't across the lake with the others.

Then where the fuck was she?

He sprang up, refusing to consider the worst at this stage, and ran the rest of the way to where the others stood. Ai sat on the ground, eyes glazed, and Blaize crouched next to her, checking her over.

"Where's Tierra?" Despite being both naturally athletic and in great condition, his fierce sprint left him breathless and panting, desperation for air mixing with fear for Tierra clawing at his lungs.

Adam glanced at him. "With Clay."

Fintan's heart rate shot up further. *Shit shit shit.* There was no time to pretty it up. "Clay's dead. We need to find Tierra."

Adam's eyes flickered, and his mouth tightened. Fintan knew his friend well enough to understand the flood of emotion those small facial moments indicated on his normally impassive face. Argus whined.

Adam's gaze swept the others. "I've sent Ymir to track the Rogue, and anyone he was with. We couldn't identify him because he hid his face. We'll stay in pairs. Search the area, Cuinn and Fintan. Blaize stay with Ai. I'll track alone."

"Are you sure you should be alone?" said Cuinn. "We don't know if they're still out there."

"Adam's like a ghost." It was the right call. And they needed less arguing, and more action. "He's right, we can cover more ground like this."

Adam acknowledged Fintan with the barest movement of his head. Tierra was important to them both. "Phones everyone?"

They all nodded.

"Check in with me by text every ten minutes. I'll check in with Fintan. Look for any trace."

"Check in with me too," Blaize said. "And hold on a second."

Ai was shivering continuously, and tears streaked her cheeks, though she hadn't made a sound since Fintan had arrived.

"Ai, can you tell us who was with the man we were fighting? Or how many came tonight with him? Or anything about their energies?"

Fintan knew she was right to gather more information before they went hunting, but the delay was almost intolerable. He needed to be taking action. His hand burned as his energy pooled inside him, boiling to get out.

More tears escaped from the girl's eyes, and she put her hands over her face. Blaize sighed, and started to stand, but before she could, Ai's muffled voice said, "They told me their energies. The male is Muladhara-Anahata and the female is Manipura-Ajna."

Ai's distress ramped up to the extent that even Fintan, with his weak empathy from his Anahata, could feel her emotions. Ai had no ability to shield, had never been taught how to manage her feelings as most energetics were taught in their basic training, and she was broadcasting to all of them terror, horror, anxiety and more.

He wanted to comfort her, but he needed to find Tierra. The addition of Ai's emotions on top of his own heated his body further, and the damp ground under his feet started to smolder.

He needed to calm down. Or at least present a calm exterior, while he raged inside. Adding to Ai's distress wouldn't help any of them.

Because Tierra was the best of them. And she was gone.

Tierra was blindfolded, gagged with material across her mouth and nose, and her ankles were tied. Her hands were bound in front of her and to her waist, so she couldn't move them. Lying on her side, she could feel every single bump in the road.

She was nauseous, and having trouble concentrating enough to draw any energy. She was grateful she'd pulled so much in before, and was using that to heal the many injuries her body appeared to have sustained when she'd been hit across the back of the head.

She had no idea how long she'd been in the car, and she'd already tried everything she could to escape. There was nothing in the trunk with her, no handy serrated edge to cut her bindings like in movies, and her throat was sore from screaming and shouting through the gag whenever the car paused at a stop light.

Her breathing was fast and shallow, and she was close to hyperventilating. She needed to calm down. If she didn't, she'd never be in a state to take her opportunity to escape when it came.

She turned to the familiar in her mind, and composed a letter in her head.

Dear Me,

I need your help. I've been kidnapped.

Any thoughts?

Me.

The process, ridiculous though it might be, gave her comfort. She gave a sob of laughter. Writing thousands of replies to letters over the years, there was always a solution, no matter how complicated. Granted, none of the letters had involved kidnapping, but there was a way forward. Somehow. There had to be.

What she needed to do was stay away from the doubts that had been plaguing her since she'd become involved in this situation. Doubts that reminded her she wasn't like Blaize, strong, an energetic Warrior, trained in offensive and defensive magics and energies. She was a Healer. Her energies had been turned towards keeping family and friends safe within the home, providing security and a sense of comfort. She could ward a home, but her own personal shields were never up to much.

Oh. Damn. Okay, she needed to work harder at keeping away from the doubts, clearly.

She hoped the others were all okay. Had anyone else been taken? No one else was in the trunk with her, anyway. Which was a good thing.

Unless they were all dead.

Source, no.

She set her mind against the idea. It was unthinkable. *Plus, no one else is as stupid as me, getting captured.*

The road surface changed from smooth tarmac to something that sounded more crunchy. Were they on a driveway? A country lane? Would they stop?

Saliva pooled in her mouth, and she swallowed, before the foul fabric stretched between her teeth soaked it up. *Source, protect me.*

She needed a plan. She had no way to attack, but she could shield herself a little with the energy she'd drawn previously. Even on this surface, the car drove too quickly for her to be able to draw on Muladhara energy when she was feeling this ill. She could, however, draw on Anahata, the energy of air. She wished she'd spent more time building it up before the fight, but she really hadn't thought it would be useful, and there was only so much energy an energetic could cache inside themselves.

She breathed in deeply, trying not to choke on the fumes in the trunk, and her own sweat and tears. The air came thickly through the gag, but she was able to fill her lungs several times. The deep breathing calmed her, and she drew energy through her Anahata Chakra, concentrating on the space between her breasts where the Chakra was located.

The car drew to a stop, and minutes passed. She kept her breathing steady. She would remain calm, and she would look for opportunities to escape. She might be terrified, but she was also determined. She had unfinished business with Fintan, for starters. She drew on the thought of him for motivation. He would be so disappointed with her if she gave up. She could do this.

Muffled voices sounded around the car, at least two.

The trunk opened with a click.

It must now be after dawn, as light trickled past the edges of the blindfold. Not being able to see exacerbated her fear. Someone grabbed her arm and yanked her to the front of the trunk. She tried to maintain a personal shield to make herself harder to grasp, but couldn't keep it steady.

She wriggled ineffectually, and got a casual backhand across the face that left her stunned. It stopped further resistance from her, as she was pulled up and out, and hoisted over someone's shoulder like a sack of flour. She was shivering, her mind so overwhelmed it was blank. She knew she needed to try harder, but without the ability to touch the earth to draw on its energy, and with her terror blocking her capacity to draw on the air, she couldn't use her energies. Her physical body was equally useless, trussed up and draped over someone's shoulder.

Breathe. Breathe.

She concentrated on that as they moved to an area where the noise of the footsteps changed – inside? There would be a chance to escape at some point. All she had to do right now was keep herself in as good a shape as possible so she could take that chance when it came. And to try and take in any information she could about her environment.

The sound of the footsteps was dampened in some way – carpet, perhaps? She was carried up stairs, a door creaked open, and she was put down on a soft surface. Rough fingers loosened her wrist bindings.

Without sitting up, she tore them apart, and ripped off her blindfold. Before she'd adjusted to the murky darkness, the door was slammed and locked.

She rubbed feeling back into her wrists, and tried to rip the gag out of her mouth. It was tightly knotted at the back, but with some effort she was able to yank it down so it was around her neck. She'd work on removing the disgusting thing later.

Could she stand? No. Her shaky legs could use a bit more rest before she tried it.

She was in a bedroom, on a bed. A window next to the bed leaked weak morning sunshine into the room. There were two doors. She needed to try them, though she didn't hold out much hope they'd open. She pushed against the wall and swung her feet onto the floor, standing slowly, a newborn deer taking its first steps.

She wobbled to the first door. Locked. She rattled it a bit, but there was no give at all. She moved to the second door, determined. It opened, and her stomach lurched. But it only led to a bathroom. Her shoulders drooped.

She sighed. Perhaps the water would help her wake up. She ran the faucet and splashed water over her face. She rinsed out her mouth, desperate to be rid of the taste of the gag. She felt a tiny bit better, but she was glad there was no mirror.

She searched the rooms. She made slow and thorough progress, twice, and took stock of her surroundings.

A small bathroom, which held precisely one bar of soap and some toilet paper.

A large bedroom. About twenty-five square feet. A bed, with bedding. A cupboard, a wardrobe, a chest of drawers. All empty, with no hangers, or anything else she could use as a weapon.

And a thoroughly locked door.

CHAPTER

26

Fintan, Adam, Blaize, Cuinn and Ymir spent the night searching the park. They didn't come across another living soul, apart from the park police, whose patrols they avoided.

Every moment that Tierra was missing more and more rage built in Fintan. His view was that she was long gone, but they had no other leads than the park.

The idea that Tierra might be suffering while they blundered around the park hoping to find a clue infuriated him. It might be a cool night, but his rage and energy kept him hot.

Ymir found a trail going away from the lake towards the outer edges of the park, which was likely to be from the person who took Tierra, easier to track because the impressions were deeper, presumably from carrying her. They led to a small beach where it looked like a boat might have been drawn up onto the shore. It seemed they'd left by sea – and none of Fintan's group was able to track across water, or had any affinity with Svadisthana, the water Chakra. They were at a dead end.

Fintan wanted to raze the park to the ground.

They continued searching, but eventually, an hour or two before dawn, Adam texted to say they needed to leave. They had to move Clay's body so park police didn't find it, or worse, a tourist or jogger.

Adam and Ymir undertook the macabre task, and drove out of Vancouver and back to Cathair Cuinn. Blaize, Fintan and Cuinn took Ai to their new hotel.

The girl still hadn't spoken. Blaize had asked her a few questions while they sat together, waiting while the others searched, but the girl didn't respond, staring into space without acknowledging the questions. There was none of the bravado that Fintan had seen in his previous interactions with Ai. It was as if the spirit had been sucked out of her.

Back at the hotel, while Blaize got the girl showered and changed, Cuinn sat on the bed in Fintan's connecting hotel room. "I think you need to try and talk to her, Fintan. You have some sort of connection with her, even if she doesn't trust you right now. You need to rebuild the connection and get through to her."

Fintan shoved his hands in his jacket pockets. Deep inside, he was cold. Icy cold. But his hands were hot, and they itched with the need to use his power. To find an outlet for it.

To destroy whoever had taken Tierra.

"I'm not sure that's a good idea." It really, really, wasn't. He wasn't stable right now. His energies bubbled inside him, screaming to be let out. Anyone could be a target if he let his guard down for a second. Ai was innocent, if foolhardy, and he needed to protect her, not put her in the line of fire.

"It's not the girl's fault Tierra was taken, Fintan." Cuinn's voice was gentle.

"I know that. I'm afraid for Tierra. And I'm angry. I can't afford to lose control, and I'm balanced on a razor's edge right now." He picked up the cushion from the arm chair and a smell of burning crept into the room. He dropped it on the bed, and scorch marks stood out starkly on the cream embroidery.

"You have to control it, Fintan. We need you." Cuinn sat on the edge of the bed, face equable.

Fintan breathed in deeply, and packed his energy down, wrapping it around his Manipura Chakra so the area behind his navel felt white hot. He might need the energy later – he couldn't afford to dissipate it. But Cuinn was right; he needed better control.

"It's fine," he said. "I just want to be doing something, not talking to a frightened teenager."

"She's our only lead. If we can't get anything from Clay's body, and we don't know where the boat took them, the only thing we have is Ai. She might be able to give us information on who the kidnappers were, why they wanted Blaize and Tierra, and where they're staying. She won't talk to Blaize. She needs someone she's familiar with. You have the best chance of rebuilding trust." Cuinn put a hand on Fintan's shoulder, wincing only slightly as the heat from Fintan's body penetrated though his jacket and then Cuinn's hand.

Cuinn seemed rational, reasonable. How much effort was it taking for him to stay that way, when Tierra was like a sister to him? Though perhaps it was just his Ajna, providing him with a logical, rational outlook on the world.

Lucky him, to have a reasonable energy.

Fintan shrugged Cuinn off and stood. "Fine."

He wished again that Tierra was here. She was the one best suited for this kind of emotional task, not him.

He knocked at the connecting door between the hotel rooms before pushing it open. Blaize paused in combing through Ai's dark hair, one hand on the girl's shoulder.

Ai was dressed in a pair of Blaize's jeans, which hung off Ai's sharp hips, and gave her a waif-like appearance. A T-shirt and a hoodie were also a little too big. She appeared the frightened child that she was, not like the belligerent goth she'd first presented as.

When she saw Fintan, her eyes widened, and her pupils dilated.

It awoke his protective instincts, but didn't calm his rage. If anything, it moved it from hot to cold – the sort of burning cold that blistered and burned. Now he had two people he wanted to keep safe.

Blaize stood, kept one hand resting on the girl's shoulder. "Fintan. Your energy is unstable. We don't have anyone with Anahata to help you if it twists. Be calm."

She stepped in front of Ai, who peered round her legs.

"I'm calm."

He wasn't. Not really. And he was worried what that might mean.

Ai stood and stumbled. Blaize let her step forward, but kept a hand on the girl.

"Are you hurt?" he asked. Concern for her flickered, but just stoked the rage further. It pressed on him like a physical weight.

She shook her head.

"Did they...?" He wasn't sure how to ask someone if they'd been drained. Especially a child. "Did they take any of your energy?"

A tear trickled down one of her cheeks.

Blaize shifted her hand to prop the girl up, mouth a flat line. Her eyes locked on his but he couldn't hold her gaze. He paced to the other side of the room. He was so hot.

He spun on one heel to face them. The girl stepped back into Blaize, who put a protective arm around her. "It's okay, sweetie. He's just worried about Tierra."

Blaize's eyes didn't match the soft tone of voice she'd used with Ai. "Aren't you, Fintan?"

"Where did they hold you?" The question burst from him. "We weren't able to track her. We don't know what they want with her. We don't know where she is."

So much for careful. A wave of energy spun out of him. He was parched. He knelt next to the minibar and grabbed a bottle of water, draining it in one long drink. The bottle it came in was plastic, and it gave way under the heat of his hand.

"Fintan," Blaize said. "Get a grip, for Source's sake."

His mind was filled with images of Tierra. Tierra being leeched from, drained. Tierra being harmed or intimidated to the point this girl had been. He imagined the girl's eyes were Tierra's, frightened and in pain. He took a step towards her, wanting to help. His brain was fuzzy, heated.

"Ah, hellfire," said Blaize. She darted across the room and grabbed him. She dragged him into the small bathroom and pushed him so he fell painfully into the tub, the shower curtain slowing his fall a little.

"What are you...?"

Blaize turned on the shower and steam hissed around him, as the heat in his body caused it to evaporate.

"You're on fire, you idiot." Blaize sprayed him with the shower head. Too dazed to do anything, he half sat, half lay across the bath, his clothes soaked and charred.

Cuinn was at the door, blocking Ai from seeing what was happening. Through the steam that was filling the room, Fintan caught sight of himself in the bathroom mirror. His eyes were wild, his hair slicked down to his head with water. His clothes hung off him in wet tatters. He looked a mess.

He laughed, wild and fierce.

He hadn't lost control of his energy in centuries. He'd kept it together through battles, wars, and numerous terrifying or difficult situations.

But he'd lost it twice in the last couple of weeks, and the cause had been the same in both cases.

Tierra.

Wonderful, beautiful, kind, Tierra.

Ahhh, shit.

He was in love with Tierra.

His stomach lurched at the idea, which was both terrifying and wonderful.

He staggered to his feet. What if he never got to tell her? What if before he got to act on it, he lost her?

His mind whirled. They had to get her back.

A noise woke Tierra. A woman stood inside the room with her, the door shut at her back. Why was she there? What did she want?

Tierra sat up, and put her feet on the floor. She needed to be ready to take any chance to get out of here. But right now, even if Tierra had the wit or the energy to tackle the woman, there was nowhere to go.

Maybe she could appeal to her. Tierra believed people were good at heart.

"Help me, please. Let me go." Tierra placed her hands behind her ready to push herself off the bed and take any opportunity that came to escape. The woman would have to open the door again to get out.

The woman laughed unpleasantly. "I don't think so."

The spark of optimism in Tierra sputtered out. She got to her feet, trying not to look like a threat, which wasn't very difficult given how beat up she felt.

The woman was short, plump, and seemed to be of Indian descent. She didn't look much like the 'baddie' Tierra had imagined. But then, the War had taught her that evil came in all shapes and sizes.

"Who are you?" she asked. The more information she could gain, the better.

"Jowaki, not that that really matters though, does it? I've brought you food. If you're lucky, you'll see the Maven soon. It's for him to explain what's what."

Tierra pushed a thread of Anahata towards the woman. Perhaps she could read the woman's emotions and understand more about what was happening. They tasted ugly. Avaricious, desperate, angry. Twisted, without a doubt, so another Rogue. A chill went through Tierra. It was rare for Rogues to work together, but this was evidence it was happening.

Weak Manipura-Ajna energy came from the woman. Very weak. But then, Manipuras trained physically as well as energetically, so Tierra knew not to underestimate her.

"Why do you want me? And Blaize?" Tierra tried for reasonable.

"I don't want you. But he's got a plan for you, I imagine." She shrugged. "I do what I'm told."

She put the tray she held on the chest of drawers at the side of the room.

"Who is he? Why do you do what you are told, when you must know this is wrong? Let me go, please." Tierra no longer held out much hope the woman would listen, now she knew what the woman was, but she couldn't help but try.

"Why? Because the rewards are great." The woman leaned towards her and licked her lips. "Be happy you're not my type."

"What do you mean?"

The woman laughed and turned away.

"Wait." Tierra took a shaky step. If the woman left who knew when the next person would come. Tears burned her eyes. She was so bruised and battered, every movement she made was a misery.

The woman moved closer to the door, her muscles tense.

"Please," begged Tierra. "What's going to happen to me?"

Before Tierra could get closer, the woman slipped out, and there was a click as the door was locked.

Tierra walked to the chest of drawers and pulled the tray towards her. She poked at the food on it. There was a sandwich, an unopened packet of chips and a sealed bottle of water.

Tierra cracked the water open and drank. The water quenched the thirst she'd been trying to ignore. Then she opened the chips and ate those. She was more hesitant about the sandwich. She left it to the side for the moment.

The food and the drink helped. The sun was up fully now, and the room was light, but another visual examination didn't bring up any new objects in the room. There was nothing she could do much with, even if she knew how. She was no inventor, couldn't create something out of nothing.

She swallowed over a knot in her throat. A tear crept down her cheek. She dashed it away with her palm. *Blaize wouldn't cry.*

That was a good idea. Channel Blaize. What would Blaize do? How could she tap into Blaize? Ah. She could write Blaize a letter. And have Blaize answer. Tierra's empathy was strong – it was how her answers to readers of her advice column were so popular. She'd never tried to answer as anyone else, but it was possible.

"Dear Blaize,

I'm trapped. I have no fighting abilities, and I'm in a room with very little furniture and no exits. I've seen one woman, and I don't know why I'm here. I'm scared.

What should I do?

Tierra.

Dear Tierra,

You say you have no fighting abilities. Yet you're an energetic, and you still have access to your power. You're a strong Muladhara and Anahata. What are your strengths? Use those to figure a way out.

Blaize.

She looked around the room with fresh eyes, and less emotion. Right. There was no point in feeling sorry for herself. That wasn't going to get her out of here.

She picked up the wooden tray her food had come on and swung it experimentally. Could she use this as a weapon? It was light, and her swings didn't give it much power or momentum. She put it down and went to the window.

She seemed to be at the back of the property, and on at least the third floor. There were fields surrounding the house, no other properties, and trees to the right. The garden was unkempt, as though once it had been tended, but not for many months.

Tierra tried the window. Locked. Of course.

She sat back on the bed, elbows on her knees, chin in her hands.

As she did so, she caught sight of something on her wrist.

It was a finely woven bracelet, delicate silk cords wound tightly together. The colors were red, yellow, green and white. Pretty, but she'd never seen it before. Was this from her captors? She tugged at it, but there was no end to catch hold of, and she had no cutting edge that she could rub against to cut the cords. She tried stretching it so that she could pull her hand out, but it was snug around her wrist, with little give.

What is it? She hoped it wasn't some kind of tracking device her captors had put on her. There didn't seem to be any electronics in it though. *Perhaps it was energetic?* She sent a fine thread of Muladhara in, and got an answering ping. Huh. She tried with Anahata, and got another ping.

She regarded her wrist again. It was on her left wrist, which was traditionally the feminine side in energetics. And red was the color of Muladhara, and green was the color of Anahata. What about yellow? Manipura. It was the color of Manipura. Was that relevant? She didn't have any Manipura energy, so she couldn't see if it pinged to that. Who did? Blaize. And Fintan.

The pieces of the puzzle came together so quickly that she gasped.

Blaize had a wrist band like this. Given to her by Source. And Cuinn had one too. A matching one. The colors of their wrist bands matched their combined energies. With white, the color of Sahasara running through them.

They hadn't been able to get theirs off either, or understand exactly why they had them.

She had one bracelet. Did that mean there was another? Who had it? Her stomach squeezed painfully. Fintan was a match, with Manipura to add to the mix. Did he have a corresponding band? Her breathing quickened as she realized she wasn't sure which was more terrifying – the idea that he might have the other, or the idea he might not.

She really hoped she had the chance to get out of here and find out.

CHAPTER
27

Fintan moved between the soaked bathroom and the bedroom in a dazed, sodden state. He sat in a chair in the room where Ai was propped against one of the beds, her legs pulled close to her, her arms wrapped around them.

Blaize had thrown a towel onto the chair, and another around Fintan's shoulders, but his messy hair still dripped onto the carpet.

Cuinn and Blaize talked in low, urgent tones across the other side of the bedroom. They were all on edge. Then something caught Cuinn's eye and he came over to Fintan and grabbed him by the wrist, eyes widening.

"What?" Fintan said.

"What's this?" Cuinn shook Fintan's arm.

Fintan stopped and looked at his wrist, frowning at what he saw there. "Ow. I don't know. What is it?"

"You don't? When and where did you get it?"

"It wasn't there yesterday. Or when I got off the plane." He'd never seen it before. He gave it an experimental poke. Where had it come from? And what was it? He didn't wear jewelry. He frowned.

"What's the problem?" said Blaize from next to the bed, where she was encouraging Ai to drink.

Cuinn beckoned and she came over.

"Give me your left hand." She complied and Cuinn tugged her forward so she stood in front of the men. Cuinn turned her wrist to show her bracelet. As he was using his right hand, the tightly bound cords around his own wrist also became visible.

Fintan's frown deepened. This wasn't good. He moved his wrist next to theirs. The bracelets were identical, apart from the colors. "Uh…"

"Fintan. Who has the matching bracelet?" Cuinn spoke urgently.

"I don't know! I've never seen it before. Maybe there isn't one." Fintan's voice was strangled. This was too much to take in. He'd known he was involved in the damn prophecy, but this took it to another level.

Blaize cocked her head as she examined him. Her eyes narrowed. "Is it possible Tierra has the matching bracelet?"

Fintan sucked in a breath, his insides fluttering. Could she? What would it mean if she did? Or, Source, what if someone else had the bracelet? The fluttering coalesced into a rock, and his stomach clenched. Another woman? He didn't want anyone else. He just wanted Tierra. Shit! He wanted her. But he couldn't have her. Or could he? Did the bracelet change things? He wished his damn brain was working properly.

"Tierra? Why would Tierra have it?" Cuinn asked.

Fintan jolted in the chair, half-naked and dripping wet. He glanced at the door, considering an exit, but there was nowhere for him to go. In his flash of realization about Tierra, he hadn't considered that he might have to face Cuinn before he told Tierra herself. He couldn't see Cuinn being that happy about it, and Fintan would understand why.

If she had the matching bracelet, that was good, wasn't it? That meant his stupid behavior hadn't put her off completely. He had a chance.

Oh shit.

He was going to have to tell Adam he was in love with his sister.

Oh double shit.

He was also going to have to tell Tierra.

Tierra eventually gave in and ate the sandwich.

She needed to get out of here, but had no idea how. Her energies were low, and the level of fear she was feeling was limiting the amount of Anahata she was able to pull.

Restless, she alternated between standing at the window and sitting on the bed. She wanted to take a shower, to see if the water might freshen up her brain, but the idea of being naked when anyone might come in made her feel sick. She washed herself as best she could in the sink.

Dusk fell, and she could no longer see out the window. There were no lights in the surrounding countryside. *I wonder where the nearest town is.* How far was she from help?

Could she smash the window and use the sheets to climb down? She'd seen it in films, or read about it in books. But when she tried to find something to smash the window with, she'd come up blank. The drawers in the chest of drawers didn't come out. The furniture was all too heavy to lift. Her energetic gifts didn't allow her the power to smash the window. Which was a shame, as the energy of air could certainly help her drift the couple of stories down to the ground.

She picked up the tray, and enhanced it with Muladhara, and made it heavier. If she could even crack the window, she might be able to use her elbow, covered in the duvet, to smash it. She was at the window, deciding on the best angle to strike, when the door opened again.

This time, Tierra was quicker. She ran to the door, clutching the tray to her like a shield. She tried to barge past whoever was on their way in, but a thick arm caught her with ease, and flung her back into the room, the tray slipping from her grasp to the floor with a thud.

Tierra fell to the floor, gasping for breath, and the door slammed on her hope of escape. Worse, the man was in the room with her. He loomed over her, smiling. "Well, now. Hello, little rabbit."

His eyes were more than avaricious, they were proprietary. This man wanted her, and looked at her like she was already his.

Tierra's bones turned to water. The other woman had scared her, true, but not like this. He took a step towards her and she shuffled further out of reach. With his second step, she hit the wardrobe behind her.

"What do you want?" She pulled a feeble shield around her, and at the same time threw out a thread to see what his energies were, and how powerful he was. If his energetic powers matched his physical strength, she was in trouble.

He was an energetic match for her, Muladhara-Anahata. Was he like Indigo? Was he going to leech from her?

His powers weren't at the same low ebb as the woman's, but they weren't as strong as her own. If she could get him to engage energetically, she might be able to beat him. But she'd need to concentrate to use her own energies.

"What I already have, little rabbit – you. My colleague has had to go into Seattle to sort out a problem, so you're all mine." His voice was seductive, silky, and yet grated like nails on a chalkboard. She scooted to her feet and darted to the side, to keep out of arm's reach.

But his arms were longer than hers. One of his hands shot out and enfolded her upper arm. He dragged her towards him, crushing her up against himself. His other hand tangled in her hair, stretching her neck out like a sacrifice. She struggled in his grip, and he laughed.

He leaned down, and licked from her collar bone up to her ear. He gave her ear lobe a painful nip. She sobbed. Her free arm tried to push him away, but that made him laugh harder.

"You won't be able to fight your way out from me, little rabbit." He watched her writhing as if she were a fish on a line, caught between the hand in her hair, and the hand which was now painfully tight on her arm.

"It's not my intention to hurt you. Oh no. Anything but. I want you fresh." He threw her with casual violence onto the bed. She bounced, winded, and started to get off the other side, but he pulled her back by the hem of her top. It strained around her neck and she choked. Her hands flew up to release the pressure, and she toppled backwards. He put a knee on her closest arm, pinning it to the bed.

She couldn't think. All the self-defense she'd learned, even that which Fintan had taught her recently, had gone.

The only thing inside her was terror.

CHAPTER
28

Fintan had finally managed to divert Cuinn from talking about Tierra and the bracelets. They were hardly a priority right now despite Cuinn's belief they were a key part of the prophecy. They had to find Tierra. Ai had finally drifted into a restless sleep, and Fintan, Cuinn and Blaize talked in low voices in the adjoining hotel room. Fintan was really sick of this hotel. He'd had enough of being caged in this bland room.

"We're getting nowhere," Fintan said. He'd been turning possible avenues over in his head, and was struggling to see a way forward. His usual dispassionate evaluation of a problem was gone, and he was all fire and energy. He needed to burn some of it off by doing something, and soon.

"I found a report of a leeching of a teenage Ajna-Muladhara energetic across the border in Seattle," he said. "We don't have much detail on it, but it might be connected. Maybe I could go there and see if there are any other leads?"

Cuinn frowned. "Leechings are rare. If we get a handful a year across the whole continent I'd be surprised. So it would be quite odd to have an unrelated leeching so close by without it being connected, but equally we have no evidence it's relevant. It could be a fool's errand. Do you really think it's the best use of your time?"

"I can't stay here and do nothing," Fintan bit out. "I need to be doing something. What else do we have here? You guys can go into the ether for leads. I can't. And it doesn't look like I'm the right person to get something out of Ai. I don't see anything I can be doing here."

"I've called Nixie to see if she can come sooner," said Blaize. "I thought if we could work out who one or two of the unidentified energetics were in the prophecy we might be able to ask them for help. Or find out if anything strange had been happening to them."

"Once Adam's dealt with Clay's body, he and Ymir will keep searching the park," Cuinn said. "I'll dreamwalk, and Blaize can question Ai."

Blaize nodded. "I can use Ajna to relax her so she can access as much information as possible."

"She should be our best lead," Cuinn said. "But she's so traumatised it's hard to know if we'll get anything useful out of her."

"I'm going to call Jeb at the Anahata Guild," Fintan said. He didn't think the man would come here, but who knew, he might have a feeling, a lead – Fintan would take anything. And if they needed him in Vancouver, then Fintan would do everything in his power to get him here. He hoped to Source that Jeb's fondness for Tierra might force him out of his self-imposed confinement in Anahata, and that his injury wasn't so bad it meant he couldn't leave.

Fintan set his mouth in a hard line. He needed to do something. The prospect of dragging Jeb here was satisfying just because it was action, but it didn't feel like it would truly accomplish much.

He would go to Seattle. He would follow the lead, and find Tierra.

I won't let her down again.

Fear clogged Tierra's throat. With her arm pinned by his knee, both the big man's hands were free. One closed over her breast, squeezing it. Pain blossomed in the delicate area. Tierra struggled harder, trying to get her legs up to kick him. Her breath was rapid and her vision blurred.

"Shhhh," he crooned. And bent down, looming over her.

There was a bang on the door, and he looked towards it, jaw clenched. Tierra writhed in his grip.

The door opened, and bounced against the wall with a crash. A tall, slender woman entered.

"Dagon." Her tone was lazy, but carried a threat. "You're wanted. There's no time for games."

She didn't spare a glance for Tierra, who tried to scream for help. The man looming over her frowned, and backhanded her in the face. "Shut up."

Pain exploded in her face, and she sobbed. She could feel the imprint of his knuckles throbbing on her cheek. Dagon ignored her whimpers, and to the woman, he said, "I'm busy."

She shrugged and turned. "Not my funeral."

She caught hold of the door handle and began to leave.

"Fine, fine. Wait." He turned to Tierra, and put one hand around her neck, squeezing a little. Tears streamed down her cheeks, but she was too frozen in fear to scream.

He leant down and put a parody of a lover's kiss on her lips. She had nowhere to go, and wanted to throw up when his mouth touched hers. A whimper tore from her throat as he pushed her into the soft mattress and got up.

Before she could move away, he gave her a final backhand across the face, snapping her head to the side. Pain thudded into her cheek on top of the last strike, hot and sore. She put her hands on her face and curled up into a ball, trembling with relief at his exit.

The woman left as well, the lock snicking shut behind her once more.

Tierra lay on the bed, and cried.

She was a failure.

All the things she'd told Fintan and the others, about being able to protect herself, were a lie. She'd been captured, and assaulted. And what had she done to defend herself? Nothing. She'd frozen with fear, and sobbed like a child and let that animal touch her. She clenched her hands, her body closed in on itself.

Had she been brought here to be raped? She shivered, the trembling increasing. Her muscles were like water, and she couldn't get her thoughts in order.

No. She shook her head. She wouldn't stay and wait for that. She would do whatever it took to get out of here. She might be scared, petrified, in fact, but she would force herself to get up, and try and think of something – anything! – that might help her get out of here.

She would not let herself, and her family, down.

And she would find out if Fintan had the matching bracelet, and what Source needed from them. She was caught up in something bigger than herself, but she couldn't play that role if she gave into the fear trying to consume her.

She pushed herself shakily up from the bed, and went to the bathroom to wash her face. She took a few moments for the cold water to bring her back to the here and now. To gather herself.

Back in the bedroom, she picked up the tray and concentrated on it. She pushed Muladhara into it, grateful that it was wood and a natural material she was able to work with. She made it as dense as she could and hefted it again. It was heavy in her hand. She might have a chance.

If necessary she'd use it to hit a person, but she would try to get away without violence first. She was in mid-swing when the door opened. The tray smashed against the window with all the power she had. There was a boom, and a thin crack appeared in the window.

It wasn't enough. She spun in place, and drew the tray back to strike at whoever had come in.

Thank the Source, it wasn't Dagon. It was a woman, all angular cheekbones and a sharp bob of ash blonde hair. Tierra gritted her teeth. The woman might not look dangerous, but she hadn't responded to Tierra's previous cries for help. Tierra glanced at the door, shut, but possibly unlocked.

She set her lips, and swung the tray at the woman's head.

The woman caught it in her right hand, a modest exhalation accompanying the catch, and wrested the tray from her. "Good. That's helpful. They'll think you left that way."

She gave Tierra a little push, so she staggered and ended up leaning against the wall, then took the tray and smashed it against the window once more. A web of cracks appeared.

"I'm here to help you. I'm going to get you out." The woman was efficiently wrapping her arm in a pillow case.

Tierra was paralyzed, wanting to try and flee, to shove the woman out of the way, but seduced by this offer of help. She had no idea what was outside the door. If there were more people like Dagon, she didn't stand a chance on her own.

"Why?" Tierra would trust her gut on the answer. There was no time for analysis. She'd go to her energies, her feelings. What did they say? What could she feel?

"I'm Cassidy." The woman drew her arm back and rammed it against the window, which shattered. Shards of glass fell to the floor. Cassidy used the pillow case to clear out the remaining glass. "It's complicated. Come on."

She moved to the door with poise, but looked back when she realized that Tierra hadn't followed.

Tierra gazed at the woman, eyes wide. She needed to make a decision. This woman was known to Dagon, at least, and able to give him orders, yet at the same time, was someone who said she would help Tierra escape. It didn't feel like a trick. Though why weren't they going out the window?

"I'll get you out of here," Cassidy said. "Don't worry. The window's not the way, though. But we need to hurry, please."

Everything had happened too fast. Maybe Tierra should go out of the window? She thought she'd be able to support herself enough with air to fall and not break something.

But she might stand a better chance with Cassidy – if she was telling the truth.

Tierra threw out a little Anahata. She didn't want to waste it, as she had precious little energy. Cassidy felt like a strong Ajna-Muladhara, and the feelings she gave off appeared genuine. She planned to help Tierra. Tierra probed a little – was the woman's energy twisted? Tierra frowned. Not really. It was…dark, perhaps, but not wrong. Emotionless, as if her Ajna ruled her with an iron fist. Tierra doubted she would have been able to sense the Muladhara if she hadn't had the energy herself.

"Quick. Follow me." The woman ordered Tierra with the tone of one who was used to being obeyed.

Tierra went with her gut, and trusted. She followed the woman, and the smallest flicker of relief crossed the woman's face. *Wow, she really rivals Adam for self-control.*

The woman slipped out the door, and locked it once Tierra was also in the corridor. They jogged along to a grubby looking staircase.

"Servants' quarters," Cassidy explained, her voice low. "We rarely use it."

Tierra followed her. Cassidy put a finger to her lips. There was little light in the stairwell, but what Tierra could see of Cassidy's skin was as pale and translucent as a pearl. They went down two flights of stairs. At another door, Cassidy paused.

"I need to tell you some things. You must take them back to Cuinn. Do you understand?"

So she knew Cuinn, too. Tierra nodded, none the wiser. The woman seemed impassive, emotionless, while a roman nose and dark blue eyes gave her a regal look, despite the jeans and shirt she was wearing.

"I believe you were taken to wound Cuinn. I didn't realize what was happening until too late."

Who was this woman? And what was she to this house? "If you're not involved in kidnapping me, who was?"

The woman hesitated. "Elrian."

Tierra gaped, staring. Cassidy had to be mistaken. "Elrian? Are you sure? He wouldn't hurt me."

Cassidy laughed bitterly. "If you think that, you don't know him at all."

She unbuttoned the first two buttons of her shirt and pulled the material back to show her left shoulder. Even in the dull light of the staircase, Tierra could see the dark yellow and browns of a deep bruise. It looked like a nasty injury.

Tierra's mind reeled. Things had just got a lot more complicated.

"Cuinn, and anyone he loves, is in danger. But I think there's more going on. I can't quite get to the bottom of it – it's already gone much further than I'd realized. He hasn't let me in on his plans for a while."

Tierra needed to get back to Cathair Cuinn. This information changed everything. "Who are you?"

Cassidy shrugged. "No one important. I've done some prophecy work for Elrian. He says the prophecy work he has done shows him heading the Major Circle. But when I dreamwalk, the prophecy slivers I see show him standing on a barren wasteland, in a future lifeless Earth. If he wins ... he'll do so at the expense not only of the energetics, but the world. If he wins, he'll somehow destroy the balance."

Her gaze drilled into Tierra. "He can't win. I've been trying to persuade him to take a different approach, and I thought it was working, but he seems to have stopped sharing his plans with me."

Elrian. Elrian was behind this? The others needed to know. She considered asking Cassidy to take her to him, so she could talk to him – because surely, surely, there was something else going on here. The man she had known had been angry, and bitter, but not violent.

Not a Rogue. And a Leech.

She shuddered. She wouldn't face him alone. She'd take this woman's help, get home, and bring the others back in force. It was time to stop being fearful, and be the energetic she used to be.

"I didn't realize he'd taken you." Cassidy hugged herself and rubbed her upper arms. "He's not going to like that I've found out, either."

"Come with me," Tierra urged. "You don't need to stay here. We'll bring others. My brother's a Protector and my – my friend is a Warrior. They can get us, you, help."

"I can't. You can," Cassidy said. "Tell Cuinn to find me in the ether. I think if we work together there we might be able to find out more. I might be able to explain your escape away, I'm not sure. My place is here, either way. I can do more good here."

"But ... he's hurting you." *Why would she stay?*

"I've told you. It's more complicated than that. And he loves me. I might be one of the few people who can stop this. Help the situation." Cassidy lifted her chin. "The other two energetics you met are Dagon and Jowaki. The latter trained as a Warrior."

Tierra was struggling to take it all in. Her cheek still throbbed, the pain distant but clear. She didn't understand this woman, who she was, why she would stay, but she would accept her help, and she would take the information home.

"Let me show you my energetic signature so you can share it with Cuinn. I'll plant it in your mind and he'll be able to see it, assuming he's as strong as everyone tells me he is."

Tierra nodded. She'd got this far trusting the woman, and her gut wasn't telling her anything different.

"Before you do, let me heal you," Tierra said. She could spare a little energy if she was getting out of here. She got the impression that the woman might take more damage for helping Tierra, which was sickening as an idea. "Have you had that looked at? You might have a fractured collarbone."

"I don't know if we have time," Cassidy said.

"Give me 30 seconds." Tierra didn't need long. She placed a hand either side of the injury, and spun power. Being underground didn't help with accessing air, but she was no novice. She fed energy into the woman's body, threading it through to first understand, and then heal. There was no nerve injury, and the slightest of fractures. Tierra increased blood flow to the area, sending energy with it, soothing the swelling and speeding the natural healing.

Cassidy stood, face impassive throughout the healing, even though Tierra was sure it must have caused her pain. But given how well she hid the injury in the first place – she'd caught the tray with her other hand, but it had to have jerked the opposite shoulder too – the woman's self-control was extraordinary.

When Tierra finished and drew back, Cassidy tugged her shirt back into place and nodded her thanks.

"Now. My turn, and let's get you out of here." It was Tierra's turn to nod, though she threw up some internal shields as best she could because she might be done being fearful, but that didn't mean she was going to be foolhardy. Cassidy reached out her hand and placed it on Tierra's cheek. Cassidy's power bled into her, and her body relaxed. She slipped into a blank, meditative state, only catching the last of Cassidy's whisper before everything went black. "But you can't bring the others back here. And before you get home, you have one more thing to do."

CHAPTER
29

Fintan rang the energetic who'd been looking into the leeching in Seattle, and told her he was coming to meet her. The woman was evasive, and didn't seem that keen to help, suggesting there was nothing to find, but Fintan shrugged it off. He'd make his own decisions about that.

He took the bike, and it ate up the miles. The border crossing chewed up some time, but he stayed civil with the police there, despite the desperate inferno inside him that wanted to burn the checkpoint to the ground.

A couple of hours later he was met by the local Warrior energetic, Jowaki, at the door of a bland apartment in the suburbs.

She jerked her chin in hello. "Like I told you on the phone, the place was wiped clean. There's nothing to find here."

She unlocked the door and gestured him in.

"Run me through it," Fintan said.

"A homeless kid's body was found after a window cleaner caught sight of him through the window."

"Any leads?" He paced around the studio.

She shook her head.

"The place was wiped down, physically and energetically. The police have nothing. But you're welcome to try your luck." She shrugged.

Jowaki leant against the door frame, arms folded across her chest. Fintan knew the tension building up in him wasn't leaving much room for compassion and tolerance of others, but he was surprised how cold her attitude was about the death of the youth.

He focused on the main room. It was big enough for a bed, a couch, a small table and a TV, a tiny kitchenette, and a bathroom with shower, sink and toilet. The whole place would have fitted in the lounge area of the house where they had found the other dead energetic, and was quite the contrast.

If they were connected the MO for the crime had changed a lot, which would be unusual. His heart sank. He'd pinned a lot on this place bringing him a lead.

Jowaki, a trained Warrior he'd never met before, hadn't moved. She was annoying him. She was unhelpful, and he didn't have the patience for games today. She needed to change her attitude or she was going to be an unfortunate target for the anger that brewed inside him, sullen and terrible. He might not be able to influence people's emotions like some Anahatas, but he would be happy to try a little brutal honesty.

"You understand that there's a woman's life at stake here?" he said. "We think this is related to two cases we have going on in the Vancouver area, one of them being the kidnapping of a friend of mine."

"I did my best, but I didn't get anywhere," Jowaki said, shifting her weight to the other foot.

"Where was he? What was the position? Who found him?" he fired questions at her, and excavated the details, fighting her apparent boredom. Maybe this was her way of showing grief? Or guilt that the energetics had let this happen? He narrowed his eyes. It didn't seem likely.

The boy – he was seventeen – had been found propped against the couch. Jowaki produced photos when prompted by Fintan, who was quickly getting tired of her attitude.

"Neither we nor the police have found anything to identify him," she said.

The photos showed a horribly thin, white male, his body wasted as though malnourished. He'd been drained over a period of time. The bed had been stripped, so it was hard to tell if he'd been kept here, but the marks on his wrists indicated he had been held somewhere against his will.

Fintan stalked the room for clues. For something, anything, that could connect this to Indigo and the previous leeching, and help him find Tierra. He clenched and unclenched his fists as he thought about her. Where was she?

"Have you come across anything like this before?" he asked.

"No." Jowaki rubbed the back of her neck.

Fintan frowned and stepped towards her, into her space. "Why aren't you helping me? What's going on here?"

He didn't have time for this. He would probably need to talk to her supervisor when they were through this crisis, but in the meantime, he needed to find out what she was hiding. He didn't really care why.

"It's a one-off. The perp probably left town already." She continued to lean against the door frame, but her hands dropped to her sides, loose. The room was full of tension, and Fintan's energy crackled inside him. He wasn't sure if this Warrior understood what a dangerous game she was playing by not just offering up all the information she had.

He cocked his head and stared her down. Her breath sped up, and her fingers flexed. There was something here.

"It's not like Indigo's work," she stuttered. "I don't think there's anything here for you to find."

He sucked in a breath, and she realized her mistake in that instant, her gaze shooting towards the door. Indigo's name and actions were a secret known only to a select few. There was no reason for this woman to know it, unless she knew a lot more than she had revealed. Fire flowed through him, ready to heed his call, and he stopped it escaping with an effort.

"What are you hiding? What do you know?" He crowded into her space and grabbed her shirt, his hand burning hot. He held the energy inside him, forcing it to stay there by sheer willpower. It wanted, needed, to be used.

She froze in his grasp for a few moments, and his energy darkened, wanting to hurt her. Shit. His energy was on the verge of twisting. His body trembled, muscles jumping. He thrust himself away from her, and at the same time he drove his energy into the floor around her, drawing up a cage of flame. As he did so, he shielded himself. She hissed, but didn't attack – yet.

"Tell me what you know," Fintan said, "and help me find Tierra, or so help me, Source, I will destroy you."

So be it.

If it took his energy twisting to find Tierra and keep her safe, he would suffer the consequences of that.

Tierra woke up with a jolt. Where was she now? She rubbed at gritty eyes, and her head pounded. She was slumped against a wall in a corridor that looked none too clean. What was this place? An apartment block? Why was she here?

What did she last remember? Being in that horrible house…Dagon…and Cassidy. Cassidy! She had helped her escape. But how had the woman made her forget the journey? She was an Ajna …but she'd have to be very gifted to be able to blur Tierra's memory like that. Plus it wasn't exactly forbidden, but it was frowned upon. There were few circumstances considered serious enough to change someone's memories of an event. It was too close to mind control for the energetics.

Why was Cassidy protecting people who hurt her? She didn't seem to have been a willing participant in Tierra's capture. And yet she stayed there, with a man – oh, Source, with Elrian – who had abused her.

Tierra needed to get home. She glanced around the space and saw no danger. She wasn't restrained, and she could see a sign to a fire exit. She pushed herself to her feet, wobbling slightly, and went rigid at a sound behind the door next to her. She pressed herself back against the wall and listened.

There were two voices, a woman and a man. Both sounded familiar. Had Cassidy brought her back to friends? Or dumped her into new danger?

Tierra drew on her limited reserves of energy, and pushed a little through the door. She could at least taste their energy to see if they were energetics.

Her frail tendrils touched on the two energetics, and she gasped.

She couldn't understand it. Both energies were dark – one twisted, and the other one so close to twisting she recoiled in disgust.

But ...one of them was Fintan.

CHAPTER

30

Tierra didn't hesitate. Even though he didn't know it, Fintan had been her strength while she had been captured. Her gifts meant she was one of the few people who could stop his energy twisting, and she would not let it happen.

She went through the door in a rush, and threw herself to the side, away from where her investigation had told her the two energetics were. She needed to get to him and draw off some of the excess energy before he used it for anything stupid.

She took in the room at a glance, and frowned. It made no sense. Fintan had the horrible woman, Jowaki, caged, but his eyes were wild, his Manipura energy visible and sizzling along his limbs and torso. If she was captured, why hadn't he stood down? Relaxed? Released the energy that was growing inside him?

He turned at her entrance, and let out a huge breath. His energy wavered but the cage around Jowaki held.

ELLEN BARD

"T! It's you? How are you here? You're safe? Thank Source," he said. He took a step towards her then hesitated, his forehead wrinkled. "Just ...wait. I need to...I'm not feeling great."

His eyes were unfocused, and the flames around Jowaki rose and fell, one minute scorching the ceiling, the next tightening around the woman's waist. The cage was there, but uncontrolled, and Jowaki, sensing this, held still, eyes wide, a grey tinge to her dark skin. She had shielded to keep his power from burning her, but she wasn't a match for him if he unleashed his power without limits.

And he was losing it.

Tierra drew a shield around her, and took one more pace towards him. She had to earth him. Out of control, he could destroy not only her and Jowaki, but this whole building. He was a powerful man.

"I just need a minute or two. I'll be okay in a minute," Fintan said. He hadn't moved, but his breath was harsh, heaving from somewhere deep inside him. The sparks were more noticeable now, and static electricity surrounded his body, his hair floating around his head like dandelion seeds.

There was a bang, and the electricals in the apartment shorted, the fuse box kicking in. She winced.

This wasn't the mild reining in his Manipura had needed in the restaurant before they'd met Ai.

This was the burn of fire and the searing of wind combined. The crash of a summer storm, wild lightning and dark thunder.

If she gave him a minute, they could be caught in a firestorm. One that might not even stop at this building, or city block.

She had no time to be scared for herself. Fintan was too important.

She reinforced her shields, then darted forward to close the gap between them. He put up a hand to stop her, but she braced and grabbed it. She crumpled over it in pain as his energy crashed into her body. She gritted her teeth. She could do this.

"Fintan?" she gasped. "I need you to listen to me."

He blinked at her, the blue of his eyes darkening like the storm. "T? You shouldn't be here. It's not safe. You need to be safe. I need you to be safe."

284

His words came like a mantra, his eyes unfocused. His energy pulsed, and he tried to push her away, but she held on tight, providing a lifeline to him. She needed to keep touching his skin.

She drew off a little of his energy and winced. It burned. She was going to need to channel it better. She'd have to use both her energies.

She spared a glance for the cage of fire. It held, but the bars were fierce. She wanted to trust the control Fintan had built over a lifetime of practice to ensure the flames of his energy didn't destroy anything in the apartment, but it would take just one moment and everything would be gone. For carpet, floor, furniture – and people – to catch fire. And she couldn't even be sure if he heard her, saw her.

She couldn't let him destroy this place. And not just for the obvious reasons. But because it would devastate him.

No, she would not let that happen.

There was a draught, and some papers blew off a table in one corner. Her eyes flicked over to them, and then to the closed window.

She buttressed her shields once more, bringing in both earth and air. She wound them together inside herself. She needed earth for its grounding properties, but air for healing.

And air carried risk. His was clearly active, from the soft currents that had begun to swirl around her feet. Active, and not under his full control.

Because while air could help her to draw off the negative energy, help stop him twisting, air also fed fire.

If she misjudged this, she could be the catalyst for the very catastrophe she was trying to avoid.

The room was now so hot, her lungs burned with each breath. She blinked away sweat that rolled down her temple, stinging her eyes, and sent a thin thread of earth and air into Fintan, and for want of a better description, given it was happening on the metaphysical plane, tied it to his energies. She tethered herself to him, so she had a bridge across which she could draw the energy from him more quickly, more smoothly.

He staggered, and fell. She went down with him, still clutching him physically as well as energetically. They faced each other on their knees, their foreheads touching. Every part of her that was in contact with his skin stung, but she needed to focus on the energy. She drew off more.

His blue eyes were luminous, glowing. She stared into them, but he didn't seem to see her. His gaze, inhuman and numb, was focused behind her head.

With Anahata, the energy of air and love, as their common energy, the nature of the bridge transmitted to her his feelings as well as the energy.

She closed her eyes. If Jowaki escaped, there wasn't anything she could do. She had to focus on Fintan if any of them were going to survive this.

She tried to breathe into the pain of his twisted energy being drawn out from him, through her. It was like draining poison from a wound – but from a well that was being refilled almost as quickly as she could extract it.

A river of energy washed over her, the feelings almost as unbearable.

Loneliness and isolation. Disconnection. Unworthiness.

He wanted a family, loved them as a family. But never felt he fitted in. Never felt he truly belonged.

His energy battered her, and she tried to root herself in her earth energy as it rushed through her. A sob tore from her throat as the feelings came close to overwhelming her.

She had never known how lonely he had been. He had always been the joker, everyone's friend. But all those lovers had been to fill a space inside him, a space that deep down, he didn't really feel deserved to be filled.

The energy burned hotter, waves of heat rolling off him. She clutched at his hand, and pressed her forehead harder into his. He was immovable, unreachable.

The only way to bring him back now was to siphon enough off him. It was a race.

Source help me, please.

She strengthened the bridge she'd built between them, and was able to bring the energy out of him and through her more quickly. She could disperse it when it hit her, her energy dissipating it harmlessly. Well, harmless to others. Not so harmless to her.

Sweat soaked her body, dripping down her back, and her grip on his hand was slippery. She tugged harder, drawing the energy off faster and faster.

More feelings, positive this time. The love he felt for her family.

The love he felt for her.

The bracelet around her wrist shone, and from the corner of her eye she saw a mate on his wrist shimmer.

She gasped, and wobbled on her knees, managing to hold on at the last minute.

His love for her wasn't like the love he felt for Adam, or Blaize. It was strong, and friendship was wound into it, along with respect. But unlike for her family, his love for her wove in desire, and longing, and intimacy.

Oh, Source.

He loved her. He really loved her.

The realisation burst over her, and gave her a boost, and she was able to increase the speed at which she bled the energy coming from him. The bracelet, whatever it was, enhanced her powers, rebounding and cleansing the energy that came from his, and adding another channel to get rid of the danger.

Malignant energy rushed through her, feelings and energy and power.

She grasped at it, siphoning faster and faster, as her own control wavered. Her head ached, her body throbbed. She was light-headed, unsure how much longer she could do this.

It couldn't need much longer though, surely. She needed to draw off a little more energy, hold on for a little more time, stay conscious and in control, and he'd be safe. Herself, not so much, but it was worth it.

She sucked in a breath, and went for another desperate effort, trying to let go of as many of her walls as possible. To open up to allow his power to surge through her.

The power smacked into her like a blow.

She held on one, two, three more seconds for it to move through her, then dissipate.

He blinked.

"T? What's going on? Why are we on the floor?" Fintan said. His eyes widened as he took her in, her nearness, their heads pressed together, almost close enough for their eyelashes to touch.

Another second, that's all she needed, for the deadly power to leave him. She didn't have the words to tell him, but she needed him to stay where he was, needed that skin-to-skin for the process to be complete.

He tilted his head, and the space between their mouths lessened as his forehead lifted off hers. She panicked. If she left any of the twisted energy inside him, the cycle could restart, and she didn't have the energy to drain it a second time.

But she was so tired. She couldn't raise her leaden limbs, couldn't form words.

She did the only thing she could think of to keep them touching.

She kissed him.

Then the last of the energy flowed from him to her, and with a low groan, she released it, harmlessly, into the air.

She slumped to the ground, exhausted, sparks dancing across her vision. She held on to consciousness a moment longer, enough time to see Fintan's eyes lose their glaze.

Then the sparks blinked out, and she lost herself to the darkness.

CHAPTER

31

The silence in the kitchen was charged. The men were in their own private worlds. Fintan sat at the table and stared into space. Adam stood at the window looking out at the grounds, Argus occasionally whining at his side. And Cuinn kept himself busy in the kitchen, pulling together a meal from leftovers in the fridge. This was the kind of situation none of them could fight.

Adam had asked Fintan what Tierra's status was, but he hadn't been able to tell them much. Yes, she was in one piece. But somehow she'd expended huge amounts of energy, and she still hadn't woken up by the time he'd handed her over to Cara. He wasn't sure what had happened.

Because he really didn't know.

The kitchen, usually the heart of Cathair Cuinn, usually Tierra's domain, was claustrophobic with too much over-protective male energy churning with nowhere to go. Fintan's skin buzzed, and he was torn between bolting out the backdoor to get into the air, or busting the door of Tierra's room down.

Burning something down would also feel pretty good.

He'd gone to meet that Warrior Jowaki to follow a lead, and find Tierra. And somehow, instead, she'd found him. But what the hell had happened in between? The last thing he remembered was caging Jowaki, then feeling sick. Tierra came in, and after that, he lost time.

Until the moments before she kissed him.

By the time Fintan was fully himself again, Tierra in a crumpled heap next to him, Jowaki was long gone. It had taken Fintan a while to piece things together, time when he'd been trying to rouse Tierra, using his rusty medical skills to assess her, and making calls to her family. He'd taken stock of the scene too, though Adam had sent Protectors to investigate properly, when it had struck him that he had done this to Tierra. He'd been the one she'd had to save the neighborhood from. His disturbed, inadequate energy.

He had rushed Tierra, who his limited healing energies told him was stable, if unconscious, back to Cathair Cuinn. It had been a frantic few hours. He'd had to dump the bike and get a car, and install her in the back. Somehow he'd got them through the border, showing their IDs and joking with the guards about his sleeping wife. His only thought had been to get her to the safety of family, where she could be looked after properly. He'd hoped the sleep she was in was healing, but he couldn't reach her in the physical world or with his energies.

On the horrible drive back, glancing at her in the rear-view mirror every few seconds, he knew the time had come to stop messing around. When she was better – and she would get better, he would see to that – he would tell her how he felt.

He still didn't think he deserved her, but if there was even a small chance they could make it work, and she might accept him, it was worth trying.

He'd thought this crisis they were all facing meant he shouldn't distract them with emotions. That now wasn't the time for relationships, or love.

But it was the opposite.

It was with love – lovers, family, friends, love of all types – that they were stronger. The prophecy showed a connected group of people who were somehow woven together as tightly as this damnable bracelet on his wrist. He didn't know all the players yet, or how someone like Ai might be connected, but their strength was in unity – that was something he knew.

And in partnerships like that of Cuinn and Blaize.

Maybe, just maybe, he and Tierra could be their own version of that if – no, when – she recovered fully.

If not? If she came to her senses and rejected him, he'd still work with the group. He wouldn't risk them all for his pride.

It would hurt, he knew that.

But it was time for him to stop playing around, and take a risk.

His shoulders sagged. He'd rather fight a Rogue.

The door opened, and Cara came in.

"Tierra is awake, and wants to talk through what happened, and she'd rather do it just once. Then she needs to sleep. Come through to see her."

There was a sense of relief in the men as they trooped after Cara to one of the empty suites that she'd set up as a small medical bay with both Tierra and Ai. The room was dim. Ai slept soundly in one bed, Blaize leaned down to talk to the occupant of the other.

Tierra's usually cheerful demeanor was dulled, her energy muddied and weak. Fintan ached to rush over to her. On the journey back he'd spotted her bracelet. He was desperate to talk to her about it, but knew he'd have to wait. For the moment he'd drawn his sleeve over his, unsure if she'd seen it already. With Cuinn and Adam balanced on the very edge of reason, the last thing he wanted was to discuss his relationship with Tierra. Especially before he had had a chance to discuss it with her.

The kiss … the kiss had given him hope, even though he knew it probably shouldn't. At the same time as he'd proved himself yet again unworthy of her, unable to hold his energy together, she'd saved him, taken herself to the brink to keep him together. That kiss had been her last way of drawing out the poisonous energy from him, and meant nothing more than that.

Did it?

He raked his eyes up and down her, deliberately searing her wan image into him. He had done this to her.

Tierra huddled in bed, sitting up but leaning heavily against a wall of pillows. She was wrapped in a huge hoodie. Argus threaded his way through the human occupants of the room, and nuzzled at her, and she absentmindedly patted him once, then drew her hand back. He huffed, and put his large silvery head on her thigh.

"The Rogue took me. And one of his team members let me go. I know you'll have questions, but I need you to let me talk it through chronologically before you do. Please." Argus gave her hand infrequent licks as she opened her story.

There were nods all round.

Cara put a hand on Tierra's arm and squeezed. "Whatever you need."

Tierra drew a deep breath, and talked them through the events of her kidnapping.

When she got to the part about Dagon, tears fell. The inflection of her voice never changed, but she groped for Blaize's hand, and held it while she talked.

If Fintan hadn't been so effectively grounded by Tierra so few hours before, this might have tipped him over the edge. His stomach burned as she described the assault.

Cara nudged him. "Keep it together."

When Tierra got to the part about Cassidy, Cuinn leaned forward, forehead wrinkled, foot tapping under the table. He'd have questions, Fintan knew. But they had Tierra back now. There was time enough.

"She's a powerful Ajna," Tierra continued. "She put an energetic picture of herself in my mind so you can contact her, Cuinn. The most scary thing is that I think she was able to hypnotize me. I have no memory of getting out of the house and to where Fintan was."

She shuddered. "She must be very powerful to be able to use mind control in that way. But I don't understand why I don't know who she is, if she's that strong. How can she be under the radar?"

There were deep lines of worry in Cuinn's forehead. "There are a limited number of Ajna energetics who can do that, and I know them all. Maybe twenty max. None of them are called Cassidy."

For the first time in the story Tierra raised her gaze above the floor, and looked at Cuinn. "It's what I thought. She's dangerous. She's unpredictable, but her energy wasn't twisted. I can't work out what she was doing there."

"I'll need to work with you to access the picture she shared with you," said Cuinn. I'll dreamwalk as soon as I do."

Tierra nodded. "Fine."

"She needs sleep first," said Cara.

Tierra bit her lip. "There's one more thing. I know the name of the Rogue who's behind all this. The man who fought you in the park. The man who's behind draining and leeching off innocent victims."

Progress at last, thought Fintan. At least some good would come of this. Here, perhaps, there would be something they could take action on.

She swallowed hard. "It's Elrian. Cuinn, it's your father. He's the Rogue."

There was a long minute of silence. Tierra bowed her head. She knew that it would be a shock for her friends and family, and she wished she hadn't been the one to break it to them.

Blaize broke it. "Are you – are you sure?"

Her voice was without its usual confident edge.

Tierra nodded. Her whole body ached with fatigue. "I'm sure. Cassidy used his name, and said he targeted you and me in order to hurt Cuinn. Having said that, his two goons were energetic matches for us, so I assume we would have served as energy batteries for them as well."

"My father? But ...this is absurd. Ridiculous. How can he be a Rogue? And involved in something so monstrous?" Cuinn shook his head. Tierra wished she had the strength to hug him, but she couldn't make herself move from her bed.

"When did you last see him?" Cara asked.

"After World War II," Cuinn said. "We argued over my mother's death. It's why I left Ireland – we both needed space. I haven't seen him since. He always was difficult, and my mother's death triggered something in him. Without her, something dark appeared. But he wasn't a Rogue. His energies weren't twisted. Depressed, perhaps. Angry, most certainly. Not twisted."

"If that was him in the park, he's a Rogue now. And a lot more powerful." Adam spoke flatly.

"The Rogue's energies were a match to Elrian's," Fintan said.

Tierra didn't have any doubts, however horrible an idea it was to contemplate. But she couldn't be the person who convinced them, then held them all together right now. It was all she could do to keep herself from shattering into tiny pieces. She glanced at Fintan and wished things were different. That he could hold her, be there for her. Be her strength, as she'd been his the day before.

She knew he loved her. The energetic link they'd shared had shown her his feelings. But the boost knowing he loved her had given her had gone. Because she'd also seen his fear. His fear of being unworthy, and his fear of risking his chosen family by messing things up with her.

Only he could get over that. She couldn't do that work for him. Couldn't even if she wanted to as she was tired to the bone, inside and out.

But ... still. The memory of the kiss she'd given him, to save him, was seared into her. She held on to the feeling of his mouth touching hers, a talisman.

Much like the bracelet on her wrist. She fingered it under the hoodie, then sighed and rested her head back on her knees. It was pointless to think about. They had far larger issues to deal with. Her own comfort, or her relationship with Fintan, weren't a priority now given the very personal threat they all faced. But she didn't have much to offer the discussion.

"I don't know what to do with this information." Cuinn looked blankly at the wall. "What do you do when you think your father might be a murderer?"

"It doesn't change who you are, Cuinn. We'll find him, catch him, and maybe we can rehabilitate him." Blaize, with her own father issues, spoke fiercely.

Tierra wasn't sure she could cope with this conversation any more. She'd reached her limit. Elrian's activities so far indicated he was worse than some of the most notorious Rogues in the energetic race's history. The idea of rehabilitating him didn't seem too likely. In the past, she would have been hopeful. And if Cuinn needed that hope, she understood. For the first time in her life, she thought that the execution of an energetic might be righteous.

Because the kind of man who tortured and killed children; the kind of man who let Dagon assault his own niece?

Maybe he deserved to be put down.

"I need rest." Cara nodded and ushered everyone out of the room. Ai hadn't woken during the conversation, her sleep enhanced by Cara's healing energy.

Tierra didn't wait for the door to close. She slid down under the comforter with the hoodie still on. She scrunched up her eyes, and tears leaked from beneath them.

Cara had healed Tierra's physical aches, but the emotional ones she'd have to process on her own. When Cara had told her about Clay, it was like a blow to the stomach. If only she'd been paying more attention, maybe he'd still be alive. They killed him to take her. His death would weigh on her conscience forever.

Cara came back into the room and sat on the bed where Tierra was a lump under the covers, curled up as small as she could.

Cara squeezed Tierra's hand. "Do you want to talk?"

Tierra shook her head.

She'd lost a little of her innocence this week. A little of her faith in the goodness of the world.

She needed time to mourn.

CHAPTER

32

Tierra woke up. Morning light trickled into the room. She still ached inside and out, but there was comfort in being back at Cathair Cuinn.

And in knowing that Fintan was alive and well close by.

She pushed herself into a sitting position, and saw Ai was awake. She sat on her bed, arms wrapped around her knees, staring at the wall.

Tierra winced. She owed the girl an apology. Tierra and Fintan had really messed up there. In trying to protect her, they'd made things worse.

"Ai?" she said, softly.

The girl didn't move. Tierra lifted the pale blue comforter off herself and threw her legs over the side of the bed. The floor was cold, stone that was pleasanter in the summer than an early spring morning. Okay, so she'd take the blanket with her. She wrapped it around herself and shuffled the handful of steps over to Ai, and sat on the side of the bed.

Ai's jaw tightened, but there was no other response.

It was time to start being open with the girl. "I'm so sorry we didn't tell you about Indigo. Can I tell you the whole story now?"

Ai shrugged.

Tierra took a breath, and launched into the story, holding nothing back. She spoke of the prophecy, of Blaize and Cuinn's relationship, their bracelets, and how Indigo had kidnapped Blaize, and nearly killed her.

Ai had turned to look at her before she got far in the story, her eyes wide.

Tierra brought her up to the point where she and Fintan had met Ai. She wasn't ready to tell the rest quite yet, though she would need to soon.

"Please, ask me any questions you have," Tierra said. "I don't want us to keep secrets anymore."

Ai blew out a big breath. "I want to call bullshit. But...the stuff I saw with that guy, Elrian. He did something to me. I don't know if it was this leeching stuff or what, but it wasn't normal."

"If you want, we can hold hands, and I'll open my emotional shields so you can see what your gut says." It wasn't something done much, but Tierra owed it to this teenager, who she'd so badly let down.

Ai's brow wrinkled. "I guess? Will it hurt?"

Tierra shook her head, and offered her hands, palms up.

Ai took them very tentatively, laying her palms down on top of them. Her fingers were like twigs, so light and slender.

"Tap into that space inside you that you call your gut feel. Your 'spidey-sense'. Close your eyes if it's easier. I'll open my shields for a moment."

Ai shut her eyes, and Tierra dropped her shields, exposing her emotions to the girl, hoping Ai would be able to tap into her Anahata enough to sense them.

A long minute passed. Then Tierra felt the ripple of connection in her heart Chakra, the girl's fingers clenching around Tierra's hands.

"Oh!" Ai said, and her eyes snapped open. "I knew you and Fintan were together!"

Tierra squeaked, and slammed her shields back up reflexively, dropping Ai's hands. That had *not* been what she'd meant to share.

"Um. How do you feel about Indigo? Do you feel you can trust us?" Tierra asked.

A weight seemed to have dropped from the girl, who scooted back and rested against her headboard. "Sure. Can we eat breakfast? So how long have you and Fintan been together?"

"Er, we're not together." This was not how she'd expected this to go. She was ready for questions about possible betrayal and the tragedy of Indigo, not about her own non-existent love life. She really needed to learn how to deal with teenagers again.

"You are. You're in love with him, and even I can see he totally digs you. Also you have that bracelet thing, and I saw one on him last night that matches. Isn't that what Cuinn and Blaize have?" Ai heaved herself off the bed, and grabbed a thick robe from the side, and walked carefully to the door.

"Yes....but that doesn't mean —" Tierra, still sitting on Ai's bed, was nonplussed.

"Plus he's pretty into you. Seems simple to me. I'm going to find Cara and see if there's something to eat." Ai turned with her hand on the door. "Thanks, though. I still don't know about all this stuff, but I'll stick around for a bit."

She disappeared out the door, leaving Tierra simultaneously relieved and dazed.

And wishing it really was that simple.

After her conversation with Ai, Tierra had slept for most of the day. Now she was in the garden. Crying.

She sat on the grass outside her window, cross-legged, deeply connected to her element of earth. She tried to ignore the tears. If ever in her life she had needed to replenish her Muladhara, the Chakra of grounding, security, and safety, it was now.

Her world had been turned upside down. Physically, emotionally, energetically, she was wounded. She'd gone out into the world, broken her self-imposed retreat, and it had cost her. It had been worth it, she thought, to have found Ai.

And then there was Fintan. She'd seen the sadness inside him, the loneliness and most surprisingly, the love he had for her.

A love that he wasn't prepared to act on. Wasn't prepared to risk losing the others as family for the chance he'd gain her as a partner, despite the fact Source, or some aspect of the energies, wanted them to be together, given their wristbands.

If he did offer her the slightest opportunity – was brave enough to even open the discussion – she'd take it, and do everything she could to reassure him that she loved him back. And that even in the very unlikely event that they couldn't make it work, and they needed some time to get over it, he wouldn't lose them as family.

Dusk was falling and she got to her feet, moving deeper into the forest that surrounded the shady bower outside her room, the spring flowers peeking through and beginning to blossom. She breathed in the smell of mulch, and more tension drained away.

A voice behind her interrupted her thoughts. "Can I talk to you?"

She turned. Fintan had showered and shaved, and wasn't nearly as unkempt as he'd been when she'd seen him nearly lose control in Seattle. She enjoyed his rugged surfer look, the stubble making him seem mischievous and non-conformist, but when his hair was tidy and his beard shaved off, the angles and planes of his face made him breathtakingly handsome. Her heart gave a squeeze. She let it mourn, and comforted it. *We'll be okay.*

"Good evening, Fintan." Her voice was soft.

He stood in front of her, hands rubbing together. "How do you feel now?"

"Better. Definitely better. Still a way to go." She sighed. "But people need to stop treating me like glass. I'm better when I'm looking after other people. And Ai needs me."

"Cara's looking after Ai. They seem to be building a relationship, of sorts."

Tierra's heart squeezed again. *Poor heart. It's okay, little one. We'll rebuild our relationship with Ai.*

Fintan cocked his head. "It'll be hard for her to trust anyone for a while. She feels like she's let us – you in particular – down."

Tierra toed some leaves. "I know. It's fine. She needs time to heal too. They leeched from her. She's okay, but her crash course in the energetics has been pretty tough."

A silence stretched between them. Tierra rolled her shoulders to ease the rigidity that appeared. She wasn't sure what to say to him. *Sorry I kissed you? But you know it was only to save you, right?*

"Do you want to take a walk?" Fintan said.

"Now? It's nearly dark."

"I can help with that." He concentrated for a moment, and a glowing ball appeared above them, bobbing up and down.

Tierra stood and took the arm he offered her. They set off at a gentle pace through the woods. Cuinn's estate was quiet, their nearest neighbor miles away. They ambled along for a while without speaking. Her shoulders relaxed. *I wish we could go back to being like this all the time.*

"Matching bracelets, huh?" Fintan said.

Heat washed across her face, and she was glad that the darkness surrounded them. Okay, not quite back to normal. "I guess."

"I think we need to talk about them," Fintan said.

She wasn't sure she did. She didn't want to have to hear how, despite the universe trying to bring them together, she still had an unrequited love.

"What's to say? We know nothing about them." Tierra dragged her feet. *Maybe I can say I don't feel well, and go back to the house.*

Fintan frowned. "We know it's linked to the prophecy. And that you and I got them about the same time. And we have the same colors, which, if Cuinn and Blaize's are a good model, are the colors of our Chakras, and the color of the Source."

She shrugged. "We don't know what that means."

He stopped, and turned her towards him. He put a hand under her chin and tipped her face up. His blue eyes were dark in the light he'd conjured.

"What were you thinking when the bracelet appeared?"

"I don't remember." It had been when she'd been captured, that she knew. There had been a lot going on.

"Well, I remember what I was thinking. At least, feeling. I was feeling utterly terrified that you were hurt, or dead. I was losing control. For the second time in a couple of weeks – which was also only the third time since I became a Manipura Practitioner." He paused. "Do you know when I lost control before that?"

She shook her head. The whole forest was hushed around them, the sounds of dusk faint and faraway, the two of them caught in their own tiny, intimate bubble. Her stomach fluttered and danced, the aches in her soul banished to a far corner of her consciousness.

In the dark forest clearing, visibility was reduced, which heightened her other senses. She could smell his delicious smell, spicy and smoky, black pepper and amber. She could feel the cool breath of the wind on her arms, and the warmth of his hand, which had moved from her chin to cradle her cheek. She resisted the impulse to snuggle into it.

"The last time I lost control – apart from in the bloody restaurant – was when a teacher called Maya at the Anahata Guild told me my Anahata energy was barely worth bothering with," Fintan said. "That my heart Chakra wasn't worth their time. That I should forget about it and focus on Manipura, because there was only enough energy in me to be a Warrior, and not a Healer, or any useful or worthwhile Anahata energetic."

He emphasized the last words with anger – and hurt.

Tierra gasped at this. "Really? How could any Anahata say that to you? That's awful."

And what a way to shut a young man down. Pieces flew into place. A way to create someone who never went too deep into romantic relationships, but kept them easy and shallow. Where he didn't bother with his feelings. His heart.

"I agree. But at the time, as a young, impressionable energetic, I was upset – and those damaged feelings expressed themselves in anger. And a loss of control that burned several Anahata Guild buildings down." He laughed grimly. "Unsurprisingly, it took me longer than most to be ready for the Anahata Practitioner trial, and I passed that by the skin of my teeth. I didn't have much interest in it after that. Anahata. The Guild. I dedicated myself to Manipura, to being a Warrior."

Her heart ached for him. She hadn't known him then, though the story of how he'd burned down buildings in the Guild was a legend. *But the legend was wrong.* It had never mentioned the cause of his anger and loss of control, but rather painted him as a mischief maker who wasn't serious about the Guild. Well, no wonder.

"And matters of the heart ... I kept them light. Given how weak my Anahata was, there wasn't much use in trying to love one woman deeply. I told myself I fell in love all the time, but when I looked into myself – which I tried not to – I knew it wasn't real love. Seeing Blaize and Cuinn together has hammered that point home."

Tierra tried to back out of his grasp. She didn't want or need a break-up speech from someone she wasn't even dating. "I know you're not interested in a long-term commitment."

She didn't need that rubbed in right now. She was too fragile. She felt brittle, as if a casual word could smash her to pieces. And she wasn't sure how long it would take her to repair herself if that happened. It had just been too hard a week.

He caught her other hand, holding her in place. "That's not what I said. Yes, that's the way I used to think. But seeing Blaize and Cuinn together ate at me. And when you dropped your bombshell in Vancouver –"

Argh. She winced. She didn't regret that moment of being true to herself – mostly – but being vulnerable wasn't easy. She turned her cheek away from the heat of his hand. He let her, but his other hand held on.

"— I was shocked. I lost control, for the first time since those buildings burned down. I was ashamed. Ashamed that I needed you to stop my energy from getting out of control. It almost twisted in that restaurant, but you stabilized me, grounded me. And I burned you." He swallowed.

She hadn't seen shame. She'd been puzzled why he'd seemed to lose some of his control, but she'd put it down to embarrassment about her confession.

"When I got the bracelet, Tierra, I had just realized I was in love with you."

Okay. That wasn't a small opening. That was the whole dam crumbling. She gaped, unable to speak from the shock.

"I know you deserve more. Because everything that's in you is good and true, and wonderful. You deserve better. But I will do what I can to prove to you every day for the rest of our lives that I'm worth you taking a chance on."

Her mouth remained open as she stared at him. Then a sparkle caught her eye, and a thread of fire shot past her face, and looped around to encircle them, shooting sparks of gold and green. Fintan drew on the ether, and flowers of fire appeared between them, in every color. They were stunning.

"Be with me, and I'll create hearts and flowers every day for you," Fintan said.

The flowers flew up and apart in a small, contained explosion, creating a mini-fireworks show above their heads.

She finally was able to nod her head, words still failing her.

Some tension in him seemed to relax. "I'm going to kiss you now."

"Um, okay."

And it really, really was.

He stroked a hand over her hair and rested it on her neck. The other traced meandering circles down to the curve of her rear. She shifted her hips towards him. She looked up into eyes the midnight blue of desire, his pupils huge. He kissed the side of her neck as he brought her body flush to his. She put her hands on his hips.

Tentatively, still uncertain of her welcome, she stroked a hand over his hip and thigh. He was warm and firm, his muscles lean and hard. The muscles in his butt tensed under her fingers.

Her whole body tingled in anticipation of what she expected to be a gentle kiss. A follow on to the way she'd pressed her lips against his to save him.

But this was no gentle kiss.

When his mouth came down on hers, it was urgent and demanding. She opened in response to him, her tongue darting out to meet his. His groin, pressed against her abdomen, showed her how attractive he found her.

A great weight fell from her, and she returned the kiss with a vengeance. His mouth was hot and wild, and his hands pulled her tightly against him. She moaned, and both his hands scooped under her buttocks and picked her up.

She wrapped her legs round his waist, and he started to carry her towards the house.

"Wait," she said, breaking the kiss.

His breath came quickly, and the look he gave her was a mix of desire, concern and puzzlement. "Do you want me to stop?"

"Yes. I mean, no. I don't want to stop, but I don't want to go inside. I want to stay out here."

"You want to ... make love ... outside? For our first time?" he asked.

She nodded. Her whole body felt electric, the nerve endings on fire, a match waiting to be lit.

He gave a little laugh, and laid her on the soft forest floor. They tore each other's clothes off, and he covered her body with kisses as she writhed on the ground. He knelt above her, the flat planes of his body delighting her as his pale skin caught the moonlight. He was hard and ready, and she couldn't wait another second.

She'd waited most of her life, after all.

"Please, Fintan."

He stroked himself, teasing her. "This?"

"Yes. That."

He put his hands either side of her head and entered her. She gasped and they moved together, bodies joined, until the match was lit and the woods were illuminated once again by fireworks.

They walked back to the house hand in hand, the night still quiet around them. Fintan felt his usual sense of security and calm at Cathair Cuinn multiplied tenfold. He glanced at their hands, joined, her left and his right, their bracelets next to each other.

They only managed a few moments back in her room before there was a knock on the door. "Tierra, love? Can I come in?"

It was Blaize's voice.

"Of course."

The door opened and Blaize said, "Family meeting, I'm afraid. Adam wants to get everyone on the same page."

"Ai, too," Tierra said.

Blaize raised her eyebrows. "Is that wise?"

"We need to build trust with her," Tierra said. "That means sharing what's going on. All of it."

They picked up Ai from her room, where she'd moved from the makeshift infirmary, on their way back to a warm and inviting kitchen. She greeted them cautiously, but with a lot less anger than before.

They joined Adam, Cara and Cuinn, already at the table. Blaize sat next to Cuinn, and Ai perched on a chair next to Cara, and fed occasional titbits to a contented Argus. Tierra sat opposite Adam, and Fintan stood behind her, massaging her shoulders.

There were a few knowing glances from the women and Cuinn's lips pressed together in a slight grimace when Fintan and Tierra sat down.

Adam leaned back in his chair and he tilted his head, seeming to weigh something up.

Fintan swallowed. He probably owed Adam an important conversation. Soon. But if Tierra had accepted Fintan, then he had better get to work on proving his worth to all of them.

"Something you want to share?" Adam said.

Okay, maybe that conversation would be sooner than Fintan had expected.

Fintan lifted his and Tierra's hands, displaying the bracelets. "Yeah. I'm in love with your sister. And for some reason, she's going to give me a chance."

He kind of wanted to add "Please don't kill me," on the end, because if Adam wanted to land a punch or two, Fintan wouldn't stop him. He loved the man like a brother, notwithstanding his relationship to Tierra.

Adam's eyes narrowed and very deliberately, he placed his hands flat on the table. He stared into Fintan's eyes for a long moment, while Fintan's shoulders tensed. Argus rested his weight on his front paws, ready.

The room was silent. Eyes wide and puzzled, Ai glanced between them and tried to work out what was going on.

Tierra rolled her eyes. "He's fine, aren't you?"

"Why wouldn't I be? My sister just chose my best friend to date." Adam leaned back. "And she's free to choose whoever she wants."

Fintan let out a relieved breath. Argus huffed and lay down, head on paws.

"He probably shouldn't fuck it up though," said Adam thoughtfully, appearing to speak to the air.

Fintan rolled his shoulders, and Tierra squeezed his hand. It's not like he disagreed with Adam. Still. Their outdoor sex – amazing outdoor sex – seemed to have renewed Tierra some, so he had to be doing some good somewhere.

Cuinn brought Ai up to speed on the time since Ai had met Fintan and Tierra. The girl's posture was more relaxed, though she still had purple smudges under her eyes. It would take time for her body and mind to heal, but her acceptance of the group would go a long way to making that happen. And they would do everything in their power to support that.

"So far we have identified myself and Blaize, Tierra and Fintan, and Adam of the twelve. The rest of the faces are either blurred or Blaize and I don't recognize them. We hope that when Blaize shares the images with Nixie, who will draw them so you can all see them, we may identify more. I haven't seen you in the prophecy, Ai," Cuinn said. "You're a wild card."

Relief and disappointment warred on Ai's face. Cara put an arm round the girl.

Fintan hoped Ai wasn't involved. Because there could be another reason Ai wasn't in the prophecy, which didn't bear thinking about. Though prophecies were slippery things, never set in stone. Even if Cuinn and Blaize could work out what they thought it meant, they couldn't take any of it for granted.

Whatever happened, they would come through this, all of them. There were a lot of loose ends to tie up first – who Cassidy was, and why she was working with Elrian. Who else was in the prophecy, and what would happen when they identified them all. What the larger purpose of the prophecy was. What the bracelets meant.

At least Fintan hadn't got through to Jeb. One less person tangled in all this.

Cuinn handed out tasks. Before they would go their separate ways, they'd go into the forest and have a ceremony to remember Clay. He had returned to Source.

Cuinn and Blaize would work on the prophecies, at the same time as Blaize would work with Nixie, and Cuinn would try to contact Cassidy. Adam and Fintan would go back to their Guilds and see what information there was on Elrian's last movements. Cara and Tierra would begin to teach Ai some of the things she needed to know as a young energetic, and Tierra would look into what had happened to Ai's parents, though she'd base herself at Cathair Cuinn to do this while she recovered.

They had their roles. And they had each other.

The meeting over, back in Tierra's living room Fintan gathered her to him once more. She was feminine and warm in his arms, and despite everything happening around them, a sense of wellbeing flooded him. He was home.

She laughed as she stretched up on her toes, and he bent down, the difference in their heights making the logistics a challenge.

The kiss was worth it though. Her lips were soft, and his hands moved from her glossy, smooth hair to the roundness of her hips. She was luscious. Her body was so inviting, so womanly.

He growled, and pulled her down with him onto the sofa. Her laugh was throaty now. She straddled his hips, and he made no attempt to hide his arousal. Because, despite the fact it hadn't been that long since the time in the forest, he was very obviously still enthusiastic about her being on top of him. He moved his hips slightly, and she responded with a gasp. He stretched out an arm, and drew her head down to his. She lay along his length, her head resting on his shoulder, her feet just past his knees.

She felt so right in his arms. She belonged there. He took a moment to enjoy the feel of her, to wrap them both in love, and he used a little of his Anahata to disturb the air around her, caressing her with a light breeze as well as his hands. Something healed inside him, something he hadn't realized had been broken.

He took a moment longer to enjoy the sensation and the peace.

"Did I mention I love you?"

She blushed.

Then he closed the short distance between their mouths, and forgot everything but being with her.

Dear Me,

Next time you get in a pickle, remember this:

Just because you're not a warrior, it doesn't mean you can't fight.

Just because you're not an adventurer, it doesn't mean you can't explore.

Just because you're not a hero, doesn't mean you can't be brave.

Just because you need help sometimes, doesn't mean you can't contribute.

Just because you're looking after everyone else, doesn't mean you can't look after yourself.

Let yourself be loved, little heart. Trust, build, belong.

Me x

There had been a time when he and his son had been close. But that had been before his wife's death. Against his wishes, she had become involved in human affairs. Elrian had told her to leave them to their idiocy, but her soft heart had bled for them as they fought and destroyed each other. And Cuinn had encouraged his mother. Helped her find a place in Poland where she could use her talents as a healer, along with her sister.

Then the hospital she'd been working at had been bombed. And no healer could put back together a body in so many pieces.

He hated humans.

But he hated Cuinn more.

After his wife's death, Elrian had destroyed his relationship with his son, just as Cuinn had destroyed his father's relationship with Cuinn's mother.

Cuinn had deserted Ireland, and Elrian had retreated to the coast of Galway, and spent his days looking out on dark angry waters that crashed against jagged cliffs. The gray weather and atmospheric countryside suited his mood. His dreamscape had become full of nightmares of his dying wife, a spirit who wouldn't leave him alone.

Then decades later he'd met another woman, with unusual gifts, and his life had changed.

He'd once more been given a purpose and a plan.

He had been a dreamwalker for centuries and had worked with prophecies extensively. But he'd withdrawn from life in the Guilds long before his wife's death. Since meeting his second great love, he'd completed many dreamwalks, and the nightmares had been contained to one part of his dreamscape.

The dreamwalks had shown him his destiny. He would become the most powerful energetic in the world.

If he had to destroy Cuinn and his friends to do it?

Excellent.

Elrian turned away from the broken window through which Tierra had apparently fled and strode across the room. He ignored Dagon, who looked away as Elrian passed.

It seemed Elrian had failed again. Tierra, someone he had considered easy prey, had escaped, and if the possible futures he'd seen in the dreamscape were true, the bracelet Dagon had seen on her wrist meant she was probably even now mooning over the boy Fintan. Still. If they had coupled up, Elrian would have four more chances to ensure the prophecy went his way.

But perhaps more drastic measures were required to prevent the next couple from getting together.

Though given how unsuited they were, the wild water spirit and the dour healer locked in his tower, perhaps it wouldn't be so difficult.

The Guilds and Circles

The energetics power structure is Guild based.

There are six Major Guilds, one for each of the six Chakras:

- **Muladhara** (The Root Chakra – Earth Element)
- **Svadisthana** (The Sacral Chakra – Water Element)
- **Manipura** (The Navel Chakra – Fire Element)
- **Anahata** (The Heart Chakra – Air Element)
- **Vishudha** (The Throat Chakra – Ether (Space) Element)
- **Ajna** (The Third Eye – The Mind)
  (Sahasara, the Crown Chakra, does not have a Guild.)

Each energetic has two activated Chakras, one Dominant and one Auxiliary, and it is the combination of these that influences their power, and to some degree, their personality.

Because of the huge differences between an energetic like Blaize, who combines her Manipura Dominant with Ajna Auxiliary, and one like Fintan, who combines Manipura Dominant with Anahata Auxiliary, a system of Minor Guilds also developed. There are thirty

Minor Guilds representing each combination of powers (for example, Manipura-Ajna is a separate Guild from Ajna-Manipura).

Each individual energetic therefore belongs to two Major Guilds, and one Minor Guild.

For example: Cuinn has Ajna Dominant, and Muladhara Auxiliary. He therefore belongs to the Ajna Major Guild, the Muladhara Major Guild, and the Ajna-Muladhara Minor Guild.

The Major Circle is the highest form of government with one powerful energetic representing each Major Guild, making decisions on behalf of the race. The Minor Circle, the second tier of government, is made up of the thirty energetics who lead each of the Minor Guilds.

List of Minor Guilds:

- Muladhara-Svadisthana
- Muladhara-Manipura
- Muladhara-Anahata
- Muladhara-Vishudha
- Muladhara-Ajna
- Svadisthana-Muladhara
- Svadisthana-Manipura
- Svadisthana-Anahata
- Svadisthana-Vishudha
- Svadisthana-Ajna
- Manipura-Muladhara
- Manipura-Svadisthana
- Manipura-Anahata
- Manipura-Vishudha
- Manipura-Ajna
- Anahata-Muladhara
- Anahata-Svadisthana
- Anahata-Manipura

314

- Anahata-Vishudha
- Anahata-Ajna
- Vishudha-Muladhara
- Vishudha-Svadisthana
- Vishudha-Manipura
- Vishudha-Anahata
- Vishudha-Ajna
- Ajna-Muladhara
- Ajna-Svadisthana
- Ajna-Manipura
- Ajna-Anahata
- Ajna-Vishudha

Want More?

The story of the energetics continues in Nixie and Jeb's story, **Nixie and the Healer**.

To be first to hear when it's out, visit my website:
EllenBardAuthor.com/sign-up
for updates, giveaways and inside information.

Discover Your Energetic Profile!

Want to know what your Dominant Chakra would be?
Which Guild you would belong to? What your archetype is?

Take the Chakra Quiz, and find out!

EllenBardAuthor.com/chakra-quiz

Help Spread the Word

If you loved the book and have a moment to spare, I would hugely appreciate it if you had time to leave a short review where you bought the book, and/or on goodreads. For instructions, go to the link below.

EllenBardAuthor.com/how-to-leave-a-review

Your review will help other readers discover the series, and is greatly appreciated in spreading the word. Authors like me rely on amazing readers like you to share their love of books with others.

Thank you!

About the Author

Ellen is an author who writes paranormal romance full of enchantment, intrigue and action. Her writing blends a background in psychology and her experiences traveling the world, with a love of magic, fantasy and a happy ending.

She's a Chartered Occupational Psychologist with the British Psychological Society, and continues to work as an international management consultant, which she has done for the last 17 years. She's worked all over the world in countries such as China, Saudi Arabia and Malaysia. She writes non-fiction under Ellen M Bard.

Her passion for other lands and cultures helps inform her writing, as does her desire to try new things – from art classes to Krav Maga, the self-defense system.

She's a passionate and dedicated reader, speeding through 100 or so books a year – find her on goodreads to see what currently has her hooked.

Born in the UK, she currently lives in an apartment nest in Bangkok, Thailand where she (almost!) never has to feel the cold.

Connect with Ellen:
Facebook: facebook.com/EllenBardAuthor
Twitter: twitter.com/ellenbard
Goodreads: goodreads.com/ellenbard
Instagram: instagram.com/ellenbard/

Acknowledgments

This book wasn't easy to write. I adore Tierra and Fintan, but getting their story right, and showing Tierra's journey, took time.

I am so grateful for the support and love I have in my life which meant I managed to slog through the hard bits instead of giving up. My mum, Mary Bard, and my sister, Sarah Bard, have acted as cheerleaders and amazing alpha readers, and have never wavered in their confidence this book would get done. I also have a wonderful extended family, the Dunnes and Bards who are always there when I need them.

Whilst writing, I went for the second time through the book The Artist's Way, by Julia Cameron, but with a group. That amazing knot of women, Eleanore (who was also an amazing beta reader), Liza, Dani, Laura and Paige helped me process a lot of bumps as well as sharing the joys of progress.

Anna Charbonneau has acted as beta reader, friend, coach and supporter, and her love of the series has helped me to keep going and help Tierra's story live.

Thanks also to Katie Bullas, another brilliant beta reader, and my writing friend Nyla Nox. Other wonderfully supportive friends include the stalwart Graham Morley, Justin and Ed (and Honey!) and Helen Clark.

Thanks also to Peter Bainbridge (there helping both at the start of the book, as well as when it was done!) and my aunt, Ellen Dunne, who helped do the final proofs of the book.

I listened to the first two albums by 'Oh Wonder' pretty much on continuous repeat while writing Tierra. Their gentle energy, connection-focused lyrics and acoustic melodies are very Tierra.

Finally, thanks to my Fox. In real life, the story doesn't end when you say "I love you", and I'm delighted to be creating our story with you (and tinyfox). Thanks for helping me get Tierra past the finish line. We both know this one wouldn't have happened without you.

Ellen Bard, July 2018